I0760428

A COURT OF FIRE AND FROST

A ROMEO AND JULIET RETELLING

LEGENDS OF LOVE

DANIELA A. MERA

ELAYNA R. GALLEA

authordanielaamera@gmail.com

elayna.gallea@gmail.com

First edition December 2021

Second edition October 2023

Book Cover Design by GetCovers

Interior/Case Laminate art by Shane Nel

Map by Daniela A. Mera

ASIN (ebook): B0CFM54ZV5

ISBN (paperback): 978-1-960343-15-4

ISBN (hardback): 978-1-960343-12-3

Created with Vellum

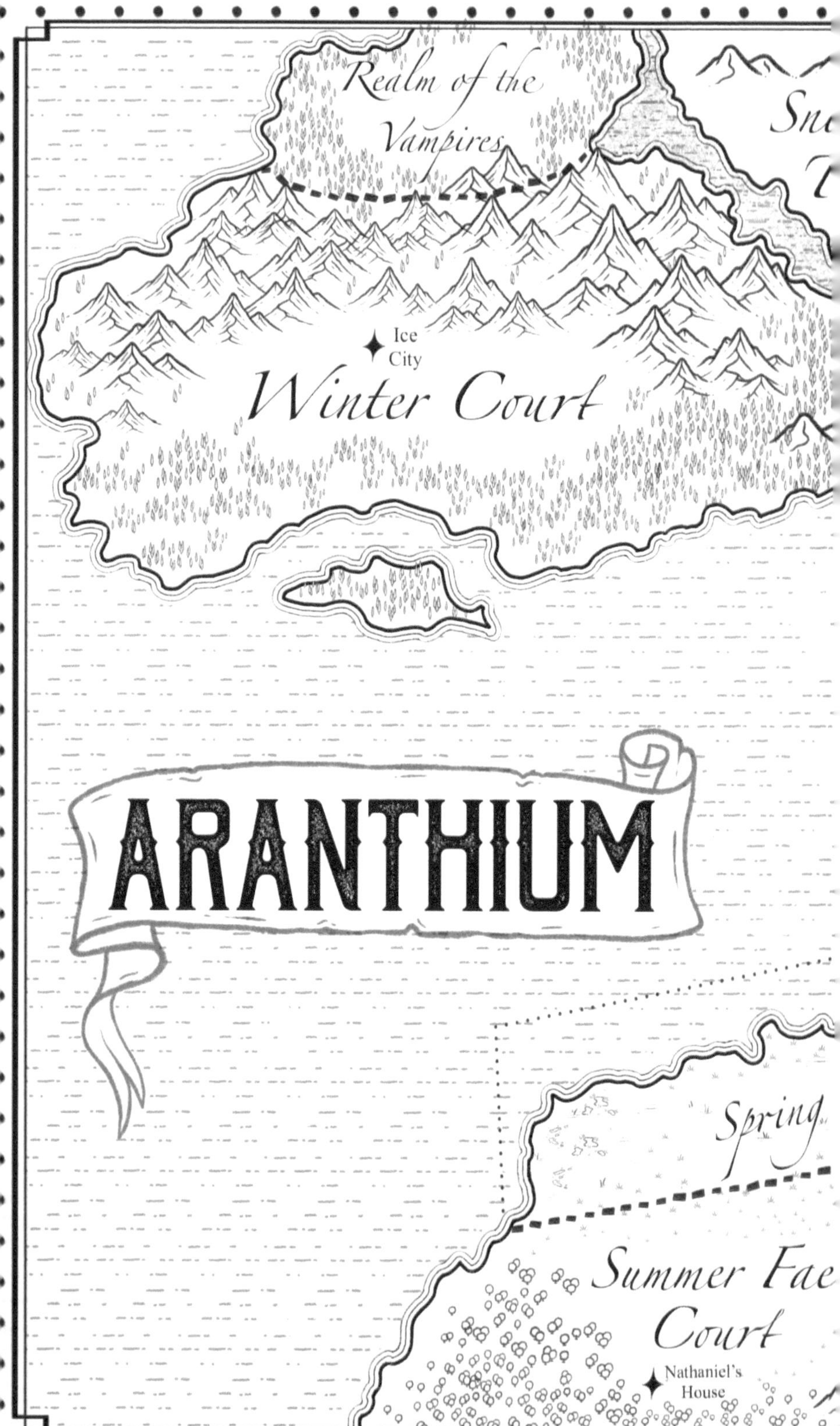
Realm of the Vampires
Ice City
Winter Court
ARANTHIUM
Spring
Summer Fae Court
Nathaniel's House

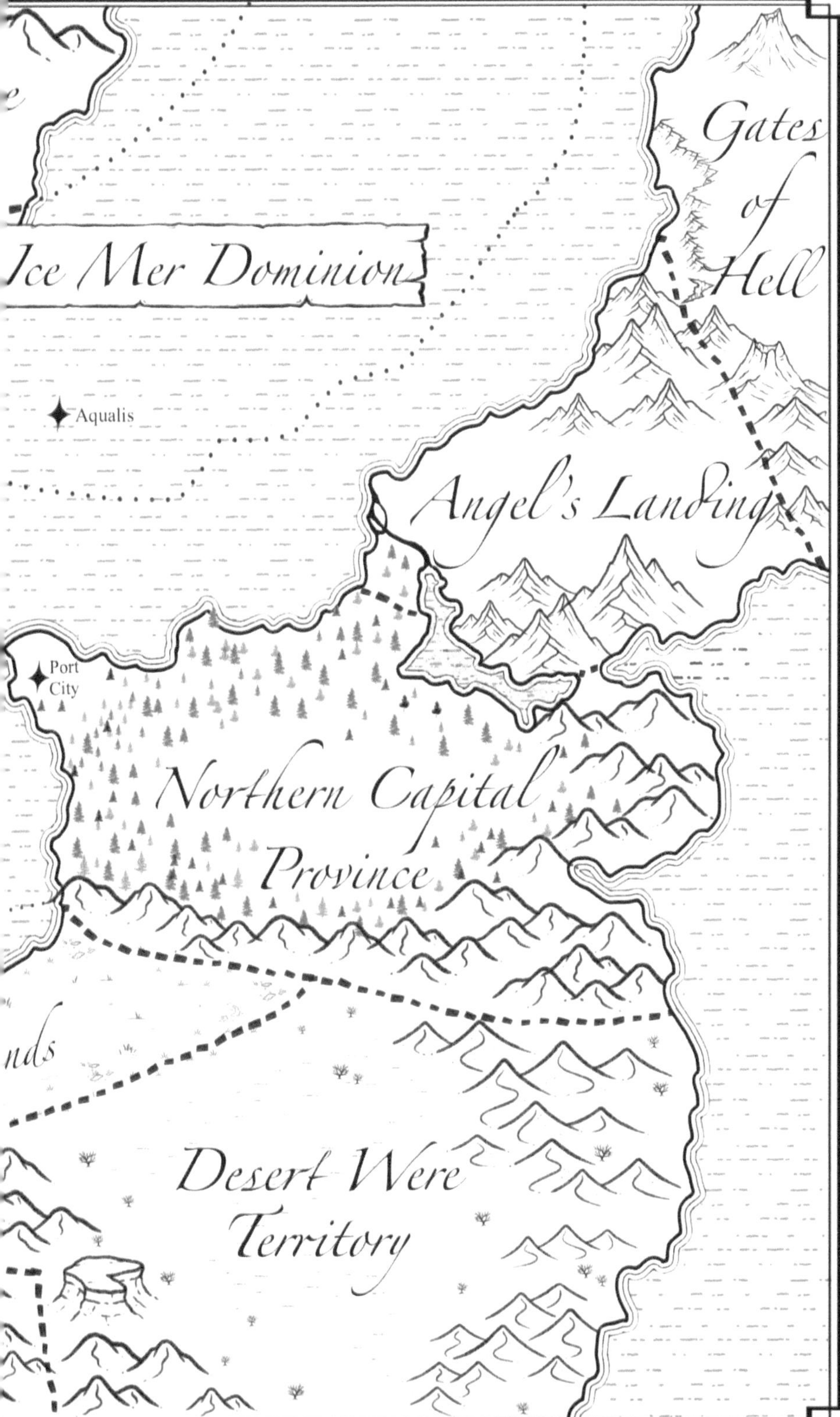

Gates of Hell
Ice Mer Dominion
Aqualis
Angel's Landing
Port City
Northern Capital Province
Desert Were Territory

SUGGESTED READING ORDER

Legends of Love novels are a part of an interconnected stand-alone series. You can read in whatever order you'd like. However, we'd suggest:

A Court of Fire and Frost

A Court of Seas and Storms

A Court of Wind and Wings

Welcome to Aranthium

Dear reader,

Before beginning this story, we want to take a moment and acknowledge that this book is New Adult.

Cursing, violence, substance abuse, mentions of parental abuse, and open-door sex scenes are present.

We care about our readers very much. Please, protect your peace.

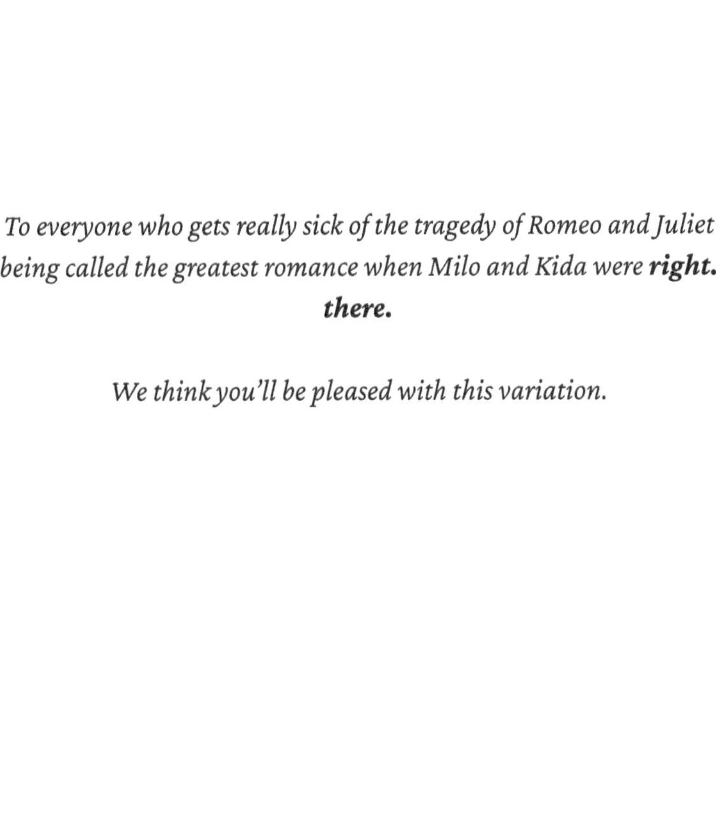

To everyone who gets really sick of the tragedy of Romeo and Juliet being called the greatest romance when Milo and Kida were ***right. there.***

We think you'll be pleased with this variation.

PART ONE

CHAPTER 1

GET UP

NATHANIEL

"I'm never doing shots with Marie again." The slightly slurred words slip from my lips, sounding like drums to my alcohol-addled brain. I bury my face into the pillow and ignore the spinning world around me.

It's an impossible task.

The same series of vibrations that pulled me from sleep sound from under the pillow. They gently reverberate through the feathers and buzz against my cheek as if they aren't committing a heinous crime by shaking my already fragile head. Gods, the hangover is no longer imminent. It is here. Dragging myself from the depths of sleep is like a ghost trying to reanimate a dead body—a nightmare in more ways than one.

My eyes slide open.

The red light on my alarm clock sears my retinas, and I groan. Forget never doing shots again. At this rate, I'm never going to drink again. I've barely been asleep for two hours. Why am I awake?

I'm about to give in to the call of sleep when a sudden and

overwhelming sensation of dread washes over me. It's oddly in time with my still-buzzing phone.

Which is... bad. It finally hits me that my phone shouldn't be ringing at this ungodly hour.

Frustration is a pulsing, throbbing ache as I push my head away from the pillow. I fling back the forest-green coverlet, and the matching pillow quickly follows it. They fall on the floor with a soft *thud*. I claw at my FaePhone just as the screen dims.

Shit, shit, shit.

The word is in a continuous loop as I pick up my phone and unlock it clumsily through squinted eyes. My room is still bathed in jet-black shadow, and the only detail I can see is the too-bright rectangle three inches from my face. It is 3:04 a.m., and there are... twelve missed calls?

BOSS AKRON

"Damn it all to Lethe," I exhale. One tap on the screen, and I move the phone to my ear.

The ringing tone blasts against my ear, and I cringe. A marching band is making a home in my head.

"Sprigg, thank the gods you're finally awake," Boss says. Irritation and sarcasm bleed into every syllable as he continues, *"There's a barge coming in.* Right. Now. *You needed to be here ten minutes ago to receive them."*

"Can't Marie bring them in? It's my day off," I slur, scrubbing the sleep from my eyes. Though I'm slowly dying, she's probably fine. Vampires have a much better alcohol tolerance.

"You're the new guy. You gotta do your time and hope someone else quits and gives you more privileges." He laughs, the sound like a hammer to my skull. Like my pounding headache is a joke.

I don't say anything. My brain hurts trying to process what he's saying. I've barely slept for three hours, and now he wants me to come in to work?

"*Sprigg,*" he seethes. I can just see him clenching and unclenching his fists. "*Get. Here. Now.*"

He doesn't even wait for a reply. He shouts at someone else and hangs up.

I stare at the phone. "Bastard."

No one would ever say my employer is kind. Working at the docks was the first opportunity to present itself to me in Port City. I'm not planning to stay forever. It's a stepping stone to other things, a way out of the Summer Court.

"Just a stepping stone," I repeat to myself as I slide out of bed and stick my head through the neck of a thick, beige sweater. My limbs are shaking, both from the hangover and lack of sleep.

A shooting pain runs through my ear. I curse some more. The chunky wool knit is snagged on one of the six golden rings threaded through the point of my right ear's cartilage. After extricating myself, I shove my arms into the sleeves.

"Flora, lights," I call out.

No response.

Right. I'm too poor for AI systems. I smack the light switch near my bed. A flicker of pale gold light bathes my shitty apartment from my singular lightbulb.

Raking a brush violently through my hair, I yank on a pair of black sweatpants. No need to try and impress anyone at three in the morning. In all likelihood, I will only deal with people for a few minutes before I'm left all alone in a frozen office with a pounding headache. Prior experience has taught me that new arrivals at this hour won't so much as glance at me once I give them clearance to dock.

It takes me exactly four minutes to be ready and out of the door of my studio apartment. It's a ten-minute walk from the docks—a frigid *ten minutes.* The entire block around my seventeen-story apartment building smells of fish and the salty mist that has left white stains over all the stucco.

Frigid air slams into me the moment I step outside. It seeps inside my fingers, and they're numb in a few heartbeats. I brace myself, fold my arms, and start running. Maybe I look like an idiot, but I am *cold*. Soft white clouds fill the air with each exhale, and I curse myself for not grabbing a jacket to go over my sweater.

This kind of weather is still new to me. While it sucks, there is also something about the crispness of the frigid air that attracts me. The gods only know it isn't the city itself. It isn't beautiful. It isn't warm. It isn't even filled with friendly people.

Even so, the cold makes me feel like I am home. It embraces me, filling a hole I never knew existed.

My family doesn't understand. My mother and sister still live in the Summer Court, and they've made no secret about their displeasure at my decision to move. Before leaving, I got my degree from Summer Court University in economics, but it wasn't for me. I hated it.

I always knew my real adventure would be here in Port City. After a hundred years of endless sunshine and getting drunk off Flower Dew, my life had become boring. I figured it was time for me to be somewhere else.

I haven't looked back since I moved.

When I reach the enchanted steel docks, the cold intensifies. I stop running. Bitter, icy air chokes me. It burns my lungs, as sharp as the ice floating in the water. A thick mist curls and twists through the air like a heavy shroud. Vision is nearly impossible, even for a Fae.

I slowly make my way up the walkway while panting, the path familiar even in the middle of the night. With each scrape of my boot, metal groans. My ears pinch at the sound, but I try not to wince when I think of clear, hard alcohol and how much I want to vomit.

Unlocking the door to the crappy office, I step inside. It's just as cold here, the walls barely more than scraps of wood. I hold out a hand and pull on my magic. Orange erupts from my palm, and a flame sparks to life. It crackles, the sound pleasing to my ears. Within a few minutes, the office is warm enough that my teeth stop clattering. Boss enchanted the entire place so no one can break in, but apparently, he draws the line at employee comfort.

When I was younger and stupider (six months ago), I asked him how to turn on the boiler system. In response, he laughed. *"Being cold makes you lot work harder."*

Then, as if to make his point, he sent me to work in the cold, frigid air for the rest of the day.

If I'm being honest—and I have to be, thanks to my Fae genetics—he's kind of a bastard.

Late-night receptions make me nervous because of a string of thefts along the coast from one particular asshole with a unique calling card: one drowned being and one with a slit-throat. He's been officially titled The Pirate of Death. I imagine some witch came up with the name because it reeks of coarse language and cliche. If we get robbed, I hope I'm the one going to take a swim with stone shoes.

Through the tendrils of mist, I glimpse a steel-gray mid-size ship with barnacles all along the bottom. The vessel approaches the dock quickly, though there is no rumble from a motor.

The Pirate of Death's boat is said to be at the height of modernity, though. Sleek. Fancy. Nothing like this piece of crap that looks like it will fall apart from a single gust of wind. The breath whooshes out of me, and my shoulders relax when I realize: it doesn't belong to the thieves. Thank the gods.

Despite the less-than-beautiful quality of the boat, there is still something menacing about it. My fingers grip the sill of the thick, grime-coated window as I watch the boat slide into the dock. Two males walk down the plank, their swagger evident even from here.

Instinctively, I brace myself for an unpleasant conversation. I'm not a burly Fae and don't particularly enjoy confrontation.

Maybe I should've picked another career path. It's too late for that, though. The sailors are already halfway to the office. The moon shines on them as they approach, illuminating the swirling white tattoos that cover their faces, necks, and pointed ears. Their skin is as black as the night, and the markings are so bright they almost glow. White puffs of fur line their face, and light blue suede covers their torsos, legs, and feet.

If the markings on their faces aren't enough of a clue, the garments tell me all I need to know about them. They are from the Winter Court. Fae Folk from the North. At first, they stare at me with steel in their black eyes. Their forms are so powerful I have to remind myself not to cower.

Power runs through your veins, too, Nathaniel.

I might be a lowly shifter Fae, but I am strong enough to work at a dock, and I have a decent well of fire-based birthright power. I also go to a gym. Sometimes.

Consciously reminding myself that these Fae are powerful because of the brutal landscape in which their court resides, I stand straight and paste a charming smile on my face.

While I puff out my chest and prepare to address them in my best customer-service voice, the shaved side of my head burns. Yes, cold *burns*. In moments like this, I try to remember that I *actively choose* to live in the frozen wasteland that is Port City.

“You are the dock master?” one of the Fae says. His tone tells me precisely what he thinks about me, and I bristle instinctively.

“Yes, sirs. How can I help you today?”

The two sailors glance at each other and then back at the boat, but they don’t say anything.

Splendid.

After a moment, I ask, “Are you planning to register the shipment or pay for discretion?”

“Paying,” the other one grunts.

These two look like they have never set foot in a party during their entire existence. Perhaps that is for the best since I always end up at parties. Maybe it is my Summer Fae blood. Maybe it’s just my desire to have a good time.

A trait these two gentlemen with sticks up their rock-solid asses don’t share.

Taking out the clipboard with a small stack of forms, I hand it over to the Fae.

"Follow me." I gesture for them to step into my office. The flame is still burning in the corner, and both Fae wordlessly brush past me.

Just as I turn to follow them, a third form leaps from the boat to the dock. Smaller than the other two, with pronounced curves, this one is a female. I bristle. Rarely do females come on ships. Sailors are a superstitious lot.

When she moves, the mist parts, as if the air obeys her somehow. I can't tear my eyes away. She is absolutely, unequivocally magnetic.

What is she doing?

The question is on the tip of my tongue, but the words get caught in my throat when I get a better look. I want to tell her that being here is dangerous, that jumping from the boat onto the icy dock is idiotic, and that she could fall into the icy water and be pulled away by the current before she can surface.

I want to say many things, but everything fades when she bounces to her feet. Her loose curls blow in the icy wind, and she looks like a wild huntress stalking her prey. The white puffs of air clear before her, as if they, too, recognize her powerful grace. She tilts her head and smirks at the wind as though it obeys her. Maybe it does? I stand there dumbly, forgetting how several of my limbs work. It is as though I have never seen a woman before.

She is beautiful. Stunning.

And I...

I am staring at her. Like an idiot. I'm stuck watching as she pulls a body out of the boat.

A. Body.

Fae, by the looks of them. Several ropes are wrapped around his body, and he's out cold.

Who is she?

The question freezes on my tongue, and I'm stuck watching as she grabs the bound Fae at her feet and yanks him behind her.

I swallow, excited and terrified at once.

Dammit. If she kills that Fae here, Boss will return the favor. Either that or turn my left pinky into a living paperweight. A shiver runs through me. I *hate* warlocks. They are freaky, and their powers don't make sense.

Momentarily forgetting about the clients in my office, gravity drags me closer to the captivating woman.

"I wouldn't kill him if I were you," I say, trying to maintain my casualness. Hopefully, she doesn't hear the hitch in my voice.

Standing this close to the mysterious female, my heart is thudding. Long, pointed ears peek out from beneath her curls. She, too, is Fae and, therefore, cannot lie.

Ice-blue eyes look up at me, and for a moment, I cannot breathe. I cannot think. How could I, when faced with such beauty? Her eyes are like glass, peering into my soul.

I lose myself in the depths of her irises.

Elaborate white tattoos run over her face, and her white and blue uniform is so tight I can see the lovely curves of her body. The tone of her muscle is... distracting. And gods, it's attractive.

I don't think I've ever been so attracted to anyone before in my entire life. What would it be like to run my hands over her? To touch her soft curves and feel her melt beneath my touch?

She laughs. The sound is wild and guttural, and it makes my muscles tighten. “Why would you think I am going to kill him?”

Not an answer.

I purse my lips. My eyes flick down just to check that she has no visible weapons. My eyes scan her legs and hips. While they are magnificent and worthy of a marble statue, there is a distinct lack of knives, guns, swords, and whatever else they used in the barbaric north.

I flush when I realize she is watching me.

Oh gods.

I blink.

She blinks.

An awkward silence stretches between us before she laughs softly.

“Fear not, Fae. I will not kill him here.” Her accent is rich and lilting. It draws me in even more. Like a spell, I almost miss the Fae trickery of her words.

Almost.

I curl my fingers. He won’t die here, but... She will kill him at one point.

Still lacking the ability to speak, I nod.

Be charming, you idiot. You are a Summer Fae; for the Gods’ sakes. Delight and surprise are literally what your people do.

Despite my rousing pep-talk, my mouth opens, and nothing comes out.

Her head tilts to the side, studying me. The corners of her eyes crinkle, and she tries to hold back a smile. Oh, gods. The sweatpants.

Would it be too much for the ocean to swallow me whole?

More awkward silence stretches between us. After a few

extended heartbeats, the tattooed Fae looks past me into the office.

I want to do anything to keep those icy eyes on me. "So..." I start, wanting to redeem myself, perhaps even casually introduce myself, but the moment never comes.

One of the men steps out of the office. "Little Twig, come and get your money, or we will leave without paying!" he shouts.

The other sailor grumbles something offensive, and they both laugh.

Feeling like a total ass, I mumble, "That's me, I think," and hurry inside.

I expect her to follow me inside, but when I glance over my shoulder, the wintery beauty has vanished into the mists. Her "cargo" is gone as well.

My heart sinks into my stomach. I will probably never see her again.

CHAPTER 2
I AM INTRIGUED
ELVA

I wouldn't kill him if I were you.

Laughing to myself, I watch the soft-hearted Fae retreat. Something about the male draws me to him; my eyes don't want to move. His russet-red hair blows in the early morning breeze and the way he walks...

I'm drawn to him.

Waiting until he disappears into his tiny office, I heave my bundle over my shoulders. The way the Fae moves intrigues me, but his words make it clear that he has never stepped foot in the Winter Court.

My mother would tear him limb from limb before he even realized what was happening.

Still... I am intrigued. Not many things intrigue me these days.

What kind of Fae asks for the life of someone he hasn't even met?

Clearly, not someone familiar with the kill-or-be-killed philosophy embraced by most members of my court.

"If I wanted to keep this dirtbag alive, I wouldn't have come to this place," I grumble, huffing as I adjust the weight of my burden.

Said dirt-bag groans, shifting in my arms.

The sleeping pills I slipped him hours ago are wearing off. Muttering to myself about the uselessness of modern medicine, I wave a hand. Bands of ice appear around the scumbag's hands and feet, strengthening the already present zip-ties. Satisfaction roils through me as I nod at my handiwork. "Let's see you get out of that."

I have been hunting this particular Fae for the past three months, one of my longer missions, but finally, he slipped up and made a mistake two nights ago.

This Fae was particularly tricky to catch, a little smarter than most, but finally, the idiot had gotten smashed and slipped up. He proved the point that I always tell my benefactors: every Fae has a weakness. Find it, exploit it, and wait for them to fall prey to themselves.

Works every time.

After all, I've been around for a long time. Sure, technology has changed. But a bastard is still a bastard, even if their clothing has changed. If anything, the evolution of technology has made my job a lot easier. Being out of the Winter Court, access to technology is as easy as snapping my fingers.

I silently bound across the dock as I head to my destination. My skin crawls as I think about why I was sent to retrieve him.

This particular asshole has a taste for little girls and whiskey. Two things that definitely shouldn't go together.

Forty-eight hours ago, I had been tossing in my bed when my FaePhone chimed in the middle of the night. Casting aside any pretense of sleep, I rolled over and unplugged it from my charger before flipping it on. Pressing my finger to unlock the top-of-the-line technology, I scowled as I took in the picture this slimy Fae had posted on social media. His audacity shocked me.

The caption beneath the photo read:

> LIVING IT UP IN VEDON #TOOCOOLFORSCHOOL #FUNWITHFAE #PARTYHARD #THREESOME

In the picture, my prey was wearing too-tight leather pants with a white dress shirt unbuttoned just enough to allow his curly black chest hair to peek out. He wore an overly large belt buckle, clearly overcompensating for something. He looked like a greasy fifties film star.

The worse thing, though, hadn't been his disgusting appearance. That was the two skinny human girls hanging off his reedy arms. They couldn't have been a day over sixteen. The photographed humans gazed adoringly at him as if this Fae were the golden-skinned Raphael Zeus himself, not some skeezy, low-powered Fae.

Shuddering in disgust, I snapped a screenshot of the fugitive and sent it to my benefactors before flying to Vedon. The city is known for three things: sex, drugs, and money.

The entire three hours I spent in the massive city were too much. I cannot emphasize enough how much I hate Vedon. It might be the worst place on the entire planet of Aranthium. I would rather spend days in the Gates of Hell with High King Hades, the DemiGod of the Dead, before I return to Vedon.

The city is in the middle of a desert, not a top vacation destination for Winter Fae. Not only that, but Vedon attracts all types of creatures looking to party away from the prying eyes of their family and friends. Fae, Vampires, Pixies, Warlocks, Angels, Were, Daemons, and even humans flock to the city all year round to gamble their lives away.

They say a picture is worth a thousand words. Well, in this case, it's worth a hundred thousand dollars.

When they hired me, my benefactors were clear they wanted

two things. Proof that this Fae bastard is a criminal, and for him to disappear. The photo was all the proof I needed.

Any self-respecting Winter Fae would never be caught dead in Vedon, the land of laughter, sin, and trickery. It stinks of the Summer Fae through and through. But clearly, this bastard is not that. Considering he is a low-power Fae with barely enough birthright magic to conjure up an icicle, it isn't exactly a surprise.

That's why it took me so long to catch him. He's a coward who rarely uses his pitiful supply of magic so I couldn't trace his magical signature. Every Fae has one. It's like a fingerprint that belongs only to them. Usually, I can track those within a few days.

Grunting as I toss the pedophile in the trunk of the SUV Blake left parked for me outside the port, I pull out my FaePhone and snap a picture of the unconscious Fae to send to my benefactors.

Me: Got the asshole.

Three dots appear on the screen instantly. A few seconds later, my FaePhone vibrates in my hand.

Unknown Sender: The funds have been wired to your account.

Grinning to myself, I slam the trunk shut. Leaning against the back of the vehicle, I allow myself a moment to smile. There is just something about catching slimy dirtbags like this that makes a girl happy. My heart might be made of ice, but Fae justice will thaw even the coldest of hearts.

Suddenly, the hairs on the back of my neck prickle. I straighten. Someone is watching me.

Who would dare?

I flip around, gasping as I catch sight of the red-headed Summer Fae from earlier standing a few feet away from me.

"Found you," he says with a wry smile.

"Can I help you?" I ask icily, crossing my arms in front of me. "Where I come from, it's considered rude to sneak up on a lady."

Raising his brows, he glares pointedly at the trunk before looking back at me. "Do *ladies* tie people up and throw them into their trunks in the Winter Court?"

"This one does," I say, winking at the male. There is just something about him that makes my insides curl. Strange. I haven't felt this way in... a very long time. I take care of my needs, of course, but always with one-night stands. With everything that is going on, I can't risk anything else.

Hilariously, the Fae appears speechless. White mist clouds around his mouth as he stares at me. Even so, something about him is magnetic. I am drawn to him, despite everything else. He doesn't belong in Port City, and I...

I have ice in my veins. The white tattoos running down my face are proof of it. The Winter Court is in my blood, whether I want it or not.

Get a grip, Elva.

I have to get out of here before I do something stupid, like ask him for his name.

No names. No people. I cannot leave any ties. Not if I want to stay hidden.

The reminder of what I am running from–*who* I am running from–is enough to spur me onward.

"If you'll excuse me?" I walk around the SUV, bending down to pull the keys from under the front wheel well.

Thank the gods, Blake is dependable. Remind me to give the Vampire a raise.

Glancing behind me, I notice the Summer Fae still hasn't left. He is standing there, his body seemingly at ease despite the cool nighttime weather. I snort as I note his running shoes and black sweatpants.

He's definitely a Summer Fae. No self-respecting Winter Fae would ever be caught in something like that.

The air swirls around him as he stands, unmoving. I turn on the car, connecting my FaePhone to the car. The moment it beeps, I select my favorite soundtrack. Everyone knows humans make the best country music. Turning the sound up high, I blast my music.

Bopping my head in time to my favorite tunes, I lower the driver's side window and wink at the Fae. He stares at me, wide-eyed and open-mouthed, as I peel out of the port and into the night.

I have things to do.

A Fae to dispose of.

There is no guilt within me. No shame. My actions are necessary. The world will be a better place without this particular Fae in it.

I do my duties mechanically for the next few hours, my mind straying back to the red-headed Summer Fae. By the time the sun rises over the water, the world has one fewer pedophile, and I'm a hundred thousand dollars richer.

Usually, this is when I begin celebrating. A glass of wine, some chocolate cake, and a night curled up with a book is how I like to celebrate a job well done.

But today, my mind keeps circling back to the Fae from the docks. Like a magnet, I am drawn to him. I want to know more. This strange feeling pricks me between my shoulder blades, like an itch I can't quite scratch.

Who is he?

CHAPTER 3
WATER WITCH ABSINTHE
NATHANIEL

One week later

Lights pulse above my head as Marie shoves a shot in my direction.

"To us!" She lifts the glass, knocking it into mine before downing the amber liquid with a hiss.

Holding the glass cup between my fingers, I follow suit. "Salud!"

The alcohol burns as it goes down before settling in my stomach. Marie grins at me, her razor-sharp fangs glittering in the low light of the bar. My eyes flick to the space around me.

The place is clean enough to get drunk in, but the smells of sweat, swamp water, and old beer permeate the walls. A sticky sheen covers the tables, and I know better than to put my ass on a chair in this establishment. Water Witches decorated the bar with ferns and moss, and several of them stand on display, pouring drinks and brewing potions to heighten one's senses.

"We should dance!" Marie shouts over the heavy beats of the music.

I smile but shake my head. Marie was the first Vampire I'd ever met. Her kind rarely frequented the Summer Court, preferring the cooler climate of Northern Aranthium. It wasn't a massive surprise since Vampires prefer the lack of sunlight.

When I met Marie, I thought she may have been among the most beautiful females I'd ever seen. Her willowy limbs and too-pale skin had been enchanting. Her fangs promised pain in the best way. I liked that she loved to party just as much as I did. We'd drunkenly kissed once or twice, but then she told me she "wasn't interested." Besides, she's a master at playing games.

As I watch her smile and laugh, a strange sensation clumps in my stomach. For some reason, the only person I can think about is the mysterious Winter Fae. She has haunted my dreams every night since we first met, and I keep replaying our conversations repeatedly.

A smile tugs at the corners of my lips, and I scan the room again, checking just in case the Winter Fae has somehow found her way to this dive bar.

Marie flips her blood-red hair over her shoulder, exposing the elegant curve of her neck in the tight black dress she is wearing. She leans over and whispers in the ear of the human man that she brought to the club.

Her eyes keep flicking over to me as if she wants to ensure I'm watching. This game, which she's been playing for several months, has long since grown boring. It's the reason things between the two of us never go further than drunken kisses and dancing. Marie wants to see how far I will go to win her over. She told me as much one night.

I'm over it. She is no better than the Fae who party day and night in the Summer Court.

I check the clock on my FaePhone. It reads a quarter to midnight, and I beckon the bartender over.

A Water Witch comes immediately. She is swaying to the

music, a bored smile plastered on her lips as she asks, "What do you need?"

I straighten my back, weirded out by her tone. "Water, please."

The bartender returns in the blink of an eye and slides a clear cup in my direction. I chug the cool liquid. My shift is set to start in less than two hours, and while I don't mind a shot or two to loosen me up, showing up to work inebriated would be a huge mistake.

Marie and the human are now walking to the dance floor. The other people in our group, Adam, Georgina, and Clarence, are shouting at each other, trying to decide what drinks will get them rip-roaring drunk the fastest.

Adam's large black wings occupy half the space at the bar, and he keeps slapping me in the back with them.

I shook my head. Angels. Never respecting anyone's personal space.

If this were any other night, I would eagerly join my friends. Getting drunk is rarely dull.

Bowing with a flourish, the chains hanging off my outfit clink together, and I say, "Alas, I must return to the Warlock's steel prison."

In unison, they let out an irritated whine. I open my arms wider, basking in the attention as I turn around. I swagger out of Water Witch Absinthe, waving one last time before I exit. It's a busy night, and a dozen cabs drive by before a shiny yellow car pulls over.

The driver, a Warlock with cat-like eyes and furry ears, stops at the curb.

"Where to?" he grumbles over his shoulder as I slide into his backseat.

"The main docks next to Fourth Street." I give him directions as I buckle my seatbelt.

The Warlock nods. "And what will you give me?"

Of course. There is always a catch when it comes to a Warlock. I sigh, running a hand through my hair. "I'll pay you your rush rate in dollars *or* a secret that no one else knows upon safe delivery to the docks."

He nods and spreads his hands wide over the steering wheel without touching the vinyl plastic. The car starts up, and the shift stick moves without physical prompting. I am relieved that the Warlock has agreed to my terms of payment. The driver picks up his FaePhone, sliding through a social media app as the car speeds away to our destination.

Warlocks. I roll my eyes and pull out my phone. Only ten percent remains on my battery, and I let out a long sigh.

"Can we turn on the radio?" I ask. I'm feeling vintage.

He grunts, and a button he doesn't touch clicks.

The newscaster's high-pitched voice is loud as she drones on about the usual fear-mongering in the world. This certainly isn't my choice of entertainment, but it's not like I have much else to do now.

"*... the Northern courts are in a political uproar. From the Fae to the Ice Mer, people are struggling with the defection of the royal family's heir after ruining a series of important trade deals between continents. Riots have erupted in every major Northern city... hard to know exactly what is happening with the intervention of the military forbidding Northerners from leaving or communicating with those in...*"

Anxiety and tension are twin weights pressing down on my chest. Breathing is harder. The silence would have been better than this. Hearing about riots and danger doesn't bring me any joy. As a general rule, Summer Fae don't engage in conflict. We create. We enjoy life. When conflict inevitably arises, we sidestep the actual problem and drink until the problems no longer seem as bad.

As the newscaster continues, I shut my eyes. Immediately, the image of the mysterious Winter Court female comes to mind. Does she have family in those riots? Is she worried about them? After a week of dreaming about her, I am fairly sure I will see her again tonight.

My entire body is jittery. On edge. Feverish warmth and excitement pound through me.

The rest of the drive goes by in a blur, and I only snap out of my stupor when the Warlock parks the car. He turns off the news before looking over his shoulder at me.

The Warlock raises a brow, and I can feel him considering whether I am worth asking for a secret. After a moment, he huffs a laugh and names a monetary sum. "Don't stiff me, or I'll cut off your ears."

I shake my head at the mindless threat and throw the cash at the driver, thanking him for the ride. As I climb out of the taxi, I sigh in relief. I don't have to remember if there are any secrets no one knows. If I were to tell a secret that someone knows, even accidentally, it would end *very* badly.

Anticipation builds with each step toward my office. I put one hand in my pocket, nervously lighting and extinguishing a flame between my thumb and forefinger. The repeated action is soothing, and some of the tension in my shoulders dissipates.

I draw my hand from my pocket when I open the office door and snuff out the flame. My employer sits behind the desk, sifting through a large stack of papers. What kind of name is that? Boss? He believes himself to be so much better than me that he never even told me how to address him otherwise.

"Sprigg. Perfect. You're here on time." Stating the obvious, he sniffs the air once with his long, crooked nose before his purple eyes look at me accusingly. "You were drinking."

The words aren't phrased as a question, which is good. I can't lie, but I can easily choose not to answer sentences like that. Instead, I shift my weight from one foot to the other.

The Warlock pinches the bridge of his nose with long, pale fingers. After a moment of obvious deliberation, he looks at me. I don't know how I can tell—without irises, his eyes are just purple voids—but I just feel the weight of his glare.

A full minute passes before he leans back in the chair.

"I suppose your kind has existed for thousands of years and operates an entire court half-drunk. I won't do anything this time, but try to be more discreet next time."

I nod. There isn't anything else to say.

He inhales sharply. "Seriously, you smell like you rolled around in the bar." He raises an eyebrow, but I don't take the bait.

My business is my own.

He stands to leave and points to a stack of papers. "I expect these to be finished before the end of your shift. Make sure the northern clients do their paperwork before they disappear."

Thrill spreads through my body like water from a hot spring. Northern clients. She is coming. I hesitate, and he notices.

"What?" he growls.

Dammit. I wanted to ask about the clients in a casual and not-at-all creepy fashion. Unfortunately, the chance of doing that just went out the window. I blurt out, "Is there anything I should know about them? The clients, I mean. They seem–"

"Don't finish that sentence." The Warlock's eyes flash violet, and a shudder runs through me. "I don't pay you to ask questions."

"No, but–"

"I would stay as far away from them as possible. Northerners are a savage people. Their government will just as soon kill you if you are seen talking to them."

That threat shuts me right up.

He nods. "I see you understand." He walks over to the door, putting his hand on the knob. "One last thing, do not look at their paperwork. Those documents are for my eyes only. Remember, Nathaniel, I will know if you do it."

Nodding tightly, I settle in the chair. "Understood." Enchanted papers. Losing my eyeballs. The usual.

A shudder runs through me as he swings open the door, and a brisk wind blows through the office.

The door slams shut behind him, and I run my hands over my arms. To say that the Warlock is very unnerving would be an understatement.

Lighting a new flame in my hand, I stare at the brilliant red and orange light as it casts small shadows on the walls. Worry and anticipation grow into a twisting knot in my stomach with every passing moment. I eyeball the enchanted papers from a distance. My desire to know the Winter Fae's name is at war with logic.

In the end, I decide not to risk it.

I quite like my eyeballs.

THE CLOCK ON THE WALL READS NEARLY 4:30 A.M. DESPITE HAVING slept in this morning, my body is worn out. Disappointment runs through me, and I keep glancing out the windows.

The dock is still empty.

I finished all my paperwork hours ago, and now it's just me and my thoughts—a dangerous combination on a good day.

An artificial water droplet sounds, and I pick up my phone.

Adam: You miss all the fun, prick.

Four picture messages follow of the group doing more shots and screaming the lyrics of whatever bullshit song is playing. Suddenly a video message from Marie comes through of her grinding against her human.

I roll my eyes and put my phone away.

Then, I hear it.

The door clicks, and my head shoots up. I swivel the chair around. Exhaustion is forgotten, and my jaw drops open.

The Winter Fae stands in the doorway, wearing the same clothes as before. I thought I'd remembered her perfectly, but seeing her now...

She defies memory. Her hair isn't simply black; it is ebony, with veins of dark red. Her eyes are as pure blue as paraiba tourmaline. The tattoos are still stark against her dark skin and almost shimmer in the firelight. Full lips quirk up to the side.

I have been around for a while. I know what I am saying when I say that no woman, dead or alive, will ever be as beautiful as her.

Then, like the stupid Fae I am, I open my mouth.

"Hi," I say dumbly.

Hi!? Suddenly, eloquence has no place in my mind. I am reduced to nothing in her presence.

"Hello again." A tight smile spreads across her face. "I thought I would take care of the paperwork this time." She grabs one of the metal folding chairs from the corner, dragging it to the front of the desk. She plunks down, crossing her toned legs. I hadn't had the chance to admire them properly during our last encounter.

I'm happy to note that they are perfect, like the rest of her.

"Where do I start?" Her voice is strong but quiet in the small place. It's the kind of voice a millionaire uses when he speaks about humility.

I slide the papers across the desk. The palpitations in my

chest are going to kill me. Pointing to the first one with a pen, I whisper, "Right here."

Is it getting too hot in here?

"Thank you," she says softly. Her voice is like music to my ears. She looks at the papers before her and doesn't say another word as she fills out sheet after sheet. There is no flirty eye flicking towards me, no attempt at conversation, just unparalleled focus on her task.

This is the first time I have seen such meticulous attention to detail. I can't help but marvel at her mannerisms. Watching someone fill out paperwork has never been so captivating. This is the highlight of my day. My week.

A few minutes in, she tugs at each finger and pulls off her leather gloves. Her hands are covered in the same white ink.

"Gods, it's hot in here."

I blink. It isn't just me.

A mumbled agreement makes it out of my mouth. I can't manage anything else because my attention is fixed on those amazing hands. This nameless female keeps her fingernails short and neat, but her fingers still have an elegant, lyrical quality.

I could spend an eternity watching her hands. They dance across page after page, and I am completely and utterly enthralled.

Filling out paperwork is such a mundane task. I don't know how she puts up with it. She's a Fae–shouldn't she be doing something better with her time? I don't know many Winter Fae, but I would assume that they had better things to do than this.

Her eyes flick up again, and my heart skips a beat. "Do you mind?" she asks.

My eyebrows draw together, and she jerks her head toward my flame.

My eyes widen. "Oh! Of course." I snap my fingers, and the

flame shrinks to the size of an acorn. I shoot her a sheepish smile before she returns to the papers.

Questions bubble up inside of me. There is so much I want to know. So much I need to know. Does she have another person as cargo? Did she kill the last one? How can she focus so intently on something so dull? Will she try to trick me?

So many questions and so little time.

Perhaps the most important of them all: What is her name?

I want to know everything about her. Her favorite color. Food. Drink. Does she do anything to pass the time?

Has she been dreaming about me like I've been dreaming of her?

Probably not.

I huff a laugh, and she looks up again. "You're odd."

I nod in agreement, biting my tongue to keep the questions inside. If she thinks I'm odd now, a barrage of questions won't help her views of me at all.

All too soon, the mysterious Winter Fae finishes her last signature. Sadness wells up within me as I retrieve a sizable black envelope from the drawer in the desk.

Reaching for the papers, our eyes lock, and I am bewitched. I want to dive into her eyes.

The most unnerving part is the way she does not break eye contact. She doesn't seem uncomfortable at all. Seconds go by, and we remain unblinking, holding each other's gazes. It's strangely intimate. Personal.

The temperature of my flame burns brighter and hotter with each passing second. I want to look away because I generally don't seek real intimacy, but the more primal part of me wants to be seen by her. To know her and let her know every part of me.

I don't even know her name, and yet I would reveal my deepest, darkest secrets for a moment of her time.

A bead of sweat trails down my forehead, breaking my

trance. A ghost of a smile flashes across her face, and she reaches out a hand. Snowflakes pop into existence, and she extinguishes my flame. The room instantly returns to a normal temperature.

My eyes widen, and something like satisfaction stirs in my chest.

Fire and ice.

She reaches for the envelope. I am acutely aware of how she avoids my hands. Something daring takes root within me, and I can't help myself. I graze a fingertip against her thumb. Those blue eyes find mine again. My heart swells with feelings that are too big for my body. Am I really this starved for attention?

No. My gut tells me this is something special, something unique.

The female's face doesn't shift at all as she stands to leave. She gently pulls her fingers away without saying a word.

Regret stirs within me, along with something else. An intense feeling of impending loneliness. I don't want her to leave. I have to think of something...

"How many people have you killed? Did you bring another tonight?" I blurt out rather loudly. My self-inflicted mental beating starts up instantly.

She lets out one breathy laugh. "You talk too much." Laying the papers in the black envelope on the table, she meets my gaze again.

My heart stutters.

What is wrong with me?

I don't have time to get control of myself before she turns to leave.

"Don't worry. I will see you again," she says over her shoulder.

"When?" I call after her.

"Hard to say, Summer Fae," she calls over her shoulder.

Boss's warning about northerners runs through my head, but I don't care what that old man thinks right now.

She saunters along the steel walkways and pauses in front of the ship. I watch her through the gray-glass window for as long as possible.

For a second, I think I glimpse her looking back at me—the profile of her long lashes and round nose—but the frozen mist swallows her whole as she leaps onto the railing.

When I can no longer see her, I walk to the chair where she sat and graze a hand across the backrest while picking up the envelope. A small piece of paper flutters to the ground, and I immediately bend to pick it up.

Did she forget something?

It is folded in half.

Tucking the enchanted envelope under my arm, I spread the note open with my thumb.

You have very nice eyes.

My free hand flies up to touch my eye, wondering what she could find so unique about the same amber-colored eyes that hundreds of Summer Fae have. The phrase is so... direct. Not like the Fae I know at all. It is so... honest.

I put the file away hastily before pulling out my golden wallet. Separating one of the leather pockets, I carefully place the little note inside.

CHAPTER 4
BACK TO REALITY
ELVA

"*Are you listening to me at all?"*

A tinny voice comes through the speaker of my FaePhone. I glance at the silver rectangle resting on the counter while I munch on freshly baked cookies and daydream about amber eyes.

Those damn amber eyes have been infiltrating my thoughts for days, distracting me. I almost missed a job because my head was in the clouds. It is that man—the Summer Fae. Something about him has been haunting me every waking moment for the past two and a half weeks.

Did he get my note?

Sighing, I keep my mouth shut and sip my coffee.

I can't lie, and even if I wanted to, I'm talking to my best friend—well, really, my only friend—Helena. She's a master at figuring things out from afar. We've known each other since we were younglings, and she's the only connection I've kept with my old life.

"*Hello?*" Helena starts speaking again. *"This is important. I'm asking you if you will return for the Summer Solstice."*

"When I come back, you'll know." Not an answer, but since I have no intention of returning to my mother's iron grip, it's the best one Helena will get.

"*Fine*," she grumbles. "*I have to go. I can hear my new butler, Alastair, calling for me.*"

"Enjoy the swim, Helena," I say around a mouthful of chocolate chip cookies. "I'll call you if I can."

No promises.

Never any promises.

Saying our goodbyes, we hang up the burner phones before I jump in the shower. I let the hot water run over me. The steam eases the perpetual tension that seems to live within my shoulders. I lather myself in a cooling peppermint body wash, enjoying the scent as it slips over my body.

Lifting a hand, I trace the white tattoos permanently scrawled across my dark skin. They are a reminder. Of my heritage. Of the promises I made to myself.

And a reminder of all the things I'm running from.

"You are not some common *Winter Fae," my mother scolds me as I march into our home and pull off my fur-lined coat. "You can't run about the world and ignore the Northern court. It's not appropriate."*

"I don't care about being appropriate, Mother," I reply icily.

This is the third time we've had this argument over the past week.

She examines the new tattoos on my hands and face, raising a manicured white brow. "Clearly not. Are you still cavorting with that fishhead?"

"Her head isn't the part that looks like a fish, Mother. Helena is one of the Ice Mer Princesses, and you have a treaty with her father."

"She's not a good influence on you," Mother snaps. "Helena likes humans. She dreams of visiting the South. She's far too much like that uncle of hers. Hades hasn't been the same since his wife died."

"Mother!" I gasped. "His wife died *in the Rebellion. He's a Demi-God! You can't say things like that."*

My mother ignored me. Typical. "Maybe I should send an ambassador down there, rethink a few things in our—"

I roll my eyes and huff. She stops speaking, glaring at me with her cold blue eyes. She always gets like this when I talk about having or wanting friends. Anything that could cause a rift between us is considered a threat. But I can care for more than one thing at a time, unlike her. "Goodbye, Mother."

Flinging my coat on the nearest chair, I huff and walk down the long lobby and into the chef's kitchen.

The head chef Theodore, a Warlock who specializes in all things delicious, wordlessly hands me a giant slice of chocolate cake covered in an exorbitant amount of frosting the moment I enter his domain.

He waits until I've devoured half before sliding a cup of milk across the island at me. I wave a hand at the glass, and ice crystals form on the glass. Once it has reached the perfect temperature, I take a long drink. Iced milk can cure a thousand problems. I should know. I have many.

"Everything all right, Elva?" he asks, his voice low.

Theodore's been helping to look after me since I was a youngling. He always knows when I need something decadent and filled with chocolate.

"Not really," I reply, tracing circles in the icy condensation around the glass. "I don't want to talk about it. One day, Theodore, I will get out of here."

My phone rings, the shrill sound transporting me back to the present.

"You'll have to wait," I mutter under my breath.

Showers are one of the few things I enjoy in this life.

Standing under the rushing water in my shabby shower, I let the now-frigid water run over my naked body. Most Fae would get out by now, but I'm impervious to the cold. It's in my blood.

After another half hour passes, my skin has begun to wrinkle. I finally step out and dry myself off using one of the frayed towels my asshole Vampire landlord left for me. "All-inclusive" apartment, my ass. My mother's icy heart would stop beating if she saw the shack I call my home.

I can afford better, but why should I pay for an expensive apartment when I'm rarely home?

Toweling off, I glance up and see myself in the mirror. My long black hair is piled on top of my head in a messy bun, accentuating the sharp points of my ears and my ice-blue eyes. My white tattoos stand out from my dark skin, practically glowing in the dim lighting. They run from my face down my upper body, curving down my arms and breasts before disappearing beneath the towel. If I were to remove it, I would see the tattoos running to my hips before they disappear. I have none on my legs. Yet.

A project for another day.

My phone dings from the bedroom, reminding me of the missed calls.

Sighing, I leave the bathroom.

"Back to reality, Jerry," I say absentmindedly, addressing the cactus on my windowsill.

He doesn't respond for obvious reasons.

Picking up my phone, my eyes widen. "Dammit, Jerry. I have four missed calls and a dozen text messages."

Silence is my only response.

Shit. I knew I stayed in the shower too long.

Three messages are from Helena, including a video of her swimming in the glacial waters surrounding her home. Her long, gray-blue tail with pink highlights swishes up and down while she soars through the water like a dolphin. She's wearing a pearl band around her chest that glimmers in the sunlight. My best friend is joined in the video by two younglings, whose own tails flap around as they splash around ice floats.

Me: Don't tell me the twins are already swimming independently.

Me: I had no idea Ian and Giselle were so big.

I send the text, intending to scroll through and check the rest of my messages, when my phone chimes immediately.

Helena: They are. We're visiting the seals today.

Helena: I'm definitely winning the 'cool-aunt' trophy of the year.

Before I can reply, my phone chimes once more.

Helena: Heading out into the sea, hugs.

I flip the camera and send Helena a selfie of myself waving before sighing and scrolling through the rest of my messages. They're all from my boss, a variation on the theme of "get your ass in here now" and "I don't pay you so much to relax."

Sighing, I send him a passive-aggressive thumbs up before tossing off my towel and pulling on my favorite pair of black leggings and a cozy taupe sweater. The fabric is warm, and I run an appreciative finger over the hem of the oversized sweater.

Human fashion has certainly evolved over the decades. This might be my favorite style yet.

Grabbing one last chocolate chip cookie, I toss my phone in my pocket and lock the door before heading to the window. Flinging it open, I relish the feel of the cold wind on my cheeks as I stand, taking in the beauty of the night.

A clawing begins deep in my chest as my animal seeks freedom. She's always been eager to get out and soar through the nights. Breathing in deeply, I summon her before leaping out of the window. I relinquish control over my body, allowing my snowy owl to take shape. The wind blows underneath my wings, holding me tight in its grasp.

The feeling of freedom overwhelms me as I soar through the city.

Three hours later, I'm regretting that last cookie. My hands are on my hips as I stand in the cramped warehouse, staring at the blueprint my boss laid out before me. Running my tongue over my teeth, I wish I had taken the time to brush them before flying out. By the sounds of it, I won't be coming back for at least a day.

"Tell me once more why we're doing this?" I run a finger over the blueprints of the two-story home. By all appearances, it's a regular dwelling. Not exactly my usual job.

My boss glares at me, his eyes sharp despite the late hour. "Because we're being paid to do this. Money is money." He spits, a disgusting glob of saliva landing on the grimy floor in a glob. My insides shudder in revulsion.

Gods. Humans are the worst.

"What's my cut?" I don't even lift my eyes from the paper, committing it to memory.

My employer rattles off a number, and I whistle.

"Exactly." The grin is evident in the human's voice. "Besides, we're bounty hunters, not the morality police."

Morality police.

As if. Human ideas of morals are far different from Fae ones. This human and I have a tenuous working relationship, at best.

Mostly, I ignore his ridiculous antics, finding the rowan berries he sews into his clothing amusing. Once, I saw him stuffing salt into his pockets. As if those could ever stop me.

They might work on lesser Fae, like the dirtbag from a few weeks ago, but not me. Very little in this world can stop a Fae like me.

When the human hired me, I made it clear. No questions about my past. All he knows is that I come from the Northern Courts, and I'm a powerful Fae who happens to be good at killing. Sometimes I catch him side-eying me as if he thinks I will glamour him or something.

He's wrong. If I am going to kill him, it won't be using magic.

No, if I am going to glamour someone, it will be someone far more interesting than a middle-aged human with a beer belly who thinks he's some sort of god just because he can hold a gun and not shoot himself in the face with it.

Idiot.

"Fine," I spit out, swiping the blueprints and tucking them under my arm. "What do you want me to do with the target once I have him?"

"Take him to the usual spot," he replies.

This evening just took a turn for the better. The Summer Fae's face flashes before my eyes, and a little thrill wiggles in my stomach.

I nod, looking at the large clock hanging on the back wall. 7:00 p.m.

"All right. It looks like it'll be another all-nighter for me."

The human rubs his beer belly. "That's why you get paid the big bucks."

Among other reasons.

"You want him alive or dead?" I ask flatly. I don't like having to inquire, but I am used to death. I've gotten good at doing it quickly and cleanly.

"Alive, this time. Make him see reason, then dump his ass. He can find his own way home." Raking his hand through his greasy hair, the human belches loudly. It is all I could do to stop from shuddering in disgust. "Blake is already expecting you."

I hum, double-checking that I have everything, before shoving my phone in my pocket. I toss my hair in a ponytail and wink at my boss. The coward takes a step back, a look of fear on his face.

I huff a laugh and flick my hand. Instantly, I extend my magic, brushing his cheek with my icy touch. I haven't moved, but I can see his face paling as he remembers who he's dealing with. I could make him do whatever I wanted, and we both know it.

Just reminding him who's really in charge here.

"You got it." Winking again, I swing on my heel, marching out of the warehouse without a farewell. No need to discuss payment.

He knows to send me my cut as soon as I send him the proof. He's already seen what I can do when I'm angry.

Buzz-buzz-buzz

Swatting my phone in my pocket, I send whatever idiot is calling me to voicemail. This is not the time for a social call.

I have my eyes on the target, a Summer Fae with long blond hair tied into a man-bun at the nape of his neck. Perched in the rafters of his small bungalow, I'm sitting in the shadows while I wait him out. I have the perfect view of my target as he walks around without a care in the world.

The Fae's pointy ears are sticking up over his hair, and even from here, I can see that he is bedecked in an ostentatious amount of jewelry. He has at least five earrings in each ear and large rings hanging off each of his eyebrows.

He looks about thirty years old, but he could have centuries under his belt. There's no way for me to know without talking to him. The Summer Fae is currently walking around shirtless, giving me a prime view of his sculpted chest covered in tattoos of flowers and butterflies. Not precisely menacing, but who am I to judge any Fae's looks?

According to information my boss sent to my FaePhone, this man is tricking local musicians into coming to Summer Court and performing for the local Fae. Once they arrive, they find themselves bound to service for eternity.

It isn't necessarily against the law for Fae to *encourage* humans to come to the courts, but it is most certainly frowned upon when humans get caught up in a favor and are bound to the land. Something about the mistreatment of humans, their rights, blah, blah, blah.

How very *human* of them to care about others. In the Winter Court, the only thing that matters is power. Self-preservation is a natural instinct–the only instinct–that matters in the court of my birth. Even familial ties mean nothing when it comes to staying alive.

It's every Fae for him or herself.

Perched as I am above the Summer Fae, I have the perfect view of him as he plops onto his couch and turns on the television. Sighing, I rest my head against the wall.

Come on, hurry up and fall asleep already.

He hits the lights and turns up the volume. I choke on a laugh when the theme music for *The Real Life of Pixies* comes from the TV. The reality tv series follows seven Pixies as they trick poor, unsuspecting humans into performing ridiculous acts for them.

Helena would love this show. She's always had a soft spot for humans. That's one of the reasons my mother hates her so much. There is no room for softness in the northern courts.

By the third straight episode of *The Real Life,* my prey's yawning every two minutes. I'm not surprised. There are only so many pixie antics someone can take before falling asleep from boredom. They call it trash TV for a reason.

Forty minutes later, the sound of snoring fills the air. The Fae has no idea I'm here, and he's sleeping peacefully.

Fool.

Using the dim glow of the television to guide me, I slip down from my resting place and hang onto the rafter. My muscles tighten, and for a moment, I dangle above him. A crack comes from the next room, and I pause.

No one else should be here. I checked the place thoroughly, but still...

My heart is hammering, my hands gripping the rafter as I dangle above the unsuspecting man. Twisting my head, I stare at the open doorway, where I heard the noise.

Then a soft *thud* fills my ears.

A dozen curses roll through my mind as I release the rafter, landing silently on crouched knees. The sleeping Fae snores, and I step away from him towards the direction of the sound. Within half a minute, I am standing in front of the doorway. My hands are balled into fists, my magic at my fingertips, and I peek into the other room.

It's dark, the only light coming in from a streetlight, but I hear a strange sound coming from against the wall. Narrowing my eyes, I hold my breath as I crouch.

Green glowing eyes meet mine, and the breath whooshes out of me.

"Damn cat." Extending a hand, I run it down the feline's back before turning around. Walking on silent feet, I hurry back into the living room. Triple checking all the doors and windows, I make sure we're alone.

When I'm satisfied the cat is the only other living being in this home, I get to work. Slinking back to the Fae, I fish a slim needle from the pack on my back. Walking to the back of the couch, I slide the silver tip into the back of his neck.

He draws in a sharp breath, but before he can do more than shout, "What?", I press the plunger.

Moments later, he is deep in a medicated sleep. Pulling out zip ties from my back, I bind his hands and feet together before I heave him over my shoulder.

"Goodbye, kitty," I say at the door. "Have a nice life."

No response.

The cat and Jerry would get along well.

Twenty minutes later, the man is stuffed into the back of my nondescript SUV. Blaring country music, I drive to the dock and toss the keys to Frank. The Winter Fae is scowling as he stands in an empty parking lot near the docks, his hands stuffed in the pockets of his fur-lined coat. Despite his grouchy demeanor, he's one of the few Winter Fae I trust, and he always works these jobs with me.

"Get him on the boat, and let's go," I say gruffly. My bones are weary, and the cat has made me jumpy. I'm tired, and it's already been a long day. The only thing keeping me going is the thought that I'll get to see that Summer Fae again.

A groan catches my attention as the blond Fae lands on the deck. The serum is wearing off, but I wave a hand before the man can do more than moan. Ice encases the lower half of his body.

He swears, the sound muffled through the gag.

"What was that?" I asked, crouching beside him as I lifted the corner of the gag.

He snarled. "Let me go, you Fae bit–"

Waving a hand, I released the gag, and his eyes bulge. "And that's enough of that."

Covering the wordy Fae in a layer of frost, I glare at him as his brown eyes stare up at me with hatred. He mumbles something else beneath the fabric, but I ignore him.

"Don't worry," I smirk, baring my canines at him. "My orders are to keep you alive. It's just a little frost. It won't kill you."

Leaving the male shivering on the ground, I get up and grab the railing. The wind blows in my hair, the cool breeze a lyrical song to my Winter Fae soul. Snow is our brethren, and the cold is our partner in crime.

As the boat moves, a sense of peace warms my icy heart. It begins as tiny as a snowflake, continuing to grow as we approach the city. Something about the port is calling me, beckoning me forward.

CHAPTER 5

NOTES AND THE LACK OF NOTES

NATHANIEL

A shipment has come in every Thursday at 2:00 a.m. like clockwork for three months. It has become my favorite day of the week. I've stopped going to parties on Wednesdays because the adrenaline from my top-secret appointment is thrilling enough.

The Winter Fae female does not know how long I spend molding myself into the image of cool, calm, and collected before she comes. Apart from the first few times she arrived at this hour, she's never been late. My heart picks up as the time nears.

Right on time, her ship pulls into the dock. Sometimes she has other Fae or humans assisting her, but she is often alone.

Those are my favorite times.

I grin. Within minutes, it's clear that tonight is one of those times. She leaps off the boat, landing on the icy dock without a care in the world as she saunters towards my office. The Winter Fae opens my door, and her lips form a gloriously genuine smile. I can't help but return it.

Tugging off her gloves and sitting down, she speaks first. "I have business in the city tonight." She pauses and eyes my over-eager face. "No cargo."

I know the drill, pulling out one of the lighter of the two stacks left behind for her.

"I feel sorry for whoever you are visiting tonight." I wink, feeling playful.

She smirks as if my advances amuse her, but she keeps responding. "Yes, well. You should be."

Leaning back in the chair, I shove my hands into my pockets. My left-hand fingers connect with the wallet that holds precisely four notes from her. She never mentions them, and I don't dare bring them up for fear she will stop leaving them.

My thumb traces over the worn paper edges as I watch her across the desk. Better than any reality TV show.

She is *real*. From her curly hair to her dusty boots.

I shift to the front of my seat. It is time for our casual five-minute conversation, where she will reveal herself once again as quiet, thoughtful, and powerful.

It is nothing like the wild, shallow conversations I have with Adam... or Marie.

These conversations always start with me saying something, mostly because I can't help myself, but she doesn't seem to mind. "So, tell me about your glamour. Do you use it?"

She draws her bottom lip through her teeth as though weighing her answer. "The Winter Fae have glamours and... other powers. I use it when necessary."

The answer sends a shiver skittering down my spine. It is painfully obvious that she is a bounty hunter. Very dangerous, but everything about it... I like it. Her confidence and strength are flames, and I am a lowly moth.

"Summer Fae are dreadful with glamours. They glamour anyone and anything they can to get a moment's amusement. Everything is a trick for them." Is that bitterness creeping into my voice? These are feelings put to words, not even thoughts I have fully formed yet.

"Is that why you left?" She arches a thick eyebrow.

I wag a finger playfully. "Tsk, tsk, tsk. No, darling. When I say Summer Fae, I *most definitely* should be grouped in that category." The word *darling* slips out before I think better of it and amusement dances over her eyes as she tilts her head slightly. It unnerves me.

"Are you glamoured now?" she asks.

I flash a smile. "For you? Never. Perhaps if we could see each other at a more reasonable time, maybe I could show you everything I'm capable of." My cheeks grow hotter, but not from embarrassment.

Her brows knit together.

I groan inwardly. *For Fortuna's sake,* I curse. *There was no way she didn't understand me. Gods.*

She tilts her head to the side. "What are you capable of? Do you have more birthright magic than glamour?"

Her red lips quirk up, and I realize she is getting some sort of pleasure out of watching me squirm. However, knowing this makes no difference as I again fall from dashing Fae to fumbling idiot.

"I'm a-a shifter Fae, so y-yes." I stumble over my words.

She leans forward. "Really?" After hesitating momentarily, she asks, "What's your animal?"

"Osprey. Weird for a Summer Fae, I know," I blather on. There's something about her that makes me want to tell her everything and anything. Delight lights up her face, but then, like the idiot I am, I continue, "I loathe shifting. I haven't done it at all since I've been here. No one even knows that I can shift. It's not a secret, per se... but I don't go shouting about it from the rooftops."

My shoulders relax, and I take a deep breath before I look

back at her face.

She's frowning.

Dammit. Is she... disappointed in me?

I wish I could take back what I said.

The metal chair creaks as she leans back. Her face has turned unreadable. "That's a shame. Birds are incredible shifting animals."

"Oh, are you—"

Her FaePhone buzzes on the table, but the brightness is set so low that I can't see who is calling. She answers and hurries out the door without even looking back.

I tap my finger on the desk for a moment before I realize she has finished the paperwork and will not return.

Expectantly, I shift the papers around without looking at them.

Tonight, there is no note.

My ribs grow tight, and my stomach clenches seconds before the nausea begins. My shoulders sag, and a feeling of intense disappointment roils through me.

CHAPTER 6

HE IS A LIGHT TO MY DARKNESS

ELVA

One year later

I soar over the port, letting my snowy owl take control as I glide over the city. It's late, and the stars are covered by thick, gray clouds that roil over the horizon. The moon is little more than a sliver, and a cold wind blows beneath my wings. It's dark, but I can see everything perfectly. The icy breeze ruffles my feathers, and I fly higher and higher in the sky.

I can feel my owl's joy. It tastes like the winter air. Cool, refreshing, and crisp. My snowy owl's body is small but powerful. With each flap, my stomach flutters in anticipation, and the wind propels me forward like I weigh absolutely nothing.

Doing this–flying–brings me small snippets of peace. I need these in my life. The gods only know everything else is rough. But this.

I love flying. It's exactly what I need.

Even though I haven't admitted it to myself, I know where I'm going. It's the same place I've flown over and over again for the past year.

Sometimes days or weeks will go by without me coming back. Other times, I make the trek night after night.

By now, I know the skyline of Port City like I know the back of my hand. My destination is always the same. I am drawn to the place like a magnet. It's been nearly four months since we last spoke, Fae to Fae.

I need to know if the Summer Fae is still there. There is something about him...

He is a light to my darkness.

We've had so few interactions in the past year, barely speaking since I slipped him that first note. And yet, every single touch, every passing glance, has been written on my heart. Thoughts of the mysterious Summer Fae have taken up permanent residency in my mind. He haunts me day and night.

Time is a strange thing. For the humans that live among us, time is precious—a commodity they value. Many of them treat every second as though it could be their last. And for them, it might be. Their lifetimes are unfathomably short, whereas Fae can live for eons if we are careful.

I'm not careful.

The fluttering in my stomach stops and is quickly replaced by a painful tightening. If being Fae means living up to the expectations my mother has for me, then I will kill. I will fight. I will live on the brink of danger and spend my days alone. Whatever the cost, I will do it.

Because I had learned a long time ago that freedom had no price that was too high for me. I would pay anything for my freedom. Better that than becoming the Fae my mother wants me to be.

What good is the ability to live a thousand years if I hate my life?

I swoop low as a stray seagull darts in my path. My squawk is a warning that the brainless fowl ignores. My owl's instinct takes over, and I open my talons and stretch my wings. Within moments, the bird is in my grasp. Death is moments away. And yet...

No sooner than my feet have brushed white feathers than my insides freeze.

My Fae brain is loud and clear. I don't want to kill this poor bird. It did nothing to me. Not really. And it deserves to live.

The shock of what I am about to do locks up my wings, and I drop like a stone. Plummeting toward the ground, the air grows damper, and the briny smell of salt becomes nearly overwhelming as I approach the ocean at breakneck speeds.

Flap! A demanding voice in me screams.

My wings obey without question. I am a faithful warrior, and there is still a certain tone of voice that gets me every time.

Once I find my wings again, I hover in place for a second. My lower lids blink rapidly, and I breathe through my beak. My heart races in my chest.

The smell of sunshine hits me like a wave, and I turn around.

I see the Summer Fae.

He is talking with the silver-haired Warlock. My head tilts to the side, and tingling in my chest tethers me in place while I watch him laugh and point to one of the boats tied to a wooden post. The words are pouring out of him in a way that has never happened between us. His gestures are wide, loud, and confident.

If I could've, I would have smiled. He is charming. The way that his head tilts back when he laughs at his own joke makes my blood feel like fizzy wine.

The Warlock looks over his shoulder as if he can feel me staring at them. In an instant, I am shooting back toward the sky.

I need to get out of here. The daydream has ended.

My heartbeat slows down, and a hollowness tunnels throughout my entire body. It is moments like these that crack the ice in my heart. The hairline fracture is terrifying. At a time, hunting the lowest beings of all species warmed my icy interior.

The thrill of freedom is no longer enough. With every being I kill, every soul I torture, a piece of myself is chipped away. I am passionate about protecting those who cannot protect themselves, but my life has been reduced to nothing else.

Sometimes I wonder why I bounty hunt at all. Take out one abuser, and a murderer pops up in their place. When I started, I told myself it was to make the world a better place. The riches were just a bonus.

There's a bank account with my name on it somewhere in this land filled to the ceiling with piles of money. But riches do not cure loneliness. Cold metal doesn't warm my frozen heart.

The only thing that makes me feel alive is seeing that mysterious Summer Fae. He is the spark that is keeping me alive.

I don't know him, but he is my entire reason for living.

I veer off toward a small island where I set up a temporary shelter while waiting for a contact. The temperature has already dropped to frigid temperatures, and a glass-sugar dusting of snow coats the coniferous trees. When my feet touch the solid ground, I am grateful for it.

I like being a bird. I have been raised to view it as a point of pride. I can almost hear my mother's voice when I close my eyes.

"Not all Winter Fae have a shifter animal, darling." She runs her manicured finger down my face in her version of a kind gesture. It takes all my self-control not to flinch despite the burning. Her long nail is sharpened like a claw, leaving a red mark on my face. "Treat her well; she will help you grow your power."

Despite our many differences, I have always kept that piece of my mother's advice in my mind. My owl is a part of me, and she has far fewer worries than I do.

I unroll the canvas bedroll I stashed in an icebox and work on making an igloo. It's not cold enough to last long term, but my magic should keep it for the night at least. The frost doesn't hurt me like the Southerners, but I've grown accustomed to more temperate climates. A damp chill reaches down into my bones and settles in my joints. They feel stiff.

My hands stretch out before me, and I close my eyes. Magic takes focus, so I take a deep breath. In through my nose, and out through my mouth. However, instead of feeling the delicate white strains of power flowing through me, I see hair the color of flames. Amber eyes focus on me from the other side of the room.

Enough, I think and open my eyes. My heart has other plans. Instead of seeing the frosty ground before me, I see my palms. They tingle as if they remember the last time I'd seen the Fae, and our hands had repeatedly connected.

His touch haunts me.

What would it feel like to hold his hand? Better yet, what it would be like to hold him. To touch him and feel his hands on mine...

Does he dream of me as I dream of him?

A strange restlessness takes over my body as I squat down and continue the deep breaths. I cradle my head between my hands.

I need to sleep. I need to rest. I have a meeting.

And yet...

I sprint across the cold ground. My feet pick up speed as I flex my powerful thighs and jump. In seconds, I've shifted back into my owl. My heart soars, feeling like I've set it free.

My wings grow sore as I race back to Port City.

The scents and sights change and my instincts take me to a place I know well. Metal, salt, and magic flood my senses, and I swoop to land on a fishing boat. The vessel bobs up and down on choppy water. It's dark, though, that matters little to a naturally nocturnal animal. I scan the area, my sights landing on the office nearby. Both flame and artificial lighting stream out. I don't have to get closer.

I see the mysterious Summer Fae sitting at his desk, filling out paperwork. There are bags under his eyes and deep shadows that seem to follow him around. His shoulders are drooping, and he keeps rubbing his eyes.

Why is he so tired?

Concern floods through me for this strange, nameless Fae. I flap my wings, trying to shake off the odd sensation. I need to snap out of this!

This is *not* an appropriate emotion for a Winter Fae.

It's for the weak.

And weakness is deadly.

I hiss, flapping my wings and stealing one last peak at the Fae before launching myself back into the night.

I shift and climb into my bed when I arrive at the igloo. Sleep claims me almost instantly.

Light and fast fingers run over my skin, dancing across my flesh. He touches my lips, my breasts, my hips. His hands are hotter than mine, carrying traces of fire, and my entire body tightens in anticipation.

A moan slips from my lips. "More," I beg him.

The flame he cast burns above us, and his pale face glimmers in the firelight. His skin is starkly contrasted to mine... opposites in every way. His auburn hair hangs down like a curtain, and though he has no name, I know him as I've known no other.

He bends, kissing me slowly. Softly. It's not enough. He's teasing me, but I don't want that. I want all of him.

I surge forward, wrapping my hand around his neck and drawing him towards me. I need more. I need it all. My tongue probes his lips, and they open for me. He tastes of fire and sunshine and life. Our lips and tongues and teeth tangle, but it's not enough. I need more. I need him all.

In the next breath, our clothes are gone. Or maybe they weren't here at all. It's hard to know in this land of dreams. Either way, his pale body is pressed against mine. He fits me perfectly.

Warmth runs through my entire body, and I'm hot. Too hot.

I writhe beneath him, and his hand dips between my legs. His fingers tease me once more. Again and again, he touches me until all I can do is arch my head back and scream.

He captures my mouth with his, swallowing my cries of pleasure.

Heat runs through my body. I'm hot. Too hot. Flicking my hand, I cover us both in frost. It melts in mere moments.

The nameless Summer Fae chuckles roughly. "Tell me, darling, what do you want?"

I reach between us, my hand dancing over his length. "Everything," I said, squeezing lightly.

The sound he makes is half-relief, half-delight as he rolls us over and slides between my legs.

Once again, I'm hot all over.

Our hands, mouths, and bodies tell a tale older than time.

When it is over, we lie in each other's arms until the sun rises over the horizon.

CHAPTER 7

A DATE WITH DANGER

NATHANIEL

Sunlight is struggling to find a way through the gray clouds overhead. The mirror reflects my sleepy reflection in my ant-size bathroom. There's barely enough room to turn in a full circle in this glorified coat closet. My mother would never approve of me in such a small space. I grab an eye cream from the medicine cabinet and pray it will work miracles on these damn circles.

I'm happy to be off the night shift, but the purple bags under my eyes say I still haven't quite adjusted to the change.

My mind wanders while I brush my teeth, and I wonder if it's time to start taking vitamin D capsules. I'm not...

Well, yeah, actually. I'm in a full-blown bout of Seasonal Affective Disorder.

The Winter Fae and her crew never returned. There are precisely zero Winter Fae outside of their mainland anymore. The borders have been closed on both sides of the world. Whispers spread in the corners of this city about the dangers of Northerners. People say that if you see one, it is prudent to give up all sense of decorum and run for your life.

Based on what I have seen in the news, I am sure they are right, but I am confident that my Winter Fae was different. My heart picks up speed, and I decide that it might be time to start partying again. I never even had this woman, and yet I am dreaming of her.

This is a problem.

There is no one in my world who is so authentically themselves. There was something in her that my soul recognized over a hundred quick meetings and small touches. I don't know the details of her life, nor she mine, but I am sure that if we could only be given the chance to get to know each other, we would recognize each other for what we are: Two parts of the same whole.

Summer Fae aren't as outwardly violent as Winter Fae, but I know her darkness has a purpose. I like that.

Even if I am wrong about everything else, at the very least, I can say that every person she brought with her was a disgusting creature. Of that, I am sure.

It's 8:48 p.m. on a Friday, and I am staring one of Hell's sentinels in the face.

I make the mistake of voicing my thoughts about the nameless woman to Adam, who now thinks I am insane. He and his new boyfriend, Marcus, have taken it upon themselves to set me up with every eligible female they know. Just because they, an Angel and a Daemon, have somehow found love despite the odds, now they think they're experts in the matter.

It has been a very long and painful process. Mainly for the females. I got set up with two Were Women, one human, and an

Autumn Fae with orange hair and green eyes. Each is funny and generally fantastic, but I am... not great. Within fifteen minutes of meeting each one, I know it won't work. I am not in the head-space to be what they need.

They are lovely women. But they don't have dark skin, long black hair, and scrawling white tattoos on their faces. They aren't *her*.

It's adding to my seasonal depression, but I think the couple has finally given up. Now I am free to make my own terrible decisions.

Hence my choice to sit across from Marie. Completely sober. She has shown up for this date. She brought me to Vitta Bella in midtown. It is trendy, with floating candle votives lining the walls and sparkling under the glass ceiling. Foliage is every-where, creating cozy spaces for each table to eat in privacy. It is the nicest place I have been to since moving here nearly two years ago.

Her sin-red lips curl up as she glances at me while reading the menu. She's selected a dark-green velvet dress with pointed shoulders, a plunging neckline, and a train that trails several inches behind her. She looks like she belongs in the Vampire Realm, toying with thralls and playing with mortals.

It's a spectacular dress; she has worn it to commemorate a significant change.

On the other hand, I am wearing a simple button-up with my gray suit-pants from work. We are seriously not on the same page, and I wonder if she even notices.

Her arms slide forward, and the smell of roses and amber assaults my olfactory senses. The gold edges of the menu glint in the candlelight.

One of Marie's elongated canines slips out from her bottom lip. "I still can't believe you are here. My friends were sure you would never say yes." She bites her lip, and I swallow hard. This feels wrong. Desire swims in her eyes. I feel nothing for her. “It seems you are ready to play with fire.”

I'd much rather play in the snow, I think, and huff out a single laugh.

“What is so funny?” she quirks a red brow.

I shake my head. “Nothing, sorry. Just a stray thought,” I say quickly as I hold out a hand apologetically.

She purses her lips in a way that is probably supposed to be sexual. “Am I amusing to you?” Sensuality drips off of every syllable.

“No, I was just thinking of some... thing.” I almost say *someone*, but Marie is the jealous type. I don't want to cause a scene in the middle of this full restaurant.

But it might be too late for that.

Marie's eyes narrow. “Why are you here, Nate? After all this time, why did you finally say yes?”

I inhale sharply. I didn’t like being called Nate. Acid pools in my lower stomach as I try to craft a response. “Because I thought it was time to give it a proper shot.”

“Give a proper shot to what, exactly?” She swirls a long black fingernail around the crystal wine glass in front of her as the waiter set down the stuffed-lobster appetizers we’d ordered.

Nausea continues to build.

“Dating, being in a relationship,” I say quickly. I am not lying. I want to date. Just... not her.

"You want to date me?"

A direct question. "No," I breathe. My gut is telling me to get out of here. I suddenly can’t remember why I thought this date was a good idea.

Marie's face hardens, and she stops fingering the wine glass. A long moment passes, and I shift in my seat. The air between us is thick and tense as she leans forward.

"Good."

My eyes widen. That was not what I expected her to say. "Good?"

The Vampire's expression is very serious, and her eyes have a dangerous glint. “I am not a great girlfriend, but I am an excellent one-night stand.”

Suddenly, her hand drops to my knee. I swallow, and she starts sliding it up to my thigh.

I reach down and grab her hand. “Marie. Seriously? I don’t want to get kicked out of this place.”

“Awh, come on, Nate. You will like it, I promise. Marcus told me all about those *other females*.” Her expression clouds. “They were all pretty, but I know they didn’t satisfy you.”

Suddenly, goosebumps coat my arms. How does she know what they looked like?

“Marie, what are you talking about?” I am still clutching her hand, and I tighten my grip. “Have you been following me?”

Those canines come back out, and I want to throw up. For a moment, I think of the bounty hunter. She walks with power, with dominance. She is self-assured and captivating. The Winter Fae is nothing like Marie.

For one thing, she would never touch me without my permission. Certainly not in a crowded restaurant. And to admit to stalking me?

This has gone too far.

This woman in front of me is no longer my date. Now, the Vampire is someone to be dealt with. I straighten. “Marie, enough. I’ve changed my mind. Whatever you think is happening here is over.”

She is absolutely, certifiably insane. Marie twists her hand, bringing my wrist to her lips. Her cold lips kiss right over my pulse, and she inhales deeply. “Oh, come on, there’s a bathroom over there—“

"Not interested," I say, trying to pull my hand out of her grasp.

She is strong, and instead of letting me go, she runs her tongue up my skin.

I shiver in disgust. Gods. This is what men want when they go for Vampires, right? Danger, mystery, lust, obsession. If so, Marie is doing a great job.

But I don't want this. I can't be this guy, having an emotionless one-night stand. Even as the thoughts enter my mind, I feel like a sack of shit.

Marie's eyes are almost completely black. "*Nate*, no one refuses me. I am offering you gold, and you are acting like you don't need it. I have been watching you and know you need this."

Unbidden, a memory of the Winter Fae laughing at me tripping over myself comes to mind.

Marie inhales and freezes as if she can taste my emotions. Vampires are powerful empaths. Her eyes shift from black to glowing red instead.

"Who. Is. She?" she demands, her voice low.

Part of me wonders how far she is going to take this. "Someone I can't have. It doesn't matter, Marie." I yank my hand back, and this time, she lets go. "I'm going to head out, this was a mistake."

She sneers, but her eyes return to normal, and she looks like the Marie I've come to know. Almost as if the spell she was trying to weave broke before she finished. The Vampire sneers. *"You've been claimed."*

I roll my eyes. "Okay, Marie."

I wait for a second, but her expression has gone from fire-hot to unreadable. She has frozen me out. A long, awkward moment passes.

Grabbing some bills from my wallet, I throw them on the

table. Standing up, I push in my chair without even biting the food.

As I pass by Marie's side, her hand grabs my elbow. "Wait, it's not too late." That same lustful stare rakes up my body. "I can still have my fun. I will try dating you. But I have conditions. If either of us ever feels like it's not worth it, we end things, we—"

I've heard enough nonsense for the night. I rip my arm free.

"We're better as friends, Marie. I'm sorry."

I can't lie. I am sorry.

CHAPTER 8

WE KNOW WHO YOU ARE

ELVA

I stare at the flimsy printer paper in my hand, running my fingers over the words as though it will somehow change the message.

We know who you are.

Five chilling words and no signature. There isn't a whiff of magic on it. My heart beats faster, and I try breathing it back to normal.

Ten minutes ago, I found the piece of paper resting on the tile floor of my apartment, as though someone had slipped it under the door and run away.

Bits of the mug Helena had given me as a going-away present are still scattered across the ground from my shock. Green tea seeps into the cracks between the stick-on vinyl tiles.

My heart pounds like a racehorse, and my calming breaths turn ragged.

"It's fine," I say aloud, trying to convince myself. "Pack your things, get out of the city, and find a new place to live. You've done this before."

The tone of my voice isn't helping anything. My insides rear up at my lie.

It's not fine.

Nothing is fine.

My eyes keep going back to those two words.

We know.

I don't move. I barely breathe. No one had ever come to my house before.

Silky strands of ice mix in with my blood. Delicate white lace forms on the windows and crystallizes over the furniture. The temperature in the room plummets as the words reel through my mind.

We know who you are.

Solid chunks of ice form all around me as panic takes over. My hands tremble, and blackness edges out my vision.

We know.

Who are they? I think of every being I've killed. There isn't a single job that comes to mind where I didn't take every precaution with my identity. Thoughts stick in my brain as if they're also affected by my magic. With every second that passes, destruction takes over my apartment. Panic becomes my reality as I lose my tight grip on my magic.

Within a few minutes, every piece of my shabby furniture is locked in an icy, frigid embrace. Icicles form on the peeling paint, and frost crawls over the ceiling tiles.

The lights flicker, darkening as ice encases the hot bulbs. They sizzle before a series of *pops* fill the air, leaving me in darkness.

Jerry, my cactus, is surrounded by frost on his windowsill. Ice is creeping up the sides of his brown clay pot. He's observing the destruction, his silent disapproval clear.

But I can't stop.

We know.

I hear the coffee pot in the kitchen crack as snowflakes begin falling from the ceiling in a flurry. My body hurts. Every muscle aches, and I can't feel my fingers or my toes.

They know. Someone knows who I am.

Which means...

Pull yourself together, Elva.

Pushing my hand against my chest, I force myself to focus. I summon the only thing I can think of: the Summer Fae male. I can see him in my mind's eye as I struggle to regain control.

The flame he always has burning in the corner of his office comes to life in my mind. It unlocks my joints, slowing down the blizzard. Pain floods in. I used too much power too fast. Even for me, what I'd just done was a lot.

Breathe.

Picturing his beautiful eyes, I release my grip on my magic. The throbbing ache in my body brings me to my knees. Seconds become minutes as I fight to let go of the ice running through my veins. Slowly, so slowly, the temperature creeps back up to normal. The ice and snow melt, leaving six inches of water on the ground.

At last, my magic is back under control.

And I am soaked from the waist down.

Sighing, I sit in the water, just trying to breathe. When I finally look up, I find everything has fallen from the walls. The only thing still standing is the small cactus on the windowsill. "Shit. Jerry."

The plant sits unmoving as water drips from its outstretched limbs.

"I know, Jerry. It's my fault." I sigh, standing up. My entire body protests. Glancing around, I take in the now-destroyed apartment.

I don't have much in the way of material possessions. I hurry to the bedroom, finding that the frost didn't destroy everything in here.

Thank the gods.

It takes me less than ten minutes to change into a pair of black leggings with a matching hoodie and throw all my remaining crap in a duffle bag.

Jotting an apologetic note for my landlord, I throw a couple of pieces of gold on top before placing it on the counter and crossing to the front door. I hesitate for a moment and turn back to grab Jerry.

"You're coming with me."

Cactus in hand, I pull my hood as far as it will go over my head, covering my curly hair and telltale pointy ears.

For the first time in my long life, I'm grateful my mother is so ashamed of me. It ensures that very few people know what I look like.

Running into the stairwell, I take the steps three at a time as Jerry and I head to the underground parking lot. My owl strains to be released, but this isn't the time for her.

Three flights pass without issue when suddenly, I hear a voice in front of me.

"Oh, hey there, Apartment 416," a female voice says.

Groaning, I halt my descent. Sure enough, the perky Warlock from apartment 227 stands a few steps below me. Everyone in the building refers to me as 416. It's convenient. 227 is a five-foot-nothing Warlock who seems to imagine herself as everyone's best friend.

I've been sending her "leave me alone" vibes for several years, but she can't seem to take a hint.

The Warlock studies me, then raises a brow. "Are you going somewhere?"

Dammit. A yes or no question.

"Yes," I reply, my voice terse. "Now, if you'll excuse me?"

I gesture to the stairwell that she is blocking with her too-perky tiny body.

"Oh! Of course. I'm heading that way too. What a coinky-dink, don't you think?"

The Warlock giggles. *Giggles* in *my* presence.

"Sure," I grunt, shoving past her.

Unable to take a hint, the Warlock blathers on about some insipid apartment building gossip as we head to the underground parking lot. I tune her out as best I can.

"... 016 is sleeping with 302, but she's engaged to 112!"

"No." I gasp, trying to infuse as much shock into my voice as possible. Then, summoning as much dryness as I can, I glare at her. "I don't care."

That seems to finally hit home with 227.

"You don't?" Hurt clouds her face, and her eyes somehow get wider. "Well, you didn't need to be such a bitch about it."

Finally. I smirk. I'm almost proud of her for that little outburst.

We've reached the underground parking lot, and the Warlock peeks over her shoulder at me before sighing. "I'm sorry I called you a bitch. I hope we can still be friends, 416."

We were never friends, I say to myself.

I let out a long exhale. I am never going to see this chick again. Why not be kind for a moment? "Fine," I breathe, stepping past her to grab the door.

227 walks out beside me, grinning as though being my friend is the best thing she could have ever imagined.

My stomach twinges, and warning bells sound in my mind.

The lights...

Where are they?

The parking garage is pitch-black.

"What's happening?" 227 asks from my side.

"Wait," I breathe. I should be able to see. The hairs on my neck stand up, and I reach out to grab my little friend.

The space at my side is empty, and my hands clutch at empty air.

My heart races. My hands tighten. Muscles all over my body ache with a vengeance. My power isn't what it should be right now. My little outburst in the apartment was more draining than I had originally thought.

A loud noise comes from the space in front of me.

I jump, my hands curling into fists as Jerry falls to the floor with a clatter. My eyes widen as the lights in the parking garage slowly come back on, one at a time. They illuminate the lot as a shuffling sound comes from behind one of the cars. I hurry forward, my eyes widening as the Warlock stumbles towards me.

"Four... sixteen."

I grab her, feeling an unnatural warmth around her middle. Something sticky coats my fingers, and my stomach drops. I pull my hands away. Blood. The scent of iron fills my nostrils, and my head pounds harder.

We know.

Reaching deep inside me, I attempt to summon an icicle. My magic is exhausted, and my power comes as a trickle instead of a raging river. I glance around and don't see anything.

But someone is here. I can feel them.

I begin to run, making it past three cars, when suddenly, a bag is jammed over my head, and something sharp punctures my neck.

I punch and connect with a stiff muscle. A masculine grunt.

Good. I kick a leg once and then adjust my aim to land in the space between his legs.

The definitively male voice cries out as my foot makes contact. However, there is no time to celebrate because I still can't see a thing.

“Damn, give me the cuffs," the rough voice demands as he grabs my wrists and cinches them together. His grip is rough, and I know it'll bruise.

My vision is dark and blurry.

"No," I groan, trying to pull myself out of his steely grip. Whatever he means can't be good.

I reach for my owl, but a burning fuzziness impedes my mind.

Throwing my head forward with the intention of breaking my assailant's nose, I scream.

Or at least, I try to.

In reality, my voice comes out as a mangled mess, and I'm met with air as he ducks his head. I try to pull my hands away, but the man's grip is too tight.

Behind me, I hear footsteps. "The other one is dead."

No. More ice floods my veins, but this one is painful and unfamiliar. My chest constricts.

I kick out, but my foot meets air.

And then...

A cool metal weight lands on my wrists, and time seems to slow. A clamping sound ominously echoes through the parking garage before the burning sensation hits. It starts in my fingers, then it spreads through my entire body.

Fire. I am on fire. Every part of me is burning, and my vision has gone completely black.

Iron.

Agony ripples through my body, and I scream as the iron burns my skin.

My magic, my owl. The iron binds them. I can’t reach them.

A sob escapes my lips as an eerily impersonal voice breaks through the echoes of my agony. My body is failing. I cannot move any longer.

"It's me. We have her."

All awareness fades away.

PART TWO

CHAPTER 9
HELP ME
ELVA

One month later

Darkness has become my new reality. My only reality.

That and pain.

The iron cuffs are like fire on my wrists, burning with the fire of a thousand suns. I have lost all track of time. Minutes, days, weeks. None of it means anything to me anymore. I've been in this hole for so long that I can barely remember my own name. Occasionally, someone throws me a bottle of water and some scraps of bread.

That's it.

My life is reduced to being fed like a gods-damned dog.

Then I hear it.

A scraping sound comes from above me. I tear at the iron on my wrists until my fingers are bruised and bloody.

"Help me!" I scream, desperation leaking into my words. "Please, help me!"

For a long moment, there is no response.

Then, a crack of light appears above me.

My heart races. For the first time, something flickers to life in me.

"Help!" I screech even as I cover my eyes from the blinding light. "Please, help me. I've been kidnapped."

A cruel laugh comes from above me, and a shiver runs through me. "Oh, I know exactly what happened to you."

A knot forms in my stomach. "Who are you?" I ask, my voice cold.

The voice titters. "No, I don't think you get to ask any questions yet."

Something clatters to the ground next to me before I can do anything more than scream. I hear a *hissing* sound. Instinctively, I cover my mouth with my bloody hands.

But it's too late. A sickly sweet scent enters my nose, and everything feels wrong. Foggy.

Time slips away from me as I drift in and out of consciousness. Hands land on me. Bright lights. People tug on me. The darkness is summoning me. Cold fear runs through me. I try to scream, but nothing works. My voice is nothing more than a whisper.

And then, I'm thrown over someone's shoulder. A moan escapes my lips as they laugh. They drop me on the floor, and I curl in a ball.

A door slams shut.

I'm surrounded by darkness once more.

CHAPTER 10

MORBID CURIOSITY AND MILD OBSESSION

NATHANIEL

Three months later

"... P*olitical unrest in the North has reached an all-time high with the royal Winter Family facing the choice of abdicating their rule or producing another heir to eventually take the throne. With each passing day, more public executions occur in the streets.*

"The Alliance of Northern Courts has officially risen, with an Arctic Werewolf pack taking measures to take down the lockdown of all borders. King Phelix has been suspiciously quiet the last few months. The question on everyone's mind is, will the Northern Courts' citizens abandon their homes when the wall falls? Or is a revolution coming..."

I pause my music momentarily while my feet continue to pound on the treadmill. Plucking a wireless earbud from my ear, I watch the flat screens lining the wall in front of the elliptical machines.

My eyes focus on one screen as a Spring Mer reporter reads off the world news.

Watching the news and *working out at the gym? Gods, I have gotten so dull.*

I can't really help it, though. This dreary port town is buzzing with anticipation of what will happen in the coming months. We are the nearest city to the Winter Court, which lies directly across the sea.

Morbid curiosity and mild obsession with a female whose name I don't even know has me watching any available news from that region. If she has Witch Blood in her, that would make more sense. Maybe she bewitched me and that's why I can't get the Winter Fae out of my thoughts.

I shake my head. This irrational protectiveness is strange, but I can't help myself. For a second, my heart drops and I wonder if she is one of the people being beheaded or hanged in the streets.

Looking back on memories of the cargo she always brought into the port, I also wonder if she is the one doing the killing.

She is a strong woman. I remind myself. *She can take care of herself.*

That doesn't settle the unease rioting in my stomach, though.

I stop the machine and start walking back to the automatic spout that fills up my water bottle with a motion sensor.

The familiar whirring sound from the stream of water fills the air as I stare at a corner. My eyes unfocus as I enter an odd headspace where no thoughts exist. This usually happens after I get stressed out.

The buzzing of my FaePhone draws me from my strange brain-limbo. I look at the contact card.

MOM, LUCINDA IS CALLING YOU

I sigh and pick up the phone.

"Hey mom," I say casually. My voice is considerably higher than usual.

"Nate, darling, what are you doing right now?" she asks.

I roll my eyes, and bite back saying, *Talking to you, obviously*. I really don't like being called Nate. "What's going on? Is everything okay?"

Her high-pitched voice is slightly too loud for the phone, like she still isn't used to talking to me this way despite phones existing in our court for nearly a century. *"Sweetheart, I asked you a direct question. You're evading me. Are you evading me?"*

I shift my weight and the stream of water automatically stops. A yes or no question had to be answered directly. "No."

It's easy to hear her smile even through the phone, *"Good, blood of my blood. Now, tell me, are you busy? No evading."*

"No." I huff lightly and screw the lid on. I hear her breathing. "Gods, mom, just tell me why you called."

She titters. *"Will you be busy in the next two weeks?"*

I consider for a moment, trying to think if there are any big parties that will come up between now and then. To my dismay, my mind is totally blank. This is a trap, but I have nothing to protect myself.

"No, I'm not busy in the next two weeks." My heart is beating faster already.

"One last thing and then I'll let you go, okay?" she says, and I don't respond, still wishing she could just get on with it. *"Flesh of my flesh, blood of my blood, you owe me for bringing you into this world."*

Yup. Definitely a trap. I let out a long breath, walking to the lockers. The damage is as good as done, so I might as well find out what my torture will be.

"Yes." I breathe and pinch the bridge of my nose.

She squeals with delight. *"Perfect. I've sent a messenger with some Iter Dust so that you can spend the Summer Solstice with us."*

I can't help the groan that escapes my mouth. I completely forgot about the holiday.

It has been two years since I left home the night before solstice, and I haven't been home since. I suppose that now is as good a time as any to return. "Great, anything you want me to bring from the city?"

"How about you bring all your things so you can move back home and marry a Summer Fae?"

I am in Hell. Tension bunches up my shoulder muscles. "Bye, Mom,"

She starts talking again, but I hang up and walk over to the showers so that I can finish getting ready for the day.

ADJUSTING THE COLLAR OF MY FRENCH BLUE SHIRT, I CHECK MY HAIR IN the mirror one last time before heading into the conference room of a tall skyscraper that Boss has rented to meet with very important shipping clients.

The Winter Fae had apparently recommended me so highly that I received a promotion not long after their last shipment. I am now Boss' second in command.

It is good work for me. I am a dashing, charming Summer Fae, and schmoozing people is in my blood. Plus, in what should have been an added bonus, I work during the day. No more late night runs. Sadly, it doesn't make me very happy. All it means is that I have no chances of a midnight rendezvous with the Winter Fae.

Boss still won't tell me her name. He told me that if I ever grew the balls to kill him or trick him out of his own position, he would reveal this apparently top secret information. I had scoffed, but I think he was serious.

Opening the glazed-crystal door, I slide in and turn up my

glamour. I rarely *love* glamouring myself, but I need this deal to go well if I am going to ask for time off.

My palms, which were sweaty a minute ago, are now dry, and I know from experience that the wild look in my eye has turned to a tenacious glint. My glamour is exactly what rich Aranthians want to see in their shipping broker.

I paste a smile on my face. “My absolute warmest welcome to each of you, esteemed leaders. It is a pleasure to see factions of the Were, Mer, Fae, and Vampire sitting at one table.” I pause momentarily, taking the time to look them all in the eye, even if they scare the shit out of me.

“Each of your delegations possess highly valuable commodities that we are hoping to take to the larger market. Historically, many of your groups have warred against each other or even hidden access to these items. We hope that with your help, everyone at this table will become very, very rich.”

I pause for effect, taking time to walk leisurely around the room. A few greedy huffs of laughter ripple around the group.

I motion to the left, and a row of assistants who had been waiting by the southeast wall spread out, placing crisp white papers with pristine black script in front of each leader.

Papers in hand, I continue. “In front of you, you will find an NDA. Please sign before we begin. Your privacy is just as important to us as your money.”

Flashing my teeth in the most alluring way I am capable of, I wait. The Mer leader, Esmeralda, is an aquamarine female with long, green-gray hair is seated near me. She turns, the water in her electronic aqua chair splashing softly, as pupil-less teal blue eyes meet mine. She smiles, revealing razor sharp teeth, before winking at me.

My heart skips a beat, and I choke back a cough. I quickly recover when I realize everyone has finished. “Thank you for your cooperation. We will begin.”

The billionaires sift through the packets full of detailed lists of commodities that will be discussed alongside their estimated value in gold, silver, and copper.

The Vampire leader, Garret Thorn, makes his eyes go wide enough to match his thick, designer glasses. There's something about it that feels excessive, but the action seems to match his personality. Thorn has an aura of absolute violence around him, and Boss already warned me of the danger he poses.

The Were leader, Dante, is the only one whose expression remains calm and collected throughout the meeting. I would go so far as to say that he is disinterested, even. It's as if the amounts listed don't amount to enough money to bail out every Northern refugee.

Dante is... interesting. He's wearing a puff jacket and jeans, as if he didn't have a care in the world. If I hadn't been to meetings like this before, I would've thought it was a grunge look. Now I know that this type of relaxed, curated outfit costs more than my studio apartment rent for an entire month.

Taking out the tablet from a drawer under the mahogany desk, I pull up the presentation on the big screen so that we can begin.

The Vampire locks eyes with me, his navy blue suit adjusted to fit over his large body. I can see the blood lust in his eyes. Or maybe greed.

It is hard to tell these days.

CHAPTER II

BLACK OPALS

NATHANIEL

The negotiations have lasted nearly a week, and they have been every bit as cutthroat as I imagined. Yesterday, Boss stopped in briefly to announce the big-ticket item of the trade talks. Half the room shifted nervously in their chairs. Sure, talking about importing pearls the size of boulders to carve into furniture was appealing, but nothing compared to what we are talking about now.

Black Opals.

The most expensive commodity in Aranthium.

These gems, veins of dazzling color, are impossible to find and worth a hefty price of 10 million gold per carat. Despite their name, they are brilliant and swirling shades of blue and green that Fae eyes burn slightly when looking at them.

The real value of these gems, though, is not their insane price tag or their blindingly beautiful appearance. It is the magic that runs through them.

Anyone who possesses magic can use them, giving the user powers ten times their Fortuna allotted birthright. The problem is, in order to use the magic for more than a few moments, you need an actual gemstone, not just slivers of the material.

It is said that these are the gems of DemiGods. Several reports of dubious validity state that High King Hades created them from darkness.

I don't like fictitious tales.

Impossible as they may be to find, they are even harder to mine as they are prone to breaking. To top it off, if there is too much sedimentary rock around them, the magic is suffocated, giving them an even shorter shelf life once they are wielded.

"We have an entire storeroom filled with samples," Dante says. "We've been accumulating them for about two hundred and ten years." There is a smug gleam in his eye as he looks at Garret, as if this is him getting back at the vampire for centuries of oppression and bad blood.

"What?" Thorn yells. "You've been doing this in secret for centuries?"

Dante laughs, the sound tinged with echoes of violence. "They are *my* wolves, after all. It is only because of their predator instincts and excellent eyesight that we were able to develop this mining process." He lays his hands flat on the table. "Frankly, you should be happy I'm telling you at all."

The room falls into total uproar.

Unbidden, the Winter Fae's face crosses my mind and I think about the state of the North. Perhaps, I can make a deal and get a small portion of Black Opals to give her. She might need it in an emergency.

Three people shout out exorbitant numbers, as if the bidding had already started.

I tilted my head to the side and study Dante. Everything about him is designed to make others underestimate him. But I see him, and I know.

Danger lies beneath his skin.

Something bubbles up in my stomach, making me feel very apprehensive about looking directly at him.

I shove it down, amp up the exhausting shield of my glamour, and take back control of the room.

The sound of cheap glasses clinking against each other is the only thing I can hear over the ballad blasting from the crappy speakers.

I'm back at the dive bar, Water Witch Absinthe, surrounded by my usual group of friends. Adam, Marcus, and... Marie.

I guess you could call Marie a friend.

I am paying because, well, I'm loaded now.

The negotiations did not go poorly. In fact, they went so well that the day after the billionaires left, taking their violent tendencies with them, Boss called me into his office. The Warlock grinned, pouring me a glass of Fae mead so smooth, I could bathe in it. It was so old that my ancestors could be considered babies in comparison. He told me he would grant me whatever I wanted at that moment.

My chest tightens, and my fists clench. Every bone in my body wants me to ask for the Winter Fae's name, but my body compels me to ask for the week off.

The Warlock's mouth drops open and a look of shock crosses his face before he tilts his frosty head back and bursts into laughter.

"You, my friend, are the best Fae I've ever met." He claps a huge hand on my back. There is a mischievous glint in his eye.

Instantly, I knew I made a mistake. I might never have an opportunity like that again, and I wasted it on... Lucinda. Bitter resentment coats my mouth with a bitter flavor, making my stomach roil.

"Gods, they play such sad music here," Marcus complains.

I nod. The Water Witches have renovated again. The smell of kelp and salt really draws out the odor of stale urine. "*Morose* is a better word. And I kind of like it."

What did they call it? Ethereal new age or something.

"Awh, you have to go see your mommy tomorrow, don't you?" Marie edges closer to me with a shot in each hand. "If you're scared, you could come to my place. I can protect you." Her fangs slide out.

I roll my eyes. "Lay off, Marie. I think I saw some humans walking in. Why don't you bother them?" I have doubts that vampires can even get drunk after spending so much time with this female.

She pretend-pouts, but I see that same strange flash of real disappointment in her eyes. "What's gotten into you? You've been such a bastard lately. Are you changing your personality to impress that Winter Fae you used to pine over at the docks? Come on. How long has it been? Over a year since you last saw her?" Marie makes a disgusted sound. "Pathetic."

Everyone at our table becomes eerily silent. Marcus and Adam look at me with careful expressions.

My cheeks grow hot in a way that has nothing to do with alcohol, and I look directly at Marie. "Who are you to say I've changed? I was never more than a toy to you, anyway."

She snarls in response. "Don't you dare start with that shit, you arrogant ray of sunshine. Need I remind you your kind is weak, holed up in their 'sunshine tech court' because they are afraid of the world? I thought you were different." She glares at me with something two degrees shy of pure hatred. Slowly, she scans me from head to toe before saying, "It turns out you're just another male who can't take the cold."

She whips around and walks over to the group of human men.

No one speaks and I feel so... embarrassed? Ashamed? I don't know. All I know is that I want to get the hell out of here.

My chair scrapes against the ground as I shove myself. No one says anything as I throw a handful of gold on the table and storm out of the bar.

I don't call a cab. I walk straight to my apartment, stewing. My heart is pounding and my shoulders ache from a week filled with tension.

I'm so tired of this place... Maybe Lucinda will finally get what she wants. Maybe I'm ready to go back home and stay there.

CHAPTER 12
EVERYTHING HURTS
ELVA

I'm losing track of time. It's possible that months have passed at this point.

They've taken to drugging my food and water.

I tried to refuse it at first, but there's only so long a Fae can go without eating or drinking. Longer than humans, to be sure. Without nutrition to feed my magic and strengthen my body, I will slowly wither and shrivel up like a sun-dried husk in the middle of the desert that is the Gates of Hell.

I'm not okay with that.

I've tried talking to my jailers, but for the most part, they ignore me.

There's been a female Autumn Fae walking about, but she hasn't come anywhere near me. I hear her voice in the hallway outside my cell, speaking in hushed tones and giving orders. Whoever she is, the rest of them seem to defer to her.

The room is dark, and the room smells like mold. Underground, likely. I can hear creatures skittering around at night, and I stare at the strange albino rats with beady red eyes as they pour out of a crack in the wall. Their long, naked pink tails trail behind them, sometimes swishing and curling as they search for any leftover crumbs of my food.

I stay on my cot, and their animal instincts tell them not to join me if they wish to live. I don't sleep during those long hours, I just stare. They might be disgusting, horrid, vile creatures, but even shackled, I am the biggest predator in this cell.

Weariness is my reality. My bones hurt. Everything hurts. I barely remember a time in my life when I wasn't in pain. Using magic is but a dream now.

I am so tired. Tired of sleepless nights. Tired of my stomach that has been stretched too tight. Tired of the burns on my wrists serving as a cruel reminder of my lack of magic.

There's a solitary lightbulb hanging from the ceiling that constantly flickers on and off. They've left me a cot with a threadbare blanket and a peeling leather mattress.

An aluminum toilet and matching sink stand in the corner for me to use. Disgusting smells come from the open drain, filling the air with another layer of grime.

Today, I think I have had enough. All the rats have returned to their home, and I pick up the broken broom head they gave me to deal with their droppings.

As if.

Prisoner and servant.

My mother would have a heart attack if she knew. Broken broom-head in hand, I wait.

The soft grunt of a greeting comes from outside, and I know one of my captors has arrived. Prior experience tells me I have about two minutes to pry the sink off the wall. I can use it as a weapon if I get it off before they realize what I'm doing.

I think. My mind is moving slowly these days. But I have to try.

My hands search for the bolts on either side of the sink and twist. I've been working on these for at least six days, which is delicate, especially since the walls are made of iron. I hold my breath to avoid the revolting smell. Using my body as leverage, I heave. The soldering groans and the sound echoes through my cell. My heart falls into my ass.

Loud. It's far too loud.

There is no choice now, I either get this off the wall, or they beat me again.

I heave again as cold sweat beads on my forehead. Just as I tug once more, the door bursts open. A burly Vampire marches into the cell, and in his hand is a strange gun.

"No!" I shout.

But it's too late. He presses the trigger, and a dart pierces the soft skin of my neck. The poison spreads through my veins like ice, and my movements become sluggish.

“You won’t be moving these again,” he snarls at me, baring his fangs as his eyes turn completely black. “Wash your hands in the toilet tank.”

Despite my drug-induced daze, I try to move the sink again. I kick, trying to shove it to one side. The Vampire watches for a second, and I even slam my body against it, resulting in a myriad of purple and blue bruises, but it doesn't move an inch.

He is right.

Time slows as I fall back onto the floor. I can only pray that I wake before the rats come.

Just as my eyes go blurry, I see the Vampire rip the sink off the wall and leave.

The smell intensifies, and I gag.

Whatever drug they used this time isn't strong enough to make me fully unconscious. I am unable to move. Hours pass, and I lay there.

No one ever comes.

My brain is still wide awake, and it buzzes with endless thoughts.

If these people belong to my mother, I'm unsure why I'm still here. She's cruel, but I'm reasonably sure she would have had me carted to her when she found me.

No doubt, she has a lavish prison already prepared for me. Only the best cell for her heir. Helena and I used to joke that our parents were cut from the same cloth.

Her father is known in the seas as the Wicked Ice Mer King, Cruelest of the Cruel. King Phelix is the most evil of the three DemiGods who reign in Aranthium. His other two brothers, Raphael Zeus and Aidoneus Hades, are rumored as no less powerful but significantly more... fair in their treatment of their subjects.

My mother? She lives up to every single aspect of a Winter Court Fae. She's ruthless and cunning, devious to a fault. Her shifter animal, a white snow leopard, is frighteningly large and can snap a person's neck in one crunch. I've seen it happen.

No, if this is my mother, I would already be locked in my icy tower, awaiting my long-dreaded coronation. I know she plans to compel me into a loveless marriage the moment I arrive as punishment for my misdeeds. I've already escaped one such marriage. There's no way I can do it twice.

My owl is screaming inside, trying to claw her way out. I've never gone so long without shifting, and it feels worse than the iron cuffs.

I can't imagine living the way that Summer Fae male does. He hasn't shifted in over two years.

His osprey must be in so much pain.

Shaking my head. I try to imagine what his shifter form looks like. What it would be to fly next to him, soaring over the ocean together. My owl hums at the idea of flying next to another Fae, sharing wind currents, and experiencing life together.

The Fae I claimed without his knowledge.

I keep replaying our limited conversations in my mind,

dissecting every word, glance and note we shared. They're the only thing keeping me sane. I picture him in my mind, tracing his features over and over again in my drug-induced haze.

By now, I know every inch of his face. I memorized how his eyes look as he gazes at me filling out paperwork, thinking I don't see him.

I don't even know his name.

But I feel like I know him.

CHAPTER 13
HOME, SWEET HOME
NATHANIEL

The thick, rich fabric rustles around me as I wake up in my canopied bed. The smell of lemongrass assaults my senses, and I open my eyes. Bright colors fill my eyes, and when my vision darts back and forth, the wildflower wallpaper moves as if I were sitting in an actual field. This is what I think hallucinating would be like.

I mean, I could be. In the Summer Court, mushrooms will bloom anywhere. They like heat and magic. The bag of Iter Dust is still in my hand, just in case I change my mind about staying for the whole visit.

I sigh. The world around me is bathed in greens, reds, and yellows. Lucinda hasn't changed a thing in my room since I left. Seeing the paintings from my 'artistic phase' hanging on the walls, alongside a chipped Faerie lute dangling from a hook on the wall, I wonder if my time in the Port City was but a pipe dream.

Acid pools in my stomach as I wonder if everything had just been a dream. An enchanted vervain trip gone wrong. What if I never left this place?

What if the Winter Fae was just a figment of my imagination?

My limbs go cold, and ice replaces the fire running through my veins.

I pull back the covers, pressing my bare feet into the carpet. The warm, moss-soft material squishes between my toes. Real. That's definitely real.

I see the boxers I'd bought in a Port City department store, and my stomach's twisting worry evaporates. I let out a long breath, running a hand through my auburn hair.

It is real. *She* is real.

"Get your shit together," I whisper to myself. Today, I am forced to dress up in blades of green grass and dance till I drop.

The Summer Celebration is supposed to last an entire month. Summer Fae sleep through the morning and wake up in the late afternoon, when the sun is brightest, to party through the warm night until the sun rises. Then we do it all over again. And again. And again.

No one works during this time. My whole life, I have watched more Fae end up penniless and exhausted after these parties than at any other time of the year. In the past, humans were glamoured and tricked into becoming servants. They worked until they died.

My stomach clenches again. Many of our parties have been founded on similar tricks and tragedies.

I hate thinking that this is a part of my people's history, but not as much as I hate the fact that people say since we don't need to acknowledge the past since we have fair labor laws now.

Lucinda (Or 'mom,' as I refer to her out loud) is devastated I won't be there the whole time. When I arrived, I stepped around the truth and said that Boss wouldn't let me have so much time off. The truth is, I hadn't actually asked. Mom had only compelled me to come, not stay, after all.

I just really struggle when I go home.

Sometimes, when I am around my mother and sister, it's like all the progress and growth I made going out on my own vanishes. It's too easy to be irritated and unkind with them.

I move to the bathroom and start washing my face.

Undoubtedly, I will be introduced to dozens of Fae females. I once made Lucinda swear she would never compel me to marry, but that doesn't mean she won't try other methods. Honest, I'm pretty sure it has something to do with my parents being separated. Mom wants so desperately to see me happy and settle down with someone. She believes in love.

What a joke. Dreamers believe in love before the realities of the world settle upon them.

My mother wants me with someone who won't weave a series of conditions into a marriage that will dissolve the second one of them is hurt or irritated. Despite hundreds of conversations (fights) about this topic, she doesn't understand that my best bet is not finding a partner in a culture where conditions, tricks, and loopholes are considered normal.

Maybe I should do something unexpected and schedule a meeting with a family therapist while I'm here.

A laugh bubbles up inside of me, and I huff a laugh at my own joke. There are no therapists or counselors in the Summer Court. Here we glamour, drink, and trick ourselves out of problems.

I tug on my first outfit from a nearby milkweed-braided hanger. Lucinda purchased everything and has coyly refused my offer to pay her back. She doesn't enjoy owing me things, even though I swear up and down there will be no debt. Gifts do not exist in the Summer Court, just endlessly complex favors.

She buys me too many outfits, undoubtedly hoping I will miraculously decide to extend my stay with her. There is a part of me, deep down, that would love to do that. Despite it all, I love Lucinda and Cherie.

Love is a challenge when it's conditional. I want grace from my mother, and instead, I get consequences. Maybe consequences are good every now and again, but after my father Andrius left, I was a sad youngling. In the years that followed, I definitely did a lot of stupid shit.

Shaking my head, I take a deep breath. *Keep it light, Nathaniel. You'll have a better time if you can just relax.*

I wash up quickly. The servant has already drawn a lemongrass-scented bath.

Got to smell the part, too, I guess.

After bathing, I change into an eccentric outfit. *Technically*, fashion standards in the Faerie Courts are made to fit their seasons, but they are still outrageous. Thankfully, we mostly only dress like this for our solstice unless you are one of those Fae-fluencers.

Pulling on the moss-green tights that *are literally made of moss*, I put on the pointed green shoes and wrap the band of tall grass around my middle. My chest peaks out from behind the emerald-green blades, but my arms and collar bones are completely exposed.

Gold bangles are wrapped around my biceps, and a designer Le Baba Morgaine gold circlet nestles over my forehead. I have re-shaved the side of my head into intricate patterns and my russet brown hair puffs out in soft curls around the gold.

I flex my muscles in the mirror, watching myself vainly.

I look ridiculous, but by Fae standards, my mom will have a ball dealing with the prospective partners.

Our house's rich, cherry-wood banisters are gleaming with polish, and the stained-glass windows depicting the Summer God bathe the room in a thousand shades of green. For a moment, my chest tightens, and I remember that not everything in this home was miserable.

Sometimes, I can taint my own memories.

Cherie is waiting at the bottom, dressed as a summer-ripe peach. Her brown hair shines with golden undertones, and her cheeks, eyelids, and lips are expertly painted to match her voluminous dress. Layer upon layer of translucent tulle trails around her. She positively glows.

I haven't seen her since I got back, and I can't fight the smile that breaks out.

"Nate!" she screams and bombards me with a bone-crushing hug.

"Hey, Cherie." I push her back, putting her at arm's length so that I can inspect her once again. "You are... wow. Why are you so dressed up? It's only the first day of our celebration."

Her smile vanishes, "Listen—"

"Nathaniel!" my mother coos loudly from the hallway. Both Cherie and I wince. "Look at how absolutely amazing you look. So masculine, *so Fae*. Every *single* Fae will have their eyes on you tonight. Oh hell, what am I saying, even the married ones. You've gained some muscle! Your father never liked to do anything when we were married. I am so..."

She's still talking, but I tune her out. It isn't even a conscious effort. I have heard this spiel so often that my brain can't handle it again.

"Nathaniel? Hello," she drawls, and I snap back into reality. "Did you even hear me? No? Well, I said, did you hear the good news?"

"What good news?" I ask, and my eyes snap to Cherie, who is now fidgeting with her dress uncomfortably.

"Oh! You haven't heard then." Lucinda shifts while she reaches over and twirls a loose lock of my hair. "I thought Cherie would tell you." She pushes her lips together in an exaggerated motion as she lifts her shoulders and clasps her hands. "Cherie will be one of the first to get married today."

"What?" I burst out just as she commands, "*Flesh of my flesh.*"

I freeze. She is compelling me to listen, something Fae can do to those with weaker minds... or their children. "Your sister is getting married today; isn't that happy news?"

My jaw is released from its locked position, but my face remains blank. "Yes, it is wonderful. Congratulations, Cherie."

Lucinda is pleased enough that I can let my whole body relax.

Cherie looks at the ground, "Yes, *it is* wonderful." She meets my eyes, and a glimmer of... something hopeful shines. "His name is Mattias, and *he* is wonderful."

I freeze. Somehow, I'd never considered that my sister would get married. She grew up in the same house as me; heard the same lectures from our mother.

Something twists in my stomach. Yes, she is getting married, but *I didn't know.*

"Why didn't you tell me?" I demand, searching for answers in her clear, amber eyes.

"You never asked. In fact, you hardly ever call." Cherie wrings her hands, and a pang of guilt is a bullet slamming into my chest.

My mom watches me with an uncomfortable intensity as I lean in. "I thought you were dating that Spring Mermaid," I whisper. "Delilah, right?"

Pinkness tints Cherie's cheeks. "Honestly, Nate, that was over two years ago. Do you even care about me at all? I can date and marry whomever I like."

An awkward pause ensues, and I shift uncomfortably as my mother slips out of the room.

"Cherie, I didn't mean..."

She interrupts me, snapping, “It is possible to have more than one preference.” Her lovely amber eyes narrow.

Aaannnddd... full circle. I’ve upset Cherie. Now, this feels like a proper family reunion.

I dip my head, and my cheeks heat. “Yes, you can. I’m sorry, Cherie. I didn’t mean to hurt you.”

“All right.” Cherie eyeballs me.

I’ve never apologized before, but that’s what happens when you spend time with people who aren’t like you. It feels good to reclaim some of the person I am becoming.

The tension in the room dissipates slightly, and I reach over. "Can I hug you?"

Cherie looks dubious before nodding. I wrap my arms around her, squeezing tightly.

"Congratulations," I say earnestly.

"Thank you, brother."

“Ready to leave?” Lucinda re-enters the room and seems relieved that Cherie and I aren’t yelling at each other.

“Yes, Mom,” we say in unison. Like a couple of younglings. Cherie grins and nudges me with her shoulder.

“Excellent, the carriage is here.”

THE ‘CARRIAGE’ IS ACTUALLY ONE OF THE NEWEST ELECTRIC CARS, BUT who am I to argue?

The Winnowing Forest is the ideal place for Summer Solstice celebrations. The large, spacious fields filled with canopy trees and breathtaking flowers in every color provide comfort and privacy if needed. It will only last for a week before it is destroyed.

We pull into the parking lot, and a large toad-like man ushers us to our space. I get a better look as we pull in and realize that he is, in fact, a toad.

"No place like Summer Court," I murmur.

"What was that, dear? Oh! Look! That is where you will get married!" Lucinda squeals.

Cherie and I follow her gaze to the enormous, blush-pink peonies that have been flipped upside down. They have been enchanted to stay in that position, their huge stems pointing up to the sky to function as Marriage Huts. My jaw drops. Nearly two dozen peonies are lined up with two petals swooping to either side of their walls, creating an entrance.

Only a Summer Fae couple can get married at these celebrations. The party that ensues will be dedicated to all of them.

Faeries don't get married in front of other people like the Were or Humans. Since Fae can't lie, there is no reason for more than two people to witness their vows. And even then, the witnesses are more of a formality. A legality, in this modern time.

I assume Lucinda has encouraged this match between my sister and someone I have never met. She will likely be the witness from our side of the family.

The doors on our high-tech car open upwards, and we make our way out of the vehicle.

Lucinda immediately sees someone she wants to talk to, and Cherie takes my arm.

My brows raise. "Don't you need to go find your betrothed? You'll need to get to the marriage huts soon."

She lays her head on my shoulder. "We will find him together."

We walk in silence for several moments. "Nate, I know I should've told you. But to be honest, I wasn't sure what you were going to say. I didn't know what you would think of me. Marrying a male, and all."

I stop in my tracks. “What? Cherie, I love you. Really love you. It doesn’t matter who you marry, I just want you to be happy.” I face her. “Truly happy. Not for anyone else but you.”

The unspoken words pass between us. She knows I worry she’ll end up like Lucinda.

“Really?” Her eyes glisten with unshed tears.

“Really.”

“Then, Nate, would you come and be my witness? I know Mom was supposed to do it, but she’s so happy that I’m getting married that I doubt she will care.”

My throat closes, and I suck in a breath. “Cher, I’ve been an ass. I don’t deserve this kindness, but I would be honored.”

She grins and kisses me on the cheek. "You have been an ass, haven't you?"

We both laugh.

Another hour passes before we go into the Marriage Hut. My sister and mother go off for a conversation, leaving me alone with my sister's soon-to-be husband.

"Mattias, right?"

The Fae nods, and I look him over. The fading sunlight illuminates his tawny-gold skin as he stands uncomfortably still, holding his elbow with his opposite arm. He is utterly awkward, and I can’t help but laugh. Leave it to Cherie to find the misfit in a court of charmers.

Mattias has brought his father with him. An equally awkward Fae I recognize as a scholar. His half-moon spectacles sit on his nose, but when he smiles, I can feel the room warm up with love.

Within moments, my mother hugs Cherie. "Good luck, my dear!"

Moments later, my sister is standing in front of Mattias. The way they are looking at each other.

My heart squeezes. *There's no way... No way that Cherie found true love. Not in this place.*

They stand close, almost embracing as they hold each other's arms. Leafy vines with small, white flowers appear out of thin air and wrap around them.

There is no priest. No representative from the gods. The ceremony begins as my sister opens her mouth.

"Mattias, from this day forward, I promise to love you, give of myself, and hold you closely. *For this life and the life to come.*"

I go deathly still. No one uses those words in a Summer Fae marriage. Giving someone that kind of power over you is far too dangerous.

Tears spill down Mattias' cheeks and his voice cracks. "Cherie, I am yours. Give me what you will when you can, and I will do the same. I will turn away all others for you *in this life and the life to come.*"

My jaw drops open.

There are no tricks. No conditions that will eventually lead to separation.

It's impossible.

The vines glow, and the newly vowed pair embrace each other with a sweet, tentative kiss.

Struck dumb, I watch them whisper in each other's ears.

The Naming.

They not only give each other no conditions, but they also give each other their True Names. In doing so, they have given each other the ultimate power.

With True Names, a being can force a Fae to do anything. Of course, it's rooted in the traditions in every court, but it has become almost unheard of in the last five hundred years.

I want to curse Cherie for being so stupid, for giving someone so much power, but... he gave her his Name as well.

There is complete and total vulnerability between them. A place where love can be nurtured, where love can flourish.

Tears prick my eyes, and I see Mattias' father also crying.

I have been wrong about this place. Maybe there is love to be found here.

Maybe.

CHAPTER 14

I'M NOT A GOOD FAE

ELVA

"I'm going to kill you." I whimper, kneeling on the floor next to the iron door.

My head rests on the wooden frame, the only part of the wall that doesn't burn my skin every time I touch it. Despite the weekly ice baths they keep dropping me into, my hair is greasy, and my skin is covered with a slick layer of grime.

I've grown so weak that I can barely stand on my own anymore. Sitting is easier.

The hard cement cuts into my knees. The pain is a welcome reprieve from the fog of my mind. It reminds me I'm real.

I haven't left this position in hours, and my voice is weak from the lack of food and water.

"The second I get out of here. That's a... promise."

The threat is pathetic, even to my ears, and I wish for my magic.

"Do you hear me?" I muster as much strength as possible and yell at the top of my lungs. "What do you want from me?"

There's no response.

The only reason I know someone is here is because I can see

one of them from my position near the door of my cell. Sometimes they don't close the door after my feedings. Not anymore. I'm so weak, I cannot move.

"It's cowardly to keep me trapped here, drugged and in irons. Come and fight me like a real male!" I slur.

Nothing.

They don't listen to me. They don't even acknowledge my words. Gods, they treat me like the rats that infest this hell hole.

This is some sort of punishment only Fortuna could dream up. If I were to see the tapestry of my life, I imagine this stretch of fabric would be grey, dotted with the bright pink of rat eyes.

The bastard's back is to me, and he's watching a news channel on his FaePhone. He is shoveling donuts into his mouth, and I groan. Sprinkles are falling all over the floor as he eats.

Slob.

What I wouldn't give for something like that instead of the bread and questionable stews they keep giving me. On the good days, they toss me a piece of rotting fruit.

There aren't many of those.

I inch closer to the door opening, straining my ears. The volume is so low that I can only hear snippets of what's being said.

"...riots every day... death... contracts... no news... money..."

The only thing that still sometimes works properly is my brain. Today, I'm feeling remarkably lucid.

The newscaster drones on and on, but honestly, everything she says sounds the same as it always has. I've been alive for a long time, and I've come to two conclusions.

One, Aranthium is a messed up place to live.

Two, some beings are just evil.

You get rid of one, and two more pop up in their place.

Maybe they're born bad, but I know evil can be shaped. You can take a good being and pour enough anger, enough bitterness, enough sadness into them so they become the thing they hate.

I should know.

I'm not a good Fae.

Maybe I was when I was first born, but being a youngling in the Winter Court taught me that feelings are dangerous and caring is for the weak. I was raised to believe I was better than the other Fae in our court because I had more power.

Getting close to anyone meant they could be a danger to my birthright, so my mother made me push everyone aside. Her fear of emotions meant I grew up alone, with only myself for company.

When my father died, I cried for the last time in my entire life. Tears are a weakness. One that I can't afford.

My friendship with Helena was my first revolt against my mother's icy grip, but it wasn't my last.

Every time I look down at my tattooed hands, I'm reminded of every time I pushed back against her. Usually, that's enough.

But now?

Now she's getting in my head.

When I get really weak, I swear I can hear her berating me for everything I've done wrong.

I told you, Elva. Her snide voice bounces around, sometimes whispering, sometimes yelling. I can't tune her out. *I said you would get hurt if you left me, and look where you are now. You failed. I was right.*

Groaning, I fall back. An indeterminate amount of time passes before I drag myself back to the tiny cot. I have no strength left to pull myself up, but I try. My jagged fingernails catch on the fabric of a lumpy pillow. I yank it down and cover my head.

This is still better than the Winter Court, Mother.

At least I'm allowed to have feelings here.

CHAPTER 15
I WANT TO FORGET
NATHANIEL

I don't remember the rest of last night. The last few images that are still accessible are hazy. Even then, I probably wouldn't even remember Cherie's wedding and the celebration afterward if they hadn't shocked me out of drunkenness.

Mattias spins Cherie around. She is laughing so hard that I am worried she isn't breathing properly. Lucinda is off with her group of social butterflies (some of whom literally have butterfly wings) gossiping about who tricked who, her daughter's perfect wedding, and of course, who Andrius is with now.

The dancing circle forms and I am among the first to jump in. We spin so fast that the world tilts sideways, and the contents of my stomach threaten to make an appearance. The wild melody comes to a close. Filled with laughter, all the Fae in their bright, outrageous costumes break away from the ring.

Something about Cherie's wedding has softened my heart, and I even accept when the female next to me with the lily petal pantsuit asks me to dance.

We drink and dance with abandon.

I pirouette around with her, elevating her small body above me in a frivolous pas de deux. *No sooner has Petal Pants come back down than a bit of black, curly hair catches the corner of my eye. I stop dead in my tracks, and my entire body freezes. My heart, my lungs, my feet. They all stop working. It is like diving headfirst into the frozen ocean at the docks.*

My female partner tugs on me violently, unwilling to lose my attention.

But I am already lost in the memories of the Winter Fae. All the merriment is extinguished and suffocated by the rock-solid ice of the North. Months of news reports stream through my mind.

That sensation, the dulling of the heat and my fire, still clings to my skin. It is terrible. Bitter cold sweeps through my body and a whole flock of butterflies riot in my stomach. Sweat beads along every surface of my body. I disappear behind a tree and put my head between my legs while I breathe deeply.

I blink away, trying to distract myself from the nausea. Even now, I'm haggard as I pull on the cape shaped like moth wings.

The servants paint my face gold, and I bolt down the stairs without food. Lucinda and I rush to the party in an electric car glamoured to look like a log. Cherie, who I looked for instinctively in the early afternoon, has already moved into the home she had purchased with Mattias.

My mother's house felt small, empty without my sister. I know neither of us have lived here for a while, but change doesn't sit well with me.

I am eager to see my sister at the celebrations. Lucinda prattles on the entire way to the forest, but I barely hear a word she says. In my mind, I see the public executions aired on television. I picture the Winter Fae's head rolling across the iced roads. It terrifies me.

My palms are clammy as I tangle them in the folds of my cloak.

Eventually, the car stops. We have arrived.

"Where's the mead?" I say curtly, barely setting foot on the ground and cutting off whatever nonsense Lucinda is spouting about some female I danced with last night.

A server appears out of nowhere with a snap of his fingers, hands me a large glass, and then vanishes.

I want to forget tonight, too. And the night after. And after.

When I open my eyes, I'm leaning against a tree a short distance from the party. The air is warm, and the jewel-like stars twinkle in the sky. I'm close enough to smell the feast but far enough away to feel a calm, peacefulness come over me.

How did I get here?... And why *in the* hell *am I not drunk?*

I take a few seconds to realize a vibration is coming from the pocket of my velvet trousers.

BOSS AKRON IS CALLING YOU

Why is he calling me?

I press to answer.

The Warlock's gruff, masculine voice conveys his anger from thousands of miles away. *"Sprigg, I know you are out cavorting. Are you drunk?"*

I really wish I could say yes. "Surprisingly not, sir. But I'm hoping to be in the near future. What do you want?" I grimace at how harsh my voice sounds.

But, to be honest, he's calling me on my vacation, so he deserves it.

"You need to come back," he grunts.

"What?" I blink and look at the velvet foliage drooping low in front of me. I study the veins of the leaves, trying to figure out where I had passed out.

"Nathaniel, *focus. I need you back here. I got a call from my contact in the Winter Court. There will be an arrival in about three hours. They said you were the only one who could receive the shipment."*

The large toadstool to the south tells me that I am in the part of the forest which had been used by the Faun Dancers yesterday. The grass is trampled and shredded from their hooves. "I—"

"Don't even think about saying no. I know I'm cutting your vacation short, so I will make you a new deal. You can return right after this and have as much time off as you want, full salary."

I pause. My hand traces the buttons on the side of my FaePhone. It is a very attractive offer.

But I have something else in mind.

"No," I say.

"Sprigg, you know how much this made your career. Keeping my contacts happy is vital. I—"

I trace the silk joggers that end in cloven hooves. I don't even remember putting this outfit on, but I must've channeled the dancers from last night. Hence my location. I suck in a deep breath. "I don't want paid time off."

For him, everything is about money. To be fair, money is important. My quality of life is better with enough money to eat, and to pay for a proper apartment with an AI system. But I have more than enough money now.

More isn't going to make me happy. It won't remove the panic attacks and the loss of feeling in my toes and fingertips.

More money won't bring her back.

"Okay, out with it. What do you want?"

My Fae instincts flare at the sound of desperation in my employer's voice. He's lucky I'm in the mood for a deal. "You can't say no, or I won't come."

"... I'm not giving you my company," he blurts out. He speaks so quickly, it takes a second for my mead-addled brain to process what he is saying.

Once the full message is received, I smile. He is squirming. "It has nothing to do with money. But you have to promise me. I know you can lie, so our contract must be bound through magic."

Several seconds pass before he lets out a long breath. Deviousness is the song in my blood as it rushes through my veins and makes my cheeks hot. It almost feels like generations of Fae share a raucous toast in Fortuna's Afterlife. I won't be the first one to break here.

"Well?" I say with a grin that feels feral.

"Fine. I promise," he chokes out.

My chest puffs up. "Promise what?" I drawl.

An irritated sigh comes from the receiver. *"I will give you whatever you want as long as it doesn't involve money or taking over my company."*

I grin and stand up. "Good. I'll buy some Iter Dust. Be there in a half hour."

I'm already lowering the phone when I hear him yell, *"Wait, what do you want?"*

I quickly raise the device to my mouth. "I'll tell you when I see you."

"You f—" he starts, but I end the call.

My mind is clear enough for me to stand, and a laugh starts in my stomach and bubbles up in a riotous sound. As soon as I am back on my hooves, I start speed walking back to the eastern quarter of the forest.

Steering through the crowd, I spot Lucinda fawning over Cherie's outfit. I march up to them, slightly breathless from the elation.

"Mom, Cherie." I nod to my family before grinning. "I'm leaving."

Mother's pale amber eyes go as wide as saucers. "No, wait. You can't go. You promised you would come."

I smile. I am not a Fae fool. The promise I made was very clear and left no room for loopholes. "And I did, but that was your only condition. If you try to compel me, I will never speak to you again." My mother's mouth is still open, and I glance at my sister. "And Cherie will never speak to you again."

Cherie starts, but she has always been a sweet sister. She bites her tongue and nods. We've always taken care of each other when it came to Lucinda.

Our mother's mouth opens and closes, and a look of absolute shock is frozen upon her features. I grin back at her before turning on my heel and walking away.

"Send me my things! I'll come to visit soon!" I call. Even I am surprised. I have no idea exactly *when* that will be, but I do want to come back.

When I reach the parking lot, I find the strange Toad Usher.

"How much for some emergency Iter Dust?" I say.

"Where to?" the bulbous male croaks.

I stare at his skin, which is shiny from his mucous coat. I've heard of snail slime serum, and I wonder if it is as good for the skin as the commercials say. "Port City, near the Frozen Sea. I need to get to the shipping docks."

"Three hundred gold pieces," he says.

I am tense. It's an outrageous cost for enough Iter Dust to travel that far, but I don't have time to waste. I withdraw the electronic card from my waistband and wave it over his phone.

He checks his notification and nods. "It's done."

The toad hands me the pass, a small bottle filled with the overpriced powder. I unstop the cork and unceremoniously dump it over my head.

I'm smiling so broadly my mouth hurts. It doesn't matter. In less than three hours, I will see the Winter Fae again.

Face to face.

And this time... I will learn her name.

CHAPTER 16

A DARK NUMBNESS

ELVA

My captors are growing tired of me. They whine and bitch about me when they think I am asleep. They whisper my fate between themselves into the frozen air.

As if the icy air can't sense what I am. As if it won't bring their words straight to my ears.

Though I can no longer use my magic, it still calls to me. It brushes across my skin, trying to find a way in.

What began as multiple meals a day are slowly becoming less frequent. Some days, they refuse to feed me altogether. The pangs of hunger in my stomach, which used to keep me up at night, have faded to familiar aches. My muscles have deteriorated. The skin beneath the iron cuffs is raw, crusted with days of blood, and sticks to my bones.

They laugh at me when I ask for more food.

Rage heats my blood and makes my vision tunnel. If not for the iron around me, I would have killed them all long ago. There are eight of them in total. I've been here for so long that I know them all.

I have finally learned the Autumn Fae's name: Veronica. She's gotten sloppy with how she barks out orders. When my door hangs open, I see her dark chocolate hair and chestnut eyes. Those vixen eyes often flick to the burly Fae male. I think he is her partner, but I can't be sure.

There's a pair of Vampires donning black leather suits. I still don't know their names, but yesterday they dragged a couple of human teenagers in front of my cell after I called them "blood-suckers" and turned them into raisins so I could watch.

A Were pops in occasionally, but he seems to be separate from the rest of the group and rarely speaks to them.

The Fae keep three humans around all the time. They wear masks. No one uses their names, relying on their guns and drugs to keep me in line.

I hate the drugs more than anything else.

They've upped the levels of medication in my food, and it's harder than ever to stay alert. A heavy fog has taken permanent residency in my mind. I can barely think, let alone feel. A horrifying numbness is taking over the pain. Nothing is right.

I am alone.

I am beginning to believe I will die down here. Even my owl is feeling the effects of the drugs and iron. She's barely clawing at my insides now.

Instead of feeling relief that the pain is lessening, all I can feel is dread.

My captors refuse to talk to me, but from what I've overheard during my lucid moments, they're some type of fanatic group whose objective is to overthrow both the Summer and Winter courts. It's laughable, really. If they knew how much I hated my birthright and they had asked me to help them instead of kidnapping and drugging me, we might have been on the same side.

It's too late now, though.

I don't know how much longer I can last. Even now, I can feel everything fading away. My birthright magic, a gift from Fortuna herself, is little more than a long-lost dream.

Even my precious memories of the Summer Fae male are fading, his features becoming less defined as I succumb to the drug-induced hazes. Sometimes I imagine he is coming to rescue me, but I know it's all in my head.

He's probably forgotten all about me.

I don't blame him.

I'd forget about me, too, if I could.

CHAPTER 17
THE DEAL OF A LIFETIME
NATHANIEL

I'm standing outside the high-rise apartment building in the middle of Port City. Raindrops are splattering on the ground behind me, and I hold a black umbrella above my head. Thank the gods, I changed into regular clothes at my apartment before arriving.

I press the buzzer, and moments later, an ugly deep voice blares over the speaker. "*Good evening. Who are you looking for?*"

I blink at the politeness. It's not at all common in Port City. "Um, I'm looking for Boss Akron. The Warlock."

I'd earned his last name after working for him for years. He was still a bastard, though.

"*Ah, very good. Your name, please?*"

I lean forward, ensuring that I am heard. "Nathaniel Sprigg."

"*One moment.*"

I tap my foot against the wet sidewalk. That stupid grin is still pasted on my face. Feeling so excited about receiving a shipment is irrational, but I can't help the butterflies flitting around in my stomach.

It's been such a long time coming, but I will finally know her name by the end of tonight.

A Fae can be happy about things like that.

A full minute passes before I hear, *"Mister Sprigg, Mister Akron has accepted your summons. You may enter."*

I know he can see me, so I bow. I wait a few extra seconds so he can take down the enchanted wards that would suffocate me like a fish out of water if I walk through them too quickly.

The large black and brass door clicks, and I close my umbrella before twisting open the handle.

Entering the lavish building, I am greeted by a pixie the size of my thumb. "Mister Sprigg welcome. Follow me, please," the male says gleefully. His wings resemble hand-spun sunshine, and his uniform glitters under the crystal lights.

He escorts me to the correct elevator. My eyes trail around the room. Everything about this place is crystal, gold, and white marble. All excellent materials for wards to hold on to. The tiny figure doesn't converse as he sends me to the correct floor and supervises me in the elevator.

I smile and hand him a gold piece as I enter the alabaster-carpeted hallway. Boss owns the only room on this floor, so figuring out where to go is a simple task.

My terrifying employer opens the door as soon as I step in front of it. He's dressed in a black, knee-length satin robe that I definitely never, ever wanted to see him in. Gods, as if I didn't already have enough nightmares about the man. His white hair flicks up at the sides, and he eyeballs me. "This had better be good."

I swallow hard, averting my eyes. "I'm here about the favor, sir."

"No shit. Make it quick, I am busy."

In my effort to look away from him, I notice two wine glasses on the long, modern dining table. My eyes trail to the side, and I see the electric aqua-chair. My eyes widen in recognition. *The Mer leader.*

"Get on with it, kid. I don't have all night," Akron growls while he watches me.

I take a deep breath, tightening my grip on my umbrella. "I need the name of the female Winter Fae."

His expression darkens, and he clenches his fist. "You bastard." He rakes a hand through his white hair, and his purple eyes bore into me.

I don't move. I won't. These are my terms. I've waited too long to know her name. On my way here, I convinced myself this is the right thing. This might be my only chance to get this information, and I won't squander it.

I am rooted in place as I stare at the Warlock's pupil-less eyes.

"Sprigg–"

"We have a deal," I practically growl. My voice is hard, and I'm proud of how my words don't shake. "This has nothing to do with money."

A minute passes in excruciating slowness. The *tick, tick, tick* of the clock is taunting me. The tension in the room grows until breathing is practically impossible. My heart pounds, and the Warlock's hand twitches at his side. I can see him considering whether he should break the terms of our deal. Whether the consequences of doing so would be better than agreeing to my terms.

"You Summer fool," he seethes, "hasn't anyone ever told you that sometimes secrets are vastly more valuable and deadly than money?"

A pit forms in my stomach.

"We have a deal," I repeat simply. Holding up my hand, I spark a small flame in my palm. It's a simple threat, but I need something to remind him who I am. He might be a Warlock, but

I'm not entirely powerless, either. The flame is orange, and the scent of burning fills the room.

We both stare at the fire for another minute.

Then, the Warlock sighs. "Well, it is a foolhardy deal. I only know her first name."

My heart speeds up at that. Her first name. Something. Anything.

I haven't seen her in months, and yet I can conjure her face in my mind's eye.

Finally, I am getting somewhere.

"What is it?" I ask.

Akron shakes his head. "Her broker never told me her last name. But that doesn't mean I don't have my suspicions. If you are smart, you will stay far away,"—he pauses, eying me carefully—"and you will never waste a deal like this ever again."

"Spare me the lecture." I sigh. My patience has long since run out, and those butterflies from earlier are turning into nervous knots. I've waited too long, dreamed of her far too often to let this go now. "I need her name, and then I will go to work."

He sighs and shifts his weight. "Fine. Her name is Elva."

"Elva," I breathe. The name is little more than a whisper as it leaves my lips, yet it sounds like fireworks in my mind. Everything at that moment feels *right*.

Her name is Elva.

I say her name again and again, rolling it around on my tongue as though it were a fine winter wine. Crisp, chilled, and completely and utterly perfect.

The name suits her. I couldn't imagine anything else fitting her better.

My employer growls at me, "Shut up. Don't say that out loud. That name is dangerous. Now, get the hell out of here and wait at the docks."

I nod. I want to thank him, but I know he'd get angrier.

Somehow, his foul mood doesn't phase me. It can't. Nothing can bother me right now. I walk out of the apartment as though I am floating on air.

Today, I will see her.

Elva.

Hours feel like minutes, and seconds take an eternity to pass. Everything is off. I can't concentrate. I can't do anything. Waiting is my new reality. My only reality.

Her name is Elva, and I am going to see her today.

I don't look at my FaePhone. I don't read. I don't listen to music. I just sit.

Waiting.

The time that she is scheduled to arrive nears. I am like a child waiting to unwrap their Winter Solstice presents. It can't come soon enough. I pace the room, glancing at the window every few moments.

When the steel-gray of the ship finally breaks through the perpetual mist, my heart stutters. My entire body vibrates as I stare at the familiar boat.

At that moment, I can hear everything. Smell everything. The waves slapping against its hull. The shouts of the small crew as they pull the ship in. My ears even pick up the distant sounds of the gulls crying in the sea. The salty brine of the ocean assaults my nose as I give up all semblance of calm and rush out the door with the paperwork in hand.

My eyes are wide, trained on the boat, as I wait.

There is movement on the ship. My heart flutters. But the form… it's too big. Too burly to be her.

A male Fae jumps onto the dock. Another quickly follows him. They turn and talk to each other, and I just wait. Where is she? My eyes are trained on the boat. Surely she will come next.

But one minute turns into five, which becomes ten.

My fingers feel like they're about to fall off. I forgot my

gloves. But I don't light a flame. I don't do anything.

"Where is she?" I murmur.

Then, there is movement on the ship. A form emerges from the fog, and my heart skips a beat.

It's not her.

This last male strides towards me, the dock shaking with the force of his footsteps. He stops a few feet away from me, nodding his head. "Sprigg."

My mouth is dry, and bile rises in my stomach. Something is wrong. I know it like I know my name.

"Elva..." I murmur the word.

The Winter Fae stiffens. "Frank, actually." His voice drops, and he glares at me, stepping closer.

I hug my paperwork to my chest as if that will protect me against the burly Winter Fae's wrath. "Have you seen her?"

Frank glares at me. "What do you know of Elva?" His words are laced with venom, and my spine tenses.

Danger! The Summer Fae within me screams, warning me to avoid this conflict. But I won't. For her, I will do anything. Talk to anyone.

I need to know Elva is alright.

A large fist snakes out and grabs the neck of my sweater. "I asked you a question, dock-boy."

Ah. Now I recognized Frank. He had come here before. I swallow, tightening my grip on my clipboard. "I don't know much," I said truthfully. "I just thought she would come to see me tonight. They told me that she recommended me for this position."

The Fae furrows his brow, and a hoarse chuckle escapes him. He relinquishes his grip on my sweater, and I stumble back. "No, that wasn't her. That was me. I like you because you're not a hard-ass."

My mouth falls open, and I have lost the ability to think of words. My mind is swirling with a million thoughts. Before, I had been concerned about her dying. But now?

Now I *knew* something was wrong.

If she thought about me even a fraction as much as I thought about her, she would have come back.

Unless something had happened.

Against my better judgment, I blurt out, “Where is she?”

Frank’s brow rises. He studies me for a moment before shaking his head. “That I can’t say. She quit six months ago. Just stopped showing up.” A moment passes before he gestures toward the paperwork. “Is that for me, or...”

“Oh, yeah...” I had over the clipboard, wrapping my arms around myself.

Six months ago.

My stomach roils, and suddenly, my entire body feels like it's made of ice. He’s wrong, I know it. She didn’t quit.

Something has happened.

“Hey, what do I put here?” Frank’s mouth is contorted as he stares at the paperwork. He reads off a few lines, and I tell him what to write in a daze.

He thanks me again, smirking at my stupid expression, and stalks back to his boat.

The boat pulls out as I stuff the paperwork into my backpack. Grabbing my wallet, I take a look around the place. I won’t be coming back. I’m getting answers today, one way or another.

The door slams shut behind me just as Adam is walking towards the dock.

“Oh, hey, Nathaniel!” he calls out. “There’s a new bar in town, do you want to go tonight?”

I shake my head, hoisting the bag on my back. “Sorry, can’t!”

He protests, but I tune him out as I break into a steady run.

I am going back to Akron’s apartment and I won’t be leaving without any answers.

CHAPTER 18
WE'RE LEAVING
ELVA

"Get up, you lazy Fae." Veronica's voice comes from above my cot, breaking through my drug-induced haze. Everything is numb, and nothing matters anymore.

"Has it been a week already?" I mumble incoherently. My tongue feels thick in my mouth, and my eyes feel glued shut as I try to force myself back to consciousness.

I could have sworn they took me to shower only two days ago, but after the months I've been trapped down here, I've lost all sense of time. The iron cuffs on my hands feel like the heaviest of weights.

My owl barely calls out to me at all anymore.

Veronica laughs, the sound bone-chillingly cold and remarkably similar to my mother's. I shiver at the sound and instinctively draw my limbs into myself. My stomach protests the movement, cramping as I press my legs against my chest.

“No, you stupid Winter bitch.” She kicks the cot, and it rattles beneath me. “We're leaving.”

Leaving.

"You're letting me go free?" My drug-addled brain is having trouble keeping up with her, and I blink slowly. "I promise I won't tell anyone anything about you."

The Autumn Fae scoffs, smirking at me as she waves a finger. "Don't be a fool. It doesn't suit your complexion." My jaw drops open, and I search within myself for a speck of anger. Of outrage.

I find nothing but ice.

Veronica laughs, and the sound is tinged with violence. "You're coming with us."

Terror, fresh and new and different from the fear I've been feeling all these months, washes over me. It tastes bitter, and my mouth puckers. My limbs tremble, and my stomach becomes a tangle of knots.

This is it. I can feel it in my bones. They've decided I'm not worth it. They're going to kill me and dump my body.

My hands turn clammy, and silver rims my vision. "No, please." Tears slip down my dirt-stained cheeks, and shame curls in my stomach.

It turns out that when faced with my death, I am not ready. I need more time. There are things I need to do. A Summer Fae I need to see.

"Don't kill me." Pushing myself into a seated position, I clasp my grimy hands in front of me. The iron cuffs clink as they bang together, and I shudder.

If I had more energy, I'd be disgusted with myself. What an un-Fae thing to do.

"Kill you?" Veronica arches a brow, and she chuckles. "We're not going to kill you, you ice-blooded fool. What a waste of months of hard work keeping you contained. We're moving you."

Moving me.

I blink, unclasping my hands as the knot of terror unwinds within me. "You're not going to kill me?"

"Gods, no." She laughs, reaching over and grabbing my arm. "You're much too valuable alive. Now come on."

"What do you mean?" I ask.

In response, Veronica's long nails pierce my skin, and she yanks me to my feet. "You ask too many questions."

Before I can respond, a pair of hands land on my back. Veronica shoves me, and I stumble forward. A searing pain burns through my arm as it comes into contact with the iron wall, and I scream. Agony roils through me, and a sob escapes me as I tear my arm away from the iron, cradling it against my chest.

Veronica titters and shakes her head. "And they said I should be careful with you. You're weak, pathetic."

She grabs my arm, her nails digging into my tender flesh as she drags me out of the cell. I stumble after her, my movements jerky and limbs sore from disuse. She drags me through a darkened hallway, past two shut doors before pulling me up a tight stairwell. My lungs are burning, but she doesn't slow down.

A heavy metal door sits at the top of the stairs. Without stopping, Veronica wrenches open the door. Brilliant white rays of sunlight fill my vision for the first time in months, and I shriek, "It burns!"

Turning around so fast I can barely track her movement, Veronica snarls as she pulls back her hand. "Shut up!" Her hand flies through the air, landing on my face with a flash of pain.

I scream again. The sound echoes through me, but this time...

This time, the scream is different. There is pain, but there is something else.

Veronica has pushed past the numbness that has taken over my body. She has broken through the ice I'd built around my emotions.

And now bright, searing anger ran through me.

I look at the Autumn Fae, and I seethe.

I'm going to kill you.

Her violence has awakened a part of me that has been asleep since they started drugging me day and night.

"Be quiet, or you'll regret it," she threatens before shoving me out of the stairwell into the brilliant sunshine.

The moment I step outside, I know where I am. Only one place in Aranthium has biting, frigid winds like this. Only one place that has snow that glitters when the sun shines on it. Only one place where my breath crystallized in the air.

I'm in the north.

Shivers run through my body as my teeth start to chatter. My clothes are little more than rags now, and I'm not wearing boots. My socks are soaked in seconds, and my toes curl at the dampness that seeps through the rough material.

A long white van squeals around the corner; moments later, the door slides open automatically. Veronica shoves me, and I land on my stomach.

The vehicle is exactly what I'd expect kidnappers to be driving. A sticky gray carpet covers the floor, and empty takeout containers are strewn about the disgusting vehicle. There are only two seats. The back of the vehicle is empty, save for a lumpy blue blanket and the piles of garbage strewn about.

And me.

Seconds after I land on my stomach, the scent of rotten food becomes nearly overpowering. Bile rises in my throat as I look around. I get on my knees and look around.

A human male sits in the driver's seat, and I stare at him. He's new... or at least, he's not one of the captors I recognize. The man is thin, with a handlebar mustache and matching gray hair. His brown eyes study me through the mirror, staring at me with a mixture of pity and interest. He's wearing a flannel plaid shirt with a white tee underneath, and blue jeans.

"Who are you?" I ask.

He doesn't answer. He doesn't do anything except turn up the music. Moments later, Veronica climbs into the passenger seat.

"Let's go," she says curtly, buckling her seatbelt. The human nods. With a grunt, he throws the vehicle out of park. I am thrown to the ground as the van screeches away, and dread pools in my stomach.

Whatever is happening, I know it can't be good.

HOURS PASS AS MY CAPTORS DRIVE AROUND. I TRY TO KEEP TRACK OF MY surroundings, looking out the front window, but after a while, all the snow-covered trees begin to look the same.

One thing is for sure: I was right. We are in the Northern Court.

Where? I don't know. Of all the Fae lands, the Northern Court holds the most territory. Dozens of mountain ranges are next to icy seas and lakes. Snow-covered forests span hundreds of acres, filled with thousands of animals. Brave souls live in small cabins or tiny towns throughout the Northern Court.

There is one city. One major metropolitan area. One place I never, ever want to go again. Ice City. My mother's home, where she reigns.

We are definitely not there. None of the signature icy buildings are in sight, and I can't spot any of her minions. Thank all the gods for small mercies.

Rubbing my arms over my legs, trying fruitlessly to encourage some heat to enter them, I try to stop my teeth from chattering. It seems that months without my magic has made me weak, and the cold is seeping into my bones.

Every part of me hurts from being manhandled into the vehicle, and my bladder is about to burst. I shift, moving my legs and trying to adjust for comfort, but there is none.

Eventually, I risk speaking.

"Excuse me?" I ask, my voice barely more than a whisper. "I need to use the bathroom."

"Not my problem," Veronica responds sharply, her body firmly facing forward. She doesn't even look at me as she speaks, and that insult hurts more than anything else.

A minute passes, and we drive over a bump. The back of the car lurches, and I am moments away from soiling myself. In all these months, that was one line I never crossed. One thing that I kept for myself.

And this Autumn Fae bitch is going to make me soil myself.

Despair tries to well up inside of me, but I push it down.

"Please," I whisper, letting some of my despair leak into my voice. "I really need to go."

The human is trying to avoid looking in the rearview mirror, but his knuckles are white on the steering wheel.

Silence fills the vehicle, the pressure growing in my lower stomach, as minutes pass by. I think they're back to ignoring me when the sound of crunching gravel fills my ears.

"Gavin," Veronica hisses, slamming her hand onto the dashboard, "what in the seven circles of hell are you doing?"

The driver shakes his head. "I'm not going to let her piss herself, Ronnie. It's not right."

Veronica reaches out, grabbing Gavin's arm. "The boss says—"

"She's not a dog, Ronnie!" The driver shakes off her grip, glaring at the Autumn Fae.

My eyes widen as I watch the two of them. Everything out of their mouths is important information, and I have learned more in the past two minutes than I had in months.

Someone else is in charge here.

If I ever got out of this situation, I would definitely utilize that rather vital piece of information.

"He isn't here right now." Gavin turns off the ignition and hops out of the van. The vehicle shakes when he slams his door.

Seconds later, a gust of freezing icy wind enters the vehicle as the side door slides open. The human looks at me, his brows furrowed as he beckons me forward. "Come on, young lady."

I stare at him for a split second before making up my mind. I am no young lady, but if this man is willing to help me, I would go with him.

My legs stumble as I hop out of the vehicle, but I straighten within moments. Snow-covered pine trees are everywhere, and the road stretches deep into the forest. The sky is clear blue, but there is snow on the horizon.

I can smell it. As I breathe in deeply, cold, fresh air enters my lungs. It fills a part of myself that I hadn't even known was empty. With every second that passes, I feel more like myself. My brain is clearer. I can think properly for the first time in months.

"Come on," Gavin says gruffly. "Over here."

His shoulders are hunched as he stomps through the snow, and I follow him into the woods. Rubbing my arms together as best I can with the irons on my hands to ward off the chill, I start to form a rudimentary plan.

Maybe, just maybe, if I can play this right, I can get away from these people.

Gavin leads me into the forest, and I duck beneath an evergreen tree. Snow crunches, and I peek around the trunk. His back is turned for privacy, and he's standing about a hundred feet away from me.

After caring for my personal needs behind a tree—much better than the alternative—I bend and gather snow in my hands. I wash myself as best I can and run some of the cool substance over my face and neck.

It's freezing, and my heart stutters as the snow lands on my skin, but I'm cleaner than I have been in months. While I wash up, I run through my plan.

"Hurry up!" Veronica's ire is evident as she yells from the van. "We need to go!"

My time is up. Wiping my hands on my leggings, I shift around the tree.

"Coming!"

My eyes flit around the woods, searching for exactly the right tree. Some are too big, others too small. But finally, I spot the perfect one a dozen feet away. Trying to infuse my steps with nonchalance, I walk toward a large rotting log covered in sharp, jagged edges of wood. Against every instinct that tells me to be careful, I keep my arms against my side. My foot connects with the log, and I don't fight the fall as my legs connect with the fallen wood.

My mouth falls open, and the breath is knocked out of me as dozens of tiny lacerations slash across my skin. The acrid scent of blood fills the air, and a squeal that is not at all exaggerated escapes me. Step one: complete.

Staggering upwards, I pull myself up against a tree as Gavin turns around.

"Oh!" His eyes widen, and he frowns as he looks at my face. "Are you okay?"

This is it. This might be my one chance.

Sniffling, I think about all the terrible things my mother has ever said to me. A tear trickles down my cheek as I remember her calling me a "worthless Fae" for daring to stand up for one of the poor Pixies she was torturing for fun. Another one slips out as memories I had long suppressed surface.

Once the floodgates open, the tears I had shoved down for

months escape me. I do nothing to stop them, pouting my lips as a shuddering breath escapes me. I don't have to fake the trembles wracking through me as I twist my hands together.

"Not really," I whisper, holding my hands toward him. "It's just that I've had these cuffs on for so long, and my wrists are chafing so badly." I whimper, "*It hurts.*"

Gavin looks at me, his eyes filled with concern. He draws his bottom lip through his teeth, clearly troubled. "I'm not really supposed to..."

"*Please.*" I bat my lashes at him and try to make myself seem unassuming. Hunching my shoulders, I bend over and let a shuddering sob escape me. "Just for a moment. I'm sure it would be fine. Then I won't ask again."

He shifts on his feet, staring at me, before turning around. Veronica is on the other side of the van, talking to someone on her FaePhone. The wind is blowing, and I can't hear what she is saying, although curse words make it to my ears every so often. I feel sorry for whatever poor soul is on the other end of that call.

Sighing, Gavin reaches into his pocket. "Fine."

A spark of warm hope comes to life in my stomach. Gavin pulls out a thick, silver key, and I suck in a breath. Time seems to slow as he places the key in the cuffs.

My heart is a drum pounding in my chest. My eyes are lasers, watching his fingers slowly turn the key.

A second passes that feels like an hour, but then I hear it.

A soft click fills the air.

I gasp, my heart thudding in my chest as the thrum of magic in my veins returns to me. It isn't quiet. It isn't slow.

My ice magic rushes into me like a powerful wave. Tingles run through me, from my head to my toes, and I feel like myself for the first time in months.

And not a moment too soon.

A shriek fills the air as Veronica turns around. Her eyes widen as my cuffs fall into the white snow, disappearing from sight instantly.

"No!" she yells.

But it's too late.

I inhale deeply, letting my magic return to me like an old friend. I can smell everything. Hear everything.

My fingers tingle as I draw on the well of my birthright power. My hands twist in the air, and a dagger made of ice appears in my fingers. Gripping my weapon, I slam it into Gavin's chest. A bone-chilling strangled cry escapes him as bright red blood blooms like a winter rose on his gray plaid shirt.

He staggers towards me, raising his hands. "Why?"

"It was me or you," I whisper. Reaching out, I brush a hair back from his face as he falls to the ground. "I'm sorry it had to end this way."

Truth.

I would have rather not killed him. He didn't seem like an overly bad man.

But when faced with my life or his, I would choose mine every time.

A crunching comes from behind me, and I turn. Magic tingles in my hands, and I clench my fists around a new dagger as I eye Veronica. The Autumn Fae looks out of the elements here, and the gun in her grip only makes her seem even more out of place.

Modern weapons have no place in the North.

Eyes filled with violence meet my gaze. "I can't let you leave," she snarls.

At that moment, I know only one of us is leaving this place alive.

"It's not your choice," I reply.

Not waiting for a response, I summon the entirety of my birthright power. I dredge it up from the depths of my soul, and my veins tingle with the strength of my magic. It pulsates within me, and I can practically taste the frigid, icy power rushing through my veins.

It's been years since I've used most of my power. The amount of magic needed to survive outside of the Northern Court is child's play compared to what I grew up with.

But right now, I will use everything I have. My mother didn't raise a fool, after all. I had created an opening for myself, and I will not let it go to waste.

Waving my free hand, I release my grip on some magic. The temperature plummets, and Veronica screams as gusts of wind surge out of me.

My heart pounds as snowflakes the size of fists descend upon us. A blizzard like no other fills the air as ice and snow fall from the clear blue sky.

My magic *sings* within me.

"I will kill you!" Veronica shouts. She walks into the blizzard, intent written on her face.

She wants to get close to me.

I let her. I want to see her face when I win.

The moment she gets close enough to see the whites of my eyes, I exhale. Releasing my grip on the dagger, I release my grip on my magic.

Ice-cold water pours from my hands, slamming into Veronica. The moment the water touches her, it solidifies. Within moments, thick, opaque ice encompasses her body from the neck down.

"You bitch," Veronica seethes.

Her words wash over me like water.

She's not wrong. I am a bitch.

One who is going to survive and make it past this day.

The Autumn Fae's eyes are still moving, still watching me as I walk toward her.

"I wish this could take a lot longer. I would love to repay you for all the wrongs you have done to me." Shaking my head, I sigh. "But alas, I have things to do."

Turning my back on Veronica, I twist my hand as I walk away. My lips tilt up as an ear-piercing scream echoes through the forest. Birds fly up in the air, shrieking in alarm as the sound of shattering ice fills my ears.

When I turn back, the only evidence of Veronica's existence is the blood-covered ice now strewn around the clearing.

Heading back to Gavin's body, I reach down and draw his eyes shut before searching his pockets and pulling out the keys to the van.

It's time to go.

CHAPTER 19
WHAT DO YOU KNOW OF ELVA?
NATHANIEL

I approach the glass door with silver trim, and press the button that rings the intercom to buzz me in. *"Mister Nathaniel Sprigg? Again? Sir, this is highly irregular. Please wait while I ask Master Akron."*

I can hear the ugly voice tut-tutting before he takes his finger off the microphone, and I questioned every life decision that led me to this point. Several minutes go by, and I'm getting desperate. The enchanted glass door and I have entered a staring contest. It dares me to go for it, break the glass, and run to my employer's apartment. I don't doubt I would die in seconds if I actually tried it.

Plus, I shouldn't be thinking that glass doors can issue dares.

I pace back and forth, but I immediately stop when the sound comes over the speaker.

"Mister—" the doorman starts, only to be interrupted by, "Nathaniel!"

The small speaker screeches due to the unexpectedly loud sound. I freeze. That's Akron taking over. I want to cower from him. He will be furious with me, potentially murderous, but it's worth it.

"As you can imagine, I am busy and do not want to see you right now. You have two seconds before I turn you into a dung fly."

I lean forward, "Yes, sir. But it's urgent. It's about the Winter—"

"*Enough,*" he hisses. No sound comes out of the speaker for a few moments. "*Okay. Get your ass up here, where it's safe.*" The sound cuts off with a loud screech, and the enchanted door swings open.

I am not greeted by the pixie this time. Instead, one of Akron's personal bodyguards in a black suit and sunglasses takes me by the arm and jerks me forward.

"Woah, *woah.*" I yank my arm back. "I won't try anything. I can walk just fine."

"Boss's orders." He tightens his grip on my bicep and pushes me into the elevator.

It is at this moment that I realize I am in deep shit.

The Warlock is one of many powerful men in Port City, but that doesn't mean he doesn't have time to ruin me. He controls all of Wyrm Heights and the Lower East Valley, which are the richest and poorest areas of town.

I knew this when I came here, hell; I knew this when he hired me. But he has always been decent to his workers, relatively speaking. He wouldn't... kill me.

I think.

I hang onto that last thought as I cross the collection of priceless Undersea paintings from the Ice Mer Court. All around, their ancient hues shimmer in the dim glow of the gallery. Blue, green, and purple paints blend into one—the ocean's salty swells are masterfully brought to life on the canvas.

My knock-off designer boots make barely whisper against

the hard floor, yet the whole place seems to hum with contained energy. It makes me pause as I reach out to touch the glass protecting one of the masterpieces.

"No touching," the bodyguard grumbles.

I yank my hand back. I had noticed the hum of Boss' wards before, but now I wonder if the paintings themselves are imbued with some sort of distant magic of the King of the Ice Mer. Everything from the Mer is mixed with some sort of siren song.

At that moment, I could swear the weight of the ocean is in the air. It's a heady gravity that draws me deeper into myself and the stories hiding beneath the waves. I suddenly long for those unknown places, and the strange creatures that swim under the moon's shifting lights.

Gifts from his lady-friend Esmeralda, no doubt.

My angry employer opens the door wearing the same robe, except this time it is open quite far down, revealing the purple warlock marks, which are now glowing. They pair nicely with his murderous eyes.

Behind him, lounging in her aqua-chair, is Esmeralda. The Mer Leader. From her file, it appears that she is of royal Spring Mer descent, but her father was an Ice Mer. The leadership is insular–only contained to King Phelix and his offspring. Given his divine parentage, cousins are mostly out of the question.

She wears nothing more than a sheer gown. Her face and body are covered in iridescent blue-gray scales, while her arms and legs are covered in silvery-gray. Her tail and hands are a smooth, shiny aquamarine, while the rest of her is a pale, ashen gray. This is way more of her than I saw in our meetings. Her aqua and gray hair flows down to her waist. Her teal eyes glow with the light of a thousand stars, and she is reclining while she watches my boss with a feral kind of pleasure.

She smiles, and I try to avoid looking at anything other than her face.

Sucking in a breath, I push past Akron.

You have a death wish today, a voice inside of me warns.

“Where is she?” I bark, my voice echoing through the silent room.

He fixes me with a hard gaze, sending his bodyguard away and slamming the door shut. His eyes slide past me and settle on Esmeralda.

“Where is who, Akron?” Her voice is no longer pleasant. Instead, it's a menacing rasp.

“Elva,” I said, not waiting for anyone else to answer.

Esmeralda gasps, and her eyes flash with rage. Her underlids blink over hard turquoise eyes as she hisses out her question. “What the hell do you know about her, you filthy little Fae?”

I take a deep breath. “She’s in trouble.”

The mer moves so fast, I don’t even see her do it. Within the space of a heartbeat, a clammy not-there, but somehow very real, hand clamps around my neck. My throat squeezes. Water mixed with magic fills my mouth, and I gag against the influx of death into my body.

Esmeralda’s lip curls, and her magical grip tightens, “How do you know that?”

I choke out a single word, “I... I just know.” The water lessens just enough for me to speak, though the consonants gurgle in the back of my throat.

“Esmeralda, stop.” Akron sounds exasperated. “He’s not with the resistance. I would know, I have him followed.”

My stomach turns over, and my heart stops beating as Esmeralda turns to face him.

A nasty choking noise escapes my throat. I struggle to say, “You what?” My voice is barely above a watery whisper. I claw at intangible hands.

“Are you sure, Akron?” she says, eyeballing me.

Blackness edges my vision, and each spoken word becomes increasingly murky as the seconds pass.

"Yes," he says.

I have no doubt he is evil... but so is she.

If Lucinda and Cherie knew the kinds of people I associate with, they'd be appalled. A small voice in the back of my head makes me question whether this life is really better than the Summer Court.

Then Elva's face flashes before my eyes, and I know it is.

After another long moment, the hand loosens around my neck. I tumble to the floor, coughing up water. Akron and Esmeralda keep doing that strange whisper-shouting while I gasp for air.

My throat burns with the sting of salt water. On the ground, something glints.

It's an earring, a gold hoop with a Black Opal shard inlaid into it like an eye. My eyes widen and I slide my hand towards the earring. It matches the one Esmeralda has in her other ear.

The opal lies glittering in the dying sunlight, taunting me towards it. It's not all black. There are swirls of browns and reds, blackish clouds with flecks of gold, and just a hint of blue.

Akron takes a step towards me. Coughing to distract him, I snatch the small piece of jewelry as fast as I can. I stumble to my feet, clutching my prize in my mouth.

A whir comes from the aqua-chair, and Esmeralda looks at me. There is no apology in her eyes for what she did to me, and I don't expect one.

"Repeat what you hear in this room, and I'll have you filleted." Esmeralda's unnerving eyes studied mine before she says, "The Princess is in trouble, but there is no way for you to know that. She has been taken. We think it is the resistance, but we can't be sure."

My brain catches one word and holds it close to my chest. Princess.

Dozens of news reports cycle through my brain. All of them had mentioned the heir to the Winter Court throne who ran away, their heir who disappeared.

There's no way... right?

Even as I ask the question of myself, I realize I'm being foolish.

Of course, there is. The Northern Courts are so secluded and secretive that they've never released photos of anything but executions and the court leaders. Princesses and princes don't last long in the Winter Courts.

Elva must've fought to survive her entire life.

A strange emotion bloomed in my chest—a tenderness and desire to protect. I'd never felt anything like this before.

"Where have they taken her?" I ask.

"The North," she replies. "We suspect she is in Ice City, but it is impossible to get there right now. Even with Iter Dust."

Only Fae can use that dust, so I can be sure this is a dig at me.

But Esmeralda doesn't know I'm also a shifter... For a moment, I am grateful I've never shifted in the city. I told no one but Elva that I was a shifter.

I don't know why she's telling me this, but honestly, I don't care.

The Mer looks at me with pity, like she knows Elva is already dead. Akron's lips are in a tight line, and I see the purple magic licking his fingertips.

There is no doubting his violent intent.

Time to get out of here.

I stand up. "Thank you both, I really—"

"Don't thank me, jackass. You're fired," Akron bites out.

I search his expression for any signs of regret, but his eyes remain a cool, steely purple. The tension in the room is palpable, and I can almost taste the bitterness in the air. The longer I stand here, the more my heart races. Sweat is a river dripping down my palms. Akron is rigid, and his fists are balled at his sides.

I know there was no time to push for answers. I need to go before things get out of hand. My fate was sealed the moment I stepped foot into his apartment.

A palpable anticipation of violence looms over us. Every second I stay increases the likelihood of serious injury.

Without another word, I turn and run out of the room. I slam Akron's front door. It seals itself shut, leaving me to wait while the elevator crawls like a snail. The guard says nothing as I burst into the lobby. Freedom is so close, but I still feel Akron's presence pressing around me like an unbreakable spell.

In seconds, I'm in the street, sprinting to the docks.

The sun is cracking over the horizon. Most residents of Port City are rising to start their proper jobs, which I no longer have. I tear one of the cheap metal hoops out of my earlobe that I bought with Marie over a year ago, throw it on the ground, and replace it with the Black Opal stud.

Urgency is a pumping, urgent call in my veins. As I near the docks, I see the swing shift personnel leaving. Adam is still at the booth, checking shipments and watching those who enter the docs. His long white wings are folded behind him. Both are thoughtfully placed to provide a stable surface for the paperwork he completes with his stubby work-worn fingers. The light from the fluorescent tubes reflects off his short black hair and creates a halo around his perfectly sculpted features. He spots me and tries to wave me down. I don't have time to stop or argue. I need to find Elva, especially if she is in danger.

“Nate," he calls out the window. "You can't be here! I just got a call from Boss. He said to shoot you if you came near the paperwork.”

I keep walking. "Good news for you, I won't be near the offices."

“Come on, I don’t want to hurt you!” Adam is chasing after me as I pound across the metal grate flooring. "I need this job. You know how much I owe from the Sprite Races. If Boss turns me out, the creditors will get me in a week," he pleads.

I stop just as I reach one of the boardwalks and turn around. "Adam, I care about you. Just hold your gun like that and keep shouting. Akron won't do anything if you tell him I glamoured you."

His eyebrows draw together as if I am speaking a foreign language. He tightens his grip on the dart gun and points it at me. “I’m not joking; this is your last chance, so either you turn around, or I’ll shoot you with a tranquilizer,” he says firmly.

My heart thumping wildly, I see the uncertainty in Adam’s eyes. He’s my oldest friend in Port City, but I'm no longer sure he wouldn't be willing to shoot me. Money changes people. Having connected those dots, I take advantage of his hesitation.

Reaching down, I yank my shirt over my head and toss it into the lapping water.

Adam’s face blanches as his eyes go wide with shock. “Dude, what the hell are you doing?”

A smirk is the only response I give him before I take off the rest of my clothes and even my FaePhone. His gun shakes slightly as he watches me like a deer in headlights.

With a sense of reckless abandon, I run toward the edge of the dock. Fear grows inside me. I may be making a massive mistake by jumping. However, it's too late to turn back now.

I can do this—I hope.

Taking a deep breath, I launch myself off the dock, praying that this will work.

For a moment, I fall and curse. I’m heading straight towards the ice water, stark naked.

My magic crawls over me a fraction of a second before I hit the water. It's foreign after so much disuse, but it still works. A flame sears through me. My body changes, bones break, and my wings stretch wide.

I let out a loud *squawk.*

One wing skims the top of the water, and an immense sense of freedom and power fills me. Even though I haven't shifted in years, I instinctively know what to do and take off in Elva's direction.

Adam's cry is faint in the distance, but his gunshot is not; a tranquilizer dart barely misses me as it sails over my head, making me panic and fly even faster. My newfound wings carry me swiftly, allowing me to gain altitude and speed away from danger quickly.

The wind rushes around me as I beat my wings harder and faster. I soar above the harbor, feeling a sense of invincibility that comes with flight. It's exhilarating—the way the air carries me higher and higher until the sounds of Adam's shouts fade away completely.

I pray that Elva is all right.

Elva.

Elva.

I speak her name into the wild using a language only birds understood, hoping the air will carry my call to her ears.

CHAPTER 20
MY OWL IS EAGER
ELVA

As soon as I climb into the driver's seat in the van, I lock the doors behind me and breathe. I run my fingers over my bare wrists, relishing the feeling of skin under my touch.

My thoughts are running a million miles a minute.

Who were they?

Who is the man Veronica mentioned?

Where in the Northern Court am I?

Thinking about the female Fae brings a smile to my lips.

She held me captive for months, drugged me, and kept me away from my magic. I don't feel any remorse for killing her. She got what she deserved. I wish I had had the time to make her death last longer, but alas, I have more important things on my plate.

First and foremost, food.

I'm starving for some proper food. Rummaging through the van's glove compartment, I find three pieces of gold and a credit card. Sighing, I leave the card behind. No use taking anything that I can be tracked with.

Rummaging through a duffle bag I find in the back. It must have belonged to Veronica. Unzipping the bag, I wince as a rainbow of glittery fabric explodes in my vision. Scoffing, I pull out a few skimpy pieces of fabric before tossing them aside.

She clearly didn't believe in comfort over style because almost all the clothes in here are skimpy low-cut dresses designed to please the male gaze above all else.

Not my cup of tea.

I settle on the one non-skirted item in the duffle bag, a long-sleeve leather jumpsuit with a diving neckline that reaches almost to my navel. Throwing aside my leggings and hoodie, I shimmy into the material, fighting to make my curves fit. The only redeeming quality about the garment is the color. Black. Unassuming. Just the way I like it.

Now that I've checked every square inch of the van and taken what I needed, I unlock the vehicle and step outside. The road is deserted, which tells me that even though we're in the Northern Court, we must be far from Ice City.

Thank the gods.

I stand in the frigid air, double-checking my pockets, before summoning my owl. The staying spell was one of the first things I mastered as a youngling, so I know my clothes and possessions will still be on my person when I shift back.

My owl is eager.

I can feel her clawing at me from the inside as I stretch out my arms. As easily as breathing, I shift. My skin ripples, and my owl breaks through, the seamless transition over in a blink of an eye.

The wind calls me, and I screech in delight as my animal is finally free from my flesh's cage. Flapping my wings, I soar over the snowy forest. The wind blows beneath my wings as I relish the feeling of flying after all this time in captivity.

Freedom.

As I soar through the sky, I catch sight of another bird nearby.

Food.

I swoop lower to get a better look at it. It's a cardinal, and it hasn't seen me yet. The bird is flying low to the trees, its red feathers a bright spot against the sheet of brilliant, fresh snow. The cardinal calls out, its voice shrill against the quiet forest.

It's too beautiful to eat. I dip a wing in greeting before flapping my wings.

To the left, I can see a far-off mountain range, the peaks are ja gged and covered in snow. Three peaks are taller than the rest, their heights easily double that of the surrounding mountains.

The Western Mountains.

Hissing at the sight, I shift my wings and head toward the east. I wouldn't go towards that mountain range unless my life depended on it. Even for a powerful Winter Fae like myself, it's a dangerous place to be.

Besides, there's only one place in my mind.

Port City.

I need to see the Summer Fae male.

Well, first, I need to eat. Preferably something made of chocolate.

Then I need to see him.

Far off in the distance, my eye catches sight of something across the forest. Flapping my wings, I fly closer to get a better look. Grey chimney smoke billows into the sky, the scent laced with that of warm bread and spices.

Soaring on the currents, I head towards the promise of food.

An hour later, I'm seated at a red half-moon booth in a 24-hour diner. The fluorescent lights are bright as the busty brunette Vampire wearing a frilly white apron hurries around, taking orders and delivering food to the four other customers in the diner.

I'm sitting in the corner furthest from the door, my hand braced around a cup of coffee as I pick at a slice of apple pie.

They didn't have any chocolate cake. Not even any chocolate ice cream.

Figures.

It's certainly not the worst thing to have happened to me recently, but it's not great. At least my stomach is full and no drugs are in my system. Silver linings, and all that.

"Can I get you anything else, honey?"

I look up to see the server standing before me, her hands on her hips as she looks kindly down at me. My lips tilt up as I caress the warm mug between my chilled fingers. "No, thank you."

"Are you sure? I haven't seen you around these parts before." She leans over, coming in closer as she refills my coffee, lowering her voice. "Is everything okay?"

I raise my eyes, taking in the Vampire's demeanor. She looks sweet, but I can see a glint of hardness in her eyes. No doubt she would betray me in a heartbeat if she knew who I was.

Everyone always has ulterior motives in the Northern Court. My mother has built her kingdom on pillars of fear and betrayal.

Shaking my head, I stare at the table. "I'm fine, thank you." I suck in a breath. "Actually, there *is* something I'm interested in. How far are we from the sea?"

She raises a brow. "I didn't know Winter Fae were interested in fishing."

Shrugging, I take a sip of my coffee. "Maybe I'm in the market for a new hobby."

"It's about a two-hour drive that way." The waitress points out the window in the general direction of the east. "Do you need a ride?"

"Nope." I shake my head, trying to lift my lips into a believable smile. "I'm all good, thanks. Just the bill, please." Lifting my coffee mug to my lips, I take a sip and lean back, hoping she takes the hint to leave me alone. I don't want to have to cause a scene.

Thank the gods she doesn't push the issue. She walks away, heading over to chat with the burly Were at the counter while she fiddles with her apron. The server laughs overly loudly at something the Were says, flicking her brown hair behind her shoulder.

They've been flirting on and off for the past hour, and it looks like the Were is ready to take things to the next level.

This is my cue to leave. I have my own male to locate. Not to mention an unknown group that is hunting me to deal with, but I'm choosing to focus on one thing at a time.

Throwing back the rest of my coffee, I wince as the warm liquid coats the back of my throat. Slamming down the mug, I slap my three gold coins on the table and stalk out the door. The waitress barely looks up from her flirting once she sees the glimmer of the gold I've left on the table.

I walk out into the cold, throwing my hair into a bun before mumbling the staying spell and shifting into my owl. The moment I take flight, I head towards the sea.

I can feel the Summer Fae's magical signature. I know he's there.

He will be there.

He has to be there.

CHAPTER 21

NAKED AS THE DAY YOUR MOTHER BIRTHED YOU

NATHANIEL

There is no way that people enjoy doing this, I think to myself after a few hours of flying across the icy ocean.

The novelty of shifting has worn off relatively quickly, and I am left repulsed by my own instincts. Every time I see a fish, I have to fight the urge not to plunge down and devour it. I hate fish when I'm in my regular Fae form. I have no desire to feel what it would be like to slide it down this small, bone-crushing beak.

I'm left with mental images and sensations instead of conscious thoughts. My body reacts, and I gag. Luckily my wings flap just fine. It seems that all those months at the gym give me some strength in this form, but I have no endurance.

I constantly feel too big for my body.

Am I flying for a purpose? Yes.

Have I hyper-focused on completing that task and forgotten to eat *and* sleep? Also yes.

Gods above, I am a mess. I swerve to the right and somehow manage to roll my bird eyes.

I am soaring above the landscape, the wind beneath my

wings propelling me closer to my destination. Sunlight glints off my feathers, and I stretch my wings even wider.

But then, in the distance, I notice another bird in the sky. It is a large white bird, barreling through the air with fierce determination. I watch as it closes in until I recognize the unmistakable silhouette of a snowy owl.

Shit. Ospreys are predators, but they have natural enemies. Pure instinct tells me that this is one of them.

I flap my wings and rise in elevation, trying to leave the owl behind. The large puff of white feathers veers up toward me. My wings tense, and I tuck my feet in tighter to my body in case I need to swerve to the side. The bird is likely hunting, which could be dangerous.

This is bad. Very, very bad.

I am a terrible bird. Maybe I should've spent more time practicing this form.

Not the time, I chide myself.

I veer to the left, trying to get out of its way. My heart pounds as I realize the owl has adjusted its course to match.

It's only a hundred paces away and moving fast. Even in my terror, I can't help but admire the rapidly approaching creature. The feathers are so stark-white that it looks like a flying snowball. The black-brown speckles that line its face define the predator within. It looks like the animal you see winning a photo contest on social media, not something that exists in real life.

I would've sat and admired it longer if it wasn't about to crash into me.

My animal brain short-circuits, and I stop flapping my wings.

Mistake.

My steady flight turns into a free dive straight into the icy water. Thick, preened feathers help protect me from the bitter cold. Under the water, my eyes sting from the salt as I momentarily glimpse the blue-green water around me.

...Now what?

I have no plan, and there is little time to consider making one before a pair of claws grabs my back. I am yanked from the icy ocean. The snow owl's talons hold my body in a vice grip as my muscles strain and contort to reach the predator's claws, but the effort was futile.

A feeling of embarrassment engulfs me while desperation and dread flood my chest. The words "I am going to die" echo in my mind as we fly over the dark, tumultuous sea.

I stop fighting.

This is it.

The wind whistles in my ears as we fly higher and higher, and I accept the truth: I'm not the hero I thought I was. I had tried, but I wasn't powerful enough to save myself.

I have been a pathetic, delusional fool.

I will never find out what happened to the Winter Fae.

The endless blue gives way to brown and white. As I stare at the snow-dusted pine trees, something switches inside me when I realize we are moving closer and closer to the ground.

Another strange voice, potentially my conscience, enters my mind and says, *"The thing about this is... that you're not actually a bird, idiot. You can switch into your Fae form."*

And then I remember my clothes. The ones I had stripped off before taking flight.

Damn. It.

If I'm going to survive this and find her–find Elva–I really need to learn how to keep my head on straight. But for now, I just needed to focus on surviving.

I pull on my magic. My skin tingles as it ripples. Feathers vanish and are replaced with my long auburn hair and golden-tan skin.

My scream filled the air as I felt the sharp claws of the owl tear into my skin, plunging me through the air. Twigs and branches snapped with each impact, sending a wave of pain across my body with every jolt. Finally, I hit the ground and rolled in the powdery snow beneath me, my limbs splayed out in a tangled heap. The snow crunches under the weight of my body.

It is so deep that the powder covers my back and legs. As the wind blows, it swirls in circles, creating mini-tornadoes. I taste it, and it is clean and pure, like drinking from an ice-cold mountain stream.

I push myself up, trying not to shiver so that I can check on the owl. I don't think it will attack me again, but I'm unsure. There, perched on a high branch of the old oak tree, is the large snowy owl. Even from a distance, I could see its deep brown eyes watching me, unblinking.

Groaning, I shout at it. "I don't suppose you could bring me some clothes, you nasty creature!"

As I stared, it suddenly spread its wings and launched into the air.

Midway through its descent, the owl's body ripples and shifts–its feathers spread and are replaced by a blanket of black curls that spill over clothed female shoulders. A pattern of intricate white tattoos appeared on her face and arms, instantly recognizable as the mark of a Winter Fae.

Shit, shi—wait.

"It's you," I gasp.

My heart is racing, my head is light, and I'm fairly certain I've never been this confused or happy in my whole life.

Where has she come from? Even as I ask, I know I don't care. She's here. After all this time.

"Why are you naked?" The female I've been looking for asks, raising a brow. I think I see a tiny smile dancing on those beautiful lips.

I turn bright red from the tips of my ears to my collarbones. I'm torn between feeling embarrassed and relieved and happy that she is alive. That she is *here*! How is she here?

"How are you still wearing clo—?" My eyes catch on her attire. She stands before me in a sleek black bodysuit. The leather hugged her curves and made her appear almost statuesque in the frosty light.

"Damn Elva. What *is* that?" I can't help the long gaze I give her, the way my eyes trace the lines of her body, only to land on her face, where there is a look of pure shock.

That's when I realize I've said her name. To her. For the first time.

It's not like it's her True Name, but Fae tend to be very sensitive about names in general.

"How do you know my name?" she demands. Her eyes bore into mine, and a white-hot fury radiates from them. The heat of her rage is a sauna, even though she stands feet away from me.

A deep red blush creeps across her cheeks, and I'm not sure if it's from the embarrassment of seeing bare flesh—some Fae are very shy, indeed—or something more sinister.

Before I can answer her, she cuts me off. "You know what, never mind. I can't talk to you when you're standing there—naked as the day your mother birthed you—in the snow."

"You've never wanted to see me naked?" I joke, quickly shutting her up. A smirk plays across my lips as I relish the momentary shock which paints her features round and innocent. She opens her mouth to protest and promptly shuts it again. She reminds me of a fish for half a second. An exquisite fish, in a very tight black jumpsuit.

Then the air is heavy with anticipation I wasn't expecting while she studies my face. A flash of curiosity, or maybe desire, lights her eyes. The meaning of my words shifts from lighthearted to suggestive.

Elva takes a step back, forcing herself to move away from me, her voice tight as she says, "I'm going to find you some clothes." And just like that, she's gone, leaving a chill in the air that I can feel deep in my bones.

In the silence, I light a fire with my magic and wonder what I had done by coming here to find a strange Fae I barely know.

CHAPTER 22
YEAH, HE'S CUTE. BUT...
ELVA

Three hours earlier

I'm running on pure adrenaline as I flap my wings, soaring over the tiny towns and villages below. They're scattered between long stretches of forests filled with snow-covered pines. As I fly, I see moose and deer running wild through the forest, along with several eagles and falcons soaring overhead.

I ignore them. With every second, I'm coming closer to *him.*

The vast expanse of water is before me. Shades of blue swirl under me. My owl's vision is sharp, and I can discern every shade, every slight deviation in color. The cerulean mixing with the azure and cobalt, the shapes of the marine animals swimming underneath as they go about their lives, even thin chunks of ice as they float over the open water.

On a different day, I'd stay to explore. But not today.

Today, I'm going to find the Summer Fae. I can feel him. With every flap of my wings, I'm getting closer to him. His signature is a beacon, summoning me forward.

He's the only thing on my mind.

Nothing else matters.

Eventually, there is nothing below me but water in all directions. I can see the faint outline of Port City in the distance, but there's something else.

Something...

An osprey.

By the gods. It's him.

I want to scream and yell and cry.

He's safe. He's alive. And... *he said he never shifts, but here he is now.*

Excitement floods me as I swoop around in the sky, screeching loudly before setting him in my sights.

The closer I get, the more I can make out his form.

He's beautiful.

His long curved beak sits atop a majestic face, a white band stretching from under his beak to his belly. I can make out two legs of the same color tucked behind him as he flies. His wings are brown, spread apart as he flaps...

Terribly.

That's the worst flying form I've ever seen in my very long life.

Has no one ever taught him to fly?

It's a miracle he's made it this far at all. He appears to be a few minutes away from careening into the sea.

I would have snorted if I were in my Fae form right now.

As it is, I hiss as I dive straight for him. He's going to need some help to finish the crossing.

I close the distance between us quickly. I caw, swooping about with hopes that he recognizes me.

One hundred feet.

Fifty.

Twenty.

Then he... dives into the water. Like an idiot.

Maybe his osprey form has addled his senses?

What is wrong with him?

Is he hunting now?

I dive after him, grabbing his back with my claws and hauling him out of the water. The glacial liquid is freezing, and I hiss.

He's fighting me, biting at my claws for a few minutes before falling limp in my grasp.

That's unexpected. I thought he'd at least fight.

But seeing as how I was begging that bitch Fae Veronica not to kill me just this morning, it's understandable.

The shoreline is in sight now, as the endless pine trees covered in layers of snow become bigger with every beat of my wings. There's a tiny fishing village near here, but I aim for a secluded forested spot.

As I dip lower, the osprey moves in my grasp. Suddenly he... *what in the name of the gods is he doing?*

He shifts into his Fae form mid-air, his feathers rippling and giving way to skin. Squawking, I let go of him as soon as he's over the snow and perch on a branch above. I can see red slashes down his golden back from my claws, and sorrow ripples through me before I dip my gaze lower and realize-

Where are his gods-damned clothes?

He starts yelling. "I don't suppose you could bring me some clothes, you nasty creature!"

Nasty creature?

Wait.

He doesn't know what I am—who I am. Maybe I've just imagined everything? I play every single interaction we ever had quickly through my head, but I don't know.

Sighing, I jump off the branch and shift, landing perfectly in the snow.

His eyes, those beautiful, captivating eyes, go wide as he

stares at me. I can feel his gaze surveying me, and it takes every ounce of willpower not to lower my gaze.

The male's eyes go wide. "It's you," he practically whispers.

Of course, it's me. *Wait.* I have a more pressing question.

"Why are you naked?" I spit out, trying to hold back a discomforted laugh trying to rise within me.

Gods, I am so awkward. That's what happens when you grow up in near isolation. If it weren't for Helena, I probably wouldn't have spoken to anyone.

He stares at me, and I note the peachy-red tone that blooms across his face and ears. "How are you still wearing clo—?" He stops suddenly and gives me a long look. "Damn, Elva. What *is* that?"

I'd forgotten about the leather jumpsuit I'd taken from Veronica's duffle. I look down at my outfit, adjusting the fit before his words settle in my ears.

Elva.

He said my name.

I stare at him with wide eyes. "How do you know my name?" I demand while taking a step forward. My cheeks go hot when I catch a long strip of pale skin. I shake my head. "You know what, never mind. I can't talk to you when you're standing there—naked as the day your mother birthed you—*in the snow*."

He grins.

Damn, Summer Fae. His face lights up in such a carefree way when he does that. A dimple dances on his cheek.

"You've never wanted to see me naked?" he says, wiggling his strange red eyebrows.

Seeing him naked had been on my mind more than once. But I don't say that, though. I just stare at him.

He laughs. "I knew you got my jokes!"

I blink, my mouth opening and closing as I try to think of something to say.

I've got nothing. It's too hard to think while he's naked, with only snow covering him. I'm a bounty hunter of the world's worst criminals, and I'm tongue-tied because of one Summer Fae male who can't even shift properly.

Ridiculous.

Get a hold of yourself.

Finally, my brain starts working again.

"I'm going to find you some clothes," I say.

Before he can reply, I shift into my snowy owl and flap away. On my way to the sea, I saw some clothes hanging on a line in the village not far from here. It won't be a long trip.

I fly over and grab a large red flannel shirt off the clothesline with my beak. In my claws, I carry a pair of black sweatpants and a pair of large runners. I hear people cursing behind me as I fly away with their belongings, but I mentally promise to pay them back.

In the long list of crimes I've committed, stealing a few clothes is the most innocuous thing I've ever done.

I bring the clothes and shoes, dumping them on the Summer Fae before shifting to my two-legged form. Fabric rustles, and I run my hands through my hair.

"Thank you," he says. His voice is low and sends shivers down my spine."Don't worry, darling; it's safe to turn around now. I won't corrupt you any further."

"What if I want to be corrupted?" Instantly, I groan. *There* is *something wrong with me.*

Slapping my hands over my eyes, I wish the ground would swallow me whole. I've never been this awkward in my entire life.

"While I appreciate your thoughts, Elva, I don't think I will be corrupting anyone right now after my extended stint in the snow."

There it is again. My name. It grabs me, squeezing a part of my heart that I thought died in the cell. No one uses my name. It's like a spell, drawing me towards him.

Turning around, I slit open my fingers and peek through the gap. He's standing a foot in front of me, smirking as he stares at me.

"How do you know my name?" I force the words out, deciding that since the ground isn't going to open me up and swallow me whole, I'd better get my head on straight.

He runs a hand through his hair, shaking off the wayward snowflakes that have accumulated on his head. His russet hair sparkles in the sunlight, drawing my gaze.

"It's a long story," he says, shivering. I realize icicles are forming on his hair, his body unacclimated to the cold of the Northern Court.

"Gods, you must be freezing," I say, extending a hand to touch his face. His lips are turning blue in the cold, his skin icy.

"I'm not warm," he says as a gust of wind blows by, shaking the branch above them before a pile of snow falls on his head.

Gods, I'm so stupid. Summer Fae aren't built for the cold.

"Can you summon a flame to warm yourself up while I find us some shelter?"

He starts, as though the idea of using his magic hadn't even occurred to him.

"Oh, yes. I can." With a flick of his wrist, he summons a large flame. Almost instantly, he sighs, the warmth bringing color back to his frigid face.

My lips tilt up into a small smile at the sound. "I have an idea," I say. "Wait here and warm up."

HALF AN HOUR LATER, I TRUDGE THROUGH THE SNOW TO WHERE I LEFT him. The Summer Fae is thawed, his flame shining brightly against the early evening violet sky.

"Come with me," I say, twisting my hands in front of me. Something about this male makes me feel like a youngling all over again.

He follows me wordlessly as I lead him into the grove of trees to the clearing where I've been working. He stops short, and I watch nervously as he runs his hand over the smooth icy dome that I've built. A small tunnel leads to the larger interior, with a hole at the top.

"Do you like it?" I ask, biting my lower lip. "I know it's not much, but it'll provide shelter for us until we can figure out a plan, and—"

He holds up a hand. "It's perfect, Elva. I've never seen an igloo in real life before."

He ducks his head and crawls through the entrance. "Are you coming?" He calls a moment later.

Nodding, I take one last look around the clearing. We're surrounded by snow-covered pine trees and nothing else. It's perfect.

Grinning to myself, I follow the Summer Fae into the igloo. He's sitting in the middle of the small circle, a tiny flame floating above his hand.

"This is amazing, Elva. Thank you."

I sit down next to him, leaning against the back of the igloo, and stretch out my legs.

"So... what's that long story?"

CHAPTER 23

TELL ME MORE

NATHANIEL

Elva is looking at me expectantly. I'm unnerved to see how thin she has gotten. Her skin is dull like she's been forced to stay inside. I think about what Esmeralda said about her being imprisoned here. It makes me shiver.

I blink and rustle my hair. "Um, if you really want to hear it, you're going to find out just how long I've been... yearning for you." I wince at the word. It's such a personal thing to admit.

Her eyes are wide, eager even.

No, I know that expression. I've seen it reflected in my face. She's hungry for connection. It is not something I have seen from her before. But I have also never been inside an igloo with her, surrounded by potential enemies in the middle of the North.

"Can I ask you something else before you start?" She doesn't acknowledge the tenderness so clearly shining in her eyes.

"Anything," I breathe, reaching up to hold one of her stray curls between my fingers. I don't even realize it until it's too late.

"What's your name?"

I let out a reactionary laugh. Here I am using her name gratuitously, and I've never introduced myself. We have spent so much time referring to each other without it... It would be a shame to spend another minute like this.

"Nathaniel. Some people call me Nate." I shrug. "I don't know if I have a preference."

She tilts her head to the side. "How about... 'Nathan'?"

She says it with reverence, and I grin. *Elva and Nathan.*

"I like it. But don't expect me to come up with a nickname for you. Elva is the most beautiful word I've ever heard."

She exhales, and pure joy breathes out with her. Her lips wobble as if she's fighting a smile.

"So, the story? I was promised to hear about how irresistible I am."

"Wait," I start, "Was that a joke?" Our laughter fills the small place, and somehow we settle beside each other, our shoulders and arms touching.

It felt normal when it happened, but now we both realize how close we are. I want to relieve some of the tension, so I start speaking. "I guess I can start with the last time we saw each other. Over two years ago. I kind of got into the news. Like watching the news. It was partly to keep up with shipping details for work... But mostly, it was to see if I saw you. Or news about the Winter Fae."

It's a really dark detail, but I'm surprised when she is the one to brighten the mood. "This is where we get to the pining, right?"

Thank the gods that my Summer Fae instincts finally kick in. "No, the pining started the first time I saw your ass bent over your bounty on the docks."

She shuts up and pulls her knees to her chest.

Feeling smug, I continue. "You might have noticed that Akron, my employer, enchanted the documents to protect your name. I never knew what to call you. I tried to ask a year ago, but... it didn't go well." *Understatement.*

"My mom, Lucinda, compelled me to go to the Summer

Court festival for the solstice. While I was there, I got a call that you would be coming. Only it wasn't you, it was Frank." I pause as all those emotions flood through me. "For months, there had been this... awareness inside of me that something was wrong. But I had nothing to go on, no address, name, or number. I was going insane. I went back to Akron, and he was with a Mer woman. She told me what had happened to you. I just... lost it. I came straight here even though they tried to kill me."

My eyes brim with inexplicable tears, on the cusp of tumbling out, as I get to the next part. "I hate flying. I hate my animal. But it was the only way to get here, to find you. I was planning on rescuing you, but it turns out you were much better at doing that than me." I laugh, my skin red-hot with emotion.

"Are you okay?" she asks. I can sense that she is unsure of whether she should touch me.

"Are *you* okay? You must've lost over twenty pounds."

She crosses her arms over her stomach as if trying to hide her smaller frame.

"Hey, don't," I say. "I'm sorry. I just want to make sure you're okay. You are seriously the most beautiful thing I've ever seen." I can't help taking her in my arms and pulling her close to my chest.

It's such a protective thing for me to do. I want her to feel safe. "It's okay, we're together now. It's going to be okay. We can get through this."

She's in so much pain, I can feel it as she slowly starts to shake in my arms. She's so different from what I thought. Of course, she's still powerful, but this vulnerability, the sweetness? This was something I could only dream of.

I can't fix this, and I don't want to give her any promises I can't keep. That's why, when I speak, I am absolutely sure of my words.

"Shh... I'm here. I will not leave."

She doesn't cry as she twists her hand in my sweater. She knows I cannot lie.

She looks up at me, and I can't help myself. I brush my lips across hers and repeat my words. "I will not leave you, Elva." This time, they are quieter but even more convicted.

The kiss was so quick, so normal that I want to do it again just to make sure I hadn't imagined it. But the ball is in her court. She is the one who will have to instigate the next one. *If* there is going to be a next one.

There's a plum color to her black skin, and I can't tell if it's from embarrassment or desire.

"Tell me what you're thinking," I whisper.

She just stares at me. I hold my breath.

"Why do you hate your bird?" she asks.

Oh. *Oh*.

"You're full of questions. Haven't you been suffering for the last few months?" I test the waters to see how she'll respond to my probing.

She bites her lip. "Yes. And now you are here, inexplicably. I don't wish to talk about myself–I wish to know you."

I blink. If this would... help her feel better, then I can keep talking. I don't particularly like diving into my past, but I want to make her feel better. "Well, once upon a time, there was a man named Andrius..."

I tell her about my father, who I inherited the bird from.

Once again, I am laid bare before her. But this time, I am glad I still have my clothes on.

CHAPTER 24

THE PERSON I'VE BEEN WAITING FOR

ELVA

I sit there in silence as Nathan pours out his story to me. The grief is written all over his face as he opens his soul to me. It's strange and marvelous. When did I become this person?

Very few beings in my life have ever stuck around long enough to learn anything about me, let alone to share with me anything about their lives. Helena is the exception that proves the rule. I'm hard to care for.

And yet, he pined for me.

That thought alone pushes me to press a light kiss on his cheek as he speaks. His gaze flutters to mine, the smallest of smiles gracing his lips, before he continues.

"When I was a youngling, before Andrius left us, he would say that he would take me flying. I begged him to take me, but he always put in small conditions that I didn't really understand at the time. Little things, like he would only take me if he was home exactly at a certain time. One minute too early or late and...well, you get it."

He's speaking softly, his shoulder is resting on mine as we sit side-by-side. The warmth of our bodies is causing the snow to slowly melt before I refreeze it.

"Eventually, I told myself he refused to take me because I was too young."

He pauses, his face distant, before he rubs his hands on his temples. "As I got older, I realized he didn't want to take me flying because he didn't want to be around *me*. He refused to use his shifting powers. Having an osprey and being in the Summer Court was like a brand saying that we weren't pure Summer Fae."

Nathan shifts, a muscle in his jaw twitches. His brow furrows and I get angry. This is one of the longest conversations I've ever had with him, but seeing him struggle to speak about his childhood...

It is like looking in a mirror that shows me the past.

My head cocks to the side.

For some reason, Fortuna has brought us together. For happiness or sorrow, I don't know. But it is in that moment, when Nathaniel looks at me with those piercing eyes, that I realize he's the person I've been waiting for.

"Nathan," I whisper, running my thumb across his cheek, "you don't have to tell me."

He gathers me in his arms, so I'm facing him. There is no room between us. "I want to," he says huskily.

"After a while... he twisted his marriage vows with my mother. He broke their bond and her heart. It's still shattered to this day. Before he left, he told me that all of this was *my* fault. That before my sister and I came along, they were doing just fine. I was a reminder of the freedom having children had taken away from him, and the fact that he had 'impure blood.'"

"Oh Nathan, I am so sorry." Without thinking, I shift in his arms and press my lips to his. I want to bring him comfort in the same way the thought of him comforted me all those long months.

Our first kiss was tentative, but this one is filled with deep emotion. The moment our lips touch, he groans, sliding his hand behind my neck to pull me closer. Despite our location in the North, he smells like summer and somehow tastes like sunshine personified. His tongue flicks out, and he tastes me like it's all he's been thinking about since the first time we met.

Grief and anger pour out of us, twisting together, as the weight of what his father did is released into the open air.

He shifts, pulling me onto his lap, as the flame he controls behind me grows in increasing intensity. There is a faint dripping noise coming from somewhere behind us. His lips move from mine, his gentle kisses exploring the planes of my face before he kisses a trail down my neck.

"Nathan," I gasp as a large droplet of water lands on my forehead. "You're going to melt the entire igloo."

I see a look of shock cross his face as he pulls his eyes from mine up to the walls that are currently dripping with melted snow. The ice is so thin, we can see the moon above us now, shining through the translucent ice.

He flushes, his ears tinged with an adorable pinkness, before he waves his hand and extinguishes his flame. "Can you fix this?" He asks, blushing.

My eyes drift over the igloo, assessing the damage, before nodding. "Give me a minute."

I shift off his lap, moving to crouch on my knees in the center of the igloo. Water is beginning to pool on the ground and it dampens my knees.

He sits back, his legs tucked under his arms, as he watches me intently.

I wave a hand, summoning ice to solidify on the inside of the igloo, before I call forth a blizzard, packing snow on the top of the structure all around us. I send a gust of wind up the middle of the igloo, making sure that air can still come in and out of the structure.

Satisfied with the renewed strength of the building, I shift backwards and look at him. "You lost control of your flame," I say, smirking.

"It's hard to concentrate on it when I have a beautiful Fae in front of me."

He thinks I'm beautiful.

It's not comfortable to sleep in a tiny igloo.

Last night we had been up late as the moon shone into the igloo, illuminating our faces as we talked. We shared sweet kisses and talked about nothing in particular.

"Nathan," I had murmured, laying down on my side, my head propped up on my arm as my eyelids grew heavy. "Don't melt the igloo again."

He had laughed, his hand brushing away a stray hair off my cheek, before he lay down across from me, not touching me at all. "I promise, I'll keep it under control."

My lips had tilted up as I drifted off into a deep sleep.

The next thing I know, the sun is shining into the small structure, the sound of chirping birds pulling me out of my slumber as I moan. "I don't want to wake up," I mumble, pressing my cheek into the warm pillow. It's soft, and the fleece is smooth under my touch.

Wait.

What pillow?

My eyes fly open. My vision is filled with red and black

stripes as I realize that sometime over the night, I crawled over and tucked myself against Nathan, using his body as my own personal heater. A heavy weight rests on my back, and I lift my head to see that he pulled me tight against him as we slept.

My cheeks flush, embarrassment flooding through me as I pull away from him, intent on crawling away while he sleeps. Before I get more than two inches away, his arm flies up and brings me to him. His eyes flutter open as he presses a quick kiss to my forehead.

"Good morning, Elva," he whispers, his voice still raspy from sleep.

"Morning, Nathan." My lips tilt up as I take in his gaze, his eyes dark with desire. " I'm glad to see you didn't melt our igloo overnight."

He grins and wiggles his eyebrows. "I'm willing to try again if you are."

"As much as I'd like that," I say as blood rushes to my face, "I really have to... step outside for a moment."

Seeming to catch my drift, he releases his grip on me and helps me up. "Oh, of course. Please, go right ahead."

Once I've taken care of my morning routine, I stand up and stretch. It's a beautiful day. The blue sky is clear, and the sun is already shining.

Just as I'm about to go back into the igloo, I hear voices coming from not far away. They're faint, but I picked this spot because it was secluded and no one should be near.

"Nathan," I whisper. "Come here."

He hurries out of the igloo, a fireball in his hand as he pops out of the tunnel. I glance at it, raising a brow. "What is that for?"

"Just in case," he says before extinguishing the fireball.

"You might need it yet," I say, sighing. "I think we're in trouble."

His eyes widen as he goes into a fighting stance. I would have found it attractive if it wasn't for the seriousness of the situation. Nathan stops moving, his hair blowing in the light breeze as he goes preternaturally still, listening. I can almost feel him spreading out his magic, trying to hear what I did.

Seconds tick by into minutes, but still he doesn't move.

Finally, he looks at me. "Someone's coming," he breathes, eyes wide. "We need to go, Elva, now."

CHAPTER 25

CRIMSON LIQUID STAINS THE SNOW

NATHANIEL

Training at the gym has made me strong, but having muscles doesn't mean I have automatically become a warrior. I try to remember some things I'd seen other people doing in action movies.

Core tight, legs shoulder-length apart, elbows bent.

Yeah, I think that's right.

I summon a small flame and seek some semblance of shelter in the trees.

"You know that this would be easier if we could just shift and fly out of here. We could leave before they find us."

Elva is right, but I don't really want to do that right now. Yesterday was a bit of a disaster.

Three distinctly male voices float over to us once again. Whoever they are, their voices carry the promise of violence. I can feel it tingling in the air, brushing against us as they move through the snow.

"They are in that igloo. We have two options. First, we can smash the top and have them surrounded. Second, we can lure them out and take them out individually," one of them says.

"What about the male that she is with? Do we take him too?" Snow crunches under their feet as they move. They aren't as stealthy as Elva.

"No, the orders were to kill him on sight."

My fiery blood fills with ice. My fear is reflected in Elva's ice-blue eyes.

"*We need to go,*" she mouths from the other tree.

I wave my arm down my torso and whisper, "I don't know how to shift with my clothes."

She rolls her eyes, the first sign of irritation she's given me since I've seen her.

"You've got to be kidding me," she whispers back as she comes beside me. She crosses her arms and stares at me. "Okay, then we will need to kill them."

"I've never killed anyone before." I feel silly admitting it to someone like her, but it feels relevant to our current situation.

She tightens her lips into a thin line and nods. I don't expect it when she grabs my hand and squeezes it as if she understands this will be hard for me.

Jerking her head to the side, she ushers me forward. I follow as closely as I can behind her.

The group of three mercenaries comes into view. They are Winter Fae, dressed similarly to Elva, and looking hungry for blood. For the third time in twenty-four hours, I am scared for my life.

I really wish I would get used to it. But my body can't seem to catch a break.

The good news is that they haven't realized we are outside, listening to them.

Elva puts her hand up, motioning for me to wait. I nod, rooting myself to the spot. In her right hand, an icicle sword forms with a trident head on the butt of the hilt. It is a terrifyingly menacing weapon. She raises the hilt high about her head and lets out a wild yell as she charges.

I've never seen anything like her when she fights. Each movement is perfectly timed to fight off not one but all three mercenaries at once. One of them, with shaggy grey hair, gets close to hitting her with a blade, but she effortlessly summons a shield of ice, and the sharp edge bounces off with a ringing vibration.

Another of them lunges, but she quickly jumps out of the way. The third tries to sneak up behind her, and she deflects his weapon easily. It's hard to follow all of her motions.

She is no novice with weapons, and she moves with ease. They drop like fruit flies, and I am shocked.

The last one spots me in the tree and charges. I freeze, unable to move as the mercenary approaches. He is wheezing, but he still looks menacing.

Before I can summon more than a paltry flame, Elva materializes out of thin air and cuts straight through his throat. Hot, sticky blood splatters on my face and hands. I gasp, frozen in shock.

My heart is racing, but I can't move.

"Are you okay?" a muffled voice asks. I can hear it, but it sounds like it's underwater.

"Nathan, are you okay?" The voice is louder this time, and a pair of hands shake me violently. My teeth clatter together as I nod, but I don't know if my body moves.

My feet are moving, one after another. I am sure of it this time. She drags me to a different place, away from where we are.

"Hey, we need to leave. You are going to need to shift. I'm going to see if I can put a spell over you. Can you shift?" I nod, still dazed.

I reach inside myself, past the panic attack, and find my

shifter animal. I pull on my magic. The shift starts, and my mind focuses once again. It's powerful.

As a bird, I take off, soaring into the sky.

My adrenaline fuels me to follow Elva. For the first time, I taste what it feels like to be entirely in control of my life.

CHAPTER 26

HE IS STRONG AND RESILIENT

ELVA

We've been flying for over an hour, and I can tell that Nathan is just starting to calm down.

The look on his face when that Fae's lifeblood splattered on his skin keeps replaying in my mind. He was afraid.

Is he afraid of me?

That thought frightens me more than anything else possibly could. He knew what I did for a living... but being faced with something is a lot different from knowing it. I shift on the wind, cawing to make sure he follows, as we fly towards the one place I know no one in their right mind will follow.

Stay with me, Nathan, please.

Glancing behind me, I see his osprey form flapping along. He's gained better control of his bird, making his movements less clunky.

Gods. I hope my staying spell worked on him. Otherwise, he might not last the night, even with a fire. Every moment that we fly brings us deeper into the North. It's so cold that I am suffering. I have no doubts that, as a Summer Fae, he might die in the biting cold.

The sun is shining all around us, and as we fly over the pine trees, I spot a river running through a clearing. Perfect. I haven't eaten since the diner yesterday, and I'm so hungry.

Cawing, I swoop down and land on a nearby tree. Nathan follows close behind, although I can see confusion in his osprey's eyes.

I look around for a moment before I spot my prey. There. I see a tiny field mouse in the snow, its brown fur a bright spot against the white blanket surrounding us. I swoop down, and a few minutes later, the mouse is gone, and my stomach is happy.

Nathan hasn't moved. His claws are digging into the branch deeply enough to leave a mark. I caw, extending a wing to get him to come down, but he shakes his head vigorously.

I didn't even know birds could do that.

I hiss before flapping my wings and launching vertically into the air. Once on the branch beside him, I nudge him with my wing. He barely moves, seeming frozen to the spot.

The river below us is teeming with fish. I nudge him again, but he doesn't move.

Gods, if he dies of hunger with a food source right before us, I'll never forgive myself.

Deciding to take matters into my own hands, I fly down to the river and grab the first fish I find in my claws. It flops around, its scales shining in the sunlight, but I manage to bring it up to Nathan's perch without issue. He stares at the fish, his bird eyes blinking wildly.

I can practically feel the disgust rolling off him in waves, but eventually, his hunger must win out. He eats the fish; slowly at first, but then he picks up speed and devours it until it is all gone.

Refreshed and nourished, I nudge him with a wing once

more before we fly back into the skies. The weather is perfect for this activity..

After hours of flying and two more hunting stops, we finally reach our destination. The mountainous peaks are high and snow-covered, and I spot a cave mid-way up one of the steep slopes. I dive towards it, a glance telling me Nathan is following.

We land in the cave, and I instantly return to my Fae form. I hear rustling from behind me and then a whoop of joy.

"Still fully clothed!" Nathan is laughing behind me. The sound warms me as I turn around.

Sure enough, Nathan's outfit is present and accounted for. His tight red flannel shirt displays his lean, muscled arms as he rubs the back of his head.

That's a shame, I think, before blood rushes to my cheeks.

"I'm glad it worked," I say instead, turning slowly on my feet to take in my surroundings.

The cave isn't deep, and it's very dark. Without being asked, Nathan ignites a light in front of me that moves alongside me.

His fire magic comes in handy.

I walk to the end of the cave quickly, realizing that it stretches back fifteen feet before closing off completely. It looks as though someone took a school bus and placed it on a mountain. It's long and narrow, but it's safe.

Footsteps crunch behind me. "Where are we, Elva?"

The tiniest hint of a smile creeps on my face as he says my name. It sounds so right, so natural.

What would my True Name sound like on those lips?

I turn around, rubbing the back of my neck. "We're in the Western Mountains," I blurt, hoping that if I say it quickly, maybe he won't know how bad it is. Those hopes are quickly dashed. Nathaniel's face leeches of all color.

For a long moment, he says nothing. That's worse, I think. I'd rather he get upset. In the silence, there is room for bad thoughts to grow. Doubt. Maybe he doesn't want to be here with me?

He lights a fireball in his hand and watches it as it grows, shifting between large and small. The flame entrances him. "I've heard of this place. Even the Winter Court Fae fear the mountains because of the dragons rumored to live underneath."

Nodding, I reach out and touch his hand. At my touch, he looks up and extinguishes the flame. I force a smile on my face. "No one has seen a dragon in centuries. They're probably all gone. But the rumors surrounding this place will keep us safe."

I hope. I don't say it out loud, but I'm afraid he can hear the doubt in my voice.

He smiles at me, but his eyes are dull and *wary* as he looks around.

We spend the evening setting up a meager camp inside the cave. We do not need firewood since Nathan can summon a flame, and I can quickly summon water.

Food is our biggest priority. Outside the cave is a bush full of delicious winter berries, but they won't keep us alive in the long run. Tomorrow, we will hunt and make a plan.

When the sun has set, we settle down in front of the fire. Nathan's back is against the cavern wall, and I'm lying between his legs as he brushes my hair back from my face and traces my tattoos with his fingers. He kisses them softly, his lips brushing over my fingers before he wraps my hand in his.

"You were incredible today," he says, rubbing his thumb over my palm. "Utterly and incredibly amazing."

Shock flickers through me, and I push myself up to look him in the eye. "I thought... I thought you were afraid of me."

"I could never be afraid of you, darling. There's something enticing about a woman who can kick ass so efficiently." As if to prove his point, he pulls me in for a kiss. Everything else fades away as one kiss turns into many. I get used to the feel of his hands and his mouth. One night stands don’t require so much kissing, and soon, hours slip by.

Eventually, we move apart as yawns begin to intersperse our kisses. We lay down on the rocky floor, settling in for the night.

"You'll have to teach me that staying spell," he whispers, reaching across and running his fingers down my face.

I grab a finger and press it to my mouth. "I will."

Minutes tick by, and his breathing steadies. I think he has fallen asleep when he begins speaking once more.

"Oh, and Elva?" he breathes.

"Mhmm?" I murmur, my eyes shut as the warmth from his fire spreads through my body. My limbs are heavy, and sleep is moments away.

"I hate fish."

CHAPTER 27

YOU HAD A WHAT?

NATHANIEL

The cold mingles with my skin, but my fiery blood makes up for it. I don't enjoy the constant dampness it causes on the surrounding ground. I roll over, only to find mid-roll that Elva's thick curls are splayed across me.

I carefully gather them up and ease her over so that I can get up and practice flying. Carefully, I shift to my other form, and I spread my wings as wide as they can possibly go before launching into the air. Wind rushes past me, and the sky is clear.

There is something about being in my bird form in the snowy mountains. The cold stifles my heat and focuses my mind. I enjoy training my wings. It *might* have something to do with Elva inspiring me.

I'm surprised at how much it hurts my back muscles. It almost seems rude. I veer to the left and try not to panic as the wind shifts in my wings. I am learning that if I trust my instincts, flying comes easily.

Soon, I settle into a rhythm, and my thoughts clear out as easily as emptying a waste bin. Circling back to the camp, I look down at where we stayed the night. There is something so beautiful blooming between us in these moments. When I look at Elva, I know she feels it too.

Cherie was my best friend growing up, and she was the first person I ever fully loved. She is a good sister. But... Elva is different. From the moment I first saw her, she's entranced me. I'm learning that there are many kinds of love–family, friends, partners–and I am better off knowing so many different variations.

I descend to the ground but don't shift right away. To my surprise, Elva is in her owl form when I reach the semi-secluded area under a combination of trees and bushes.

It feels odd to see each other like this. The companionable silence we are slowly coming to know flickers to life. I am hyper-aware of each shift of her feet, each ruffle of her feathers. She is acting... anxious.

Confusion washes over me, and I hop over to her and extend my wing around her body. I don't cover her form, but she shifts closer to me. It is beautiful and sweet. It feels good to seek refuge with each other in this way, even though I know it is time to talk about what happens next.

Perhaps it is odd to stay there as a bird for as long as we do, but there is something intimate about it. Something that solidifies the friendship between us in a way that I had never expected or imagined.

I am the first to shift. I extend my arms to either side, showing off my new ability to keep my clothes.

One moment, she is watching me through a cocked head, and the next, she stands beside me, her hair rustling in the breeze.

I want to reach for her, but I know that the second I touch her, all sense of urgency will fade in the excitement of being next to her. Touching a real-life being instead of a dream.

I break the silence first. "What now?"

Elva lets out a long breath. "I honestly don't know."

"Why don't we start with you telling me precisely what is happening?" I have always gestured with my hands when speaking, and I can't help how my thumb and index finger come together to emphasize 'precisely.'

"I am the heir to the Winter Fae throne."

"So I gathered."

She glares at me, and I put my hands up in defense. I have to consciously fight myself against making a witty quip.

"Three years ago this month, my wedding was supposed to take place," she says. "I was engaged to the Crown Prince of the Ice Mer, Henrick. He's my best friend Helena's brother. I didn't want to marry him, and I didn't want to become queen. So I... left."

Something like disappointment washes over me. It is ridiculous, and I have no right feeling... jealous? I think that is what it is.

I think what hurts me most is the fact that she had been forced into something.

Unsure of what to say, I wait a few more moments, wondering if I should say something else.

"My mother is... not a good person," is the next thing Elva says.

I figured as much. Still, it's jarring to realize that Winter Fae are brutal, even to their own family members. "These people that are coming after you... they're hers?"

After a moment, Elva nods. "I haven't been in her territory for years. But now... I'm here, and she wants me back."

My brows furrow. "Is she the one who took you?"

A bitter laugh escapes Elva. "No. Ironically, that was a completely separate incident. But my mother's magic is powerful, and she can sense my presence. I'm afraid..."

Her voice trails off, and I brush my hand against hers. "Afraid of what?"

Elva inhales sharply. “I’m afraid that this time, there will be no escaping her. It’s me or her. I know it in my soul.”

I hitch a breath, but Elva keeps going. “Which is why I’m going to kill her.”

Just like that. Treasonous, deadly words slipped from her mouth. I stumble. “You are?”

She nods. “Yes.”

My mind whirls. “And then you’ll... take the throne?”

“Maybe.”

“*Maybe?* Elva, you want to kill one of the major monarchs, destabilize a whole court, potentially the entire continent, and you don’t even know if you want the throne?”

“I—”

I am shocked when I keep speaking. This isn’t like me, but being around Elva has changed me. “Do you at least have someone else to take your place?”

Her silence is response enough.

Perhaps I have spent too much time working in trading, but I know how bad things are on this side of the ocean. I know how dangerous and precarious the pseudo-peace is.

“Don’t talk down to me. I know what things are like where I grew up. I am not an idiot.”

That shuts me up. She is right. I am being an ass.

“Hey, I’m sorry. I didn’t think.”

“No, you didn’t, Summer Fae.”

“Hey,” I start, “don’t push me away for one stupid thing. I’m not a prince. I’m not a perfect man. I’m an asshole and capricious, but I think I have shown you more than once that I am not going anywhere.”

She bristles at my words but doesn’t make any moves to leave. That’s a good sign, right?

I rake a hand through my hair. “Look, I know I’m coming on strong, but I can’t help but feel like this is exactly where I am supposed to be. So, let me in. Tell me what is going on, and I will do what I can to help you."

She looks at me long and hard. "We need to go to get supplies. And you need to get a weapon." I bite my lip. A hint of a smile comes up at the corners of her mouth as she adds, "And you will need to learn how to use it."

I laugh. "Off to infiltrate the Winter Court it is."

The tension still floats between us, but I feel good about what I've said.

... I mean, mostly.

We fly into a small town with exactly ten buildings scattered about. It is almost laughable. I spotted an Everything-Mart with glowing green lights.

I had heard they have these here, but it still feels surreal, surrounded by the brutal landscape.

Laughing in my mind, we descend toward a particularly thick collection of pine trees. When we land and switch, Elva pulls my hood over my head.

"Try not to let them see your eyes. Or your face."

I smirk and waggle my brows. "I am an excellent charmer."

"Nathan, listen. They will recognize you as being not from here in a heartbeat. We don't want that to happen. We don't know what kind of warnings have been put out. I need to go around and see if I can find some weapons. As good as fire and ice are, it always helps to have a backup."

I smile and nod, hoping she can't see the nervousness shifting beneath my casual expression.

I pull the strings on the hood, making it even harder to see inside, and push through the swinging glass door.

It creaks as the hydraulic door stops and closes. I try to change my gait. I'm not sure if it will do anything, but it can't help to try. One of the small green baskets with wheels comes into view, and I snatch it up.

The neon lights overhead make everything look awful and slightly blue. When I pass the aisles, I try to make out the contents by looking at the bottom shelves. Not a soul speaks to me.

I think that's good.

We pass the section with cheap winter clothes. I hate the style, but I know it is for the best. Reaching out, I grab a few things for Elva and me, including a few travel-size shampoo bottles. Just because. I don't know when we'll use them, but they seem like something she would like.

After throwing in a series of snacks and non-perishable food, plus backpacks, I find myself wandering down the electronics aisle. We could use a cheap burner phone.

Several of the televisions are on, all playing the same news footage. The reporter is stiff, and he speaks robotically. There is something intrinsically off about him. Pictures flash in front of the screen. I get my first glimpse of the Winter Court Queen as she walks into a meeting with Ice Mer officials.

The reporter clears his throat and shuffles some papers awkwardly. He's either very bad at his job or very nervous about something. "We interrupt our regularly scheduled programming to bring you breaking news." He glances off the camera for a moment. "The queen has just received pressing news. The princess, who has been missing for several years, has finally surfaced."

A gasp comes from the attendant behind a nearby counter. "I thought she was dead," the Fae says.

She isn't. Elva is alive and well. I step closer to the television to hear the reporter better.

"...been detained by rebel enemies from the South for a considerable time. As of yet, her whereabouts are unknown, but the queen assures everyone she will promptly find her heir and put her on the throne where she belongs."

He continues speaking as pictures of Elva flash across the screen. She is bloody, crumpled in the corner of a cell. In another picture, she is looking at the camera, but her eyes are watery and glassy, like she's been drugged into a stupor. Even in the images, Elva is so thin I can make out far too many of her bones. I can tell how much pain she is in.

I clench my fists so hard that I draw blood. Elva's mother might not have been the one who kidnapped her daughter, but she's profiting off it. Why? How could someone do that to their daughter?

I had half-heartedly agreed to find Elva's mother, but after seeing these pictures, I want to help my Winter Fae burn the rebels to the ground. For her, I would incinerate every particle of their worthless bodies.

Anyone who could turn such a lovely Fae into a shell of themselves did not deserve to live.

"Hey," Elva breathes at my side. Her voice is tight, and I don't know how much she's seen of the program.

I don't respond, afraid of what I will say. Words can hurt. I know that. I haven't been so angry since... since my father left. Red clouds my vision, making it difficult to see straight. I know this intense anger will worm into me, poisoning parts of my thoughts. I don't like feeling like this... and I don't like her seeing me like this. Anger pulses through me, and it takes everything I have to calm my breathing. This isn't the moment to let rage take over me.

Think Summer thoughts. Green grass. Flowers. Fresh air.

With each passing moment, I breathe more easily. I unclench my fists. The red fades.

I finally look over at Elva. She's staring at the television, chewing on her lip as she wrings her hands in front of her. Her confident, cool exterior has been reduced to an anxious mess.

The reporter says, "...We are pleased to announce that the heir will assume her role as queen in the coming months."

He keeps going, but my attention flips to Elva. The Winter Fae is shaking, clenching, and unclenching her fists.

She seethes, "I will never take the throne. Never be my mother's puppet."

Elva's voice is quiet, but the attendant is turning towards us.

Shit. We need to get out of here. The last thing we need to do is cause a fuss.

"Let's go pay and get out of here," I suggest.

Elva huffs, turning to me with furrowed brows. "Pay? Who said anything about paying?"

"I..."

"We have nothing to pay with."

The realization of what she's saying slams into me as I look at our full cart. This is new.

Elva grabs my hand and tugs me and our cart toward the emergency exit. She seems to have recovered her cool.

I have not.

My heart is racing, and my cheeks burn by the time we reach the exit.

"Ready?" Elva asks, gathering up our items and shoving them in a bag as inconspicuously as possible.

She doesn't give me time to answer before she kicks the door. It flies open, and a blaring alarm rings into the night.

"Come on!" she yells.

I follow her lead, my legs pumping as we run into the dark

night. Snowflakes cascade around us in a flurry as we escape. Shouts fill the air, but we're Fae and faster than them.

Soon, the woods envelop us both. The thrill of our small crime electrifies me, sending jolts of warmth through my veins until I can't help but let out a laugh. I shouldn't do that—we're in the gods-damned Winter Court, and nothing about this is particularly funny—but I can't help it.

"I've never done anything like that," I say breathlessly.

Elva lets out a low growl, pulling me harder until the shouts and wailing alarm are lost to the wind.

We made it.

Then, she spins around with a smirk on her face. Her eyes are ablaze. She drops her bag on the forest floor and pins me against a tree trunk. Her lips crash over mine in a hot kiss. Every part of me is on fire. I match every move of her mouth with an intensity I didn't know I possessed.

Snow is falling harder, and the world is like a white bubble around us. It's just us; for now, I don't care about anything else. Her hands travel down my sides, pulling me closer to her. The fire deepens, becoming an inferno within me.

Her teeth graze the edge of my mouth. They are soft at first, then harder, like the snow under our feet. Her tongue darts out, probing at my mouth, seeking entrance, and I part my lips willingly, letting her in.

I'm utterly drunk on her when she suddenly pulls away. "Stick with me, Fire Fae," she says softly. Her face is flushed in the cold, and her lips are swollen.

Mine.

Her hand strokes down my arm. "This is just the beginning."

CHAPTER 28
I WILL PROTECT HIM
ELVA

One month later

"Nathan, if you hold the sword like that, you'll be gutted like a fish before you can even utter a word."

He's standing in the middle of what has become 'our clearing' near the Western Mountains, holding an ice sword I made for him moments ago. The weapon isn't my most elaborate piece of work ever, but it will do the job.

I walk around him, placing my hand on his hip and slightly adjusting his stance before molding my hand around his. "Here, like this," I say, adjusting how his fingers grip the hilt. "Otherwise, you'll lose the weapon as soon as someone hits it."

He nods, lifting the sword in both of our hands, and swings it through the air. It glides effortlessly, his muscles tightening with the effort. I can't help but appreciate how the material highlights his body, nor can I ignore how his fingers hold the hilt of the sword with such strength.

He's strong for a Summer Fae.

"There, that's better," I say, squeezing his hand and appreciating the warmth emanating from his body. Despite being in the cold, he's a Summer Fae through and through.

"It sure is," he replies, tilting his head back to steal a kiss. It's sweet and quick and speaks to our growing connection.

During the past month, we've spent every day training with weapons. To say it's been a learning curve is an understatement. Nathan is one of the least violent Fae I've ever met, and I can tell that the idea of using these weapons against another living being is bothering him.

I keep replaying the look on his face when I killed that Fae right in front of him. But it was kill or be killed.

And I will kill tens of thousands of Fae before I ever let them lay a finger on him.

He's mine.

Mine to protect. Mine to teach. Mine to love.

We've cycled through a dozen weapons before landing on the short sword.

Traditional human weapons like guns are obviously out of the question since most contain iron. Even if we could handle them safely, there's nowhere to obtain them nearby.

The first few days after our trip to the Everything-Mart, we just focused on having him *not* melt all the weapons I created for him so he could practice.

After the third straight time he had melted the ice daggers I had magicked for him, we had sat down on a log to eat some chocolate chip cookies together. He had laughed when he found out my chocolate weakness, saying it was entirely unexpected.

"Your fire is amazing, Nathan. Truly, it's incredible. I grew up surrounded by snow and ice, and seeing it brings me joy."

He had grinned at my confession, showing off by shaping a rose out of flame and handing it to me, bowing. "It's an honor to be the bringer of joy for you, lady."

My lips had tilted up in response, accepting the rose. "And your fire is useful."

He nodded, running a hand through his hair as a look of concern crossed his face. "I sense a 'but' coming."

Sighing, I slumped against him. "You're right. How do you do that?"

He tickled my nose, making me smile. "It only seems to work with you, darling."

Leaning my head against his shoulder, I grabbed his hand. "But Nathan, those Fae are trained killers." I sighed, rubbing my shoulders. "You have to be able to get close enough for your fire to make a difference."

"I know, Elva," he had said, as tiny icicles had hung off his eyelashes. I leaned up, kissing them away, before making him another weapon.

"I appreciate it," I said, handing him the sword. "Let's go again."

Again.

This is the theme of our lives right now. Every day, we wake up, hunt as birds or eat some of the carefully rationed food we had stolen before going back to the clearing to train.

He's trying really hard, and I can't help but feel admiration for him.

As far as I can remember, no one ever went out of their way for me before. Even as a youngling, one of the first lessons I was taught was that you need to look after yourself. But... He's leaving everything behind to look after and care for me.

This is so far out of his comfort zone, but as he keeps reminding me, he won't leave me. It's hard for me to wrap my head around. No matter how often Nathan reminds me he isn't leaving, I still have nightmares about waking up and finding him gone.

It's too good to be true.

Growing up, I thought myself unloveable.

It wasn't a hard conclusion to come by, as my mother saw me as her heir, not as a Fae needing nurturing. She taught me early on that emotions are dangerous and not suitable for the Princess of the Winter Court.

"You can't rely on feelings, Elva. You must be firm, unwavering, as you lead this country." My mother is leaning against the roaring fireplace in a pale blue pantsuit that hugs her curves. Her black hair is braided tightly down her back, showing off her strong cheekbones as she watches me closely.

My gaze is locked on my mother's hands. My stomach clenches as I stare at the bright red hair streaming down her hands. The pale face of my only doll stares at me, her unmoving green eyes silently pleading for me to help.

I can see my reflection in a mirror on the wall. My eyes widen as I stand before her, running my hands down my arms. My thin, white flowy nightgown is not warding off the chill of the evening. Even for Winter Fae, tonight is cold.

"But Momma," I say, my childish voice sounding frail, even to my ears, "Helena gave me Rubella. She said that it's a toy and—"

My mother waves her hand in the air, coating the room in frost. I stop speaking instantly, my hands trembling slightly as I take in her steely gaze.

"You don't need toys, *Elva. You have a duty to your country and your people. What are you?"*

She pushes herself off the wall, coming to tower over me. I cower, though I hate myself for it.

"I-I..." I stammer, taking a step back.

"What are you?" She growls at me as the temperature in the room drops even further. I fight to keep still despite the cold.

"I am the princess, and emotions are beneath me," I repeat the words from memory, having heard them repeatedly as I grew up.

"That's right. And you don't need toys."

Before I can say anything, my mother flings her hand. There is a pop as Rubella lands on the fire. I suck in a scream as the flames devour my doll, the crackle and pop of the logs the only sound in the room. Soon, all that's left of her is a thin ash coating on the logs.

I don't cry until I make it back to my room. Even then, I wait until all the sounds have quieted in the castle until the moon and stars are the only witnesses to my grief.

If she hears me crying, things will be even worse.

The breaking point was when my mother announced my engagement to Henrick three years ago. Helena's older brother had always taken after their father in both temperament and life choices. Whisperings of prostitutes, lavish parties, drugs, and hitting his lovers when drunk were collected in my mind over dozens of years.

My mother loves him. His cruelty seems to echo something in her. The thought of them working together sends shivers down my spine.

When we were younglings, Henrick would constantly torment us whenever we were unlucky enough to find ourselves in the same room as him. He would seek us out, cutting our hair, or blaming broken items on the two of us, knowing he would go unpunished for whatever evil was his chosen course of action for the day.

When it was publicly announced that my life would be tied to his, I ran. For three years, I managed to remain hidden. I don't even know how she found me. But it's become clear that we can't stay in the Western Mountains forever.

Eventually, they'll find us. As much as I've worked to put up wards to keep our magical signatures hidden, my mother employs the strongest warlocks and is likely already tracking us down.

That's why we are out every day at the break of dawn, training until late in the evening.

Nathan hasn't complained once, although I see him rubbing

his muscles. We stumble back into the cave every evening, so exhausted that we can barely speak. We eat before falling asleep next to each other, warmed by the fire Nathan keeps going for us.

If we're being honest, I wish that the nights held more time for the two of us. I would give anything to recapture the heat between us after he shoplifted with me. I want him to push me over, tear off my clothes, and use those muscles on something other than holding a sword... But there's a lingering fear in the back of my mind. I claimed him so quickly.

What if Mother breaks him, just like my doll?

"Holy shit," I say, grabbing Nathan's hand and standing up. Our swords are leaning against a snow-covered pine not far from us, in easy reaching distance if needed. He just knocked me down in a fighting match.

"Nathan, I think it's time for us to leave," I pant, fingering the earring he gave me, the jewelry a constant reminder of the risks he took to get to me. It fell in the snow when I loosened the back, and he dipped to grab it.

"Hmm," the Summer Fae says, gently putting the Black Opal earring in my ear.

I shiver at his touch, still engrossed in how he smells and how my body reacts when I am so close to him. It's like I'm a flower, and he's the spring sun. He's brought me to life in a way I never thought possible.

He hasn't answered my question, though, so I ask him again.

"Do you think I'm ready?" Nathan responds, his eyes twinkling in the early morning light.

I give him a quick once-over, not hiding the desire in my eyes as I study him before wiping the sweat on my forehead. "I do. You came close to beating me."

"Just close?" he teases, snaking his arm around my waist and pulling us together.

I swat at him, summoning a light snowfall to swirl around us. "Just close."

He chuckles, leaning in to press a kiss to my lips. His lips are warm, and I lean into his touch. "When it comes to you, Elva, I'm happy to be beside you. At the very least."

My skin tingles and heat spreads through me. My core tightens, and I kiss him again. I can't help it. He warms me from the inside out, making me feel like pure sunshine. "What do you mean, Summer Fae?"

He pulls me down to the ground, landing on his back. I follow his movements, straddling him easily before claiming his lips once more. Our mouths sing an ancient song as we kiss and kiss and kiss. The snow around us melts, leaving us in a small area of damp ground.

Nathan's hands wander all over me, fleeting touches that leave me wanting more before they land on my hips. He pulls me towards him, and I feel all of him. He wants me just as much as I want him.

Wantonly, I grind myself against his arousal, sending a rush of excitement through me.

He groans, his head falling back into the snow and his eyes smoldering with desire. "It means that I don't care about fighting, or the cold, as long as I get to be with you."

He pulls me down, his hand lacing behind my neck, his mouth seeking mine.

We lose ourselves to the moment, indulging in the silence of the snowstorm as we explore each other.

Time slips, but eventually, I remember myself. Where we are.

The broadcast at the store. Mother. And... my engagement. Being back in the Winter Court is problematic for more reasons than one.

I pull away, groaning.

Nathaniel looks at me, his brows furrowed. "What's wrong?"

I sit back. "Did you hear what I said earlier? We have to go."

His eyes search mine for a long moment. "Are you sure?" he asks huskily. "I can think of a lot of ways we can entertain ourselves in the wild. We can stay here as long as you need."

"If I had it my way, we wouldn't be here at all," I say, fiddling with the tail of my braid and ignoring the ache in my lower belly. "But we are. And you were right."

He places a hand over his heart, flying backward into the snow and falling as though he's been shot with an arrow. "By the gods. Elva, did you just say I am right about something?"

Groaning, I rest my head against the tree, peeking out through lowered eyelashes as he dramatically lies on the ground. "I did," I say tartly. "But don't get used to it. I'm sure it won't happen often."

"Even once is enough for me, darling," he says before returning to life.

He jumps to his feet and pulls a flaming rose from his pocket. He hands it to me with a flourish bow. "For you, Princess."

I take it, admiring the handiwork. His creations are warm but never burn my skin.

After a moment, he coughs. "Out of curiosity, what was I right about?"

Twirling the flaming flower, I inspect it as I consider my next words.

"We can't just go charging into the Winter Court," I say. "For all I know, my mother is expecting us. Besides... if I just kill her without a plan, the entire territory will be thrown into turmoil, and I don't want to be the cause of that."

He is silent for a moment, biting his lip as he appears to consider my words. “I think that’s very wise. What *do* you want to do?”

"I think it's time we visit a certain Ice Mer."

CHAPTER 29

AND TO YOUR LEFT, AQUALIS

NATHANIEL

Aqualis is a place that is simply not made for Fae. Temporary spells are available at the land entrance, but they make me claw at my skin in desperation. I cannot think of anything other than the suffocating pressure on my lungs or the searing sensation on my neck.

When I look over, Elva is wonderful. She takes my hand and drags me into the water. At first, the saltwater stings my eyes, and the suffocating feeling intensifies. But only for a moment.

All too suddenly, I can feel water rush through new growths on the sides of my neck. They feel odd, out of place, but my chest rises and falls normally.

I stroke my fingers along the bumpy ridges as I look at Elva. *Damn*. We grew gills.

"Leave it to the Mer," I grumble, staring at my once-beautiful hands now webbed like a frog.

Elva's feet move up and down in graceful waves. She discarded her shoes on land, and a pair of brown fins now peek out under her pant cuffs, but they suit her. Everything suits her beautiful body.

The water is bitterly cold, but I cast a bubble of warmth around us, keeping away the frost. Schools of fish pass us, their scales glimmering in the murky sunlight like dozens of gems. As we descend further into the depth, the water pressure still doesn't harm us.

Lanterns of bioluminescent plants sway gently around us, their tips reaching toward the surface. Two hefty hammerhead sharks guard the tunneled entrance to Aqualis, the Ice Mer's grand city. I am positive that no other Summer Fae has ever come to this place. The Ice Mer are not very welcoming to those on their own continent.

As we pass through the streets, I am acutely aware of two things. First, Elva knows her way to wherever we are going very well. This worries me slightly because I know she was engaged to the prince–I suppose they are possibly still engaged–we haven't really talked about it. Second, there are no 'other species' besides us.

"Thanks for the heat," Elva finally says over her shoulder as we tuck into a narrow empty street. I glimpse her tattoos that glow in the marine lights.

"Any time," I say and speed up my swimming to join her at her side. "This feels peculiarly similar to flying. I feel... well, I don't feel bored."

She raises an eyebrow, her eyes dancing with affectionate amusement. "Really? Not bored? This is one of the best-kept secrets of our world. If they opened tourism here, I don't doubt there would be those who never return on land."

I scrunch up my forehead. "Yes, but don't the Ice Mer kill anyone who gets too close to their city?"

"I never said there wasn't a price to such secrecy." She fixes her mouth into a grim line.

I want to continue talking to her, but the beauty of the surrounding buildings sweeps me away. All of them are vibrant hues of jewel-toned coral. I could have never imagined how the pearlescent coating they painted on each surface made them look like precious stones. It's like walking through a treasure chest from a children's tale about pirates.

The Ice Mer are dressed in sealskins, which makes me shudder. Their skin and hair colors match the surrounding tones. They come in many shapes and sizes. The only unifying factor between them is the scaly tales that flip from side to side as they move.

The castle is in the city's epicenter. It appears to be made of abalone, but I am sure that is impossible. I just don't know how they made it look like that.

Instead of heading for what appears to be the main gate, Elva takes me to the side, and we wind our way through a series of side paths that lead to one of the castle's estates. After she leads me through a kelp forest, I spot the dark-green house.

I use the word 'house' lightly. It appears to be a mansion.

I hesitate at the gate, and Elva turns back to me. Her hair floats around her head in the water like a halo. It is nothing short of mesmerizing. I'm sure she can see the worry in my eyes, but before she opens her mouth, I claim her lips with my own.

Something beautiful and dangerous stirs inside of me. With each touch and night spent together, emotion grows within me. I am utterly defenseless against it.

She laughs, and the melodic sound is muffled through the wonky sound waves of the sea. She trails a series of kisses up my jaw and to my ear. "This is where my best friend lives. Helena."

I look into her eyes. "Your best friend lives so far from you?"

A shadow crosses her face. "We're both princesses and..." *I was engaged to her brother.*

She doesn't need to say the words. I know what she means.

For a brief second, I get a view into a life growing up that differed greatly from mine. As complicated as my relationship with my family may be, it has nothing on her solitary life, holed up in a castle and being auctioned off to the highest bidder.

I can relate to the last bit. I open my mouth to tell her–*to show her* that I understand through a shared experience. Before I can speak, she puts a webbed hand on my chest, silencing me. Reaching down, she forms a thick ice disc and hurls it through the water toward an open window.

The disc speeds through the water before slowing down after passing the window.

"Impressive, but how can we be sure she'll see it before it melts?" I ask.

"Look up." She points towards the mansion's second story, where a small window is illuminated in a glowing yellow light. "You see that light? She leaves that on for me, just in case."

My eyebrows go up, and I am delighted to be included in her world. A few seconds pass before a head pops out of the window. A cloud of silky strands that shift colors from purple to blue float around Helena's face. Her skin is the color of grey ice, but her eyes are the most unnerving part. They are bright pink.

She smiles, her full lips pulling back to reveal pointed teeth. I suppress a shiver.

"I was wondering when you would show up on my doorstep." When she speaks, Helena scrunches up her nose as if she smells something disgusting. Her under-lids blink, and then she pulls herself out of the window. Her long tail follows her movements in elegant motions as she emerges completely. She's wearing a long, translucent light green top that billows in the water, revealing a pearl-studded band around her breasts. Matching pearls are braided into her long hair, while a diadem of seashells circles her head.

She is positively bewitching. I swallow hard, thinking of how the Mer people would drag unsuspecting humans down to their deaths on a whim. I turn my attention back to Elva, who is watching me.

I take her hand and squeeze it.

"Helena, this is Nathan." Elva's voice is light, and Helena casts her a knowing look.

"So, you are real," the Mer says.

Elva raises an eyebrow at her friend.

"There was a picture that the media here tried to leak of you two kissing in the woods a few weeks ago. It caused quite an uproar because it looked like you had just stolen from a nearby store. Your mother paid a hefty fee to delete it from all databases permanently." Helena gives me a long, appraising look. "Can't have an engaged princess taking on a lover before the wedding is finalized."

Her tone is light, but even I can catch the warning in her words. Elva's skin is different shades of crimson red. For the first time, I see her as she must've been before we met. A wild, cold creature, enraged at being caged in.

Helena sees the anger and clasps her friend's bicep. The action steadies them both as unspoken words pass between them. This is a friendship that has been tempered into a long-lasting bond. I'd seen nothing like this before. I'm not sure that anyone who doesn't live in constant fear of brutality can create the trust these two have forged between them.

Helena turns to me and smirks. "So this is the male Elva has chosen over my brother."

I can't help feeling like I want to shrink. In my panic, I catch my fin on one of the decorative boulders that line the seafloor and tumble through the water. I am flabbergasted.

How in the hell did I manage that?!

Helena's smirk hardens over. She does not find it endearing as Elva does.

"Can we come inside?" Elva asks, her eyes shifting from side to side to take in the surroundings.

Helena's eyes stay on me for a few more moments before she nods and leads us to the front door.

"Hallie and James are visiting with their little fish sticks. They are out shopping for dinner they are putting on later. I suppose you both are invited."

Elva laughs at Helena's joke, but I keep my mouth shut as her stern glare bores into me. She stops looking at me, spreads her arms wide, "Welcome to my royal estate. A little small compared to what my older brother and younger sister have been given, but I am daddy's little black lobster."

I stare at the enormous room around me. Is this *small* to her? *What in the actual nine circles of hell?*

Helena catches my eyes, and I try to smile. "Nathan, be a dear and follow Barth to your room," she says. "If you're good, I'll let you and Elva keep sleeping together."

A dolphin with unnaturally human eyes comes alongside me and waits for me to make my way up the ramp. They aren't stairs. Stairs aren't necessary in the ocean, I guess.

Our furs from the surface have gotten so waterlogged and damaged from just a few hours in the salt water. A wave of relief washes over me when I see luxurious sealskins in the closets to replace the blue suede wasting away. An image of a drowned sailor intrudes into my mind's eye, and I cringe.

In the center of the room is a sea anemone bed. I wonder how I might sleep adrift in the water. Then, when my brain imagines Elva and I putting the bed to good use, I hate it a bit less.

Voices carry differently in the water. This is the first lesson I learn when I swim silently back down the stairs, warm and content. Elva and Helena are seated on a sofa made of a giant oyster shell. I have a clear view of Helena, but not my Elva.

"... I don't know what the hell you are doing. First, you abandon your position, and then you leave Henrick here waiting for you."

"Please, shut up, Helena. You don't know what you're talking about."

"Oh, come on, you think I won't say anything because I am your friend? Elva, because I am your friend, I will tell you right now that this will end horribly. You don't get to have frivolous lovers. You know the rules of the crowns. You get to marry once. He's a skinny Summer Fae. There's no way your mother will ever allow it. I'm more likely to witness his execution in the streets of the Ice City than I am to see you two married."

Elva's hands are rubbing against her forehead. She remains silent, much to my despair.

"Did you have sex with him? Is that what this is about? Is he the first one to make you feel like a female? He's the size of a twig! I swear, you are the friskiest Winter Fae in the whole damned court. I get it–you needed to get laid. I told you to sleep with someone inconsequential so you wouldn't get overly attached and you wouldn't have any problem breaking it off before the wedding. You can't try to tell me that Henrick didn't offer."

At the sound of her fiancé's name, I tighten my fists.

"Helena, stop it."

Ignoring her friend's pleading, Helena opens her mouth to bombard her some more, but Elva cuts her off.

"I don't want to marry your pompous-ass brother!" The finality in Elva's words warms the pit forming in my stomach. "Henrick is a prick who has slept with half of the royals in every court. You, of all people, know how disgusting he is. How could you even suggest I touch him?"

"Because I fear the consequences of you not being with him more. I would help protect you from the worst after you were married."

Elva flinches but continues. "You have never known someone like Nathan. Gods, Helena, when he touches me it feels like I am a living flame. My whole life I have spent encased in ice, but two seconds with him and I am burning, melting to the ground. But it's so much more than that. He is kind and gentle, but most of all, he is loyal. Which is more than I can say for you right now."

Helena's eyes fly wide open at that last insult, and I can hear by her voice that Elva knows she has wounded Helena in the exact right way.

Elva doesn't stop there. "Did you know that when he found out I was in trouble, he came looking for me? He lost everything. His job, his life, to be with me. He could be anywhere, with anyone back in that disgusting city, but he chooses me."

Helena is silent, her face plastered with shame and hurt.

Elva is brutal. And she burns for me. A smile spreads across my lips and heat pools in another part of my body.

Helena continues to stare at the ground until Elva stands and spots me.

I don't know what to do. I feel like I'm naked. So, I smile widely and say, "I don't suppose we can get Fae mead down here."

CHAPTER 30
HENRICK THE HARD-ASS
ELVA

When I imagined seeing my best friend again after all these years, I thought she'd warmly welcome us. I was wrong.

Helena is still holding a grudge that I ran out on her brother. In all the times that we texted on the burner FaePhones, she never once mentioned it. Now, it's all out in the open. We moved to the dining room, which unfortunately did nothing to relieve the tension.

Helena is seated across from us, her gaze frosty as she watches us intently. Nathan has an arm around my shoulder and is rubbing soft circles as he studies the goblet of sparkling wine in his hand. They didn't have any Fae mead.

The silence has become its living entity, occupying a fourth seat at the table as we look at each other.

"So, this is new," I say to break the tension, gesturing to the table beneath us. It is enormous and can easily seat over twenty people. The three of us are dwarfed by the chairs, their backs rising far above us.

"Mhmm." Helena nods, her gaze distant. Usually, she is the picture of poise, but today, she slumps in her chair and runs her finger over the rim of her glass. She watches Nathan out of slitted eyes.

I instinctively stiffen, shooting daggers at my best friend.

I understand her hesitation about him. I do.

Would I have ever picked a Summer Fae for myself? No.

Will I give Nathan up? Never.

Helena must read something on my face because she leans back and sips her sparkling wine. I watch her, my gaze drifting to the enormous windows behind her that open up into the city of Aqualis. The glass is enchanted and warded so we can look out, but no one can look in.

Merpeople swim by outside the window, their arms laden with packages and bags as they go about their daily lives. The faint sounds of conversations drift through the glass, sounding so conventional. They look so normal.

Normalcy has never been something I've been allowed to know.

Dinner is somehow even more awkward. Seeming to sense the tension in the room, Helena's sister Hallie and her husband made a flimsy excuse about their son Ian and disappearing before dinner is served. I never liked Hallie. She's all royal manners on the outside but pure bitch inside.

Servants swim in, bearing iridescent cloche after iridescent cloche, placing their dishes on the long table before removing the lids with a flourish to reveal perfectly cooked fish. Salmon with crispy skin and maple glaze, tuna steaks with a sesame crust, and shrimp sautéed in garlic. There's an enchantment around the food that stops it from taking on the seawater that surrounds us.

Nathan's disappointment is a wave that washes over me. He

picks at his food, eating only as much as necessary not to insult our host. The clinking of cutlery against china fills the room as every chew and swallow is amplified.

Finally, the servers swim in to clear the plates. Once the table is clear, I pick up my wine and throw it back in one swallow. It's strong and burns before settling in my body, but it gives me the strength to finally bring up why we came here.

"All right, Helena, that's enough," I say. "We need your help."

Before Helena can reply, a voice comes from the door to my right. The sound sends shivers down my spine.

"And why does my little sister need to help you, my elusive fiancé?" the newcomer asks.

I stiffen, my grip tightening on the goblet until my knuckles turn while. A crack echoes through the room, and the empty wine glass shatters in my hand. I watch in clinical fascination when I realize a piece of glass has cut my palm, causing red blood to stream out and color the water.

"Elva, gods," Nathan swears beside me, grabbing my hand before finding a napkin and pressing it against the would. His hands are warm against my clammy skin.

"Yes, Elva, *gods*. What are you thinking, letting this Summer Fae touch you?" Henrick swims around the table, his tail as black as his soul as it swishes around him.

"Henrik, you weren't invited," Helena snarls. I'm floating in the water in an instant, backing away from the table and feeling off-balance and vulnerable.

The crown prince smirks. "Yes, I was. Hallie is a better sister than you."

"That bitch," Helena says. "Go to–"

In a flurry of movement, he stops right in front of me, shoving Helena aside before leaning forward and putting his hands on the table. His black eyes are filled with violence as they glare at us.

I pull away from him as he leans in, only to see Nathan swim between us. I can feel panic rising in me like a tidal wave, despite myself. It's hard to breathe as my heart pounds in my chest, banging against the thin shell of my ribcage.

You are fierce. You are not his toy.

Henrick glares at my Nathan. "Really, Elva? Him?"

"Hello, Henrick," I say through clenched teeth as I open my eyes again. "I was hoping to avoid this interaction altogether, but here you are."

He looks back at me, his gaze promising pain. "Imagine my surprise," he says, tapping his fingers on the table as he swims in place, "when I found out my future wife was not actually holed up in some bunker with the rebels."

Shit. Shit.

How did I not consider the possibility of him being here? He spends so much time traveling.

His tail suddenly slams into the chair beside Helena, the wood cracking under the impact. I jolt backward, my veins running cold as the threat of violence fills the air.

"Do I scare you?" He laughs, the sound chilling. Helena is behind him, cradling her arm. *Don't make things worse*, she begs me silently as her eyes grow large and red.

"Well?" Henrick asks again, demanding I look at him. He once left me alone with a great shark nearly at me alive. Everything he did was to preserve power. I was afraid of him, but mostly I hated him. I shake my head no.

"That's good," Henrick says. His lips pull back, exposing rows of razor-sharp teeth. "Gods forbid my fiancé be frightened of me."

That makes me angry. "I am not your fiancé," I say, willing

my voice to be steady. "I never agreed to marry you, and I *never* will."

"Tell that to your mother," he says, winking. The gesture is revolting, making me want to peel my skin off my bones. "My dear Elva. You are *mine*. I should be thanking you for introducing me to your lover. What a fabulous wedding present."

Nathan has another moment of emboldened anger. “We’re leaving.”

I touch his arm, ignoring the stinging in my palm. He looks at me, and Henrick studies the interaction. This is my fight, not his. He has already sacrificed enough. "I am *not* yours. And I will *never, ever* marry you."

"Is that so?" Henrick asks mockingly, raising a black brow.

"I would rather die," I grind out through clenched teeth.

He stares at me, his gaze assessing, before cackling wildly. His hair floats around his face as his eyes widen, a crazed look entering his eyes. "That can be arranged, my dear. It would be a damn shame if your enchantment suddenly wore off and you couldn't breathe underwater, wouldn't it?"

Beside me, Nathan sucks in a deep breath. "You would dare threaten to murder a guest in your sister's home? Do the laws of hospitality mean nothing to you here?" Nathan’s red hair floats around him like a halo. His anger is pulsing off of him as an unnatural warmth fills the room. My Summer Fae’s beautiful eyes are now swirling with rage as they glare at Henrick, a vein popping out in his neck as he glares at my once-fiancé.

My Nathan. I claimed him before I ever knew he could be like this. My instincts had chosen correctly.

Henrick scoffs. “Those are Fae rules. Your customs don’t bind us Merfolk.”

Nathan clenches his fists. "You listen to me, you overgrown fish. *The lady said she doesn't want to marry you.* And that's final."

Henrick looks between us, his gaze steely. "Who is she going to marry?" The Mer waves a hand at Nathan, looking derisive. "You?"

My Summer Fae stiffens. "Maybe. But it's up to her to decide, not some archaic law."

I pull on Nathan's arm again, harder this time, trying to get him to look at me. I recognize the steely look in Henrick's eye, and it's promising disaster.

"What if I just take her now and make her mine?" Henrick sneers at Nathan. "What are you going to do about it, little twig?"

Fire shoots out of Nathan's hands, only to be extinguished in seconds. The water heats around us, becoming almost uncomfortable as more spurts of the heat warm the room.

Henrick's eyebrows shoot up. “So the dog can bite?”

"Elva," Helena pleads, "do something."

"Yes, Elva. Do something,” Henrick echoes mockingly. He turns towards Helena. "You've always been weak. That's why Father can barely stand to be in your presence."

He leers at me, his gaze dropping to my chest. "Mhmm,” he says, licking his lips. I want to throw up as his eyes strip me bare. The sensation is so unwelcome that I can’t stop the shiver that runs through my body. “Once we're wed, we'll have to talk about your choice of friends, Elva."

"That's enough. You will disrespect her no longer." Nathan seethes, his eyes wild. "I challenge you to a duel."

"Nathan," I breathe, swimming over to clutch his arm. "What are you doing?"

He shakes me off, standing his ground. "I won't let some big-tailed man insult you, Elva, or force you into a marriage. It's not right."

"But Nathan—" I try again. I desperately need to tell him something right now.

No. No. No.

I'm screaming inside, trying to find a way out of this mess. Before I can even move, Henrick speaks again. "I look forward to our fight to the death."

I watch as Nathan shifts towards me, his face paling before he pulls me in, and my hands fly to his face. "Elva, I—"

Suddenly, a wave of water pulls us apart, pushing Nathan to the other end of the dining room. Henrick grins, flicking his hand as he controls all the water in the room. His eyes are feral as he watches us.

"Twenty minutes. The Conch Coliseum. I'll see you there." He pauses, tilting his head before baring his teeth at Nathan. "Oh, and *Nathan*? I've never lost a duel, and I don't plan on starting today."

With a swish of his tail, Henrick leaves the room.

Twenty minutes.

That's all I have to prepare Nathan.

This is why I have never tried to fall in love. This is why it was a bad idea to have anything more than one-night stands. My life is a mess, and I'm entangled between two courts set on hurting each other.

Then I admit to myself the truth building for months. I love him.

TWENTY MINUTES FEELS LIKE BOTH AN ETERNITY AND THE BLINK OF AN eye. We swim past unsuspecting Merpeople by rows of coral houses and abalone buildings. On any other day, my eyes would have been drinking at the magnificent underwater city.

Not today.

Ultimately, I can't summon those three words to say to Nathaniel. I feel them in my heart, but they're stuck on my lips, refusing to make it out of my mouth.

"How could you do this?" I ask as we swim along to the Conch Coliseum. The large building is in sight. The coral-pink conch shell that gives the arena its name is much larger than the rest of the city. It curls up and reaches high into the water, the focal point of this part of the city. It is beautiful. Pale blue lines reach down the side of the enormous shell, each pointing to a different entrance.

Nathan is silent for a moment. "I will do anything for you," he says.

But why this?

I want to scream, cry, kick something, and then fall apart. The Summer Fae is too honorable for his own good. I push down my mother's voice as hard as possible, silencing that treacherous part of my being.

"Henrick is weaker on his left side," I say to Nathan as we swim through a side door of the coliseum. I can hear the shouts from the stadium. I float away from my Summer Fae and look out of the open entrance. I'm shocked at how many people have already arrived. Aqualis is a large city, but having so many pain-hungry spectators is alarming. I turn back to him and blow out a large bubble. "He injured his ribs on that side long ago, which still bothers him. If you have a shot, you need to hit him there."

Nathan winces, and his hair floats around him as he steadies himself with careful strokes of his hands. I remember how he almost beat me. He has talent.

"You don't think I'll make it out of the arena, do you?" he asks.

Of course, I do. The words are on my lips, and I try to force them out. They won't budge.

My silence is telling. "Nathan, I—"

He turns towards me, but instead of the anger I'm expecting, I see... kindness. "It's okay, Elva. I know you're used to taking care of yourself." He reaches down and grabs my hand, pulling it to his lips to kiss. I'm greedy and don't wish to let him go. "Let me take care of you this time. I will see you after. I promise."

Magic tingles between us as he makes a vow. I know he can feel it too. The screams are louder now, the sounds echoing through the tunnel we're in as a timer counts down in the arena.

How in the hell did they get so many people in twenty minutes?

"Come back to me," I say, pulling him for a deep kiss before releasing him. "Remember, the left side."

Nathan nods with a grim look in his eyes. After another kiss, he turns and swims away from me.

I stand in the tunnel and watch, clutching my fist to my chest. I can't bear to turn away even for a moment. A swishing of water alerts me to someone's presence before I hear Helena's soft voice.

"I'm sorry, Elva," she murmurs.

I nod, my eyes never leaving the Summer Fae fighting for my honor. "Me too." Helena has been mistreated more often than I have by her family. She has been hurt, abused, and just plain ignored. It's one of my greatest wishes that she finds someone who can bring the fire out of her like Nathan has for me. When she starts fighting back, she'll be a sight to behold.

Together, we stand vigil as the two males, Fae and Mer, pick their weapons. Henrick chooses a three-headed mace, while Nathan goes for a sword. I hear the crowd booing his choice of weapon, clearly hoping for a better show.

A buzzer goes off, declaring the beginning of the dual, as screams echo through the arena. Mer are blood-hungry folk, and this is right up their alley.

Come on, Nathan. Remember your training.

For the first few minutes, the males simply circle each other, their gazes locked as they assess their enemy.

"I pray that your Fae wins," Helena breathes beside me.

I shoot her a look of surprise. It's treasonous to support someone other than her brother.

"What?" she says. "It's not like Henrick has ever been kind or decent towards me. I'd like to see Nathan win."

Before we can unpack that statement further, the sound of metal hitting metal fills the arena, and my gaze is drawn back to the men fighting for me. My stomach twists as I watch them dance in the ring.

Reaching out blindly, I grasp Helena's hand, squeezing tightly as we watch Nathan pull his sword out of the mace's chain. The sound of metal against metal rings through the arena. The crowd is growing wilder by the second, and their energy is practically pulsing through the water.

Henrick cackles, the sound booming through the arena. He whirls the mace around his head, the water swirling like a tornado.

Faster than should be possible underwater, he darts and swings the mace around in a circle. It's as though I'm watching in slow motion as the weapon approaches Nathan.

I scream, the sound ringing in my ears, and try to swim out to him, but Helena yanks on my arm. She pulls me back, wrapping powerful arms around my middle. "Stop," she hisses in my ear. "You know the laws. You can't go in there."

The one she's referencing is bright in my mind, pulsing as I fight against my instincts to go to him. *Once a duel has been called, no member of the Northern Court may interfere. If they do, their lives are forfeit.*

"Damn Northern Court laws," I whimper, struggling against Helena's grip. "That's my... He's... Nathan." The last word comes out as a plea as I stare at him.

The first swing misses, barely. But Henrick is still advancing. Half the crowd is silent in anticipation, while the other half shouts advice. Henrick swipes again, and it lands right in his opponent's side. Nathan doubles over, crying out, as a stream of bright red blood floats into the water.

"Nathan!" I scream.

He turns ever so slightly and locks eyes with me.

Please.

I don't know who I'm begging, I just know I need him to be okay.

Even though he's wounded, Nathan seems to be still moving well. He's dodging Henrick's attacks and appears to be doing everything he can to pull Henrick around the arena.

He's trying to tire him out, I realize suddenly.

It's a great strategy, really. Brilliant. One I wish I had thought of myself. The large Ice Mer is almost double the size of my Summer Fae, and he is already flagging, the weight of the mace much heavier than Nathan's sword.

But he isn't injured.

I feel every single second, every moment, as though it was me out on the sand. My heart is beating so fast, it's moments away from exploding. Helena's arms are still around my middle, her tail brushing up against me every so often in comfort.

Remaining still, I tune out the shouts, trying to focus solely on Nathan.

Eventually, Henrick seems to lose his calm. He roars and surges forward, his teeth bared as he lunges for Nathan.

Quickly, faster than I knew he could move, Nathan spins around and swings his sword. My hand goes to my mouth as I watch it cleave through the water before slicing into the side of Henrick's neck.

Silence.

Bile rises in my throat as I watch Nathan pry the sword from the Mer's body. Blood taints the water as Henrick screams, his hand loosening on the mace. Even from here, I can see his face paling as he looks down at his neck.

"Impossible," he gurgles as blood streams from his mouth. He lurches towards Nathan as if to attack him with his bare hands. His head rolls grotesquely to one side as he moves, exposing the horrible wound to the arena.

Nathan stares at Henrick for a moment, his lips moving in a wordless prayer, before he lifts his sword and drives it through Henrick's heart. The Mer jerks once before his eyes roll back in his head, and he floats limply before my lover.

Nathan seems to be frozen in place. His sword is still gripped in his hands as blood trickles out from his side.

A stern-faced Mer who must work for the arena swims out from a hidden door in the heart of the Coliseum, their blue tail swishing as they approach Henrick's body. They check for a pulse, one of the most preposterous things I've ever seen, before shaking their head.

"The challenger has won," the Mer announces, his voice magicked to echo through the arena. The crowd has fallen silent, their gazes locked on Nathan.

Shit.

Shit.

"The Crown Prince is dead "

Suddenly, roars erupt around us as the Mer begin thumping their tails on their seats. The sound echoes through the stands as the entire building begins to shake. I know what happens next. I realize that I really didn't expect Nathan to win, not against someone like Henrick. I'm filled with so many emotions I can hardly breathe–fear, gratitude, relief. I will never doubt him again.

"We have to get both of you out of here," Helena says quickly, unwrapping her arms from around my middle. I look at her, pale and clearly in shock.

She is the future queen now.

Her voice is desperate as she straightens her spine. "Let me help you."

CHAPTER 31

IS THIS BECOMING A HABIT?

NATHANIEL

My eyes are locked on Henrick's lifeless eyes, but it's like I'm half a second behind it all. I watched the spark of intelligence fade from his eyes. I sag, and clutch the wound at my side. I feel weaker, but I've already begun healing. Blood is still floating around me, both mine and his.

Death forces me into duality, and I am staring at him but also watching my life flash before me. I throw myself into the images, the pictures of every hope and dream I've ever had, the person I wanted to become back then. The Summer Court is not violent. My father once thought me unworthy of his attention, and I believed him. University, teaching, all the things I had wanted to do were floating around me like the bubbles containing Henrick's last breaths.

The word "murderer" bounces around my brain, trying to get me to own up to the title. I consciously avoid looking at it, acknowledging it.

I should own it. I did murder the person in front of me. But I did it for Elva.

When Henrick came into the dining room, I saw how Elva changed. The confident, powerful female all but curled into a ball. I saw the emotions parade across her face. Shock, fear, a hint of agony, and then pure, unadulterated rage.

What had the male done to them? To make two females that were perfectly capable of protecting and defending themselves... It made something primal stir inside of me.

Killing the Crown Prince was the right thing to do. I can feel it in my very bones and the sting of the saltwater on my skin. But I know it will come at a heavy cost for me and this court.

A trident whizzes past my ear, drawing me back to myself. I whip around and see that the crowd Henrick had drawn is turning riotous. They aren't cheering for my victory, they continue to call for my blood.

From the door of the arena, I see Elva and Helena. Elva is trying to find a way to me. I see it in how she darts back and forth at the entrance. Helena doesn't come into the space. It's a wise choice, especially since she will be the next ruler of this land. It's dangerous enough for her to be next to Elva right now.

Guards that had been ordered not to interfere with the duel are now racing towards me, their tails stirring the water as they move swiftly. My brain kicks into gear, and I swim toward Elva. There is nothing more to do. I duck, and spin in the water when a few more weapons, steely and razor-sharp, narrowly miss my body. One scratches my arm, but I ignore the burn of saltwater in my wounds.

When I reach Elva, she yanks me with the full power of her force towards a door that Helena has slipped into. "Are you still bleeding?" she asks, breathless from shock.

The darkness of the tunnel provides a small amount of protection. It won't last long. I know they have seen where we have gone. "Barely. I'm fine, really."

She nods and swims on while clutching my hand. When we

arrive, Helena is talking to some servants in a hushed tone. The group of them looks up as I enter. I nod tersely at all of them. When our eyes meet, I see something wild and unexpected. Admiration.

"Elva, you two will wear these tunics. Leave in the middle of this group of servants. You won't be seen for a little while, at least."

Elva throws her arms tight around the princess. I am impressed at the sight of two future queens embracing. Quiet words pass between them.

The things this could mean for this continent...

The train of thought fades when Elva throws the server's cap around me, hands me a coral tray, and pulls me to the center of the servants. They give us weapons and armor to carry, the least conspicuous we could be. I know I wouldn't look twice at the royal servants.

With no further words, we leave. Every muscle in my body is tense, as if my corporeal form knew what I had done just as well as my mind. When we step into the light of the city, it is everything I can do not to shake.

It is pure chaos. A few fights have already broken out in the manhunt for me. I see bright red blood blossoming in the water as one Mer punches another in the face. Weapons are brandished by far too many. They are threatening others who would dare harbor the Prince's gods-damned assassin.

"He is an infiltrator from the South to infiltrate our government..." one voice hisses.

"With Henrick dead, his bitch-sister will take over. Imagine the changes that pus—" I tune out the bitter, hateful words as we near the castle, and I know we must run as soon as we reach it.

Most of the Mer are still assembled at the Coliseum, but soon, they will realize their searches are for nothing.

I have never felt the way I do now. I am completely sober and completely focused. It is something so terrifying and so exquisite I can't help feeling that I've been missing out. We have reached the castle gate, and one of the Mer males turns to us and hisses, "*Go now.* Stick to the coral and kelp."

We don't need to be told twice. The sanction on our spell is supposed to last another twenty-four hours, but now we have to gear up and swim.

At first, we move slowly, trying not to attract unwanted attention. Our pace increases when the large city gates draw near. I cannot help it, and I sense Elva clawing at her insides, trying to stay calm.

I'll be honest. I have no idea what she thinks of all of this... what she thinks of me. I was headstrong and irrational when I challenged him. I am playing with fire. Or maybe... maybe I am just letting the ice take place in my soul.

It feels good. Grounding.

Just as we near the gate, an explosion bubbles up from the castle. I turn back for a fraction of a second, trying to see exactly what has happened, but Elva grabs my shoulder and yanks me forward. We race through the gate just as a small team of Mer males and females ward the bioluminescent protections surrounding the city like a great wall.

They see us and immediately send the sharks guarding the gates after us. My chest tightens, but we keep swimming. I conjure all the fire in my veins to boil the water around us.

The problem with this—and it is a problem—is that we are also in the water and prone to being boiled alive. But I am not alone.

Elva hurls ice spears behind us. One of her weapons hits one of the massive great white sharks that has joined the hammerheads. Thick, red liquid clouds what happens next from view. Unfortunately for me, I can still hear what is happening.

Snarls, ferocious and unlike anything I've ever heard, fill the sea. The sharks' blood is so irresistible that the creatures are sent into a frenzy, killing each other as it leaks into their systems.

We swim as fast as we can until we spot a whale. This blue whale is heading towards the surface, and Elva again yanks me. I wrap my arms around her waist. As I do, she moves, maneuvering expertly until she is positioned as close to the whale as possible. She rapidly grabs the tail of the enormous beast. A heartbeat later, the water rushes around me, faster than before.

This feels like flying.

"Blue whales are protectors. It will not harm us," Elva calls over her shoulder. I nod, holding on tight and trying not to loosen my grip. I can't be left behind.

We are moving so quickly, my blood is a drum pumping through my veins. The light of the surface grows brighter every second.

Closer. *Closer.*

We realize the whale doesn't intend to break the water, so we will have to be the ones to let go. Elva is the one actually holding onto the whale, so she preps herself. We will need to be careful not to be hit by the tail.

She lets go, and immediately, we fail at avoiding the tail. When it collides with my back, my shoulder *crunches*. White-hot pain flashes through me. I scream. This hurts far worse than the mace to my side.

Elva holds onto me, moving, but the pain is so acute that black spots pop up in my vision. When I look at Elva, all I see is the white of her tattoos.

She is now dragging me to the surface, and I am fighting against the pain in my arm.

I am suddenly very concerned about what will happen when we reach the surface. It is impossible that we would be in the same city on the shore that connects to Aqualis. There will be no one to help us.

There is so much pain and shock coursing through my veins, the worry makes me feel like I might explode. My fears are for naught as we burst through the water tension of the surface. I see the ice floating all around us but realize that the searing pain in my neck returns while our gills disappear and we are gasping for air through our lungs.

I am fading out of awareness. I know Elva is dragging me with all her might towards a slab of ice.

"*Nathaniel*," she shouts as my eyelids flutter. "You're going to freeze!" She is out of the ice before me. Our breath is misting in the frigid air, and I can feel the cold in my bones. I want to warm her, dry us both with my magic. But when I reach inside of me, sharp pain is the only thing I find. Trying to roll over, something stabs my shoulder, and I yell.

"Shh, shh," Elva hisses in my ear, her hot breath tingling against my skin. I try to focus on that instead of the pain. "You can't scream, *dammit*. We are still on the run."

Fae heal relatively quickly, but not quickly enough to heal shattered bones in a matter of minutes. Certainly not when they are soaking wet in this freezing place. I will die of hypothermia, shock, or whatever the word is.

Something goes into my mouth. It is firm but pliable. The taste tells me of some sort of leather.

"Don't scream." I am not fully conscious, but I could have sworn her voice is softer, enticing. Or maybe I am just going insane.

I am prepared, sort of, when she adjusts my shoulder. A scream forms in my mouth, but I bite down, instead. I clench my teeth so hard that they feel like they might pop out of place.

"Shit," I hear Elva whisper. "It's going to be okay, Nathan. It's okay. I am here." She repeats the words repeatedly, a mantra to hold on to against the fiery pain.

Suddenly, my shoulder and arm feel like they are burning up. I want to cry out as worry consumes me that my power has somehow decided I am useless and will consume me completely.

My eyes fly wide, despite the desire to keep them shut. Elva clasps onto something with one hand while her other is pressed against me. She is using the shards of Black Opal. My arm is knitting itself together. A red glow encompasses me.

That is the most valuable thing between us, and she uses it on me. It's good shit too. With each second, the pain fades and is replaced with something else.

I can see we are on solid ground now, shaded by wintery bushes and pines. My body is hyper aware of just how close her body is, the way she lays on top of me with her curves molded to my own body.

"You saved me," I say, threading my hand through her wet curls and warming them just enough to let them dry. I trace the hand down her back. It is warm, comforting, and she lets out a sound of relief as her body warms up.

That sound.

I light fire around us. Nothing else matters except her. We are safe. We will be fine for the next five minutes, at least.

She leans forward, "You saved me, too." She brushes a quick kiss across my lips before pulling away. I beg her with my hands to stay, to kiss me again.

"Nathan, we shouldn't be doing this here," she growls as my finger strokes her neck. I grin. I know exactly what I am doing. The moment of levity is sweet. The wild look in her eyes as her hand meets my face is pure torture.

I grab her neck and pull her into another kiss. This ice is solid enough and is connected to the mainland. But I can't seem to continue thinking about this now. Our bodies are close, the kisses growing more and more feverish. I am careful this time; I will not melt anything.

Elva straddles me as I sit up. Her neck arches when I lay a trail of kisses down her throat. It is impossible to stop when the plum flush of her skin deepens. She grabs the collar of my now-dry clothing and pulls me over her as she lays down on the snowy ground.

She tugs me down and crashes her lips against mine, but I resist, pulling back slightly.

Her brows furrow, and she looks confused when I grin. I return to her neck and then pull down the drying seal skin on her upper body, kissing her collarbone before dipping to her chest. For the first time, I see the naked swell of her breast, full, with peaked tips. I take one in my mouth, and she gasps, hungry for me. That only adds to my confusion when she shoves me away.

I growl, and she shakes her head. "We need to keep running, my savage, fearless Elva. There will be time for a million moments of this later."

She feels the tingle of magic because of the promise, just as I do. It's a dangerous promise because she is a princess and I am nothing. But one thing is for sure, she does not fear what I did. She does not fear a murderer. I sure as hell know that there is nothing about her I am afraid of.

CHAPTER 32

I WANT OUT OF THE OCEAN

ELVA

For two days, we've been flying through the Northern Court, keeping to the edge of the icy waters. We have spotted search parties looking for us, but they do not hone in on a couple of birds circling the skies. Ice Mer do not sense magic trails like I can.

The sea that once separated Nathan and I has now become our guide through this frigid land. Our strength is waning. I can see it in Nathan's eyes every time we shift. It's been too long since we've eaten proper food and had a good night's sleep.

He won't admit to it, though. He's too stubborn for that.

After I healed him using the Black Opal earring, I summoned a blizzard to surround us. It kept us invisible from prying eyes as we made it off the ice but slowed us down.

Finally, I spot what appears to be a small log cabin surrounded by snow-covered evergreens. We fly down and shift. I release a breath I didn’t know I was holding when I note the untouched snow all around the cabin. It's well made, with evenly cut logs and a shingled roof. There's a small front porch and a wooden rocking chair with a small layer of snow. Beside the cabin is a stack of wood five feet tall, stretching the length of the small building. The air above the chimney is crisp and clear, and the only tracks I see are those of a curious rabbit. No one has been here for a few days, at least.

"What do you think?" Nathan has his hands in his pockets as he looks at the cabin, then back at me.

"We should at least see if they have a television or radio. We don't know what's going on or if my mother has yet learned of Helena's... promotion to Crown Princess."

He winces, the reminder of the duel fresh in his mind. I wrap my arms around him, leaning my head on his good shoulder. "You did what you had to do," I say against his skin, marveling at his warmth. Our exhaustion has kept the tension between us at bay, but my body begs for release. Making love in the open air as fugitives doesn't feel right–and I want it to be right. With all these dangerous emotions swirling inside of me, I need to be sure this will work. "And you saved me."

I brush my lips over his, the contact seems to pull him out of his reverie. He groans, a low, throaty sound, and puts his hand behind my neck to deepen the kiss as he pushes me against the cabin wall. I am aware that this is the first place we could have true privacy and I crave it. The wood digs into my back, but I can barely feel it through the oversized black sweater I stole from a campsite. Nathan's internal heat wards off the chill, and I run my hands down his arms, feeling the muscles he built up training.

We're a tangle of lips and tongues and teeth and it's the safest I've felt in days.

Eventually, he pulls back and kisses the tip of my nose. "Let's continue this inside," he says, his eyes gleaming.

I growl at him, but he's already pushing off the wall and trying the doorknob.

"Might as well add breaking and entering to my growing list of crimes," he says, shrugging, before pushing the door wide open. I summon a pair of ice daggers and hold them in my grip, just in case we were wrong about someone being in the cabin.

If there's something being a bounty hunter has taught me, it's that you can never be too careful. It opens easily under his hand; the hinges creak loudly, testifying to their lack of use, as the door opens. The interior of the one-room cabin is dark, but it's clearly empty.

I exhale and toss the daggers in the snow.

There's a fuzzy brown rug on the inside of the cabin that reads, 'Wait. Did you call first?' I laugh, surprising myself with the sound. Whoever lives here is my kind of person.

Nathan stands in the middle of the room, turning in a small circle as he takes in the small space. The owner of the cabin must love cartography, because the walls of the entire space are covered in maps of various sizes. There are maps of the Northern and Southern Courts, Fae territory, Were lands, Aqualis, and even the Vampire covens. It reminds me of what we need to do while we are here, cooling my passion. Nathan feels it too, because his arm withdraws from my waist while he walks to the large drawings.

Time, I remind myself. *We will have time.* After we find my mother, and we are no longer running, we will have the rest of our long existence, and I am desperate for that.

"Shit, these are beautiful."

I scrunch my eyebrows together. "Do you like cartography?" Did he do that before we knew each other?

He nods. "I went to school to be a history teacher before I moved to Port City."

I blink, storing the information. Asking questions is uncomfortable for me, I'm not good at it. "I never went to a university. They don't have them in the Winter Court."

He looks back at me and raises an eyebrow. "Did you have a governess?"

Thinking of the woman who taught me to read, fight, and plan a battle, I say, "Something like that. I was bread to lead a kingdom, not read a book."

Nathan laughs, and I find a very detailed map of the Northern Court. I cross my hands behind my back as I study the map. Soon, footsteps approaching behind me are my only warning before Nathan's arms snake around me. He rests his head on my shoulder, nuzzling my neck as we silently study the map.

"This is us," I point to a small x on the map near the Great Sea. I drag my finger further north, past seemingly endless forests to another larger X, "and this is Ice City."

"That's where you grew up," he whispers. I nod, my fingers tracing the city on the map. I don't have to turn around to know that his eyes follow my every movement.

It isn't a question, but I reply anyway as I press my body into his. "Yes. And it's where we need to go to find my mother."

"What's this?" He points to a red pin on the coast not far from here. I squint, trying to remember what I know about the small village.

"I *think* there's some sort of inn here..." I tap my finger on my chin, trying to remember. I catch him watching the movement, and I twist in his grip, winking at him. "Ah! I remember. The Polar Bear Bed and Breakfast. It's a neutral location because it falls outside of most boundaries. Perfect. I'll bet you we can access the news there too." For the first time, something inside of me whispers to leave him. He has spent so long training for me, fighting for me, I can't ask him to face my mother.

But then, he smiles at me, his lips turning up in the corners, and I put the thought aside. "I'll follow you anywhere, Elva. It sounds perfect."

There isn't any food in the abandoned cabin, but we can shower and replenish our funds. I add the cabin owner to my never-ending list of people to pay back. This must be some kind of hunting lodge because there isn't even a bed. We are lucky it has running water.

“Nathan, I need to see your shoulder,” I say once we take separate showers. It was a damn shame, but we need to sleep.

"I'm fine, Elva,” he says, shaking his head. Droplets fly off his red-gold hair as he grimaces. “Seriously, it was just a fracture... *maybe* some minor scratches."

I fold my arms in front of my chest and scowl at him. *Stubborn Summer Fae bastard.*

“Minor scratches don't require Black Opals to heal,” I say.

He frowns when I mention the opal. His shoulders droop, and he turns his back to me. “Fine,” he mumbles, resigned, as he pulls off his sweater and hands it to me. I can't help but admire how his muscles ripple, that golden skin almost glowing in the dark cabin.

I run my free hand down his shoulder. "Does this hurt?"

He shakes his head. I try another spot.

"What about this?"

Again, no.

I giggle, an idea forming in my mind. I can't remember the last time I made a sound like this. It feels so foreign and yet... so natural to do so with Nathan. He tenses under my fingers. Before he can turn around, I nuzzle his shoulder with my nose, lightly grazing his skin with my teeth. He tastes like sunshine.

"What about this?" I breathe, deepening the pressure just a touch.

He takes a shuddering breath, then two, before shaking his head. "No," he rasps, his voice husky. "That does not hurt."

"Good," I say, handing him his sweater before laughing and pulling away. "Then let's go."

"What, now?" he asks, confusion and desire warring in those beautiful eyes.

Tilting my head, I smirk playfully. "I think you said there would be a million more times for this."

He grumbles.

"I don't know about you, but I'm starving," I say.

He runs a hand through his hair, his gaze never leaving mine. "Fine," he grumbles. "But I'm going to get you back for that."

"I would expect nothing less," I say, blowing a kiss towards him as I head into the snow.

The Polar Bear Bed and Breakfast lives up to its name. It's an ancient two-story building set in the middle of the forest, its white walls accented with silver around all the windows and doors.

Snow-covered pine trees surround the building, and a shoveled walkway leads invitingly up to the front door, painted a cheery yellow and adorned with a large wreath. Even though the Winter Solstice is months away, it looks ready for the holidays. A pillar of grey smoke is spiraling up from the chimney, carrying the tantalizing smell of freshly baked bread and meat.

We shifted a few minutes ago up the road, and now we are walking in companionable silence hand-in-hand up the pathway. I lift my hand to knock, but the door swings inwards on silent hinges before I can.

"Oh my goodness, look at the two of you. Aren't you just the sweetest Fae couple?" A high-pitched voice comes from inside the house. It's too bright for how miserable the word around us has been. "Jeremiah, we have guests!"

I look down, my eyes widening as I see the source of the voice. A Vampire stands in front of me, her long black hair braided down her back as she gestures for us to come inside. Her skin glimmers as the light flits on her. Despite the tales humans like to tell in their movies, Vampires are fully capable of being in the sun, but their skin shimmers like it's made of thousands of pieces of glass.

I scan all around us, trying to find danger where there isn't any.

The Vampire's face is unusually pale, her red lips standing out from the rest of her features. She is unnaturally beautiful, almost painfully so, and has the kind of face meant to lure unsuspecting humans to her.

Of course, most laws make that illegal, but not here in the Northern Court. Here, Vampires can play with any humans they find. A Vampire running a bed-and-breakfast is the last thing I expected to see this far north. They tend to keep to their covens.

Nathan shifts on his feet behind me. I can tell that something is making him uncomfortable with the turn of events. The Vampire seems not to notice his discomfort, for she beckons us inside with a wave of her hand. "Come, come," she says, tittering. "I won't bite."

A laugh comes from behind her as a man, a *human*, walks out from the kitchen. I have to tilt up my head to look into his eyes, noting the pair of glasses hanging from his nose. He is built like a lumberjack, his greying hair speaking to his age. "Calitha, love, are you scaring our guests away again?"

"Never, Jeremiah." The Vampress grins at us, her fangs on full display. A shiver runs through me. She continues, ignoring my discomfort. "This lovely Fae couple was just coming in. We've got a pot of coffee on, and my husband here made a lovely beef stew for dinner with fresh bread, if you're interested."

Husband? It just gets stranger and stranger.

"Do you have any rooms available?" Nathan asks, still standing in the doorway. His tone makes it sound like he really hopes the answer is no.

Calitha nods, a grin breaking out on her bright red lips. "I have the perfect one for the two of you."

"Oh, well, I..." I stammer, but Nathaniel puts his hand on my arm. He sighs, resigned, before coming to stand in front of me.

"It's fine, sweetheart. I'm sure we can make it work." He leans in, tucks a strand of hair behind my ear, whispering. "I know how hungry you are, and it's just one night. They seem harmless enough."

"Okay," I say, biting my lip. "I do love the sound of some warm food."

Jeremiah undersold his stew. It is easily the most delicious thing I've eaten in months, and I shamelessly help myself to three servings. It is paired with a loaf of homemade sourdough bread, and a rare dollop of butter.

Nathan laughs at me when I ask for a third helping, but he quickly stops when I throw a quickly conjured snowball at him. Playfulness in danger should be wrong.

I should hate this. But instead, I lean into this life. Monsters and death do not surround me, I am surrounded by a warm glow. A warm glow that will extinguish forever if Nathan dies. The thought is so sudden, so heavy, that I can't put it away. It's a constant effort not to let the terror inside of me shine through.

After dinner, the Vampress leads us to our room, handing me the key to what she calls the Snow Suite as we climb a set of very narrow stairs. There's no railing, but we manage to make it to the top floor without incident. Calitha leads us to the end of a long carpeted hall, passing several closed doors.

"We don't have any other guests at the moment," she says, "but this is our best room."

I see where it gets its name when I open the door. The room is a study in shades of white, from the rugs to the ceiling and everything in between. An enormous four-poster bed in the middle of the room is covered in a large, fluffy white comforter and a mountain of six cloud-like pillows. It's the best thing I've seen in months besides Nathan.

Calitha hands us some towels and toiletries before leaving us alone. The room is warm, and despite the oddness of the couple downstairs, I feel safe.

I chuck off my boots and throw myself on the bed, sighing blissfully. "That's it. I'm not moving for the rest of the night."

Nathaniel arches a russet brow. He's standing by the now-closed door, leaning against it. An amused smile dances on his lips. He looks relaxed as he plays with a small fireball. "I'm glad you're happy," he says. "I'll be honest, I thought you would be more suspicious around these people."

I shrug and grin at him before grabbing the remote on the nightstand and flicking on the TV. It's a large-box that is sticking out of the cabinet in the corner of the room. "They aren't Mer here. They clearly don't recognize me without a crown. And... I don't know, I trust them."

"You have very good instincts."

I laugh. “I know.” Then I start pressing buttons, clearly not knowing what I’m doing.

Nathan grabs the remote from me and mumbles, “... outdated technology... miss my FaePhone...”

A newscaster fills the screen, but there isn’t any sound. “Of course,” Nathan sighs before running his hand through his hair. “Old TVs are notoriously unreliable.”

I throw a pillow at him and steal the remote back before finding the volume button on the remote. The sound blares to life, drowning out everything else. I curse as I fumble to turn down the volume.

A newscaster's monotonous voice fills the room, drawing our attention.

"...a convoy from the Ice City has been seen making its way to Aqualis. The Fae have heavily guarded the convoy, presumably carrying the Queen herself or her heir. More information on that as soon as we have it. In other news, reports have come in that the Ice Mer King is seeking revenge for the unlawful assassination of Crown Prince Henrick. There is a ten million-dollar reward for the Summer Court assassin, wanted dead or alive..."

I flick off the tv, my hands trembling as the temperature in the room drops. I fight to keep it under control, taking a few deep breaths before looking up at Nathaniel. His face is grim as he walks over to me.

"Don't you even think about it," he says fiercely, taking my hands. His eyes are blazing with passion as he crouches before me. "I'd kill him again in an instant for you."

Truth.

I lift my pained eyes to his face. "I wish you didn't have to,” I say.

"What's done is done," he replies. "Now, let's talk about Ice City."

We stay up late into the night, making a plan. Tomorrow, we will leave.

When our eyes are bleary, and exhaustion is a heavy blanket over us, Nathaniel grabs a pillow and blanket and lies in front of the door. He doesn’t trust these people, but I have spent so much time around evil people; I know them when I see them.

"Nathan," I say sleepily, blinking my eyes at him, "there's room on the bed for you. You don't need to sleep in the hall."

He smiles softly. A moment later, the mattress dips before the room goes dark. I can’t see anything, but I can sense him beside me. He leans over and presses a kiss on my forehead. "I'll see you in a few hours, darling. Sleep well."

You can’t let him come with you. The thought is so insistent I know I have to follow through.

CHAPTER 33

THE LENGTHS I'D GO TO KEEP YOU SAFE

NATHANIEL

Elva is sleeping soundly, but I am still partially awake. There is a pit at the bottom of my stomach. The regret for killing Henrick never came, but the fear of the inevitable consequences certainly has. They are hunting me. If they find me, how far would their threats extend?

Would they go to the Summer Court and harm Cherie? Lucinda? The terrifying thought is that any of this is possible. It is not just Elva and I that are in danger.

When the first rays of sunlight break through the window, I know it is time to wake my Winter Fae and journey to her city, the one she will rule over one day. She stirs gently when I shake her shoulder and grumbles as she stretches her limbs. Her cheeks are flushed from our shared warmth, and her hair is a wild mess. When I glance at myself in the mirror, I see the bags under my eyes and the worry lines streaking across my forehead and between my brows. Instantly, I try to relax them and find they stay longer than I like.

In a dynamic where two people are together—which is very much what I am trying to do with Elva—if one partner is worried, this rubs off on the other. But if one panics, the other can become eerily calm to help solve the problem. I don't want to put Elva in the position to be either one just yet. I am sure tensions will rise when we get to the Ice City.

After we pack up our meager belongings, Elva leads me down the stairs as she still rubs the sleep from her eyes. The Vampire, Calitha, and her human husband are nowhere to be seen. My stomach growls greedily when I see several frosted buns lining the main table. Neither of us conceals our excitement as we take several and head out the doors.

"I never thought I'd see a Vampire and a human happily married," Elva says lightly. Yesterday she had told me that she trusted them. I've noticed how she spends so much time watching them.

I smile gently and say, "The more time I spend with you, the more I believe that opposites can work just fine. Fire and ice do not mix, yet, we are stronger together."

She takes my hands and summons ice. It's so cold that frost bites into my palm. I return her nudge with straight fire. The ice melts into water, which turns into steam. I laugh playfully as she jerks her hand away, feigning anger.

I pull her in and smile down at her. "My dear, I believe you're smoking hot."

Her face falls into a straight deadpan, and a lick of dread makes its way up my spine.

"Don't think I will hesitate to freeze your shorts if you make joke as corny as that again." Humor dances in her eyes, and I can hardly believe she is the same frosty Fae that avoided my gazes and touches over mountains of paperwork.

After we have finished walking and eating our breakfast in companionable silence, I busy myself brushing crumbs off the front of my shirt. The seal leathers were a dead giveaway for someone like me, and I was grateful that we had found extra clothes in the closet. These aren't blue, but a deep grey, and they cover me nicely.

Elva is the first to shift into her owl, with me following closely behind. The trek will take us a few days if we fly most of it. I think I have mastered shifting well enough to make it work. Looking down below us, I see the beautiful variety of white, blue, deep emerald green, and black. I can't help but feel attracted to its beauty. I never felt like I belonged in the vast valleys of the Summer Court, but somehow, despite the freezing cold and dangerous enemies, I feel at home in this place.

I am surprised to find that the Ice City is literally made of ice. Thick blocks, similar to the igloo that Elva made for us when we first found each other, make up most of the buildings. The domed architecture is unassuming and beautiful as it stretches across the plain. It is unlike Port City, where the height of the sky-rises enabled the city planners to concentrate so many people in a relatively small space.

The white buildings almost blend into the ground, pebbling across the ground like some kind of Vampire Zen garden. The crowning element that makes this city incredible is the literal Ice Palace at its crest. It is completely opaque white, clearly frozen. It is larger than any other palace I have ever seen. The ice spikes surrounding it tell me exactly what I need to know about how inviting it is.

Tension is lining Elva's face, even as an owl. She circles toward the ground, and I follow close behind her. We touch down on the cold, powdery snow. It crunches beneath our feet as we return to our Fae forms, and the smell of intense cold hits the inside of my nostrils, freezing them. The worry is exacerbated on her face.

"Hey, I'm here." I nudge her gently.

She has completely retreated inside of herself. She doesn't respond for several moments.

"I—" she starts and stops mid sentences. Her mouth is slightly agape.

I want to ask her what she wants to say, but I get the sense that pushing her will be futile. I don't know exactly what kind of trauma she has been through, but if it made her like this, trying to force her into anything would probably end badly.

Pushing aside my instincts, I wait, despite my insides screaming to say something. My head is willing me to be patient, and I choose to follow that path. Finally, she whips around and looks at me. The fear in her eyes is so potent it's like a song playing in my head.

"I think I need to do this by myself. If they see you... if we get separated..." She doesn't finish, just shakes her head. One solitary tear flows down her cheek, and I am stunned at how emotional she is. There are no walls, no barriers, just her and I.

The tear freezes mid-way down her cheek and falls into the snow. It is so quiet between us, I hear the tear hit the ground with a light ding, like the ringing of a bell.

"Elva, that's not fair. We are going to do this together." I reach over and grab her hand. It is ice cold. More tears come, and they follow the same pattern–turning into tiny, gentle icicles before hitting the ground.

She grips my hand so hard that it hurts. She shoves me against a tree and puts her hands out before her. Too late, I realize what she's doing as thick ice surrounds me.

"Elva, no, don't do this." I plead, shaking my head.

"No, Nathan," she replies, her voice steely. "I have to do this.

Everyone is looking for me. The Ice Mer King, the rebels... my mother. They will *kill* you."

I call after her again, but she is already darting away between trees. Her owl form is likely to be recognized now, and I relax a little when she doesn't even try to use it.

Abandoned, all I can do is watch her fade.

Again and again, I yell for her to come. My throat is so raw it hurts to breathe.

Tears run down my face. I might never see her again. I never told her how I feel. The dreams I had, however foolish or hopelessly romantic they might be, might be lost now. She left, and now, I will never have the chance to know her completely.

I yell in frustration struggling against the ice. I refuse to let this be the end. Pulling on all my magic, I will my body to heat up as fast as possible. I need to get to her.

Elva made the ice thick and rock solid, knowing that I would try to break free. Despite my fire, I need time to melt through it all. And by then... it is very possible that someone important will die. I don't know if it will be the Queen or Elva.

CHAPTER 34
FROZEN IN THE MIDDLE OF THE FOREST
ELVA

Silent tears run down my cheeks as I move swiftly through the forest. Snow crunches under my boots as I vault around the trees, putting as much distance between Nathaniel and myself as possible. My heart is breaking into a thousand shards of ice. Every time I recall how he looked when he realized I was leaving him there, it shatters a bit further.

I left part of myself with him. The good part. The part that loves.

The forest is thick and small, ice-covered branches tear at my face while I run, but I don't try to stop them. Every time they slap against my skin, whenever there is a burning sting on my cheek, I push into the fractured sensation that builds in my chest.

I deserve it and so much more. Pain is the only thing I need right now. If I concentrate, I can still feel Nathan behind me, still hear him yelling at me. The ice will hold. It has to. If my mother finds him before I get to her, I will never be able to forgive myself.

We were doomed from the start. Forbidden love. It's better this way. At least, that's what I tell myself.

It's a lie.

As I run, I shove down every emotion he has made me feel over the past few years. I take all the care, the tender-hearted looks, the kisses stolen between training, the laughter, the love, and push it so far down into my core, it's little more than an ember in the depth of my soul.

Even that ember might be too much.

Helena had told me that she had found pictures and paid for them to be taken down. If she found him with me, she would make it the goal of her immortal life to make us suffer for having the audacity to care for each other.

By the time I leave the forest, the sun is rising over the horizon. I can see my childhood home. The icy spikes are looming above me. My blood chills at the sight of the Ice Palace; hundreds of horrifying memories flood my mind.

My mother, shifting in front of the entire court and devouring a Were whole for stealing food from the kitchens to feed his children. In her eyes, he was selfish instead of a community member.

A whip of ice whistles in the air as cold air kisses my back. Agony ripples through my body as hundreds of eyes watch on in silence.

Bright red blood coats the throne room's floor as servants drag out the bodies of dead Faerie she considered a spy.

And... A funeral where tears were not permitted. Saying goodbye to my father.

I take a deep breath, leaning against the rough trunk of a large evergreen tree as I adjust my clothing and calm myself down. The smell of sap and pines soothes my soul as I shove away the ghosts of my past.

You can do this, Elva.

The wind blows past me, carrying an icy blast as I stare at the palace built in the city's heart. It's still early in the morning, and most of the citizens of Ice City are still in their beds. I can see the telltale helmets of the White Legion marching past as they patrol the streets, enforcing the strict curfew my mother has placed over her citizens.

I know from experience that members of the White Legion–guards, as she calls them–all carry two swords, one on their backs and another at their sides, along with various weapons hidden on their bodies. I'd spent enough time away from here that they acted less like protectors of the peace and more like sanctioned criminals.

Usually, I would avoid them at any cost. Not today. I pull the hood of my coat down low enough to cover my eyes.

The street is mostly empty today, meaning it is one of the cleansing days when everyone must stay inside while the ice shamans work. There must have been a visit from another species because Winter Fae do not allow other species to coexist in the same city walls. Down the street, I spot a tall, bulky Fae with long black hair and the insignia of the White Legion stitched across his chest. He looks about thirty, but he could be three thousand years old for all I know. I quickly look away from his dark grey eyes so he can't see my face.

He arches one eyebrow. "Can I help you?" he growls at me, his gaze predatory as he sweeps his eyes over me. It takes everything in my body to remain still and not castrate him where he stands.

"You can take me to see the Queen," I say, keeping my voice steady despite the nerves flying through my body.

He arches a black brow and studies me. "What business do you have with Queen Ophelia?"

This is it. "I've come to tell the Queen her heir has returned." The words barely leave my mouth when his large hand clamps down on my wrist. I bite my tongue, trying to keep from crying out.

"What do you know of Princess Elva?" the guard hisses, his voice low as his fingernails dig into my arm.

"It is not," I say before summoning shards of ice to pelt the guard's hand. His grip loosens before he grabs onto his wrist with his other hand, whimpering.

He snarls, those eyes darkening despite the rising sun. But the force of my movements causes the hood to slide back. Shit, I didn't want anyone to know who I was until I arrived. Those grey eyes go wide as he looks at my face.

He immediately drops to the ground. "My lady, you are alive."

"Yes. Now, take me to my mother," I say, holding my head high. "Or the ice won't just be on your fingers." Clenching my jaw, my gaze drops pointedly to his crotch.

He scrambles to his feet "That won't be necessary. Right this way, please."

WHEN MY ESCORT BRINGS ME TO THE MASSIVE FRONT DOORS OF THE palace, The Shamans have gone outside to chant to the gods, which signals to the people that the city is free from the negative energy brought by Were or Vampires, and it is time for Ice City to wake up. The sounds of life fill the air as we march down icy streets, but the city is devoid of color. Life in Ice City is not kind.

I worry that the visiting group may have been the Ice Mer. If they have come to see my mother, then everything will be worse. That's why I had to leave Nathaniel behind. This city will eat him up and spit him out.

We get to the gates, which swing as if on their own accord. Holding my head high, I march into the icy palace, the white walls rising above me as I stare straight ahead. The weight of dozens of eyes falls on my shoulders as I march through the palace, ignoring the whispers and gasps that ring through the air in the wake of my arrival.

"The Princess," someone says.

Then the bowing starts. I openly show my disgust as I keep my gaze locked ahead of me, knowing exactly where I'm going. I turn left, then right, seeing the massive portrait of my grandfather Mikael hanging at the end of the hallway in front of me. The artist's rendering is both fierce and lifelike. As a youngling, I always ran past the frame, unwilling to let my gaze connect with my grandfather's.

He looks down at everyone who passes by, his ice-blue eyes firm as a scowl remains etched on his lips for eternity. His pointy ears stick above his white hair, a crown of white diamonds resting on his head. The artist painted him wearing nothing but a cloak of white leopard fur, his dark skin peeking out from beneath the cloak.

Just another member of my family who ruled with ice spikes and iron fist. He kept thousands of humans as slaves, allowing the Winter Court Fae to grow to the size it is now just before starting the Third Great War. My mother is a benevolent ruler in comparison.

My tutors told me he had roamed the Winter Court for nearly ten thousand years before deciding to submit to the Eternal Sleep. Now he rests, undisturbed, in the crypts below the palace.

Hurrying past the reminder of my grandfather, I put my hands on the door handle and breathe deeply. *Here we go.* Pushing with all my might, I fling the double doors open. There is no resistance, and they swing wide, revealing the grand stateroom before me.

Everything is made of ice. The walls, the chandeliers, even the intricate tiles on the floor are all carved out of ice. A massive dais stands at the far end of the room, with four grand steps leading up to the singular, enormous throne perched before the room.

It's empty.

Before I can turn around, a large white snow leopard prowls soundlessly up beside me. I freeze immediately, my eyes tracking the leopard. Its head comes up to my breasts, and its jaw is much larger than the average snow cat. It snarls, baring its razor-sharp teeth, before it comes up to sniff me.

I don't move, despite the shivers running up my spine. The snow leopard circles me, snapping its jaws. Still, I maintain my position.

Suddenly, the scent of magic fills the air. The leopard is gone, and my heart freezes over. Standing in front of me is the face of my nightmares. She grabs my arm and pulls.

"My sweet Elva," the Winter Court Queen croons, drawing her red fingernails over my skin. "Have you finally come home to beg for my forgiveness?"

I blink at my mother. Ageless and stunning, in a deadly sort of way. Today, she is dressed in a pale pink pantsuit with matching stiletto heels. Her hair, the mirror image of mine, is gathered in an intricate braid that hangs down her back. A crown of ice rests on her head, glittering in the morning sun.

"I'm not here to beg for anything, Mother," I reply, willing my voice to remain steady and my face blank. "And I don't want to talk about me. I'm here to talk about you."

She taps that manicured finger on her chin, staring intently at me. Instinct tells me to avoid her gaze, but I don't move.

"Interesting," she purrs, walking around me as she studies me. "Very well. I can't have my only daughter feeling like I didn't care about what she has to say, could I? Right this way, child." She spins on her heels, marching quickly out into the hallway.

There are no guards following her. She doesn't need them.

Power is everything for Winter Fae, and she is the most powerful of us all.

A small voice niggles at the back of my mind. *You are the rightful heir. Your power rivals hers now that you've matured. Those years spent as a bounty hunter may have made you even stronger than her.*

I shove that voice, those words, down with all my emotions. It has no place here. I don't want to be the queen if it means continuing our tradition of being a backwards, brutal, insular people.

Bristling at her words, I watch her back momentarily and calm my breathing before hurrying after her. My mind is blank as I will all my emotions away.

I am empty, a cold vessel of myself, as I walk behind her, surrounded by the icy walls of my youth. People bow as we walk past, my mother in her heels and me in my clothes that have seen better days. I keep my face straight, ignoring them.

I don't care what they say. The news of my return has surely spread through the city. Somewhere in the back of my mind, a flicker of concern about Nathan comes to life. I push it down so fast, like a dagger to my head.

My mother isn't a mind reader, but she has her ways. Her terrible, horrible ways of making you tell her anything. I've spent years trying to forget this place, and now I've walked back in willingly.

I will leave with my life, I promise myself.

Too soon, Mother stops in front of a plain, nondescript door. She flicks her hand, and a gust of wind blows the door open. A spiral stone staircase is in front of us. "Come," she says.

Wordlessly, I follow her until we reach a landing. I automatically assess the room for weapons and exits, marking my escape route. She has brought us to a room at the top of a lofty tower, and I can see over the entire city.

It's not very large, this small circular room. Two pale blue couches face each other on a furry white carpet. A white stone fireplace is built into the wall, with an enchanted fire burning blue, not orange, in its cage. It gives off no heat, somehow adding to the cold of the palace.

There is a large curved window that overlooks the forest I came from. I turn my back on it, sitting on the edge of the couch as my mother walks around the room, running her finger against the fireplace mantle.

She lifts a finger and turns it over, tutting. "Dust," she says, shaking her head.

I narrow my eyes. Her finger is as immaculate as ever.

“You’re just in time to help me with the flogging,” Mother says. “The servants will not get away with laziness in my home.”

A reminder–to me–that she can do whatever she wants without consequence. It’s always been this way. Her grasp on the Northern Court has been ironclad. Until now.

“Mother, I haven’t returned to help you flog innocent people.”

She whips around. “Innocent?”

I press forward. “I know you are looking for me. So I’ve come to claim to do what’s right.” I’m going to kill her, I pull the icicles to my hands, allowing them to grow to sharp points.

She starts to laugh.

My flimsy plan floats to the ground in embers and I am ashamed to have ever thought it would work. She will not hear me out about those fighting against us, even if I am the princess. It’s clear to me that if I don’t kill her before I leave, then I will regret it for the rest of my life. I clear my throat and step forward.

CHAPTER 35
SHE'S POWERFUL
NATHANIEL

If this were regular ice, I'd have melted it in seconds. But this ice, Elva's special recipe, was designed to harden in seconds. As I melt through the surrounding walls, the steam billows up and soaks me through and through.

It's actually terrible. The problem with this cage is that it was also designed to restrict my legs. I can't shift into my animal form because I'm not practiced enough. She has meant to tire me out.

I wonder if she knows she could kill me with all this ice, especially if she never returns.

Pushing the thoughts from my head, I try again. I put everything I have into concentrating my heat away from my hands and on my legs. It's yet another thing I'm not great at.

I swear, I think. *This entire journey has been one big exercise in the fact that I am built for frivolity and drinking. For tricks and easy labor.*

The sun crawls up the sky. It's at once too fast and too slow. It warms the top of my head, my face, and my neck. I am grateful for the extra warmth but would appreciate it more if it would melt the ice.

Being a Summer Fae has got to be the most useless inheritance of all the species that roam this planet.

The appearance of my skin stuck in the ice resembles a raw guinea fowl. One of my favorite dishes. I stare at the shiny pinkness coating me all over and drop my hands.

It is impossible to admit that this is defeat, but my body knows what's happening. I redirect my heat to keep myself warm in the literal ice. It helps quite a bit with the physical sensations, but once I am slightly more comfortable, the knots in my stomach twist and writhe in my stomach.

Suddenly, I am left with the harsh, cold reality. I cannot go anywhere.

Helplessness is an odd sensation for me, and I immediately try to turn it off, shove it down. Being helpless isn't attractive, it isn't productive.

For a moment, Lucinda's face... Mom's face... flashes in my mind. She holds me and my sister close as our father leaves our house for good. Trails of tears have streaked down her face, ruining her cosmetics made of minerals and fruit.

Andrius had turned back at us momentarily before leaving, for just a few moments to smile and wave before vanishing into thin air. If I had been younger, I might've thought he was just taking another casual business trip. His smile was so carefree, so self-assured.

That was the face of a man in control of his life.

My mom's face, though. She looked about the same as I do right now. Exhausted, wary, and resigned to give up and devote her energy to someone else.

I think I understand her better now.

I shift my weight, realizing how energized my power feels. Emotions make these things more potent.

Wait. I shift my weight once more.

Sliding one leg forward as far as possible, I move into my stance for shifting.

I try to shift. Nothing happens.

I try again, tightening my abdomen a bit more and straining my neck.

A tearing sensation builds. I can move one leg. Then the other. I am more than happy. I let out a garbled laugh of pure joy and pull on my shift. The next moment, I'm a bird.

I wiggle my long, feathered wings through the small opening I made in the ice. They won't recognize my bird here.

I am no longer helpless.

CHAPTER 36
LIKE MOTHER, LIKE DAUGHTER
ELVA

My mother is staring at me. Her ice blue eyes, mirrors to my own, are peering into my soul.

I've seen over a century of life but still feel like a youngling when I face her.

The room temperature drops as I lose control and shake.

Get a grip.

Focusing my sight on a small figurine sitting on top of the fireplace, I slow my breathing. Long, painful silence passes before the room returns to its normal icy temperature.

My mother notices my discomfort, and I see her lips tilt into a macabre smile.

"Cat got your tongue?" she purrs, stalking closer and grabbing my chin. Hard. Her nails dig into my skin, causing me to clench my jaw. "Come now, Elva. We haven't been together for years, and now you can't find the words to speak to me. I'm hurt."

She pouts, her lips painted a bright red that contrasts against her dark skin. "Would you like to play together? I'm happy to call forth the servant for their punishment now if you want to loosen up?"

Play.

The word sends shivers down my back as I recall all the 'games' my mother forced on me over the years. Lessons, she called them. Mother-daughter bonding, she said.

The whip whistles through the air before it lands on flesh, the sound of fear and pain second nature to me by now.

A tear flits down my cheek. I brush it away, but it's too late. She noticed.

"Again," my mother says from her throne, her eyes as hard as ice. "My daughter hasn't learned her lesson yet. You will do this until you don't cry, Elva, or you will be on the receiving end of the whip."

The servant kneeling before me whimpers but doesn't say a word.

I lift the whip again.

And again.

And again.

I shudder, pushing the memory away.

There was no bonding between us.

She was honing me as a deadly weapon.

The joke's on her because I know only one of us is leaving this room. And I have to get back to my Summer Fae. There are no other options.

I close my eyes, banishing my fear, before turning to face her once more.

"That won't be necessary," I say, shifting on the couch to stare at her. "We can talk."

A beat of silence passes before she purses her lips and frowns. "What a shame," my mother replies. "Perhaps we can play later."

I shake my head. "I will not be playing your games with you. I came back because you crossed the line." I clench my teeth, willing the memories of my captivity to remain hidden. "What you did can't go unpunished. I *won't* let it go unpunished."

She turns and raises a brow. "What I did?" She parrots my words, a false look of naivety plastered on her face. "My child, I do so many things each day. I'm afraid you'll have to be more specific."

I stand, my fists clenched, as I glare at her. "What you did," I seethe, "was arrange for me to be kidnapped because I refused to marry Henrick."

She laughs. The loud, high-pitched sound is eerily mirthless as it echoes through the room. My stomach clenches as bile rises in my throat at the sound. I struggle against the desire to throw open the window and shift, to fly away from here. It takes everything I have to tamp it down, to lock it into place with all my other emotions.

"I am serious," I say, approaching her. My blood runs colder and colder as I get closer to her before she flicks a hand. Suddenly, I can't move at all.

Ironic.

That's the first thought that enters my mind.

I try to move, but the ice wrapped around my legs is so thick I can't do anything but stand there, helpless.

"That's close enough," my mother says nonchalantly, tapping her fingers on the edge of the couch between us. Her nail is so sharp it leaves indents in the fabric. "I wouldn't want to hurt you before we can play, my dear."

Snarling, I don't say a word. She smirks, stepping around the couch to come behind me. I swivel my neck as far as it will go, unwilling to let her out of my sight for even a moment.

Her lips tilt up, a cruel look entering her eyes. "Yes, I like this look on you," she says. "A shame I didn't think of doing this before your wedding. Now someone has killed the Crown Prince of the Ice Mer, and that horrible friend of yours is next in line for the throne."

"She has a name, Mother. It's Helena," I snap, trying to stand tall despite the ice encasing my lower body.

My mother waves a hand in the air.

"Semantics," she says dismissively. "She's still a fish. Now let's talk about you. I'll have you know; you've left me in quite a predicament. I have an unwed heir who seems reluctant to be in my presence."

Reluctant is one way to phrase it.

"Now, I know you don't want to hear this," she continues, "but since you'll be staying here for the next while, I see no reason why we need to wait to have this conversation. The question is, will you be a good girl, or must you be forced to stay here?"

I stare at the ice around my body as I attempt to sort through everything she says.

Staying for the next while.

Not happening. I won't stay in this palace a second longer than necessary.

I won't promise not to harm her, but...

My mind spins until I find the wording I'm looking for.

"I will listen to what you have to say."

She chuckles, her eyes darkening. "I see you remember how to watch your words. I'm glad spending so much time around humans hasn't made you soft. Good." Waving a hand, the ice disbands around my legs and feet.

I sag at the sudden ability to move and collapse soundlessly on the couch. My eyes are constantly on her, as I won't put anything past her.

"Now, as much as it delights me to hear that you think I would resort to kidnapping you to get you here, I have never done anything of the likes."

"But—"

She waves her hand, silencing me. "I am not done, Elva. I didn't kidnap you, but I am pleased you returned to me. It's long past the time that we discuss how things will work around here."

"I would rather live in the nine circles of Hell than stay here and work with you." I go to stand up, but a gust of wind blows me back down in my seat.

"*That* is the Elva I remember," my mother says, tutting as she waggles a finger at me. A look of disgust crosses her face. "Henrick would have known exactly how to put you in your place. A real shame, what happened to him."

She stops, staring at me. "You wouldn't happen to know anything about that, would you? The Ice Mer King seems to have put his court in a media blackout. Not much news in or out, I'm afraid. All my spies were able to tell me was that Henrick has died. They didn't know the cause or wouldn't say it. That's the problem with all those fish people, Elva. They don't have to tell you the truth. Lies are powerful."

I shake my head, biting my tongue so hard I draw blood. The words bubble up in my throat, but I push them down.

My mother examines me for a long moment. I don't even breathe until she turns away to look out the window. I sag in my seat as I try not to tremble.

"Here's what we're going to do, Elva. You are going to remain here, in the tower." She nods to a door beside the fireplace I hadn't noticed before. "This leads to your bedroom. Guards will be posted outside your doors at all times, and you will not attempt to leave. If you do, I will be forced to act. Are we clear?"

I stare at her as snowflakes begin to fall from the ceiling. My breathing speeds up as I try to focus on her form. Her eyes are hard as she watches me.

She wants to lock me in this tower.

I'll never get out, never be able to feel the wind on my wings, never see Nathan again.

Red-hot anger bubbles inside me as I realize she will keep me here for the rest of my life, a prisoner.

She will keep me locked up simply for having the gall to come back.

The ember of emotions that I had tamped down deep below me begins to glow as I throw caution to the wind and release the emotions that link me to the world.

To him.

My Summer Fae.

I will not be trapped.

Fury bursts through the cold facade I had painstakingly created on my journey here. The veneer I had pulled over myself, the emotionless Fae my mother wants me to be, cracks into a million pieces. I can *feel* everything.

"No," I say, shaking my head. "That is not okay with me."

She must see something in my eyes, for my mother steps back towards the glass window. She raises her hands in supplication, her thin lips tilting down. "Elva, child—"

I raise my hand, freezing the air so quickly that the window shatters behind her. Quickly, I summon a gust of wind to pick up the pieces and deposit them on top of a nearby roof. The air from outside is warmer than here, and my mother shivers as I cover the room in frost.

"I am not a child!" I roar.

Advancing on my mother, she flicks a hand, trying to encase me in ice once again, but it won't work. I turn the magic back on her, forcing bands of ice to wrap up her legs and bind her in place.

"You will not trap me here again," I force out. "I refuse to be your puppet any longer."

"But you're so good at it," she says placatingly. The tone of her voice makes it sound like she thinks it's a compliment.

"Good?" I scoff. "Nothing about me is good. You made me into a monster. Do you want to know what I spent all these years doing when I was away from here? I was killing people. I worked as a bounty hunter for a filthy human, and you know what? That was still better than being here with you."

My words seem to hit their mark as I watch my mother's eyes widen. "You would rather be with a *human* than with me?"

"I would rather be anywhere else than here."

All traces of kindness, of emotion, leave my mother's eyes. Her face transforms in front of me into a cold, steely woman that mirrors the painting of my grandfather in the hall.

I smirk. "I was wondering how long it would take for you to show me your true colors," I say. "Less than an hour, and you've already abandoned the 'nice mommy' act. Is that a record, do you think?"

"Where do you get off in speaking to your mother like that?" She twists in the ice, trying desperately to break her bonds.

She won't be able to.

"You might have given birth to me," I say. "But you're not my mother. Mothers love their children, and all you've ever done for me is teach me that emotions are wrong. Well, *Mother*, let me tell you something. You were wrong. I've met someone and he's taught me that feeling is good. It's not dangerous. It doesn't make me weak. In fact, it makes me stronger than ever."

She laughs.

She has the gall to laugh at me while she is bound in front of me. "Oh, you foolish Fae. Do you think that someone could love you? You're a monster," she seethes. "I knew exactly what I was doing when I raised you. You are a creature of my making. No one could love you. You're made of ice and pain."

Every word that comes out of her mouth is one that I've told myself. She's echoing things I've said a thousand times over.

But the difference is I can feel how Nathan's fire makes me into a better Fae.

"That's where you're wrong, Mother. He sees me for who I am and loves me for it."

Deciding I've had enough of her words, I create a long dagger made of ice. It's an intricate and dangerous weapon, over a foot long, with an osprey etched onto the hilt. I weigh it in my hand, walking around my mother as I watch her.

"You can't kill me, you know," she says.

I'm trying really hard to remind myself of that right now.

"Death would be too easy for you," I reply. "You deserve to suffer the way that you've made countless others suffer. Besides, we both know you'll heal from this."

I lift the dagger, intent on driving it into her heart, causing her even an iota of pain compared to what she has done to me, when a flutter of wings coming from outside draws my attention.

No. No.

My heart is breaking.

This city will ruin him. *I* will ruin him.

Above all that, one thought keeps ringing in my mind.

He came for me.

PART THREE

CHAPTER 37

THE COLD CAN KISS MY ASS

NATHANIEL

It's pretty easy to find the Ice Castle. It is literally the most visible thing in the city. When I see the glinting ice spires reaching the sky, a wash of dread crashes over me.

I don't know exactly where she should be.

Damn the Winter Fae and their "aversion" to technology. There is absolutely no reason everything in this gods-damned city needs to be so archaic.

I am sure I won't have hours to soar up and down the castle before someone realizes I might be a shifter and not a regular bird. There will be guards watching for traces of magic.

The sparkle of ice in the sunlight fills me with determination.

Wind soars through my wings as I pass through an invisible barrier I hadn't expected. A coldness flashes through my entire body, along with a tightening sensation.

It could be the ward used by royals to keep out those who would be unkind to them or cause problems. Immediately, I panic.

The squeezing sensation intensifies, and my eyeballs and brain feel the pressure agonizingly.

Suddenly, a pop resonates throughout my whole bird body. The relief from having survived is short-lived because I still don't have hours to search every window. I may be even more suspicious now because I didn't flap away at the first sign of danger and am now pushing on.

I don't have to fly so fast now that I am close to the castle. My head darts wildly around, checking different areas where she could be. The place is *devastatingly* massive.

Below me, I see the changing of guards. They are dressed in the same elaborate fur outfits Elva wore the first time I saw her. The only difference is the heavy enchantments they must wear and the stitched silver-snow leopard they wear on their chests. I had seen these uniforms on the news before but hadn't known what Elva's shifter animal was then.

Snow leopard?

She's most definitely an owl. The way to find her unfolds before me, but I don't like it. I steel myself and brace my emotions. I know what I have to do.

I plummet toward the ground.

When I reach the frost-covered bushes, I shift back. I pull on a thread in the back of my mind, the weight of shifting intense and nearly unbearable. It has been a long time since I have done this.

My skin goes hazy and blurred as I shift my features to match those of a Winter Fae. The golden tint to my skin turns grey, my hair becomes straight and black, and white tattoos appear all over my body. With a snap of my fingers, I change my clothing to match the guards' uniform.

The glamour isn't great. If someone were to look directly at me for long enough, they might see the cracks in the magic because I am not practiced. The good news is that I won't rely solely on the glamour.

Hopefully, this will work. I pray to the gods above that this works.

The guard just released from the front gate walks ahead, and I dart after him.

Be dignified, Nathaniel. They don't saunter here, a small voice reminds me. *Back straight, strong gait.*

I try to match what my brain tells me when I finally open my mouth to speak. I don't have his True Name, so I cannot compel him. But I am almost sure I can trick him.

"Hey," I bark, willing every bit of harshness I can into my tone.

The guard whips around. I note the lack of an earpiece or anything to keep him from communicating with others. This might be the first time I don't mind the Luddite culture here.

"Where are you going?" I sneer.

His mouth presses into a straight line. He doesn't answer, and I am cheering on the inside. He won't be expecting my next move.

"Who are you?" He snaps back.

This is it, I think. Time to use my MFA in Extreme Bullshitting. I bet that if I speak with enough authority, he will answer. There would be so many guards in this enormous place, there's no way he would know everyone.

"*Nathaniel*, you son of a bitch. How dare you question me? I need your help to find someone. There is an intruder on the grounds." The words tumble out quickly. None of them are lies; I just leave out the fact that I need to find Elva, and the intruder is me.

His eyes widen a fraction of an inch, and he glances behind me. He responds to the tone in my voice and isn't expecting what is to come. "Sorry, sir. The princess returned this morning, meaning security has been raised all over the castle. The intruder must be a rebel."

I nod grimly, even though my insides are exploding.

"Where is she now? I need to get to her immediately." I cringe at my desperation, which is so clearly out of place. He doesn't notice.

"West end of the palace. The tallest tower."

I nod tightly. "I need one more thing from you," I say quickly, every particle of my being hanging on to what he will say next.

"Yes, sir," he nods once, his hands behind his back.

I grin wickedly. I truly am a bastard Summer Fae. "You will forget about this meeting forever."

The magic tingles between us. I can hardly believe it worked.

Ah, hell, who am I kidding? I knew it would work.

Before the lucidity returns to his eyes, my glamour is stripped, and I am an osprey again, soaring above him. He shakes his head as he looks at me, but I am already racing away. The tower is in sight.

When I approach, I hover at the tallest window. I can see nothing.

I drop, which is a terrifying sensation. The following window is also empty. And the next. I am panicking. Maybe the guard didn't know that they had relocated. And if they had, what was happening to Elva. I swooped to the last window. I can't see inside this one.

Which probably means it is enchanted.

And they are inside.

Without thinking better of myself, I hurl my strength at the window. I brace myself for the impact, but instead of hard, icy glass, I roll into ungraceful somersaults across a thick white polar bear fur rug. I am back in my Fae form.

When I look up, I have to blink. There are two Elvas.

No, not two. One had just slightly lighter skin and harsh eyes.

It is the Queen of the Winter Court.

CHAPTER 38
WHY DID YOU COME HERE?
ELVA

My heart plummets the moment that Nathan tumbles into the room. He shifts as he falls, his clothing still mercifully in place. His landing is awkward, though, and if I weren't scared for his life, I probably would have laughed.

I don't laugh. I do nothing but stare at him as he dusts himself off.

Damn, Summer Fae, who can't do what he's told.

I fight against every instinct that tells me to run to him. My heart is beating so fast that I am certain my mother can hear it. My only hope is that she might think it's out of fear of her and not fear for Nathaniel.

I'm running a million scenarios through my head, each one worse than the last. I only have one thought, one goal. Maybe I can still find a way for him to get out of here safely.

I will do anything to get him out of here.

My mother stares at him and arches a brow. "Why hello, pet," she says as her lips grow into a terrifying predatory smile.

Her voice is bitingly cold. “It’s been ages since a Summer Fae came to my court. Who, pray tell, are you?”

I turn towards him, trying to will my face into blandness as I barely shake my head.

He ignores me. His gaze is locked on my mother. I see his fingers flicking almost imperceptibly against his side as he observes her, keeping her in sight at all times.

At least he realizes she’s dangerous.

Blinking rapidly, I try to make him notice me. To see me one last time.

Leave, Nathaniel. Just get up and fly out of here, please.

Finally, he looks at me. His gaze is piercing as it penetrates my soul. Entire lifetimes of emotions pass between us in the blink of an eye. I warm as he holds my gaze.

For a moment, I think he might listen to me. Fly out of here before she can stop him.

Then he shakes his head. Devastation slams into me, and I can’t help the reaction pouring out of me.

“No,” I gasp. My heart is pounding, and ice begins to crawl up the sides of the room again. I see Nathaniel shiver, but he stands his ground. I’m losing the grip on the magic binding my mother as panic sets in.

A crack rings through the air, and I know it’s the ice holding her. It won’t stay for much longer.

“It doesn’t matter who I am,” he says, staring at my mother. “I’m here for her.”

My mother looks between us. She seems to grow, her back straightening, as her gaze flicks from Nathaniel and then back to me.

I watch as she bares her teeth before clapping her hands together, seeming to forget that I’ve bound her in ice. She looks almost giddy as her gaze flits between us.

“Isn’t this just perfect?” She croons. “Elva, child, when you mentioned that you found someone who loves you, you seemed to have left out the most important part. I arranged the perfect marriage with the Crown Prince of the Ice Mer, and instead of being grateful, you go and whore yourself out to a Summer Fae male, of all things?"

I fall apart at her words. They hit me in my core, pushing apart the last hold I have on my magic. The ice restraining her shatters into a million pieces, covering the floor. I sob, sagging against the couch as defeat washes over me.

Nathan clenches his jaw, his fists furling at his side.

"Elva isn't a whore," he says, his words sharp with anger as he approaches my mother. "How dare you speak to your daughter that way?"

The Queen bristles before flicking a hand and freezing over the window Nathaniel had flown through.

The scent of her magic fills the room as ice so thick that it becomes white and fills the space where the glass used to be.

My heart sinks, and a moan escapes me.

There's no way he can get out now. I see him trying to figure out what we will do. His eyes are darting back and forth. He summons a ball of fire, but my mother sends a gust of wind to extinguish it so fast it's as if it never existed.

His face falls, and she laughs, the sound mirthless. "You see you worthless male. You are not worthy of breathing in the Winter Court's air."

Nathan tries to speak, but she wraps a gag of ice around his mouth. His eyes widen as his gaze darts between us.

I try to summon my magic, but barely a trickle of it is left to access. My fear is so potent I can't do anything but watch, helpless.

I am too weak to save the male I love.

The Queen seems to sense my desperation, for she titters, her laugh echoing off the chamber's walls. "I will speak to my daughter any way I want, Summer Fae. This is *my* court, and you would do well to remember that. The only reason you're still breathing is because I'm allowing it."

I inhale sharply, and the blood drains from my face. "Please, Mother, don't hurt him," I beg. I hate that the tone of my voice gives away my emotions, but I can't stop it.

Tilting her head, she studies me. I try not to flinch at her blue eyes.

"On your knees," she says without emotion.

I fall instantly, ice shards cutting into my knees. I look up into my mother's face.

"Crawl," she demands. "Beg me to spare the life of your lover."

"Please," I breathe, looking into her eyes. They are filled with violence and hurt and pain, swirling with the deepest emotion, looking straight into my soul.

I've seen this look thousands of times before.

It's the same one that haunted my nightmares for years. The one that caused me to cry soundlessly into my pillow at night, lest she hear me wail. The last time I sobbed in front of her was when she told me my father had died.

The only parent who ever loved me. Gone, stolen in the night by some illness. I wailed when she told me the news until she flogged my back with a whip made of ice.

Only weak Fae cry.

"What will you give me to spare him?" She asks, turning on her heels to walk over to me. The ice crunches over her feet, reminding me of the sound of bones crunching in the maw of her snow leopard.

As she speaks, her tone is almost conversational. I can see the wheels in her mind turning as she watches me.

"Anything," I say immediately. I already know I will give him anything to live the life he deserves. "Just let him go."

"Elva, no," Nathaniel says, speaking around the gag as he shakes his head. Before I can respond, my mother summons a gust of wind and throws him back, his head hitting the stone wall with a sickening crunch. I can feel the impact reverberating through my bones.

A scream rips through the air as I turn and run toward him, tears streaming down my face.

"*Please*," I sob, struggling to breathe. "No."

His face is pale, cold, and his eyes are shut.

Don't leave me here.

I crouch down, placing my hand on his face. "Wake up, please, wake up." I beg him, faintly hearing my mother chuckle in the background. "I need you. *Please wake up,*" I plead with him, stroking his cold face.

Tears escape me, falling on him in tiny droplets.

Seconds tick by into minutes, and he lies still.

I hear the sound each of my tears makes as they splash onto his beautiful, unmoving face. I brush my lips on his cold forehead when his eyes flutter open.

A sob escapes me. "I thought you were dead," I choke out, brushing back his hair from his face.

"You can't get rid of me that easily," he says, his lips tilting into a small smile. Relief floods my veins as life fills his beautiful eyes.

He is going to be okay. Thank the gods.

"As charming as this is, Elva, I'm afraid I must insist I break things up." A shadow falls over me, causing chills to run down my spine. I look up and see my mother standing over me. She is wearing a cold mask on her face that I immediately recognize.

Long fingers clamp onto my arm before they yank me up. I stumble but manage to get upright. "Behave," she hisses in my ear, "and I will consider letting your Summer Fae live."

I do everything she asks. There is not an ounce of fight left in me. Not when Nathaniel's life is in jeopardy.

She nods at me, her mouth set in a straight line, and I give Nathaniel a hand up. I squeeze, trying to get him to look at me.

His eyes are hooded with deep shame and sadness when he finally does.

I want to cry, to scream, to yell.

I do none of these things except to motion for him to follow us.

He keeps glancing at me. There are so many questions swirling around in his eyes.

I'm sorry. I scream inside, pleading for him to hear me. *I need you to stay alive.*

We follow my mother down the spiral staircase, through long icy hallways, past hoards of whispering servants, and into the bowels of the palace.

"Come," she says.

Like a dog on a leash, I do. Nathaniel stumbles behind me, slipping on the icy floor. I grab his arm and help him up.

This time, he doesn't even look at me. I can see his face burning with the fire in his veins, but he doesn't say a word.

We walk for nearly an hour, our path lit by sconces, down through the darkest part of the Ice City. My mother's heels clack on the ice that gives way to stone, their rhythm accentuated by a terrifying symphony of screams and wails that seem to grow louder by the second.

Terror floods through me, but still, I walk.

Eventually, we come to a stop.

In front of us lies a cell made entirely of stone. A singular window is at the top of the space. It has a small cot, and a chamber pot sits in the corner. It reeks of death.

A large iron door stands guard in front of it.

I start shaking as I look at the cell, memories of my recent abduction rushing through my mind. It takes everything in my being not to whimper at the sight of something so terrible.

Beside me, Nathaniel takes in a sharp breath.

"Get in," the Winter Court Queen says sharply, inclining her head towards the cell.

"What?" I reply, stupefied. Every inch of my body screams at me to run, move, act.

One look at the male beside me convinces me to remain still.

I love you.

"Get in," she repeats, her eyes narrowing. "I won't ask a third time."

Tears push at my eyes, threatening to overwhelm me, but Nathaniel grabs my hand and squeezes. He sends a flicker of fire through my palm, caressing me.

I swallow, putting one foot in front of the other. A matching pair of footfalls accompanies me.

Soon, too soon, I'm in another cell.

With a gust of wind, a clang echoes through the stone dungeon as the iron door in front of us slams shut. My mother pulls out a key from her pocket, and the sound of the lock tumbling into place nearly undoes me. Only Nathaniel's quiet presence beside me keeps me steady.

"Did you think I'd let you roam free after the way you mocked me, Elva? Running around the world, doing gods-know what with whomever? I hope you enjoy your new home, child because you won't leave for a long time."

She turns on her heels and walks away, the sound of her departure growing quieter by the second.

When I can no longer hear her, my legs crumble. I slide down the wall as violent sobs rip through me. Salty tears run down my face in rivulets until I have nothing left.

Nathaniel's warm arms hold me the whole time, muttering sweet nothings into my hair as I shake against him.

"Why did you come back?" I whisper when I am empty inside. "Why did you have to come back?"

CHAPTER 39

REPULSIVE EMOTIONS

NATHANIEL

I stare at the ceiling.

"This is a real shit show, you know that?" I said to the open air. Elva huffs in the corner. She still won't touch me. Her arms are wrapped around her knees, and I see her back rise and fall as she breathes deeply.

I try to stand and wince. There are cuts on my back, and the blood is crusted against my skin. Bits of it flake off onto the stone floor. "Elva, *talk to me*. Just... look at me. *Please*."

A slight, mangled sound erupts from her. "No, I will not look at you. I can't. Not after that soldier whipped you, and my mother made me watch while they ravaged your beautiful skin." She lifts her head and lets it thud against the wall, but her eyes remain closed. "Did you know your blood steams in this air? The smell of it still clings to my nostrils."

I don't know what to say to that. I have been healing quickly, but I'd be lying if I said it didn't hurt like a bitch. My mouth opens. I want to tell her it's okay, that I'm okay, but I don't really know that. So I stop trying to stand. I just sit there and stare at her. "Did this ever happen to you when you were growing up?"

She stills. Even her breathing stops.

"It did, didn't it?" I say a bit too harshly.

The response is as good as a resounding yes. I want to tear this place apart. Being in the brutal North has awakened a primal beast inside of me I thought was long dead in my selfish, Summer Fae heart. I am acutely aware of the value of community and love.

I want to speak, to heal the silence... or at least balance it with a joke or something happy. But I cannot.

"Why are they keeping us like this? They haven't tried to ask questions; they just keep coming to beat the shit out of me." I smile as I say it, but the joke falls flat, as hollow as a dead tree.

"To punish me." Elva's voice is clear of emotion, almost as if she's numb to the cold.

"But—"

"This is why you weren't supposed to come. I would've returned, but you should've fled even if I didn't. Don't you get it?" She seethes through her teeth, "Emotions are dangerous. They have been nothing but ammo to shoot at me with."

I stare at her. "I'm sorry, Elva. But you can't act like you are the only one in this equation. I am here too; I am here because I —I—I love you. If that *emotion* is repulsive to you, then so be it. But this is worth it to me. I have searched for meaning, something real, and you are it. Deal with it, *princess*."

Her head snaps up, and she stares at me.

Even so, she doesn't speak.

Why the hell isn't she speaking?

A low chuckle comes from the small square at the iron door. My ears twitch. I know that sound.

The door swings open, and Akron, of all people, saunters into the room. He scans the space until his eyes land on me. "Sprigg, great to see you. I never knew Summer Fae could enjoy the cold so much."

His eyes linger a second too long on Elva's folded-up form. He's dressed in a thickly quilted cashmere coat. Its jet-black color absorbs the light from behind him. His purple eyes scan my face, falling on the torn fabric on the back of my shirt. "I heard they had been rough with you. I'm here to help."

Something akin to relief floods through my veins. The last time he saw me, he was threatening to murder me. Maybe he realized just how vital I am to his business deal. Either way, I know he's powerful. He might persuade the Queen to let us out.

"Akron, it's superb to see you. I never thought you would come. Look, I'm sorry—"

"Woah, Sprigg. Don't thank me just yet. I'm a businessman. This solution requires a pretty hefty fee. I'm not an altruistic person."

I clamp my mouth shut. I worked with him for a long time. There's something big in it for him.

"We'll hear your offer," I say, straightening my back. Elva is staring at him, but her eyes are slits. She doesn't trust him. I know her well enough to recognize her expressions like this.

"Not so fast, Sprigg. Let me invite you to dinner first." An unnerving smile spread across his face. He bends down, and magic from his hands skitters across my wrist as he takes hold. I grimace.

I've forgotten how much I hate Warlocks.

My former employer pulls me to my feet, but before he can move to touch Elva, I cross in front of him and wrap my arms around her. She is on her feet, but something about her feels feather-light. I don't like it, but I don't think commenting on it is wise.

"Come on, friends. I have some new clothes for you. Especially you," he looks directly at me. "Blue doesn't suit your complexion." A gruff laugh escapes him. This is part of the game. He needs to be in a good mood for us to get the best deal possible. I reach deep inside myself, past the intensity and the grief, and find the levity.

"Excuse me?" I feign some sort of offense and smooth my hair. "I'd look good dressed like bird dung."

He lets out a laugh, and I relax just a bit.

"In fact," I go on, "one summer solstice..."

The Warlock yelps with wild laughter as I tell the story, but when I glance at Elva, her face is like solid ice. Unmoving, unfeeling. I squeeze her hand and wait.

She doesn't return the gesture.

We walk down a corridor made of ice and stone, our feet clattering on the stone floor. I am constantly looking over my shoulder to take in Elva. Directly behind her are two guards grasping their weapons menacingly. I want to shout at them. *She is resigned; she won't try to escape.* I let out a long breath because the words would fall on deaf ears. They are ready for a fight and will see what they want to do.

Akron leads us to a room. The guards wait outside on both sides of the door while we take in the curtained corners of the space. A wash basin full of steaming water is in the center before us.

"Get clean and put on the clothes over there." He points to a golden rack with blue dress clothes. I groan. There is a long, revealing dress for Elva and a thickly padded suit for me resembling his outfit. He is out the door with a choppy arm flourish, slamming it against the frame.

"Alone at last," I drawl to Elva. She looks at me, and the look in her eyes is unreadable. Not even a flicker of amusement passes across her features. It has become unbearable to continue coughing up jokes only to be met with that look.

I cross to her, grab her shoulders, and crush her against my body. "I'm sorry. I couldn't let you come here alone. I'm sorry."

"They will kill you. Brutally. And I will spend the rest of my miserable life reliving it." Her icy eyes look up to take me in. There is no promise of threat; there is just calm, resigned truth.

It coils my insides so tightly that I can hardly stand to be conscious. I want to curl up and sleep, get as far away from this place as possible. For the first time since I've gotten here, I understand how dangerous this situation is.

Love has made a fool of us, and it is too late for me to laugh it off and say, "Lesson learned."

I drop my hands. They are dead weight against my sides.

"Akron will save us," I say defensively. Never mind that he had tried to kill me before. Surely he will save us now.

"He will not. My mother has done work with him for years. That's how I got the contract with him." Elva is speaking more now, which is good. Hopefulness swells in my heart as I savor the sound of her voice, storing it safely in my mind in case she stops again.

"Right then, let's get dressed before he comes back."

She nods and moves to the washbasin before undressing in plain view. I avert my eyes. There is no warmth, no heat in the space where we exist now. It is a hole clawing at my chest, hollowing out my insides.

The sound of water splashing against her arms fills the silence as I walk to the clothes.

"Nathan... I love you, too."

I turn around and find her looking down at the steaming water. The burrowing creature in my stomach stops digging for a moment. For some reason, it feels like I'm in a movie. One of those human romance dramas. There isn't any way this could be real life.

Except that she is not human and cannot lie.

"Love me... how? Like a friend? Like a brother? Like a toy you played with for a while and then grew bored with?" I know as soon as I speak the words that the questions are unfair, but I have to be sure she feels the same as me. It wouldn't change my decisions, but it might influence the ones I'm about to dive into.

She inhales deeply, lifting her eyes to mine. She's crying.

I fold my arms around her bare skin. She is dressed in pants and a band wrapped around her chest.

"It's okay; you don't have to answer. I shouldn't have said that."

Viciously wiping away a tear, she huffs. "Of course I mean it." Her voice is hard as if she's trying to hold back a heavy load threatening to break through her barriers. She clears her throat and says, "Since I already know that you love me, I need you to do something before we go."

I drop to my knees with a thud, my arms still locked around her waist. I can't resist kissing her stomach before I whisper, "I am yours, do with me what you will." My voice is gravelly, grating against the tingle of magic in the air.

"Marry me." Her voice is husky.

"What?" I look up at her. There's a vulnerability in her eyes and confidence that makes my head spin. She enjoys seeing me on my knees before her.

"Marry me, Nathaniel. I give myself to you to be yours in this life and the life to come. Never to love or be bound to another. I will gladly give it all." She loosens my arms and lowers herself until we are face to face.

She isn't crying now; she isn't hollow. It's almost as if I can see her brutal, analytical mind working through her eyes.

I'm still too stunned to do anything but keep staring at her.

She continues, "My father is dead. My mother never remarried because the Winter Court Queens are only allowed to marry once. If we are married, and... and..." she trails off, raising wide, bewildered eyes to me.

"And I'm killed?" The words taste like ash as I finish her sentence, seeing where she's trying to go. I'm not young, having lived for over a century, but speaking of my death so blatantly... my stomach turns.

Her eyes line with silver. "Yes. If you... if that..." She swallows. "I would never be subjected to another Henrick."

My mouth hardens into a line. "So, you want to marry me because I will die."

How is this the course my life has taken? How is it fair that we found each other despite everything else, and now it seems we are doomed to fail? I thought the gods cared. I thought they wanted people to be happy.

Now I know the truth.

They are cruel and sadistic, dangling love in front of people only to pull it away.

"No," Elva says vehemently. "I want to marry you because I love you."

"I love you too." My eyes search hers, and I wait for the next words. The ones hanging in the air like a death sentence. Because they are. "But?"

"But the stars seem to have cursed us. Fortuna has cursed us." She smiles sadly. "I wish... I want a long life with you. But I don't... I can't... if you die..." She struggles with her words. "I just love you, Nathaniel."

My mind is torn. I think of Cherie and her new husband. I think of the years I have spent wanting only Elva. Trying to be with other people and failing miserably. Will this be worth it?

These might be my last moments with her. Maybe what she's suggesting will help us. Maybe one of us doesn't have to die.

Maybe we can find happiness.

"All right," I speak slowly, drawing out the words. "Yes. I want to marry you."

Whatever gates were holding her emotions at bay burst open. "Thank you," she breathes a sigh of relief. Tears spill over her face and her lip quivers.

It cements the decision for me. We will probably be torn apart, never to enjoy the promises we will make, but if I can do something to protect her after I'm gone, I will.

I ignore the "gone" part. Maybe if I don't look my impending death in the face, it won't come for me.

After I've agreed, things move quickly. Elva is in front of me, our hands clasped together. Our voices are whispers, barely audible, but each word echoes like it's thunder in my ears.

"I give myself to you eagerly," I say.

She repeats the words quietly.

"I love you and will continue nurturing that love in this life and the one to come," I breathe.

Those, too, she echoes.

The ceremony is simple. Our words hang in the air. A golden light snakes around us, pulling us together tightly until there is barely an inch between us. The air crackles with magic, like every inhale is filled with the depths of our love.

Then an idea strikes me. Something else I can give her. A gift.

I move even closer, lowering my lips to the shell of her ear, and I whisper one simple word. The word that holds all the power in the world for me. She gasps, but the binding holds us together too tightly to look at her face. Her chest rises, pressing against me.

Her lips reach my ear. She kisses me, then breathlessly returns the gift I just gave her.

A Name.

I draw in a breath, and it's like I've never really breathed before. Everything is better. New. Different.

I am hers, and she is mine.

The golden light fades away, leaving us in the same room as before. We relax, our hands sliding together and interlocking.

We are wed.

Elva looks up at me and smiles. "Thank you," she whispers.

A long moment passes as we stare at each other. A world of silent understanding passes between us. No one can tear us apart. Nothing can destroy us. We've already been through so much, and our struggles are not yet over. But maybe we can have one more thing.

I won't move first, though. I need to hear her say it.

"Nathaniel," she breathes. "Kiss me. Touch me. Please."

Those words are my undoing.

In an instant, I crash into her. Her legs unfold as she lands on the floor, my body pressing down on top of her. The kisses are feverish and intense, echoing the fire in my veins.

"What do you want?" I ask between kisses.

Her hands twist in my hair, tracing the uneven growth of the once-shaved side. "Everything," she breathes. "Anything. I need you."

Gods, how I have waited to hear her say these words. My hand slides down her smooth, bare skin. She is soft in all the right places, and my desire for her grows.

A door slams somewhere nearby. I pause, my hand on her hip, and we stare at each other with wide eyes as muffled voices filter through the door.

"Bring them..." a deep voice says.

I want to groan.

Please leave, I think. If the gods are real, they will let this happen without interruption. I've waited for so long for this. To hold her, kiss her, touch her, make her mine.

"Not yet..." a female outside replies.

"... but..."

Elva's head tilts back, her neck so beautifully open to me as our chests heave in time. Her pupils are dark, and I can smell how much she wants me.

"Get Akron, and he..."

The voices move on, but it's too late. I heard what they were saying.

"They're coming," I say.

"I heard," she whispers.

Where is my fighter now? The Winter Fae who killed mercilessly? I hate what this place is doing to her.

"Come," Elva says. She pushes herself to her feet and walks past me to get her clothes. "Let's get ready."

There is an air of sadness as we move, but it's different than before. *We're* different than before.

She doesn't go behind the curtain as she slides off the rest of her clothes and works the tight leather of the fabric up. I can't stop staring. When our gazes meet again, there is a claiming hunger there. It fans the burning flame in my core.

We are married now.

I follow her lead, and she watches me intently as I wash and change. We both know if we touch it could be very bad.

Or very good.

I shake my head. We can't risk someone walking in.

Entire conversations are passing between us without a word spoken.

She is the most beautiful thing that has ever existed. The dress is too revealing, and the thought of others seeing her in it makes me want to rip something in half.

Or smash a vase.

A very expensive one.

She leans against the wall, exposing her throat to the open air. I swallow hard as my eyes skim the beautiful curve of her throat, down her shoulders...

Her eyes rake across my form, and even from here, I can see how dilated her pupils are.

"Elva..." My voice is thick with desire. The anticipation of sliding my hands down—or maybe up—causes a red-hot flush to blossom on my neck. Wicked thoughts bounce around in my head. Ones that I've entertained for years but can finally be reality.

When I think I can no longer stand it, the door opens.

I thank the gods we are on opposite sides of the room.

Akron's eyes flicker between the two of us. He sighs in relief. He doesn't know I'm the princess's consort. I smile at him.

"Let's eat!" I say too brightly, and he gives me an annoyed eye roll. He walks out the door and jerks his head to follow him. I fall in line and look at Elva again as she comes to my side. I can't resist trailing a finger along the tight fabric on her hip. She exhales quickly and tightens her jaw.

I smile and say, "It's good that you came when you did Akron. I'm starving." My eyes again drop to Elva's mouth, and the corners twitch almost imperceptibly.

I am playing a perilous game right now. Death and I are on opposite sides of the table.

But I am still a Summer Fae.

I know how to trick, possibly even cheat fate. I have much more to lose now.

CHAPTER 40
I FOUND MYSELF
ELVA

The last hour of my life has been the craziest, most insane sixty minutes of my existence.

I have never been one for taking risks, yet somehow, I not only proposed marriage to Nathan, but married him and gave him the one thing that gives him absolute power over me.

It feels incredible.

We have had an incomparable bond since the first moment we met. It's nothing like the one that binds us now. I keep sneaking glances at him as we march down the long hallway.

My husband. He walks regally behind the Warlock, who goes by Akron, his back straight as though he hasn't been whipped within an inch of his life during the past twenty-four hours. All the pain I was feeling earlier, all the sorrow, washed away after he agreed to bind himself to me.

He loves me.

I am giddy inside. This isn't even an emotion I knew existed. To be fair, I haven't had much of a chance to explore them, but I'm fairly certain this is something I've never felt before.

Laughter rises inside of me every time I glance over at him. It is as though my joy is rippling over at the thought of having bound ourselves together. This is the most un-Elva thing I've ever done.

It's all because of him. This Summer Fae male. He makes me want to be a better Fae than the monster I was raised to be.

He makes me want to be giddy. As we walk a path to what is likely certain doom, I keep glancing at this male and imagining what it would be like to have him rip this dress off me with his teeth.

As if he can sense the direction of my thoughts, he turns and winks at me.

By the gods. Summer Fae can't read minds, can they?

Blood rushes to my face, and I am grateful for my dark skin to hide my embarrassment. Gods, it's not like I'm some virginal youngling, but he makes me feel so... fresh. Beautiful. And I like that—a lot.

He chuckles, low and deep, the sound warming me as we walk along the long corridors. I somehow can't help but be elated, despite our horrifying circumstances.

Chances are, my husband will never make it out of these walls alive.

I know my mother. That cold, deep, dark rage that lives inside of her. It has always been there, but it worsened after Father died.

When she finds out we've married each other, she will be furious.

She will kill him on the spot if she finds out what I've given him.

I can't let that happen.

I won't.

With each step I take, I resolve to get us out of this. Nathaniel might be a Summer Fae, but he is *my* Summer Fae.

FINALLY, WE COME TO A STOP BEFORE AN ELABORATE SET OF TALL DOORS that are made entirely of ice.

I stare at the doors, the carvings a new addition since the last time I've been here. An enormous leopard is carved into the ice, its large paw holding down a snowy owl on the snow. The snowy owl appears to be crying out, its beak wide as it stares at the leopard.

Subtle, Mother. Very subtle.

I watch as Nathaniel stands in front of the door, staring at the carvings. A muscle feathers in his jaw as his fists clench. He scowls at the sight. I slide my hand into his, sending a burst of frost into his hand. The Warlock is talking to a Were on the other side of the hallway and doesn't notice my use of magic or the way we are touching.

My Summer Fae looks at me, and I nudge him forward. We can't cause a scene.

Not here, not now.

He seems to understand, for he nods and pushes open the door. The room is large, and a mahogany table fills the space. It can seat at least ten people, but there are only four settings at the table right now.

I raise a brow and shrug, walking over to the side table and pouring myself a generous serving of Fae mead. I throw it back, feeling it burn as it runs down my throat. As I set down the glass, my back warms up with a lick of flame. I know without turning around that Nathaniel is nearby. I pour him a serving of Fae mead and turn around, handing him the cup.

He's standing a foot away from me, and I have the perfect

view as he grins, showing me that gorgeous dimple, before tossing back the Fae mead. He grumbles in appreciation before his right arm snakes around me. I lean into his touch, but before I can do anything else, he is pouring another serving of the mead into his glass.

He taps the tip of my nose, taking a step back from me. "If you keep looking at me like that, darling, it won't matter where we are. I'll take you up on those thoughts from earlier." He ambles over to the table and pulls out a seat, dropping himself in it before tapping his fingers on the table.

I'm sure the tips of my ears are turning red as I turn away from Nathan. I busy myself with pouring a glass of sparkling Fae wine, before taking the seat beside him. I pointedly inch the chair away from him, trying not to ignite the fire I started in the bathing room earlier.

I can sense him behind me. Every time he moves, it sends flames down my spine.

Ever since we said those vows, it's as though we have become two parts of the same whole.

I am... warmer inside. As though a piece of his fire now resides within my soul.

Before I can further explore this new feeling, Akron saunters into the room and slides a chair out from across the table. With a wave of his hand, the decanter of whiskey floats over to him. He grins, a frightening toothy smile, as he pours himself two fingers of whiskey and tosses them back.

I narrow my eyes at the Warlock. I know Nathaniel said that he has worked for this... Warlock, but I don't trust anyone who has free rein in my mother's court.

He stares at us, pouring himself another dram of whiskey, before he places the cup on the table. He taps his long fingers on the table rhythmically, meeting my stare with one of his own. Eventually, he chuckles and downs his drink. I shudder.

The other male ignores me, looking past me to Nathan.

I'm relieved that his attention is off me.

A shiver runs through me, and I feel the weight of Nathan's eyes on me as I stare at the Warlock.

I most definitely do not *like this male.*

"You're far from the Summer Court, my boy. What did I tell you about her name?" The Warlock inclines his head towards me.

My husband winks at the Warlock. "Look at her. One glance, and I was smitten."

My insides melt at the admission. I feel the same way, but hearing it from Nathan's lips is something else.

The Warlock's eyes narrow. "I hope she was worth it."

I open my mouth to respond, but before a single word can make it out, the sound of clicking heels on the ice fills my ears. Their wearer walks slowly, methodically, down the halls, their every movement orchestrated to create fear.

I know exactly who it is.

Keep it together, Elva.

When my mother glides into the room, it takes everything in my body not to fly at her. The horror that twists my stomach when I look at her perfectly manicured nails and her designer pantsuit roils through me like an impending storm.

She dares to look this put together when she had my husband whipped just hours ago? Her audacity astounds me.

A flash of fire burns up my left arm, and I know without looking, Nathaniel is returning the favor from before.

Right. Focus. Get us out of here alive.

The second my mother stands in front of the table, two servers wearing my mother's livery materialize out of the hallway. One of them, a petite female Fae, rushes forward and pulls out the chair at the head of the table for her. She bows profusely, her head almost touching her knees as she backs up.

Her companion, a male, stands at attention against the back wall.

Tension fills the air as my mother stares at me, her eyes sharp as she seems to stare right into my soul.

I stare right back.

I don't let her see the way I quiver inside, the way her face makes me feel terror, the fact that until a few hours ago, I felt so broken I thought I might never be put back together again.

No. She sees none of that, receiving the cool facade I have perfected over the years.

After a few moments, she blinks and lifts her right hand. Instantly, the male server fetches a champagne flute and fills it with sparkling wine, placing it in her hand. She doesn't even look at him before her fingers curl around the flute, and she sips the wine.

Nathaniel stiffens beside me, and I will him not to say anything yet.

"I heard something interesting today, my dear," my mother finally says. Her voice breaks the silence, somehow increasing the tension as she speaks.

"Oh?" I try to sound casual, despite my racing heart.

She nods, sipping the wine as though she doesn't have a care in the world. And I suppose she doesn't.

I do. And everything I care about is sitting next to me. He is the fire to my ice, and I will do anything to protect him.

"What did you hear?" I ask, gently prodding to see if my mother will open up. She has been known to play a few games for a Winter Fae. This one, I'm familiar with. Act interested, and she will tell me much more than if I ignore her. All that gets me is a beating.

Her lips tilt up, a terrifying grin lighting her face. "Would it surprise you that I recently heard from your fiancé's father?"

Chills run down my spine, and I stop moving.

I swear I hear Nathan clench his jaw so hard, a tooth cracks.

"I would be interested in hearing what he had to say," I reply carefully.

"He told me that a certain Summer Fae male was responsible for the death of your fiancé. Dear Henrick. What a match that was."

My mother sighs, resting her chin on her hand as her eyes take a faraway look before she continues. "I worked so hard to secure that union for you, and how do you repay me? By running away and then coming back towing this *male* behind you. Frankly, I'm quite surprised he could take down an Ice Mer nearly twice his size since he barely looks capable of breaking an icicle in half. Now, the Ice Mer King has invoked the Right of Retribution."

I freeze. My blood chills as my mind races to catch up with the words that exited my mother's cruel lips.

"The Right of Retribution…" I repeat, stunned. "But that hasn't been done in over a millennium!"

I race to try to remember everything I was taught about Fae history. Sixteen hundred years ago, the heir to the Autumn Court, Hypatios, supposedly attacked and killed the Day Court's only female heir, Parthenia. As a result, Parthenia's grieving parents invoked the Right of Retribution.

They appointed a champion to fight for their cause against Hypatios. Legend has it that their champion fought Hypatios all day and night before falling to his death on the end of the Autumn Court heir's sword.

She nods, her eyes glimmering with cruelty. "I hope you've said your final goodbyes, my dear because the Right will occur at midnight tonight."

My mouth falls open as I stare at her. "Who…. who will your champion be?"

A violent grin lights upon her face. Her canines catch the

light as she swirls her wine. "Why, you, my sweet. Why else have I been training you up to be a weapon for your entire life? Finally, you can show your sweet mother everything you've learned. And after this, I am sure you will be the queen I've always trained you to be."

I shake as I shift in my seat and stare at Nathaniel. My eyes fill with tears as I stare at my husband of two hours. His hands are gripping the end of his seat as he watches me.

My heart is shattering into a million pieces as I look at him. It is as though I can see the bond between us binding our souls. It's taut, waiting to be destroyed by the cruelty of fate that is ready to rip us apart.

He must read something in my eyes, for he breaks his silence. "What is the Right of Retribution?" he asks.

CHAPTER 41
I AM NO IMP
NATHANIEL

Elva's face is drained of color, and a muscle bulges from how tightly she clenches her jaw.

My gaze flickers across Akron and lands on the Queen. She is the picture of languid amusement, lounging in her overstuffed chair with one finger lazily tracing the design on her knife. "Yes, Elva, what is the Right of Retribution?" she drawls.

My new wife bites her lip.

Queen Ophelia snaps forward in her chair, her back as straight as a board. "Elva!" She barks, *"Answer."* Her voice is low and feral.

"The Right of Retribution," my wife grinds out through clenched teeth, "is an ancient Northern Court Custom. It's a show of unity between our people. If a royal court member is murdered, they can ask the other courts to avenge the death while they are in mourning."

The Queen taps her fingers loudly against the long wooden table. "Yes, yes." She waves a hand dismissively. She leans back and smiles. The Warlock sips his wine, but his face is unreadable. "The council of Northern Courts has convened without deigning to include us. They sent Akron along with another messenger to notify us they want Elva to be the one to do it," Ophelia says.

I expect Elva to scream, but her eyes glaze over, and she retreats like she'd done in the cell.

Except this time, I am with her. I can't explain it, but somehow, I still sense her emotions, her silent presence in my mind. I know how she measures her heartbeats to avoid showing her feelings.

I reach out with my thoughts and touch her gently so that she knows I'm there.

As I watch her face, her eyes open a fraction of an inch.

I realize they are waiting for me to react to hearing that my executioner will be Elva, but I still haven't moved.

"Well, you little imp? What do you say to the council's decision?" The Queen spits.

The strangest sensation coats my mind. It's almost as if I know exactly what she wants. She wants me to react. She wants to see Elva in pain.

I won't help her. I meet her eyes and hold her fiery stare.

"I accept."

Her face contorts into something so horrible I can't help but flinch. Luckily she doesn't notice as she says, "Very well. Arrangements will be made presently." She stands, composed and cruel. "Akron, escort them back to two *separate* guest rooms."

He springs to his feet, and we are herded back into the hallway.

No sooner is the room out of sight than a loud crash followed by a series of screams fills the air. Elva's hand flings out and squeezes my own. Her terror is ice through my veins.

We don't look back, just continue down the otherwise quiet corridor and up some stairs. We don't look at each other, and we don't speak.

I sift through the options, but I know there is only one. I will die, and she will be protected from marrying again. This is what we planned when we spoke our vows.

It's all right. I repeat the words in my head like a mantra. We stop at a door, and I am forced to watch as the guards shove Elva inside.

It will be all right, my eyes tell her.

We continue to walk in silence. When we stop at my room, the Warlock opens the door, and I enter the guest room. It is lavish but devoid of identifying factors outside the Winter Court crest.

He comes in and keeps his eyes on the floor. "Look, Sprigg, I'll be straight. Things haven't gone well with the deals since I fired you."

I stare at the wall near the bed.

He continues, "I'll make you a new deal. I don't know what your relationship is to that Winter Fae princess..."

My wife.

"But if you can kill her, I'd help you get out of here. Just between us, the Winter Court's power is fading. It's time for fresh blood to step up."

I continue staring at the wall, but my mind is racing a million miles a minute. There's no way I can do this... there is no way I could kill my kin.

But he doesn't know we are married. Maybe there is a way to use it to our advantage. I move my head to look at him. "I'll see what I can do."

He smirks and saunters out the door.

As soon as I'm alone, I viciously tug on Elva's presence in my mind. I wish I could tell her what happened, but this bond lets me know she's alive.

It is barely enough. I'd much prefer to have her in my arms

for the few brief hours I've been given before we are set against each other like two feral dogs.

Before she slits my throat or stabs my heart... A dozen ways to die run through my mind, the culmination of these thoughts causing my palms to sweat.

Falling in love with Elva was inevitable. I couldn't have stopped myself even if I tried. But it seems Fortuna herself has doomed our pairing. The stars have not aligned for us, and we will suffer for it.

I shake my head. Foolishness had led me to believe that I worthy of the kind of love like Cherie or Adam had found.

I am a plain, right idiot for thinking that love can conquer an entire society's brutal wrath and traditions.

Then, as if invoking the Goddess's name had summoned her wisdom, a new thought popped into my mind.

A plan.

CHAPTER 42

DO YOUR DUTY

ELVA

I am a monster.

The soft bed rustles under me as I lay, counting the specks on the ceiling as I try to harden myself. To push away the emotions. To give myself to the ice that once ran through my veins.

Nathan tugs on our new bond, but I can't respond. How I wish I had never met him, never loved him. Love makes us fools, blind to reality. Fire and ice.

I scoff at myself. A century of training myself to live without emotions, but all it takes to destroy me is one Summer Fae coming and sweeping me off my feet. A few hours ago, I thought of our love as something poetic to be sung about and shared in those movies humans love so much.

Now, I know better.

I can see what will happen. It's all laid out for me like a terrible film. After tonight, death will be my only companion, and I will mourn Nathaniel until my worthless immortal life ends.

Our love is a ballad, a tragedy, a tale that will drive the masses to tears.

It is fitting, I suppose that our brief marriage will end in such a poetic fashion. We reached across the sea and found each other, only to lose everything at the hands of fate.

When the clock strikes midnight, savage custom dictates that I must become the thing that I've always struggled against.

Gods, I was so foolish to think I could escape my fate. Sitting around the table with my mother, watching the realization strike Nathaniel that we wouldn't even get twenty-four gods-forsaken hours together as a married couple, was the worst thing I've ever had to do.

This is what I get for trying to be happy.

With every second that ticks by, bringing me closer to midnight, I grow colder. It is as though the very flame he lit inside me is being extinguished.

I am being extinguished.

There will be no coming back from this.

For all he has trained over the past few months, Nathaniel has nothing on me.

I am a weapon honed by over a century of cruelty. I know countless ways to take a life, to make it hurt, to make it last for as long as I need.

Tick

Tick

Tick

The analog clock on the wall is my only companion now. It watches me, its face blank, as it counts down to my husband's death. I have shoved everything down, and I know that nothing else will ever matter after tonight.

At eleven-fifteen, my door swings open with a thud. A tall, thin female Angel stands before me, her long blond hair pulled into a bun as she walks stiffly into the room. She is wearing a black pantsuit marked with my mother's livery. She shuffles in sideways, her grey wings tucked in behind her as she looks around the room before sighing.

"The Queen sent me," she says by way of introduction. "I'm here to prepare you for the Right of Retribution. We don't have much time."

She pulls out a chair, and I sit in it. A steady stream of servants follow the Angel, their light chatter filling the air.

At first, they try to talk to me but soon give up.

I stare into the mirror the Angel places in front of me, unmoving, as she speaks. It's as though I'm underwater. Nothing she says reaches me.

My eyes are lifeless, pale, and uncaring.

I am nothing but a vessel of violence and death. There isn't a single thing left for me in this wretched life. I am the harbinger of my demise.

The Angel tugs on my hair, trying to tame it. She places a silver diadem on my forehead, pushing down harshly. I don't react to the pain. Icicles sprout out from it, rising inches above my head. She places metallic tips on the points of my ears that match the crown.

The nameless Angel paints my face in silver and the palest of blues before dressing me in the finest silver fighting leathers I've ever seen.

They glide over my body, hugging my every curve. My mother's emblem is on my right breast.

Earlier, I might have tried to rip it off. Earlier, I would have cared.

Now, I sit limply in the chair, letting her push and pull on me how she wills.

I stare at the mirror in front of me. I look like death personified.

I'm sure my mother will be proud.

At five minutes to midnight, all the servants leave the room. The Angel takes one last look at her masterpiece before bowing. "It will be an honor to serve you again, my lady."

Knots twist in my stomach at her words.

Again.

I will be expected to live in this wretched place after I kill the male who loves me. Bile rises in my throat, and I hurry to the wastebasket, emptying the contents of my stomach before rinsing my mouth with water.

Somehow, I can still feel Nathan. He keeps tugging on that bond, trying to get my attention. It hurts more than anything else. He is alone here, even more so than I. His family is far away in the Summer Court.

Dear gods, his family.

I don't even know how to get in contact with them. How will I ever tell his sister what happened? His mother? Before I delve deeper into the shame and horror of what I'm about to do, my mother appears in the doorway.

The Winter Court Queen is wearing an elaborate crown made of silver and inlaid with hundreds of blood-red diamonds. It is enormous, stretching more than a foot in the air. Beneath it, her eyes are cold, filled with cruelty. She is wearing a revealing gown made of the finest silk, the pale silver contrasting beautifully with her dark skin.

Her beauty is a mask that I can see right through. She smiles at me, beautiful and chilling, flashing her canines.

"Let's get this over with," she says as she studies me, her tone cruel. "You brought this on yourself, you know. You should have just married Henrick when I arranged the match."

I shudder but remain silent.

She sighs. "Have it your way. We'll talk more about this later."

Before I can reply, she throws Iter Dust over me, and the palace fades away.

We land in the middle of the Winter Arena. Snow crunches under my feet as I fight to remain upright. The Arena is open to the night sky, but there isn't a single star in sight. It's so cold that I can see my breath billowing like a cloud before me.

A boom echoes off the stands before a dozen floodlights are turned on. I squint as I try to take in my surroundings. I have never seen the arena from this angle; it is far larger than I ever realized. There are thousands of seats, but most of them are empty.

I see a contingent of Mer in their aqua chairs, Were, Daemons, and Vampires filling the stadium, along with a legion of Winter Fae. A few large wings announce the presence of Angels, but there are far fewer spectators than I would have thought.

A small mercy.

"The Right of Retribution is an invitation-only event, Elva," my mother mutters beside me. "Now be a good little Fae and do your duty to me. After this, we can talk about more comfortable living arrangements."

I ignore her, instead watching as a flash on the other side of the arena is the only warning I get before Nathaniel materializes out of thin air.

My husband is all alone.

They have dressed him in black fighting leathers, which makes his russet hair even more noticeable. His face has a grim look as he stares at the stadium, but I know the moment his gaze lands on me. His eyes widen slightly as though he is trying to send me a message.

When I don't respond, he yanks on the bond so hard I almost double over in pain. I gasp, but my mother moves before he can even take a step forward. She flits a hand in the air, summoning a pillar of ice around her. She stands, arms outstretched, as the ice raises her ten, twenty, then fifty feet in the air.

Applause rings through the arena.

"Honoured guests of the Winter Court," my mother says, using magic to amplify her voice. It echoes through the stadium, silencing the onlookers. "Welcome to the Right of Retribution. As you know, this time-honored tradition takes place when a high-ranking member of our court demands retribution. We are all gathered here to witness the fulfillment of this tradition."

A deafening roar fills the arena as the spectators cheer. Ice runs through my veins.

I dare glance at Nathaniel and see him tapping his hand against his leg.

He doesn't look scared. He looks... ready. Thoughtful. As though a million things are running through his mind.

Gods, I wish I could talk to him one more time.

They won't let us speak. It is against the customs of the Right of Retribution for the two challengers to meet.

What would I say?

I'm sorry my mother is making me kill you?

I shake my head. Maybe it's better this way. I am empty and have nothing to give him except a clean death.

The Winter Court Queen drones on for ten minutes about the rules of the fight. It's simple. Magic is allowed, weapons are encouraged, and we go until one of us stops breathing.

It is archaic, violent, and the crowd loves it. They scream and roar their approval of the process, banging their feet on the stadium floor in encouragement.

They disgust me. All of them. They are no better than my mother in their desire to see bloodshed.

When the Queen is finally done, she bows to the crowd. I don't move at all.

Under the thundering applause of the crowd, my mother uses Iter Dust to transport herself into the Royal Box that overhangs the arena. She sits on a throne made of ice, her back straight, with a scepter in her hand. When the sound has died down, she grins before waving a hand. Instantly, the pillar of ice she was standing on shatters into a million pieces.

A loud boom rings through the arena before thunderous music plays through hidden speakers. It sends chills down my spine.

Entertainment.

That's what we are now. I school my expression as weapons of every nature materialize in a large ring around us. There are swords, daggers, bows, and arrows with deadly iron tips, tridents, maces, and even lances.

There are no shields available. It would defeat the purpose of this disgusting game.

Nathaniel shifts, his stance wide, as he takes in the arsenal before us. A look of pain and anguish washes over his features as he studies me. He tugs on the bond, and for the first time, I do the same. His eyes widen, and I see a tear run down his cheek.

Never have I ever hated the Northern Court more than I do at that very moment.

"Any time now, Elva," my mother purrs. I hear irritation lacing her words.

Oh gods, Nathaniel. I am so sorry.

I am going to regret this for the rest of my days. Keeping my gaze on Nathaniel, I walk backward and pick up a long sword. It's a beautiful weapon, and maybe another day, in another life, I might have appreciated its beauty.

Today, I hate this sword almost as much as I hate myself.

Swallowing hard, I take a step, then two, closer to Nathaniel. I see him step back and reach down, his gaze never leaving mine. He grabs a dagger, his eyes wide as he holds the hilt as I taught him. I see fear in his eyes as he looks at me.

He is scared of me. He should be.

Everything within me wants to tell him to put down the weapons, that the best way to show him my love is to give him a quick death. By doing so, I am saving him from far worse at my mother's hands.

I don't, though.

I just watch this man who bound himself to me, knowing exactly who I am. The man I am now destined to kill.

My eyes track his movements as he walks around me in a circle. The snow crunches under his boots as he moves around me. His presence is like a fire behind me, and without moving, he has sent a flame to caress my skin one last time.

We move in time with each other. I take a step forward, he takes a step back. I lift my sword. He sends a ball of fire towards me. It's wide, and I can tell he's aiming to miss.

My sweet, kind Summer Fae.

There is no way out of this.

From the stands, I hear screams every time we get close to each other. The music is booming now; the beat is vibrating throughout the arena.

Ten minutes pass, then twenty, as we circle each other. I

refuse to take the first shot, and looking into his eyes, I know he feels the same.

"Let's hurry this up, Elva," my mother calls out from her box.

Suddenly, the snow we are standing on becomes slick as thick ice coats it. I know my mother is responsible for this.

The moment the ice appears under his feet, Nathan slips, his boots having no traction. I watch in horror as he slides forward, his arms flailing like he will fall.

My heart drops, and suddenly, I know I have to act.

It won't just be ice she summons next time.

I stand still, my hand on the sword, gathering ice and snow around me. Flinging out my power from the depths of my being, I create a blizzard that whips around us. I send it throughout the entire stadium, covering the entire Winter Arena in my storm.

Under the cover of the snow and wind and ice, I walk towards Nathaniel. I tug on the bond repeatedly, hoping he can understand what I'm trying to say.

I'm sorry, my love.

As I approach him, I shift my grip on the sword as tears stream down my face. As I approach, I can see his outline. The storm whipping around us covers us both with snow. My gut wrenches as I prepare to lift the sword. I am only a few feet away from him.

Just as I am about to bring the sword down to end the life of the only Fae who has ever loved me, there is a tug on the bond. It is so sharp that I halt my movements.

"Elva, love, do you trust me?" he whispers. His voice is so low, so hurried, I think I imagine it.

"With my life," I reply instantly.

"I have a plan," he says before he moves and fades into the storm.

Our words are lost to the wind and snow, my storm screaming furiously around us. The blizzard is picking up speed, snow drifting across the area, when my mother's voice booms out.

"End this, child," she growls, "or I will release the wild beasts."

The snow is flying so furiously around me. I can't even see my hand in front of my face. Fortuna never wanted us together, and we will end in a frost-ridden tragedy.

"I'm sorry," I say before releasing my hold on the storm and allowing the snow to settle on the ground before us.

When the winds die down, I see... nothing. No one is there. I blink twice in confusion as I try to find my husband. Nathaniel has disappeared. Shouts and jeers come from the stadium, and I stiffen as heat rushes down my back.

Keeping my grip on my sword, I slowly turn on my feet.

Standing directly in front of me, his eyes filled with tears is my husband.

"I'm sorry," he echoes my words, before moving to embrace me.

A sharp pain, unlike anything I've ever felt, fills my chest. The agony is so acute I can barely feel the way he is furiously tugging on our bond.

I look down, my eyes growing wide as I see the hilt of his dagger buried in my chest. My fingers release the sword, and I see it falling to the ground in my peripheral vision. The pain grows in my chest, and numbness spreads all over.

It's over.

I let out a choked sound before raising my gloved hand and brushing it down his face. "I love you," I tell him before my legs lose the ability to support my weight. I crash to the ground, letting the soft snow envelop me.

Darkness claims me instantly.

CHAPTER 43
SHE'S DEAD
NATHANIEL

Silence ripples around me, enveloping the stadium. Elva is on the ground, scarlet blood leaking from the hole I've just made with my dagger. Tears are spilling down my face as I silently pray to any gods that will listen.

"She's dead!" someone shouts, slicing through the panicked silence.

I drop to my knees next to her and whisper in her ear.

"The Fae has killed another heir!"

"Kill him!"

I am whispering faster now. Instructing her heart to keep beating slowly. Just enough to keep her alive but not enough to be detectable, I pray.

I press my hand to the soft spot on her throat, checking for a pulse. There's nothing, and for a second, I panic. I tug on the awareness between us and find her alive. Her frosty, glittering ice still coats the other end of the bond. Barely.

The end of a staff shoves me to the side viciously. I tumble into the snow, ramming my head against the ice beneath the thin dusting of powder. I groan and try to scramble up as the guard reaches for Elva.

I move to stop him, but the guard growls. His tone promises violence. I stay put as he checks for her pulse and finds nothing. He raises his hand, fist closed tight.

Dead.

Not dead, I remind myself. Hours earlier, as I sat in my room, I thought about every fairytale I'd ever heard. There was no library, so I was left to sift through my thoughts as I stared at the ceiling. I had absentmindedly tugged on the thread between Elva and me repeatedly until a thought popped into my head that made me sit straight up.

The Names.

I know her Name. I can, technically, command the speed of her heart. She won't stay alive for long, especially if she bleeds out before I can figure out how to heal her.

But I also have Akron on my side. I am almost sure he will help me. Perhaps he will even congratulate me for my ingenuity. The plan unfurls before me. It is a terrifying, impossible path, but we both get out alive this way.

I yank on the bond so fiercely, hoping for a way to tell Elva what I was thinking. I can't stomach the idea of her thinking I would actually kill her.

Silence is my only response.

I am snapped back into reality when the guard turns around and expertly twirls his spear at me. He draws the weapon back, preparing to deal the final blow, and I squeeze my eyes shut as terror floods my whole body.

Failure. This whole stupid idea has been a failure, and now I will die next to Elva.

I force my eyes open. I need to see this next part. Elva is the first thing I look at, and I am filled with guilt and despair. We deserved each other. Deserved to be happy. They don't know she still lives.

"Heal her," I choke out as the spear plunges toward me. The guard's eyes fly open.

"Stop!" a voice bellows, echoing throughout the open space. The guard freezes, along with everyone else. The scent of magic rips through the air as the screaming and chanting "*Kill the fae*" ceases.

My chest heaves, the point of the spear digging into my throat just slightly, as I catch eyes with Akron. He materializes slowly next to the guard. Not as quick and efficient as Iter Dust, but I didn't know he could travel like this at all.

He grabs the neck of the guard and tosses him to the side easily. He is terrifying, with his eyes and tattoos glowing brilliantly.

"Get up, Sprigg. You look like a damned weasel," he growls at me through gritted teeth, and I scramble to my feet. He doesn't wait for me to follow. "I can't hold these assholes forever, Move!" He barks before turning and fleeing.

He doesn't realize I grab Elva, as he's already halfway to the gate. I doubt he could move us all with such a heavy strain on his magic.

I slide my hands under her armpits and start pulling. I don't want to move the knife in her chest and cause her to bleed out faster. The adrenaline coursing through my veins has given me strength I didn't even know I possessed. She slides across the snow and ice easily.

I am running backward, looking like a rutting idiot. Without thinking, I compulsively yank our connection to ensure she doesn't die.

My whole body feels as though it's covered in ice. A stretching and rippling sensation tears through my body when we reach the threshold. A portal has been set here, transporting us somewhere else.

I am paralyzed with fear. We materialize about one inch off the ground and land with an uncomfortable thud.

Akron curses vehemently. "I knew I never should've given you her name," he says. "Why. In. The. Nine. Circles. Of. Hell. Is. She. Here?" The anger in his voice is tangible. When I look up at him, I almost shit myself. He has grown taller, and his hands shifted into claws like some creature from a nightmare with glowing purple eyes.

I swallow hard. "She's not actually dead."

"Explain, *now*."

"We are married. I kept her alive."

He doesn't respond.

I keep rambling. "She could be very useful in negotiations, which is why you saved me—"

"She would've been very useful *dead*. Don't you see, you clueless idiot? *I needed her dead.* Things are about to change in these lands, and we need the Winter Fae royalty wiped out." He trails around us like a beast stalking its prey.

My eyes widen, but I don't speak.

"My employer needs her dead so he can take control of this court," he whispers.

A lightbulb springs to life in my mind. That's why he's been trading in Black Opals. Everything falls into place. The new trading routes, his references to connections in the North over and over... my stomach drops when I think about extravagant art that had been gifted to him from the North.

"Yes, I can see you working it out in your tiny, stupid brain. Well done, Sprigg. Too bad you both will die now." He lifts his hand, a glowing purple ball in it, and launches it toward me.

I duck out of the way, panicked. He is already charging another. I need to keep him away from Elva.

Elva's heart can't start beating faster. If it does, she will bleed out.

I duck behind a tree just as the Warlock incinerates half of it. He should be able to freeze me, but the drain on his magic must be enormous. He didn't plan on me bringing Elva.

As if to show my thoughts, he launches another ball of magic. This one is considerably smaller. He fumbles with the watch on his wrist. My magic is tingling in my veins. I shift ever so slightly, and then I am a bird.

He laughs. "Ah yes, your measly shifter magic. Good job keeping that from me for so long." Another ball of magic whizzes past me and singes my wing. It hurts. I dive towards him, talons out.

I connect with his face and gouge mercilessly at his eyeballs. My claws connect with both eyes, but not enough to take them out completely. His hand strikes me so quickly that I am sent hurtling toward the snow. A bone crunches, and I scream as I return to my Fae form.

Blood streams down his face as he screams in agony. I take my chance.

"I'll kill you both!" He stumbles toward Elva.

"*That's my wife*, you sick bastard," I shout. Mustering every drop of magic inside me, I blast a stream of white-hot fire toward him. The magic does its job until nothing is left of him but ashes.

I let out a long breath.

And then, I scream and scramble over to Elva, my broken rib barking in shooting pain. She is still there, but now I cannot heal her. He was supposed to help with this.

She will die.

The depth of my grief is too deep to comprehend. In another burst of fiery anger, I am on my feet. I reach for his ashes and kick them ferociously. I tug at my hair, screaming again.

When the screams are done, I sink to my knees and sob.

Something jabs hard into my leg. When I look down, there is a watch at my feet. The band is made of leather, but the face...

The face is made of Black Opal.

Incensed, I claw at the watch, trying to get it open. I pick up a rock and start hacking toward the crystal glass. I need to touch the gemstone.

I drag myself, my whole body throbbing to Elva.

Repeatedly striking the watch, the glass doesn't do much as scratch... But the back pops off.

I let out a strangled shout.

Sliding my fingers over the smooth surface, I jump as power courses in my veins.

Knowing time is short, I reach for Elva. I don't know exactly how the Black Opals work, but I will do everything I can for her. I lay a hand on her, imagining myself a conduit between her and the power. I push the power in my veins into her, towards the gaping wounds in her body.

My heart pounds, and all of me hurts as I work, but I keep going.

This needs to work. It has to be enough.

Whispering to her, "Hold on," I funnel magic into her. My fingers wrap around the knife's hilt, and I yank it out.

The Black Opals work quickly.

Her wound closes, inch by inch until smooth skin is in its place.

I command her heart to beat as normal.

My body is weak and spent as if I have lost my blood from my body. I slump onto her, hoping that it is enough.

"Please be enough," I whisper as I lose consciousness.

CHAPTER 44
I FORBID IT
ELVA

Something heavy is lying on my chest. It hurts so much, and my lungs are struggling to find breath.

I always knew I would end up in Hell, but somehow, I at least thought I could breathe.

I try to shake my head, but the movement sends a bolt of pain through my neck.

"Gods," I curse under my breath. Even in death, nothing is easy.

My chest is heavy, and I groan, trying to force my eyes open. They're nearly frozen shut, but finally, I see... evergreen trees towering high above me, their branches reaching to the sky, where streaks of red and yellow and orange are dancing across the sky.

Hell looks a lot like the Northern Court, I think, smirking. *Fitting, but so unlike the crystal caverns I thought were watched over by Aidoneus Hades.*

I close my eyes, content to rest in peace for a few minutes, when the weight on my body shifts slightly.

My eyes fly open.

What is on me?

I push myself onto my hands, ignoring the shooting pain rushing through my body. Every curse I know of leaves my lips as I stare at my love.

He is lying on top of me, his russet hair covered in snow and ice. His lips are the palest blue, and icicles dust his eyelashes.

"No," I cry out.

This is wrong.

He shouldn't be here. I'm dead. He killed me.

I put my hands on my chest, searching for the hilt of the dagger that was there only moments ago. I remember a flash of pain before seeing Death welcoming me with open arms. It's... gone.

Memories start flooding my mind, one after the other, after the other. A plan. Nathaniel said he had a plan. Then... I was on the ground, and snow was covering me, blanketing me as my heart slowed and my lifeblood left my body.

His lips near my ear, telling me I *had* to stay alive. I had no choice, he said. The way he tugged and tugged on the bond as I drifted off.

Faint memories of being dragged through the snow start flashing through my mind before... he healed me. I don't know how, but he healed me. My brows crease as I stare at him. My wonderful, foolish Summer Fae. His head is in my lap, and I cradle him to my chest.

"It was never supposed to be this way," I say, as my tears fall freely. "Nathaniel, it wasn't supposed to happen like this."

I bend down, brushing my lips over his forehead, his eyes, his nose, as I anoint him with my tears. "You foolish male," I say, choking on my tears, "you had to get the last word in, didn't you? One final trick?"

Shaking my head, I brush back a lock of hair falling in his eyes before pressing my lips to his.

They're... not frozen.

Gods.

I yank on the bond in my mind, again and again, until I feel something on the other end. A flame, burning so low that it is barely there.

Laying him gently on the ground, I ignore the pain in my body as I press my ear to his chest. The faintest beat echoes through his chest, becoming weaker by the moment.

"No," I say, gathering him in my arms before I push myself up. Every muscle aches, protesting the movement, but I ignore them. "You don't get to do this to me, husband. You don't get to leave me in this hellhole and die for me. *I won't let you.*"

My knees buckle at the added weight, but they hold firm. Decades of training have taught me to push through when my body is on the brink of giving up, and I will not let this be the time that they fail me.

With my arms wrapped around my husband, I start to run south. I don't know where we are, but I need to put distance between us and my mother.

I shudder, imagining her anger at this moment.

Not grief. She would never grieve for me.

But she will be furious that a Summer Fae bested her, and took her weapon away. That's all I've ever been to her. I can't worry about that right now. Every few minutes, I tug on that bond between us, trying to push my awareness into him as I move. His flame is growing weaker, flickering out like a candle.

I'm so tired I can barely move. I know I can't heal him right now.

After running for an hour, I climb to the top of a hill and turn in a slow circle. At first, all I see are trees, but soon, something familiar catches my eye. Far off in the distance, nestled in the forest, I see the Polar Bear Bed and Breakfast.

"Thank all the gods," I breathe before adjusting my hold on

Nathan and pressing my lips to his once more. They're so cold, the contact sends shivers down my spine. "Just a little while longer, my love. Hold on, just a little while longer."

"Open the door, please," I beg as I kick the door repeatedly. Sounds of life come from inside the building, and I increase my efforts. "I need help," I cry out. "Please!"

My arms are so heavy, and blackness is pushing in on all sides of me. My chest wound was healed, but my body is threatening to give out on me. I've been running for hours without rest, gripping Nathaniel in my arms.

His light is fading fast.

The door swings open just as I'm about to kick it again, and I fumble slightly, leaning against the doorframe before my legs give out entirely.

"Help us," I say before collapsing on the ground.

"Can you hear me?" a voice, muddled and underwater, break into my dreams.

Warmth surrounds me as I lay on something soft. My hand twitches, relishing the feeling of silk sheets under my fingers.

There's something warm beside me, and as I try to push myself up, a small pair of hands land on my shoulders.

"I wouldn't do that if I was you," a female voice says. I know her. It's the same Vampire as before. Cali... something. My head is too fuzzy to try to figure it out. "You and your boyfriend were in a bad way when you landed on our doorstep, and you've been sleeping for the past day."

I blink, wincing as a bright white light fills my vision. "Did I make it?" I mumble, shutting my eyes against the offensive light. "Is he going to live?"

There's no reply.

Sleep is calling my name, pulling me, beckoning me to come. My bones are so heavy that I can hardly move.

"Will he live?" I ask again, more urgently this time.

A moment passes, and then another.

I can barely hear the Vampire's reply, it's so quiet.

"He will."

I shudder. Wetness slides down my cheeks as I fall back into sleep's embrace.

A soft, dim light fills the room as I blink slowly, pulling myself up onto the bed. The Vampire is nowhere to be seen as moonlight filters in through the open window.

My hand brushes against something warm, and my eyes widen as I see Nathan lying beside me. His eyes are closed, and he looks so peaceful. I can't help but lift my fingers and trace them over his features. He is so beautiful.

He is mine.

I tuck a lock of his hair behind his ear, and he shifts under my touch, his eyelashes fluttering before his eyes slowly blink open.

"Elva," he says slowly, as his lips slowly tilt upwards.

My hand flies to my mouth, stifling my cry as tears fall. They are salty and warm, running down in rivulets as I look at him.

He raises a hand, brushing his fingers down my face as he struggles to sit up against the mound of white pillows.

"Darling, why are you crying?" He asks huskily. His voice is low, raspy from disuse.

I choke on my sobs, my voice catching as I try to speak. "I thought you were dead," I reply, shaking my head. "How could you do that to me?"

He pushes himself up before pulling me against him. His arms wrap around me, pulling me close. "I would give everything for you, wife of mine." He murmurs into my hair, "I love you."

"I love you too," I say, burying my face in his chest. Sobs are wrenched from me until I have nothing left.

Still, he holds me.

Minutes slip by until the tears are long gone, and something else has taken their place. My fingers trail over him, feeling the lines of his body as we remain together. How is it possible to feel so safe and loved?

He's here. I'm here. We're both alive.

It truly is a miracle.

Eventually, I turn and nuzzle his chest. I inhale deeply, his scent filling me. He groans my name. Placing a finger on my chin, he tilts my face so I look at him. His eyes are dark, filled with deep emotion and longing. "I would very much like to kiss you right now."

How does he know that's what I want? What I need?

"What are you waiting for, husband?" I say, trying to be coy but failing miserably.

Quickly, far faster than I thought possible considering the past few days' events, his lips press against mine.

It's not a kiss. It's a declaration, a claiming, a promise of something more. It's powerful and moving and filled with intense longing and emotion. It's a bringing together of two beings who have looked death in the eyes and come out the other side. It's a promise that I can cry, and he'll always be there. I can break, and he'll put me back together. I can do anything, and he'll stay by my side.

It's *everything*.

For countless minutes, our mouths move together. He nips me, I sweep my tongue into his mouth. His hands roam over me, I grab the back of his neck and pull him towards me. This isn't gentle, but it's precisely what we need.

"Elva," he murmurs my name like it's an entire prayer to the gods. "I don't care what happens. I will never let you go."

In response, my hands sweep over him. They dip down, down, down until I'm tracing the lowest part of his stomach. Then I keep going.

When I touch him, feeling his hardness, he groans. "You're going to be the death of me, Winter Fae."

I chuckle, the sadness from earlier nowhere in sight. My fingers continue their dangerous exploration, his soft gasps and muffled curses invigorating my every movement.

My hands wrap around him, and I move to my knees. "You don't need to do this," he groans.

"I know." I lower my lips, tasting the small bead of moisture on his tip. It's salty, but somehow, tastes exactly like him.

He yells.

I smile. Pressing kisses down his length, I speak quietly. "Nathan. My husband. My love. For now until the end of my days, I swear to you, I will never leave you."

Then I take him in my mouth. He is thick, and it takes me a few minutes to find a rhythm, but soon, he clutches at the sheets and groans as I continue to work. There is something powerful in this, in making him fall apart for me. A different kind of magic than the one running through me.

He groans, "Elva, I'm going to come." He tugs at my head to pull me up.

I shake him off, taking him deeper. I want this. I want him.

"I'm—argh." He comes apart, and I swallow all of him. He's not the only one affected here. I'm hot all over, my core is tight, and moisture is gathering between my legs.

He pulls me up, settling me gently on my back.

"I don't know what I did to deserve you," he says. "But I'm going to show you how much I love you daily from now until the end of time." His eyes sparkle as he helps me out of my clothes, tossing them on the ground beside us. "Now lay still, wife of mine."

Before I can protest, he kisses a trail down my collarbone, my breasts, my stomach, and brands me as his own. When he reaches my belly button, he rests his chin on me and looks up. His gaze is dark as he studies me.

"You are so beautiful," he says. "I've waited so long for this."

"Me too," I say breathlessly.

His hand splays on my stomach, holding me down as his head dips between my legs. At the first touch of his tongue against me, I cry out. He chuckles darkly but doesn't stop.

"More," I beg shamelessly, pushing my hips against him.

He laughs, the sound rumbling through me. "So needy."

"Mmmm," is my only reply. "Please."

Thank the gods, he listens.

His mouth moves over me, finding that little bud between my legs, and he licks, sucks and kisses me until I'm writhing before him.

"I'm close," I half-whisper, half-moan.

In reply, something hot dances across my breasts.

Fire.

I can't help it. The first touch of his magic, combined with his mouth, has me screaming. My body shakes harder than ever, and I come apart for my Summer Fae.

Afterward, he slides up behind me and pulls me against him. "Sleep," he whispers. "I've got you." And I do. With him, I am safe.

CHAPTER 45
HOME
NATHANIEL

An analog clock is ticking somewhere in the room.

Who in the hell still uses old-fashioned clocks? Let alone noisy *ones?* I sigh. *Winter Fae, that's who.*

It's impossible to fault them when Elva is lying in my arms, completely and utterly disrobed. The lingering ecstasy from last night persists in the dark corners of my soul. I am as though I am lost at sea, my heart dipping with the clawing needs of the outside world and then rising to a crest every time the echo of her gasps rang in my ears.

Trying to control my breath, I trace the lines of her tattoos from her collarbones and down her arms. Absent-mindedly, I lose myself in the memory of her until I realize that my hand has disappeared under the blanket.

It is impossible to stare at her face, hair mussed from love-making and a soft smile still curling the edges of her delicious mouth, and not wake her.

Neither of us has been complete until this moment.

My fingers search through her curves, mapping out her body until I can stand it no longer. I miss her so deeply that my heart aches with longing. When she put her mouth on me last night, I just about lost control in the first few seconds.

And then when she came apart for me...

Gods, I will forever dream of those sounds she made.

I find myself leaning over her, pressing my lips to hers with the reverence of a prayer. Her breath hitches, and she stirs ever so slightly, giving me the courage to move closer, our bodies pressing together in a familiar embrace.

"Nathaniel," she breathes my name.

I kiss her, "Good morning."

She smiles softly. "With you, it is."

Her lips find mine again. Soon, our hands are wandering. She's more daring in her touches today—as am I.

"I need you," she whispers. "All of you."

As if I would ever deny a plea like that. I run my hand down her stomach, tracing the soft curves until my fingers slip between her legs. I part her legs with my knee, and she yields to my touch.

With a low moan, I push a finger inside of her. Her walls clench around me. My mouth moves to her neck, kissing and biting as I slowly add another finger.

Elva arches beneath me, her hands gripping my shoulders.

"Please," she whispers, the word a prayer on her lips. "More."

Those are the best words.

I oblige, removing my fingers. I lift them to my mouth, tasting her before shifting my hips and positioning myself at her entrance. Slowly, I push inside, relishing the way she envelops me. My hips move slowly at first, but soon harder and faster. She meets my rhythm with one of her own.

Our eyes meet.

Nothing exists outside of this moment, and the only thing that matters is this beautiful woman who has given me every bit of herself. Our souls entwine in an uncontrollable passion as our mouths move together in perfect harmony.

The analog clock ticking away in the corner is a distant sound, fading away into nothingness as time ceases to exist around us. Her back arches, and she tightens around me. We come hard and fast together.

It is only then, as I pull back that I realize the clock is still ticking away. When I'm with her, nothing else matters. And now, we have all the time in the world—an eternity to explore our love.

After we've finished, I pull away the covers and sheets, padding to the room where I find a towel. I wet it with warm water, squeeze the excess, and then hurry across the room back to where she lies, watching me. The dark fur drapes across her hips.

I hand her the towel, and reach forward, rubbing my thumb over her soft cheek.

Gods. Her skin is so smooth.

"What do you feel?" She asks, reaching up to catch my hand and press it towards her lips.

I sit down, my back propped up against the chocolate-stained wooden headboard. "That I was right."

She smiles, "Right? How?"

"From the first moment I saw you... gods, I wanted you. But more than like this." My hand slides from her shoulder, across the luxuriously soft textures of the blanket, and stops at the crook of her knee. "From the first time you sat across from me in the office, talking to me for the first time, I knew I was home. I wanted to be home."

The companionable silence she had led me to discover settles in as a look of complete content passes between us. It is like heaven for my wild mind.

One thought keeps returning until I can't help but let out a laugh. “We both know there was no way you’d ever sleep with me unless I tricked you into marriage. What can I say? I told you I was a bastard Summer Fae.”

She slides into my lap and wraps her arms around my neck. “You keep saying that, but how do you know this wasn’t my plan all along.” She grasps my shoulders before she bites my neck.

I swallow hard. “Again?” My voice is a bit too high.

She purrs in response.

I almost wish the clock was louder now.

THE WANTING SIMPLY NEVER STOPS.

I can’t stop staring at her mouth, how it closes around her fork or pulls up to smile or say ‘thank you’ to the Vampire. I’m slowly going insane.

We haven’t even recovered. Surely what we’re doing isn’t helping the healing process.

I shake my head and turn my attention elsewhere. The dated devices in this house hurt my head, and even in my crazed stupor, I can’t ignore the loud click as the television comes on. The too-perfect reporters I saw in the Everything-Mart drone on. They are dressed in gaudy, pastel-blue suits, and the Angel’s skin is so white that he looks as though he has freezer burn. The Winter Fae in charge of the weather barely wears anything at all.

We’re in the middle of another report, pasting Elva’s ashen face across the screen. The replay the same scene over and over, and at different angles. Each one of the moments when I plunged my dagger into her heart.

Then, Jeremiah walks into the room and stares at the television. His face passes quickly between us and the screen.

A sound escapes him, and the human pales.

Elva is on her feet before he can speak. Her hands wrap around his neck. "You can't tell anyone who we are," she says threateningly.

Footsteps come from behind us.

"Calm down," Calitha is in the doorway, a cooking knife in her hand, "*Princess*."

My heart is racing. How did this get bad so quickly?

"Woah," I say. "Why doesn't *everyone* just calm down? I'm really not in the mood for any more death.

Elva glares at me, but relaxes her stance.

Jeremiah steps back, hurrying behind the Vampire. She tucks her arm around him, glaring at us.

"Explain what's going on, now," she says.

Elva bristles, but I put my hand on her. These people are helping us, they deserve to know what we can tell them.

I bite my lip, trying to piece together what to say. "I'm Nathaniel, and this is my wife, the Crown Princess of the Winter Court. We are seeking refuge from the Queen."

"*Why?*" Calitha demands. "What was that report about?"

"Because I am going to take the throne," Elva interjects, something shining in her eyes. "My mother is dangerous and needs to be stopped. Change needs to come to the Winter Court."

For a long moment, the air is so thick I can barely breathe. Calitha stares at us both shrewdly before nodding.

"That's just what I've been hoping to hear. I have some people you'd like to meet." She briskly turns on her heel and walks away.

Her husband is still in the room. He crosses his arms and stares at us both. "You're really going to try to help?"

"Yes," Elva says.

He stares at us both, tapping his foot. “Alright. Then you’ve come to the right place.”

My brows furrow. “What do you mean?”

The human runs a hand through his hair. “You can’t share this with anyone.”

“We won’t,” Elva and I say at the same time.

He bites his lip. “We are with the resistance.”

I didn’t even know there was a resistance. It makes sense, I suppose, considering the horrible way this country is run.

Elva’s eyes widen. She opens her mouth and then closes it. After a moment, she says, “This is wonderful news.”

The man’s eyebrows shoot up.

I rub the back of my neck for a moment. “Hey, look, do you have a phone?” I say, and Elva turns to me, tilting her head inquisitively.

He nods. “Yes, of course.”

Elva and I are alone in the room, and I feel a twinge of guilt for how hard it is for me not to kneel and...

Focus.

“Bad news,” I say. “We need to call my mom.”

Elva’s mouth falls open. “Lucinda?”

“Yes. Wait, how do you know her name?”

She smiles as Jeremiah returns, pulling out a ghastly flip phone. “I remember everything you tell me.” I take it slowly, trying not to look like I was touching a dead rat. It is a damn miracle I still remember the number. I punch in the digits quickly, and the phone rings.

"Hello?" Lucinda's voice sounds morose, and more guilt stabs at my heart.

"Uh, mom?" I say tentatively.

"Nate?" Her voice sharpens. "Nathaniel, is that you? WHERE. HAVE. YOU. BEEN. I thought you were dead. DEAD. Cherie and her adorable husband are beside themselves. What number is this?" She stops yelling long enough to check her phone. *"THE NORTH? Nathaniel Sprigg, I am going to—"*

"Hey, Mom, calm down. I'm married. I have been away because I got married," I say, and Elva's eyes are wide at my mother's sheer volume. I smile sheepishly.

"Married? Oh, Nathan, really? It's not that Vampire you mentioned once, is it? Please, please, I don't need to wake up some morning and find you drained of blood—"

Elva quirks an eyebrow, and I say quickly, "No. She's a Fae."

"A Fae," Lucinda repeats, her voice positively entranced. She doesn't need to know she's a Winter Fae quite yet. *"She sounds absolutely beautiful. When will you bring her home so she can meet her new mother-in-law? I have some herbs to give her so you can finally give me grand-younglings. Honeymooning in the ice isn't great for the ovaries, you know—"*

I roll my eyes. I've described literally nothing about my bride. I look at Elva, who can clearly hear my mother droning on. I'm confused because instead of anger, I find Elva smiling on the point of tears.

"Can I talk to her?" My mother repeats, and I blink. Elva nods enthusiastically.

"Yeah, Mom. Sure, here she is."

Elva tentatively takes the phone. "Hello?" She says and then grins as my mother showers her with compliments and embarrassing stories.

My cheeks heat, but the look on Elva's face stops me dead in my tracks. She's had no one care about her like the way Lucinda can, even as petty as she is sometimes.

It hits me all at once. She is a product of her fears, of her traumas. It hurts to realize. I don't want to gain sympathy for the female who I felt raised me poorly, but it comes. Everything she did was born out of hope that I would get exactly what I have gotten.

I've changed a lot. Maybe she can too... Maybe she has, and I haven't even noticed.

For once, I hope my mom doesn't stop talking.

Elva leaves the room, and I hear the words, "Oh, that's nothing, one time—"

CHAPTER 46
DARLING
ELVA

I am going to take the throne.

My words echo in my ears as I lift the painted china teacup to my lips, sipping the herbaceous black tea while studying the group that has gathered around me. I hadn't planned them or even discussed them with Nathan before they came out of my mouth.

Gods. I didn't even ask him how he feels about it.

I am not good at this whole marriage business.

I might not even be a good queen. All I know is that I've been haunted by nightmares ever since I got away from Veronica and her goons, and I would do anything to help save my people from experiencing horrors like the ones I've gone through.

Shivers run down my spine as I recall the way the iron shackles felt clamped around my wrists, the painful searing as they burned away my ability to use magic, and the way the drugs ran through my system every day. Gods. I may never forget it, but I don't want to let those memories run my life. I came out the other end of my ordeal stronger, and maybe, just maybe, the Winter Court can too.

Maybe.

And that's why, now that I've opened my big mouth, we are sitting in a tight room at the back of the Bed and Breakfast, staring at members of the resistance. Calitha had led us to this space a few minutes ago, the Tea Room, she had called it, before handing us teacups that came from humans. They're small and dainty, and the flowers. Gods. They are so old-fashioned, but something about them is sweet.

Nathan and I are sitting on a small flowery settee, facing a roaring fire. His tight grip on my thigh is the only outward sign of his discomfort with the situation. His teacup is balanced on his thigh, and he hasn't moved it since we sat down.

The overwhelming emotion in my heart is happiness. I still can't believe this is real, and I keep tugging on the bond to check that he's still there.

He is.

"I will always be here for you," he said repeatedly as we learned about each other in a completely new way.

The promise echoes in my mind, making me hum with happiness. It's a welcome distraction from the situation we are currently in.

The heat from the tea burns as it goes down my throat, warming me from the inside out. It gives me something to focus on as I assess the members of the so-called resistance.

Words are far and few between, the clinking of the china filling in the silence as everyone watches each other.

Besides our hosts, there are two burly humans with multiple weapons hanging off them. They are standing sentinel at the door, their faces grim as they watch us intently.

I watch a female Were leaning against the fireplace mantel and sipping her tea. She has long chestnut-brown hair and is dressed in a tight leather catsuit. She keeps eyeing Nathaniel, and I am not impressed.

He's mine.

Instinctively, I snuggle closer to him before glaring at the female. She steps back, a feat in a room the size of a walk-in closet.

Sitting across from us is a Winter Fae male with ice-blond hair who I vaguely recognize as a low-level politician in my mother's court, and a Daemon whose black horns stick up from above his mop of curly red hair. His only contribution to the conversation thus far has been to point out that it's "freaking cold," and we should hurry things along so he can leave.

Calitha is hurrying through the room, stepping over limbs and offering little tea sandwiches to everyone.

Their eyes bore into me.

It's not like I haven't been the center of attention before, but this is different.

"So," the Were says, putting her teacup down with a clink, "here you are, Princess. Very much *not* dead." She stares at Nathaniel, assessing him before raising a brown brow. "And this is your husband?"

Incredulity rings in her voice as she quirks a brow. Nathan stiffens beside me.

"He is," I reply with finality. "He will not be going anywhere, so working with me is working with both of us. I won't tolerate any disrespect towards him."

The Were bows her head and steps back. "I meant no disrespect, Princess."

I snort, but the other Winter Fae nods before I can retort. "That won't be a problem, Princess." He clears his throat. "I wasn't at the Winter Arena, but everyone has heard of your... death. It's quite an interesting turn of events to find you here. I must say, this is exactly what we've been waiting for."

I nod and say, "Thank you."

Sighing, I place my teacup on the side table before looking

around the room and straightening my back. "I was telling the truth earlier. My mother is a tyrant, and I will no longer allow her rule to go unchecked." I grow cold as the memories of everything she has run through me.

Nathan squeezes my thigh, warming me, giving me the strength to continue. "She is too old and has lost touch with her emotions long ago. I plan to force her off the throne and take my rightful place as Queen. I would have done it if I hadn't been a youngling when my father died."

The daemon cleared his throat, glancing at Jeremiah before nodding. "About that... your father—he's not exactly dead," he spits out quickly.

I freeze. Flurries of snow appear as icicles start forming in the room. The temperature drops so quickly that Nathaniel's cup's tea freezes. Shouts are coming from all around me, but I barely hear them through the ringing in my ears.

"What do you mean?" I say, my voice frosty as panic edges into it. "Of course, he's dead. I went to his funeral. My mother told me..."

My voice trails off as a tear freezes on my cheek. Nathaniel starts to shiver next to me. "Elva," he whispers, creating a fireball before us. Its heat is barely noticeable through the cold, and a strange clicking sound fills my ears. It takes a moment, but I realize that the sound I'm hearing comes from Nathaniel's teeth as they chatter. "Elva," he says more insistently, "darling, it's freezing in here."

I shift in my seat, my eyes widening as I take in his blue lips. "Dammit," I choke out, cutting off all my magic.

I am the worst wife in the world.

Instantly, the heat returns to the room as I press my hands to his cheek. "Oh gods, I'm so sorry, my love."

He blinks a few times as color returns to his cheeks. "Don't worry about me," he says, forcing a small smile before pulling me in for a hug. He turns in his seat, his arm still over my shoulder, as he looks around the room. Nathan's face hardens as he studies the Daemon. "What do you mean, her father is not exactly dead? I was in that wretched palace and didn't see a trace of him."

Jeremiah clears his throat from his perch against the back wall. "The resistance has sources inside the palace. We have it on good authority that the King is... unwell. We believe he is being held in the Southern Tower, as the Queen is often seen going in there, but only her most trusted servants are allowed in or out."

"You mean... he really could be alive?" Hope tinges my every word as I stare at the resistance members sitting around us. They nod, but their faces are grim. "Why is everyone looking at me like that?" I say. "This is good news! If my father's alive, it will make getting rid of my mother even easier."

The daemon shakes his head. "If he's been under this... whatever it is, for decades, chances are his mind is addled. He might not even be the Fae you knew anymore."

"You don't know him like I do," I say, refusing to believe him. "Father loves me. He will help us!" I turn to Nathan, grinning. "You can meet him." Excitement fills my words, and I squeeze my husband's hand. "He will love you so much."

He smiles at me, but there is a tinge of sadness in his eyes as he reaches up to brush my hair away from my face. "I'd love nothing more, darling," he murmurs.

Pure, unadulterated joy is running through me. "So, what's the plan?" I ask.

"I can't believe this is the best tech they have available," Nathan grumbles beside me. He is clipping a black walkie-talkie to his belt, the twin to the one that I'm currently holding in my hand. He spent the past half-hour turning it over in his hand, seemingly in disbelief that these existed.

"These are high-tech for the North," I remind him again. Last night, as we lay together in bed, sated in every way possible, he ranted about the analog clock on the wall for an hour. I hadn't even noticed it, but apparently, it was offensively ancient to Nathaniel.

After having pulled apart everything wrong with the clock, he had moved on to dissecting the flip-phone, followed by the VHS player in our room.

"You're older than the walkie-talkies," I say as I pull on my white knee-high boots. I'm perched on the side of our bed, staring at him as he leans against the bathroom door. These boots are lovely and warm, trimmed with blue fur and styled to match the rest of my outfit. "Don't you remember using these as a youngling?"

He snorts. "Darling, you wouldn't believe the tech we use in the Summer Court. I'll show it to you one day. It puts human technology to shame."

"It's a deal," I say, and shiver as the magic seals the promise between us. I glance up and smile when I catch his eye. His pupils darken, and I see his gaze sweeping over me. "Nathan," I warn, "we don't have time. They're waiting for us."

He walks over and pulls me up from the bed, wrapping his arms around me before pulling me in for an intense embrace. When he releases me, he brushes his nose over mine. "I just wanted to make sure you don't forget about me," he says.

I shake my head. "Haven't you learned by now? I haven't forgotten about you since we first met on the docks. You've haunted me ever since that day."

"What can I say?" he says, jokingly. "I'm just that handsome of a Fae." He ducks out of the door, laughing, as the pillow I launch from the bed slams with a soft thud into the door. “Now, now, Princess. No time for this. Let’s go.”

Chuckling as I open the door, I launch a snowball at him before running down the stairs. He growls, chasing me out into the snow. “I’m going to get you back for that.”

I laugh.

It feels good.

CHAPTER 47
TWO BLUE EYES
NATHANIEL

I look out the window while the group meets in the next room. I am giving Elva some time to sort through the plan I had been *briefly* briefed on. She had insisted that I be there with her, helping her to take the throne that is rightfully hers.

The resistance will head in first, clear a path for us to follow, and lead us to where my new father-in-law is being kept. It sounded good. Their intelligence seems solid, and the maps are easy to follow. After a few years of working in Port City, I know my way around an excellent strategy.

After the meeting, Calitha dragged Elva away, and I have been here ever since.

Before I realized I had been brooding, the sun had finished setting behind the misty, snow-capped mountains. As much as I hate the lack of TV, phones, or music, I notice that going "off the wire," as Elva puts it, actually does wonders for my concentration.

I stare out the window at the Winter Court and repeatedly

remind myself that this will be Elva's domain, her court to rule. I will be alongside her.

And I feel like an utter imposter. The resistance members regard me warily and somewhat reverently as the person who has killed some powerful and nasty players in their game.

They don't know it has much to do with adrenaline and sheer dumb luck.

Even landing Elva... I am the luckiest bastard in the world. In reality, I am better suited to buy a bridge somewhere and set up shop as a troll tricking people out of their hard-earned cash.

In fact, that almost sounds better than becoming the consort to this place.

The problem is that Elva holds my heart in her hands. She has the power to break me in half as I've gone hollow with all the trust and openness I've poured into her, and, instead, she has filled me up. The cold focuses me, the open air centers me, and Elva grounds me.

If my heart has a face, it is hers.

That sense of being an imposter burrows itself under my skin, even though I know she trusts me. Even though I have come so far.

I am staring out the window for endless hours because I just don't know what to do with that.

I don't know how to walk around after having reached into my chest, torn out my heart, and presented it in a gilded box to the lethal Winter Fae with swirling tattoos.

An icy hand trails across my shoulders and slides down my arm to meet my hand. Each touch is an electric current.

"We leave soon," she says, leaning her head on my shoulder. When she pulls her sweater tighter, I turn up the heat across my skin and she nestles into me. I thought Winter Fae loved the cold more than anything else, but she has always appreciated a warm bed. I lay a kiss on top of her head. She's braided her hair with golden rings. I don't know where she got them from, but she looks beautiful.

"Would you like something to eat?" She murmurs into my neck.

Food. My stomach grumbles in response.

"Yes, that would be excellent. Just please tell me it's not fish. I'm serious; at this point, I would rather just go veg—"

"Relax," she smiles mischievously, "it's venison."

Great. Gamey, chewy venison.

"I've changed my mind. I would much rather eat something else." I deadpanned and waited for her to work out my words.

Her eyes widen before she flushes, leaving me feeling quite proud until she covers my face with snow. I stagger back, spitting out half-melted ice crystals.

"Honestly, can't you be serious for two seconds?" She crosses her arms, and a twinge of guilt hits me.

"I... well, I don't think I will be useful on this brief excursion. We were captured the last time I went to save you anyway."

Her brows furrow as she looks at me. "Wait, what?"

I shrug, trying to seem like I didn't just admit something incredibly personal. "All I'm saying is that I seem more of a problem than a solution."

She studies my eyes intently, adjusting herself so she is directly in front of me. "Nathan, you saved me. More than once. You've killed for me, and you still don't think you are enough?"

I rub my neck viciously, trying to avoid answering. "That was all luck," I start and immediately stop when I see the muscles in her jaw dancing.

"You killed Henrick and Akron... technically, you almost killed me." Her voice is quiet, even.

I scoff. "Come on, you don't count. You let me stab you. Sorry about that, again, by the way."

"Okay, fine, maybe I don't count, but the other two? How do you write that off? Do you know why you won against them?"

I don't respond.

"Because you are something new. They were waiting for someone to attack them in the ways they already expected. They were expecting someone like them, with their minds and strategies, to try to hurt them." She brings her icy hand to my face. "You aren't anything like them, you are much better. That is why I love you, because you have something inside of you I recognized instantly. A gentleness and a compassion that I never realized was possible."

I look over her head, out at the stunning whiteness in front of us. The Winter Solstice will happen in a month or two, and the rich evergreen pine scent excites me. This, combined with her words, brings a lightness to me.

She turns around, her hand falling from my face, and she looks out at the expanse as well. "For this reason, you will be an excellent consort to these people. This place is beautiful but dying." She grabs my hands and snakes them around her waist, hugging herself with my arms. "Be my consort; breathe life into this place just as you have breathed life into me."

I nuzzle into her neck and kiss the smooth skin where her throat meets her shoulder.

We stay like this for quite a while.

After the leader comes to get us, and I am sufficiently stuffed, Elva and I shift into our bird forms.

We are now soaring over the expanse of white, and my head twitches back and forth, monitoring how the Were, Vampires, and Daemons darted through the trees. They don't have the gift of shifting, but they make do. We have made this trip before, and the journey here seems shorter than usual. In what seems like no time, we reach the edge of the forest and stare at the Ice Castle. Calitha holds up a finger, instructing us to stay. We perch on two separate branches. My small bird heart is pumping so fast I am unsure how to calm it down.

Like small, white snowflakes, the resistance charges the castle gates. Even from here, I can see how ridiculously easy this is. They are cutting down soldiers like weeds; I even see some kneel and hold their hands up high.

What the hell is happening?

They have gotten in so fast, I am not entirely sure what this means for the plan. I shift my weight nervously and look up at Elva. She is as still as a statue. I tug on our bond, and she looks down at me. She shakes her head as if to say, 'Not yet.'

The tension in the surrounding air is killing me. Five minutes pass, no screaming, no shouts.

Then ten minutes.

Then a half hour.

I pace back and forth on the branch, and Elva flutters down beside me. She opens one of her enormous wings, wraps it around me, and then forcefully pecks me on my neck.

I let out an annoyed squawk.

I could swear she is laughing... or at least smiling.

She launches off of the branch, and I trail close behind her. When we reach the gate, I brace myself for the uncomfortable ward I had passed through before. I'm surprised to find it down.

It's almost... *as if they are expecting this.*

Dread is swimming in my stomach, constantly ramming against the stinky meat I ate for dinner. We reach the front doors of the castle. They are large, intricately sculpted ice panels melded together with magic to allow us entrance inside.

Elva shifts back, and I follow suit. I've never been to this part of the castle.

I gawk at the grandeur. It seemed like something that was frozen in time from a thousand years ago. Modern designers have yet to touch the carved wooden accents, elaborate crystal chandeliers, or silver trim in the last century.

This will all belong to Elva soon. I grimaced. This will be our home. It feels exactly how it looks: *cold*.

Elva doesn't speak or look at me, and I can see from her expression she is nervous. Tense. She leads me through two more corridors until we spot the rebels. Each one has a grim look painted across their rugged face. It doesn't bode well for me.

I am just trying to keep my breathing even and remember what Elva has told me. My difference is my strength.

Elva looks each one in the eyes and says, "Was that as easy as it looked?"

They all nod.

"Something is wrong," Calitha hisses. "This place was all but abandoned when we got here... this mission might be a bust if we can't find the Queen."

Elva bites her lip. "No, she's still here. I'm sure of it. There's no way she abandoned the ship when she's the captain of the damn cruise line. You know where my father is being kept?"

Calitha nods.

"Lead the way."

I feel more like a bystander than ever as she takes us into a grand library. Calitha stabs a painting of someone who looks like they are very, *very* self-important and tears the tapestry. Behind it is a lever.

I roll my eyes.

A godsdamn lever.

The humor is lost on me when she pulls it and reveals a tunnel.

"One of many secret passageways hidden throughout the castle. They were used for safe houses and escapes."

I nod.

The hall is considerably colder than any other part of the castle, and I try to avoid cringing at its frosty bite as we walk through it. My heart is racing, unsure of what will await us on the other side of this hall.

Runes mark the wall, and I can only assume their deep blackness comes from charcoal. When we reach the end of the hallway, my stomach twists, and bile rises in my throat.

A chamber, very similar to the cell we had been placed in, stands before us. Except along one of the four windowless walls is a very lush bed. Laying on that bed, asleep, is another black Winter Fae with a grey beard and a bald head.

Next to him, with her legs casually crossed over each other while she reads a leather-bound book, is the Queen of the Winter Court.

CHAPTER 48
THE KING OF THE WINTER COURT
ELVA

I'm not even sure I am breathing as I stand in the doorway of this hidden bedroom, staring at my father. He's clad in white silk pajamas and tucked under a heavy blue comforter. A dozen pillows are on the bed, and he's lying in the middle of the large mattress.

My father is alive.

Or, at least, not dead.

A sound of deep agony escapes my throat before I dart across the cold stone floor to my father's bedside. Somewhere beside me, I know my mother is talking, but I don't have time for her right now. She's had me for decades, and she squandered every one of them.

Her time is up. Completely ignoring my mother's presence, I gently take his hand. It's so cold.

A sob rips through me as I lean in. "Father?" I say, my voice sounding weak even to my ears. "Can you hear me?"

There's no response, and for a long moment, I fear he is truly dead.

Silence fills the room, and I can sense Nathan walking up

behind me, his heat warming my back as I lean over the only parent who ever loved me. A warm hand lands on my hip before he squeezes gently.

There are no words needed between us. He is here for me, and I need him more than ever.

Taking a deep breath, I close my eyes before leaning closer to my father again. His breaths are so shallow, but I can see slight movement in his chest.

“Father?” I repeat, squeezing his hand. “*Please*,” I sob as a tear runs down my cheek.

His hand is like ice in mine. Just as I’m about to give up and pull my hand away, the lightest touch brushes against the inside of my palm. My eyes dart up to his face, but there’s no movement.

But I know what I felt.

He’s in there.

Sobs wrench through my body as I shudder, drawing my father’s hand to my lips. “I love you,” I say over and over again. “I won’t leave you.”

In my peripheral vision, I can see two resistance members standing guard in the doorway, their hands on their guns as they watch my mother closely. She hasn't shifted yet, but we are all wary of her. The memories of public executions, of heads rolling in the streets, are at the forefront of everyone's minds. A guard, one of the Vampires, steps forward, but I shake my head.

"I'll do it," I say firmly. The guard reaches into his pockets and pulls out a pair of thick iron cuffs. They are wrapped in cloth, but I can feel the offensive metal from here. My every instinct screams at me to run, but I walk over and put out my hand. The cuffs are heavy, and even through the cloth, they sear into my skin. I bite my lips as I come over to my mother.

"It's over. Those guns are loaded with iron bullets. You won't make it off this chair if you fight or shift." I pull away the cloth and clamp the iron cuffs down on her arms. To her credit, she doesn't move, doesn't scream, but I see a bead of sweat running down her forehead.

If I had any room left in my heart for this woman, it would be breaking right now. I know the pain of this better than anyone.

From our planning, I know many more resistance members are spreading through the castle now.

None of that holds any significance to me right now.

Nothing matters except for the people within this very room.

Anger flashes through me as I shift, staring at my mother. Despite the iron cuffs, she hasn't moved from her perch on the chair, her hands calmly holding onto her book. Part of me is giving into the coldness inside me as I turn towards her.

"You did this to him. To my father," I seethe through clenched teeth.

She stares at me, her eyes cold and unmoving. I can practically see the wheels turning in her head as she watches me. She tilts her head, watching me. "For a ghost, Elva, you certainly have a lot of opinions. Do you care to explain how this is possible?"

I shake my head. "No," I say, releasing my father's hand and stepping back from the bed. I stand tall in the middle of the room, looming over her.

"No?" She repeats, quirking a brow.

"You don't get to run this conversation," I say as cords of ice wrap around her legs, binding her to the chair. "From here on out, you will answer my questions."

My mother studies me for a long moment before she gently closes the book in her hands. She ignores the bindings around her legs as she folds her hands on top of it, sitting primly in the chair beside my father. "All right," she says. "What would you like to know?"

Clenching my fists, I gesture to my father. "How about this?

You told me my father was *dead*. You watched me mourn him, and then you whipped me because I grieved for him."

Behind me, Nathan inhales sharply. Heat rolls off him in waves. I can practically feel the effort it's taking him to bite his tongue.

"You should be thanking me for that," the Queen says. "Look at how beautiful, how strong you are now. If It had been up to Edric here, you would have turned out to be some weeping, weak-boned female with no spine or ability to lead. Instead, look at you. You're incredible." She reaches forward with her hand as though to touch me.

"Don't," I spit out, as I look at her in disgust. I crinkle my nose, shaking my head as I step back. "You have lost your mind. Did you do this to him on purpose?"

She looks at him, raising her brows. "This?" She says, gesturing towards my father. "It's just a little poison, darling. It'll wear off... eventually." She cackles. "Your father was such a bore. I did us all a favor when I got rid of him."

"Tell me how to fix this," I say. "If you ever cared for me, you will fix this for me."

"Care for you? You're my heir. My job was to raise you to take care of this court and our people. And that's what I did. Caring is for the weak, the vulnerable. I taught you better than that."

I shut my eyes, feeling control slipping away, when Nathan's arms snake around my back. "Breathe," he whispers in my ear. "You can do this."

I lean into him, grounding myself in him before I open my eyes. "You were wrong, Mother. Caring is not for the weak. Emotions don't make us bad rulers." I tug on Nathan's hand, pulling him beside me. "Love is the most powerful thing I've ever felt. It has bound me to this male, my consort. Now we will take the throne."

Cold, hard fury passes over my mother's face. She purses her lips, her eyes steely. "I see I should have killed you myself when I had the chance," she says softly.

"You will never have the chance now," I say, tears filling my eyes. "After today, you will never see me again. You will never get to know my husband or any of the children we may have. I will forget you even existed."

The chair scrapes on the ground as my mother pulls on the bonds around her feet. I stare at her, pity in my eyes.

"You have a choice to make," I tell her, my voice as hard as steel. "You can put yourself in the Eternal Sleep willingly *today* or pay for your crimes against your people. There will be a trial, and *when* you are found guilty of the hundreds of horrific murders perpetrated by your hand, you will be publicly executed."

She watches me, those blue eyes studying my every move. For the first time, I see fear reflecting out of her eyes. "And who are you to decide such a thing?"

"I am the heir," I say, holding my head high. "Your creation. Come to take my throne. Only, I am nothing like you. I hope that for every moment of your life, from now until whenever it ends, you will know that I found love and that it makes me a better Fae than you could ever hope. From this moment on, I am not your daughter. You will abdicate in favor of me *now*. Your reign of terror is over."

"Is that so?"

My heart is a drum pounding in my chest. My fingers flex at my side. My magic is throbbing in my veins. I don't want to fight her, but I will. Nathaniel has shown me that people can change. What could I do for the Winter Court if given the chance?

"Yes," I nod.

She snarls.

"Don't do this, Mother." I take a step towards her. "You've done such much. Hurt so much." I placed my hand on my heart. "Hurt me."

"I *made* you."

"Perhaps," I concede. "But these are just the beginning." I gesture to the rebels. "Your time is over. Give up with grace."

I see the thoughts swirling in her head as she studies me before dipping her head ever so slightly. Nathaniel sucks in a breath, but I don't take my eyes off my mother.

"I really... I love you, Elva," she says.

My head dips. "I believe you think you did. But now I've learned what love truly is." I take another step. "Please. Don't make me fight you."

Her eyes search mine for what feels like an eternity. My heart is racing in my chest, and I ready myself for a fight. I don't want to do it, but I will. I'll give her a trial if she wants one, but I don't want to do it.

Then, a miracle happens.

The fight leaves my mother's eyes. She slumps against the chair. "I, Queen Ophelia of the Winter Court, hereby give up my claim to the throne of the Winter Court," she says coldly.

The scent of magic is in the air, and I hold my breath as I wait for my mother to continue.

She sighs, shaking her head. "I shall not fight my daughter for the throne nor stand in her way. As is her birthright, she shall reign over the Winter Court from this moment forward. May all the power of my ancestors be stripped of me and handed to her. Long live the Queen."

The moment the last word comes out of her mouth, a frigid breeze swirls through the room before landing on me. My very pores are alive as they are infused with the power of the North.

No one moves.

Seconds tick by into minutes. My mother sits there, watching. Waiting.

Eventually, I step forward. "What is your choice?"

"I will go to sleep," she concedes, sighing. "But not because you want me to. I'm bored. After having lived for over a millennium, things never seem to change. I thought more cruelty would solve the problem, but this new generation of soft Fae doesn't agree." She looks pointedly at me, sneering.

"Today," I remind her.

She nods. "Today."

Turning my back on my mother, I walk out of the chamber. "Don't let her leave," I say to the guard. He nods at me and pulls a gun from his holster. "Yes, Your Majesty."

"You have no idea what's coming to you, little one. You might find you also need more cruelty to survive," she calls after me. I keep walking.

Your Majesty.

The guard's words echo as I pace in the throne room. We left my parents an hour ago, seeking some peace. My footfalls echo on the ice as I walk back and forth, furling and unfurling my fists. Nathan is standing a few feet away from me, having followed me from the Southern Tower.

"He was just lying there," I say, gesturing wildly. "I can't... I've thought my father's been dead for a hundred and thirty years. He's been here the whole time? How could she do this to me?"

Tears prick at my eyes as I fight to keep them at bay. I rub my palms against my eyelids, pushing them away.

"Gods," I shake my head. "Every time I think I know the depths of the depravity of my mother, she does something else that makes the last thing seem paltry in comparison. Borders locked down, public executions, media control... these are all things she did. Terrible, horrible things. But this... my father... this might really top it all."

I can feel my husband standing close to me, watching me. I shake my head. "The thing is... I'm not a good Fae, Nathan." A tear, salty and warm, runs down my cheek. "How do I know I'm going to be any better for the Winter Court than she has been? There are so many wrongs that need to be righted. Where do I even start? How do I open borders? How do I make the people trust I won't have them killed in the streets?"

I bury my face in my hands, slumping against the ice that surrounds the dais. Tears run down my cheeks, dampening my hands, as I reveal one of my deepest fears to this male who has crossed the ocean to be with me.

The faint sound of boots approaching is the only warning I get before my hands are peeled away from my face. I squeeze my eyes shut.

"Elva," Nathan whispers while cupping my cheek with his hand. "Look at me, darling."

I force my eyes to look at this Summer Fae kneeling in the Ice Castle. His eyes are filled with warmth and compassion as he watches me. "You are amazing," he says. "You will be nothing like her because you *care*. Elva, you *love*. Don't you think I know what it feels like to be loved by you?"

His lips tilt up as he studies me before pulling me forward and pressing his lips against mine. The kiss is raw and full of emotion, sending electricity through my body.

Nathan pulls away, wiping a tear from my cheek. "You make me feel alive, Elva. From that very first moment, you entranced me. You pulled me from a humdrum life and gave me something to fight for for the first time in over a century. Wife of mine, you are incredible. And if you love your people even a tenth as much as you love me, I know this court will flourish under your capable reign."

I sniffle. "I hope you're right," I say.

He smiles. "Can I lie to you?"

I shake my head.

"Then you know I'm right."

WE ARE STANDING IN A LARGE STONE CRYPT DEEP UNDERNEATH THE ICE Castle. I'm shivering despite my ability to endure cold as a frigid breeze runs through the chamber. My mother is standing in front of a row of caskets made of ice, her expression guarded. Most of the caskets are closed, their residents long since asleep, but one has an open lid. It's empty. For now.

Inside is a pale blue silk pillow, a sheet covering the ice, and a blanket of the palest pink. I can't help but shudder as I think about climbing inside it willingly. The Eternal Sleep is so far off for me that I don't want to think about it for a second.

When we went back to the underground chamber for my mother, she didn't put up a fight. She simply kissed my father's hand before sighing once. "He will wake within the week," she said before waiting for me to release her bonds.

I didn't take off the iron cuffs.

"Let's go," she said. "I'm ready."

Part of me wanted to fight her for trying to take charge of this moment, but I didn't. I simply nodded and followed her to the chamber.

In this, one last time, she can be in control.

Her gaze hasn't left mine since we first entered the chamber.

"Are you certain, Elva?" she asks.

My mouth is set in a firm line as I nod. "Yes, Mother. You *will* do this, or I will put you on trial for your crimes. There will be no reprieve for the Fae who has subjected this Court and its people to atrocities for centuries. I don't care who you are."

"Fine," she sighs before climbing into the coffin. She extends her arms. I step forward, frowning, as I pull off the iron cuffs. They burn my fingers, and I drop them into an awaiting box as quickly as possible.

Seeing my mother in this room sends chills through me, but I remain strong.

"Goodbye, Mother," I say.

She smirks. "Remember, you can't come running to me when things go poorly."

With that loving statement, she shuts her eyes and mutters under her breath. I stand above her, frowning, as I wait.

It doesn't take long.

Soon, my skin tingles as thousands of ice-blue snowflakes rush through the room, hovering over my mother before settling into her skin. For a moment, it appears she is glowing, peaceful even, before they disappear.

No one speaks for a long time.

"Is that it?" Nathan whispers in my ear.

I jump. I didn't even hear him approach. "It is," I reply. "She'll remain asleep with her ancestors. I've never heard of anyone who comes out of Eternal Sleep."

He lays his head on my shoulder, his arms wrapped around my waist. "I'm sorry it came to this."

"Me too," I whisper. "But at least you're here with me."

We stand there for a long time, staring at the casket holding my sleeping mother before someone clears their throat from behind me.

"Excuse me, Your Majesty, but something requires your immediate attention."

CHAPTER 49
GET ALONG
NATHANIEL

Two months later...

I look in the long, gilded mirror and shift from side to side as I check my fitted white suit.

Fae take their wardrobes very seriously, and I'm no exception. When they mentioned I might need to be fitted for clothes worthy of a consort, I might have been more excited until I realized I would never be dressed as a grass blade again.

I guess that's what visiting home is for.

Which is where we will be at the end of the week, after I finish the next ten thousand meetings I have scheduled over the next three days. There is so much to reform, so much mess to clean up. The sheer size of it is overwhelming.

Zipping up the leather boots with a fur lining that I have taken to wearing, I fold my woolen pant leg over the top of the shoe. More businessman, less snow trekker. I nod with satisfaction.

I walk from our warm bedroom, decked out in fur over every possible surface, down a short stairwell, and into the living room. I smile as I take in the way the paintings of summer months line the walls next to photographs of Elva and I that they took for a socialite magazine.

The corners of the walls are adorned with ripe red berries and clean-scented pines. The enormous solstice tree is already set up behind the green velvet settee.

I smile. Stacked log walls are much better at keeping heat in than the Ice Castle.

I grab a coat from the wall. It's a fashionable pea coat that Elva says makes me look younger. Walking to the enormous fireplace, where an enchanted fire always burns, I pick up some Iter Dust and rub it between my fingers. In an instant, I am in the castle. The familiar chill licks my skin as I look at the long table of VIPs in front of me.

As I look at the leader of the largest Vampire coven in the region, I think about the people trading Black Opals and shudder. Those are still a problem.

The leader of the Were, Lolita, stares at me with a cold, guarded expression. She has been one of the most difficult to deal with, but I am grateful she has come. There are no official Angel communities here, but there are Daemons. The red-skinned co-leaders, Lilith and Aracnid, stared up at me. They are unnervingly agreeable, and I am not sure I trusted them. Local officials pad the spaces between them.

My eyes fall on the only open space in the entire room. The place that has been reserved for the Ice Mer King. Helena has been out of contact with Elva, and Phelix never even bothered to return the messengers.

The entirety of the Winter Court has the same aversion to

technology, but I figure that will take a few centuries to deal with. At least now, there is less shouting and growling in these meetings. My body was tired of the constant fight or flight.

They all look at me expectantly. I clear my throat and call to mind the presentation I had practiced on Elva no less than three times. She hasn't arrived yet, so I'm trying to stall by making jokes that are received with half-hearted smiles.

The Daemon leader told me he thought I was amusing a few weeks ago. So... that's something.

Finally, the doors swept open, revealing the future Queen of the Winter Court, Elva. She is wearing a suit made of snowflakes. Somehow, the fabric allows her to stay warm. Or maybe she's just used to the ice.

She smiles widely at me. She's been in charge of all of this, but this next project... It's mine.

It's been on the back burner for a few months since there was a coronation to plan, a military reform to instigate, criminals to imprison, and poverty to address, but she assures me now is the right time to bring this up.

The room is silent, and all eyes are on the Queen as she walks to the front of the room next to me. Her ice crown spikes up around her head, leaving her forehead free.

She extends her hands slightly, palms facing up. "Welcome. Thank you all for your punctuality. My husband Nathan and I are pleased to discuss a new idea that will help solidify the ideals we've been working so hard to highlight under our rule. I'll leave the rest of the time to him. We break at 12:15 for lunch." She smiles at me and sits at the head of the table, swiveling around to watch me.

I clear my throat. Walking forward, I place a tablet with a built-in projector on the table, and a few maintenance crew drag in a large, black cloth.

I shine the presentation on it, and a few people shift uncomfortably in their seats. I smile, trying to make it seem like I'm not amused.

A floor plan comes to life through my screen, and I turn back to them as I clear my throat.

"Welcome, friends. I present my plan to repurpose the ice palace into two important functioning bodies. Since the Queen Regnant is still awaiting her coronation, we haven't officially moved into the palace. I propose that we never shall. There are two of us, and no possibility that we could have enough children to fill the entirety of the space. We are quite happy in the state house where we currently live."

I take another deep breath while Elva smiles encouragingly. "I propose splitting it equally between the government and a public university." Everyone is listening closely now. "Before we vote, I have a few things to clarify. Does anyone have questions?"

The Were leader speaks up. "Yes, why a university? Most of our younglings go abroad if they want higher education or pick up a vocation."

"This university would be free and allow our younglings to stay here and have those same experiences... closer to home. We wouldn't have only Northern teachers," I say, and a few leaders look offended. "Of course, we will still have them, but there will be a balance."

"I suggest you tip the scale a bit more if you want us to agree," the Vampire leader says. I concede.

"And what will your role be with this university?" Lilith pipes up.

I smile. I've missed negotiating. It's something I'm very good at. "Truth be told, I would like to be its director." I scrub the back of my neck.

A small smile crosses Elva's mouth. When I told her, she surprised me with a small gift the next morning. A pair of glasses —no, they were definitely spectacles—was sitting on a velvet cushion. When I put them on, she all but squealed as she threw her arms around me and covered me in kisses.

The list of inappropriate things she's done to me while calling me 'professor' is concerning.

I clear my throat again, glad the cold helps me avoid blushing scarlet, and begin fielding more questions before settling into my charming self as I present the finer details of the plan.

I think I'm settling into my role.

SIX LE BABA MORGAINE DESIGNER SUITCASES LINE THE WALLS. FIVE OF them are mine. Elva rolls her eyes.

Her hair is down, and she's dressed in a flowery blue summer dress. I didn't even know she owned such a gown.

"Hey, I have to meet with the Summer Fae government. They will take you at face value, but if I'm not dressed my absolute best, they might as well skin me alive. With words."

Elva laughs. "Yes, well, I have a feeling I will spend most of this trip wearing next to nothing."

I quirk up an eyebrow, and she swats my arm. It actually hurts, but I keep a straight face. "No, I mean the heat. My coronation is in three weeks, on the Winter Solstice. How in the hell will I adjust from tundra to muggy heat?"

"Permanent snow cloud over your head?"

"Right, Nathan, because that will make such a good impression on your family."

I smile and squeeze her hand. I'm not entirely sure how to use the Iter Dust to get all the luggage, so I just... sort of... half-lay on it and hug the rest. Elva is laughing so hard tears stream down her face. She picks up the powder and throws it at me. I smile weakly.

The next moment, we are in the Summer Court pickup station. Elva is facing the opposite direction, and she stiffens at my side. I whip around to see the perceived threat and find my mother sobbing. Next to her are Cherie and her son-of-a-scholar husband. I smile. I'm going to have a conversation with him about the university.

I squeeze Elva's hand, and between us, we roll our suitcases across the ground. My mother bolts past me and pulls Elva into the tightest hug I've ever seen.

Elva hesitates for a moment and then wraps her arms around her as well.

Lucinda keeps slobbering over Elva's bare shoulder, and I try to pull her away. She's hysterical, going on and on about how she "feared it would never happen."

"Mom, *shut up*. You're being ridiculous," Cherie hisses at her.

Lucinda wipes her eyes viciously, smearing her cosmetics further. "I'm only concerned about your happiness. You tell me what you worry about when you have younglings."

I laugh and cough at the same time. "Mom, calm down."

Having children is not exactly our number one priority right now. We have things to work on. Elva would be an excellent mother, but she needs to sort out her own feelings about her mother before we can get there. I do too.

The advertising screens are flashing through different images around us, and I find myself disoriented. Too much time in the Winter Court, I guess.

When 'the carriage'—electric car—takes us back to my mother's house, the vividly happy and wild memories are way more prevalent in my mind.

The thing about love is that it makes you want to bring out

the best in everything around you. I don't think that's a bad thing at all.

When we walk through the door, I'm touched to see that they decorated for the Winter Solstice. My mom pauses. "Dinner tonight?"

"Look, I have to go meet with the Summer Embassy with Elva, and I just really don't know what time it will be—"

"Flesh of my flesh," Lucinda starts, her eyes narrowed. I already feel my body starting to tense.

Elva notices immediately. "What do you think you're doing?" she interjects.

Lucinda breaks her focus, the intense expression melting away. "I... I'm his mother. I want to spend time with both of you."

Truth.

"By compelling him?" All the softness is gone from Elva's face, and my mother shrinks back. "It's abusive. You don't compel your adult children to do anything; I will not stand by and watch. If you want us to be a part of your life, and we desperately want to, you will have to learn new ways to treat your children."

Cherie's mouth hangs open, and my mother looks as though she's been slapped.

Lucinda slowly nods.

The silence is intensely awkward. There's a funny mixture of guilt and pride in my chest. Guilt that Lucinda feels embarrassed, and pride because of how fiercely protective Elva is. She really is the best thing to ever happen to me. Sometimes having someone come in and help clear out the cobwebs in families is good.

Just when I'm about to break the silence and offer for us to stay somewhere else, Lucinda speaks again. Her words are careful and precise. "I'm happy you both are here. When would you like to get together for a small party?"

Cherie and I look at each other, stunned. Mattias is just happy to be here.

Elva grins. "How about tomorrow night? I'll help you plan. I've heard your family is a big fan of fish."

We all start laughing. There's so much joy crammed into this moment we all might burst.

Mostly, I'm just so grateful. I've never really felt that before.

Shortly after we unpacked, we find ourselves in the office of the Governing Council. We don't really have royalty in the Summer Court, it would be far too easy to trick and control them.

There is no receptionist to receive us because the smart room has been designed and programmed to take care of us easily. Elva is really freaked out by it. I just think it's cool.

She squeezes my leg as the door opens automatically to the counsel room. "Are you ready?"

She knows why I'm nervous. It's not the negotiations.

We stand up together and walk in hand-in-hand. Elva has placed a royal circlet around her head, the insignia now two soaring birds... a snowy owl and an osprey. I hadn't asked her to do it.

The reason for my anxiousness is sitting in the middle of the table. An inconsequential place for a big station. His russet brown hair is so long it reaches the mid-section of his back. He sits up so straight he looks like he literally has a stick up his ass.

Anger and embarrassment swirl inside of me.

"The Queen Regnant and her Consort have arrived." The artificial voice is speaking through hidden speakers around us.

Everyone is smiling, so bright and cheery. I hope Elva can see the daggers in their eyes, the calculations of wondering exactly how to trick us into some terrible deal.

“Welcome, Nathaniel and Elva. Everyone, meet my son and his wife, Her Highness Elva.”

I’m so tense that I can hear my bones creaking as I walk. Now that I am someone with power, I am worth his time.

“Andrius, council.” Elva nods to everyone graciously.

The first order of business is trade routes and then a travel agreement between our Fae courts. Surprisingly, the meeting goes very well. Elva, unsurprisingly, is even-keeled and sees through all of their baiting. It must be infuriating for them. One member briefly brings up the crown prince that I killed, but it is quickly swept under the table as a problem for a later date.

At the end of the meeting, everyone stands, and there is a bit more of the lightness in the air. I am grateful, even though I spent most of the six hours locked in there, avoiding Andrius’ staring.

Just as we are leaving the building, I hear footsteps walking quickly towards us. Andrius is standing there, a forced smile plastered on his face.

“Can I have a word with my son?” He says to Elva.

“Son. You really like using that word now, don’t you? Too bad it gave you a violently sick reaction for the last century and a half, no?” I spit out. A very bitter flavor has coated the insides of my mouth.

Andrius pouts, “Oh, come on, I was never very good with the baby stuff.”

“I most definitely was not a baby when you began being cruel.”

“Nathaniel—”

“No, just stop. I don’t want to hear it. You’re too late. I wish you the best but stay away from my family and me. You are nothing to us anymore.”

He stares at me, stunned, for several moments before I turn and walk out the doors. I find Elva’s face upturned and her arms out as she stands in the last rays of light. She looks golden, like a goddess.

She pries open one of her icy eyes, studying my expression. “You okay?”

“Yeah,” I say and snake a hand around her waist, kissing her temple. Her skin is warm. I growl a little with delight. “Let’s go back and hang out with my mom?”

“Oh?” She looks at me devilishly. “I heard about some springs near here from your sister...” Elva’s eyelashes skim the tops of her cheeks as she looks at the ground. What in the hell had Cherie discussed with her? I pale at the thought.

“Let’s go. We have the entire week with them,” I say, taking her arm as I nod. “After all, this is technically our honeymoon.”

She laughs. “We had one of those in our house.”

I roll my eyes. “I would like one where I’m not freezing my ass off.”

She grabs my face and kisses me hard. “That, my love, can be arranged.”

We don’t ride off into the sunset, but damn, it sure feels like we are as we take the car to this mysterious place of Cherie’s.

Ironically, for a moment, as I wipe a bit of sweat off my brow, I miss the Winter Court. I am happy to get back to the big party. I’m curious to see what the Winter Court will become when celebrating their new queen.

Elva looks at me and finds me watching her. A lovely smile crosses her lips, with no trace of hardness in her face or eyes. She is ruthless, brutal, and broken, but together we are healing. We are moving to a better future.

And I’m just so grateful. So. Damn. Grateful.

CHAPTER 50

A CORONATION FIT FOR A QUEEN

ELVA

The Eve of the Winter Solstice

"I'm telling you, I feel like the dress makes me look like an enormous snowflake." I take a sip of the Fae mead, enjoying the quiet of the evening after what has been a series of very long days filled with endless meetings. The reforms seem to be taking effect well, and what little resistance we've encountered has been fairly easy to subdue.

I continue, "When the seamstresses put the gown on me, I had to stop myself from laughing. It looks ridiculous. It is made from yards of fabric and tulle, and it stretches out at least ten feet behind me. It's just so... not me. What would you think if I wore my favorite black leggings and sweater tomorrow instead?"

A choking sound comes from beside me as Nathan spits out his drink. He grabs a napkin and coughs into it. "Dear gods," he says once his throat is cleared. "Elva, I hope that's a joke."

At the same moment, Lucinda, who is sitting across the table from us, screeches. I didn't know that Fae could make sounds like that. "My dear, you can't... you just... you must look the part," my mother-in-law says, her hand on her heart. She looks one second away from fainting and taking the entire tablecloth with her.

Lucinda has been staying with us in the Winter Court for the past month, and it's been heartening to see the way she and Nathan have been getting along. With every day, I see them mending their relationship more and more.

She turns to her son and widens her eyes at him. "Tell her, blood of my blood. She must wear the gown. I just checked on the seamstresses yesterday, and it's so lovely."

Nathan narrows his eyes at his mother. "I won't tell my wife what to wear," he says before downing the remaining Fae mead from his silver goblet. We had dozens of crates of the beverage shipped to the Northern Court for the wedding, and he practically danced when the first crate was unloaded.

He leans in to nuzzle his nose against me before lightly kissing the shell of my ear. "You know I'd be happy if you showed up naked." He winks at me, and I lightly slap his arm.

"Nathan," I hiss as color rushes to my cheeks, "our parents are here."

Looking up from under my eyelashes, I see my father chuckling as he sips his drink across the table from us. "You're married, Elva. I know what happens in a bedroom."

"Oh, my gods, Father." I breathe, my attention turning to him as I fight the urge to bury my face in my hands. I didn't know it was possible to feel so embarrassed by people you love.

He laughs loudly, and the sound warms my heart. Ever since my mother went into the Eternal Sleep, I've had the very best physicians caring for him day and night. It took some time for him to heal, but he is finally seeming more and more like himself.

When I asked him a few days ago if he wanted to reclaim the throne instead of me, he shook his head adamantly. "I would much rather watch you, Elva. This is what you were born for. Let me enjoy my retirement."

Before I could reply, he wrapped his arms around me and pulled me in for a hug. Despite his frailty, he still towered over me. His arms were warm and strong as they held me close.

Our relationship still feels so new, so untested, but I am enjoying every single second of it. I am relishing the feeling of being loved by a parent for the first time in over a century.

Lucinda clears her throat, seeming to have recovered from her near-fainting spell. "Elva—" she starts, but before she can continue, Nathan's pocket begins vibrating. It's so loud and out of place that everyone stops speaking immediately.

He pulls out the flip phone, checking the screen quickly. "Cherie is almost here," he says excitedly. I don't know if he's more excited about his sister showing up or the fact that she and her husband have promised to bring him a new state-of-the-art FaePhone from their home in the Summer Court.

His excitement over technology is infectious, and he is already planning on decking out the university in all the latest tech. "We need to have the best if we want to attract people from all over Aranthium," he had argued in front of the council last week. It had taken some convincing, but he finally got the go-ahead to order whatever he wanted from the South.

A few minutes later, Cherie and her husband use Iter Dust to arrive directly into our living room. Nathan jumps up the moment their feet land on the carpet, and he runs over and gives her a hug. It isn't long before I'm pulled into the embrace, their arms wrapping around me tightly.

Soon, the Fae mead is flowing, and we are all seated around the fire, warm blankets tucked around us to help ward off the chill. A large evergreen tree is in the corner of the room, the silver decorations glittering in the firelight. Piles of gifts are under the tree, waiting to be opened tomorrow.

We stay up late, with the moon as our companion, laughing and sharing stories. My husband holds me close and draws mindless swirls on my arm with his free hand. Every so often, he leans in and presses his lips against mine, to the backdrops of cheers and screams from our family.

As the midnight chime strikes on the clock, I lay my head on Nathan's lap. My eyes are closed as he brushes back my hair, sending warm sparks through my body. With each touch, my heart sings in a way I never thought possible.

Love has filled every crevice of my broken soul and melded into something new and beautiful.

I am happy.

The Winter Solstice

"Are you certain you don't need anything else, Your Majesty?"

I shake my head, meeting the eyes of the slim Winter Fae in the mirror. Her curly brown hair is escaping its bun as she bends down, fluffing out my train behind me. She has been trying to make this monstrosity of a gown somewhat more feasible to walk in for the past thirty minutes and hasn't gotten anywhere. At this point, I will accept that it is an impossible task.

I sigh, careful not to disturb the elaborate braids running down my back. "No, thank you, Margerie. I'll call for you if I need anything."

She bows before backing out of the room. My gaze flips back to the mirror. I still can't believe this is me. I am wearing a crown made of pure ice, the spikes of the crown reaching high above my head and tapering off in snowflakes. Margerie spent hours painting my face with blends of silver and gold, and my tattoos are standing out from dark flesh. I barely recognize myself.

The gown is cumbersome and decidedly over-the-top, but I don't have much of a choice for a Fae celebration of this magnitude.

I'm so wrapped up in adjusting this frivolous gown I miss the flicker of movement in the mirror behind me. Strong arms wrap around my middle, cinching the voluminous tulle, before Nathan embraces me. I laugh as he turns me around before pressing his lips up against mine. His kiss is languid and unhurried, his movements slow and appreciative.

He is wearing a suit made of white, the colors made to match my dress perfectly. His hair is brushed back, one side newly shaved in honor of this day. A band of silver wraps around his forehead, gleaming in the firelight.

When he pulls away, I see a glimmer in his eyes as they crawl over me.

"You look stunning," he says, his eyes dark with desire as he watches me. This male holds my heart in his hands, and there is no one I'd rather be with on a day like today. He swallows, pressing a kiss to the corner of my lips. "Your husband is a lucky bastard."

"He is," I say. "But I'm fairly certain my mother-in-law will murder him if he makes me late."

Nathan chuckles, brushing his knuckles over my cheek before bringing my hand to his lips and pressing a kiss to the back of my palm. "You're right. We wouldn't want to anger her." He winks, offering me his arm. "Besides, I have a Winter Solstice gift for you. It's in my trouser pocket."

I gasp. "Nathan, we can't do that right now. Everyone is waiting for us."

He laughs, a big hearty sound that fills the room and brings a twinkle to my eye. "Darling, as much as I'd enjoy that, I do have a gift for you." With his free hand, he reaches into his pocket and pulls out a black jewelry box. "I have had this for you for a while, but today seemed like the right day to give it to you."

He cracks open the lid, and my mouth falls open. "It's beautiful," I breathe before extending a hand. My fingers glide down the diamond, admiring how the carving is so lifelike. "Will you put it on me?" I ask.

"It would be my pleasure." He goes behind me and shifts my hair before unclasping my necklace, draping his gift over my neck instead. He kisses the back of my neck before peaking over my shoulder. "It looks even better than I thought."

"Where did you get this?" I ask, admiring the translucent diamond flame as it lays between my breasts. It hangs on a chain so fine that it can barely be seen against my skin.

"I know a guy," he says, winking. "When I asked him if he could make something that symbolizes joining Summer and Winter together, he jumped at the chance. Do you like it?"

"I love it," I say before turning and kissing him deeply. "I love you."

"This is it," Nathan says, holding onto my arm. "Are you ready?"

I breathe in deeply, taking a look around the room. The throne room is filled with guests. Humans, Vampires, Were, Mer, Angels, Daemons, and Fae have all flocked to witness our coronation. I look around the room to see if Helena is there, but my heart sinks when I don't see her. Despite having sent multiple messengers, I haven't heard from her.

I will have to find out what is going on with her. Our sources tell us that King Phelix has returned to the Ice Mer lands, but we haven't heard from Helena since Henrick's death.

Shouldn't the Crown Princess of the Ice Mer be easily accessible? Something tingles in the back of my mind to check in on my oldest friend. We may have gotten into a spat over Nathan, but she is still my best friend. I tuck this away in the back of my head as I look ahead of me.

Straight ahead of us, at the end of the long red carpet laid out on the floor, are two new thrones made of ice. Behind them is a large blue banner embroidered with our new emblem. The snowy owl and osprey, entangled in flight over the sea. I had it commissioned as soon as we began planning the coronation, and I couldn't be happier to see how it turned out.

Evergreen wreaths hang all over the room, and silver streamers and baubles hang from the dozens of trees brought inside to celebrate the Winter Solstice. Hundreds of gifts are resting in mountainous piles under trees. I made sure that there was one for each guest, wanting everyone to stay happy.

An incredible aroma is coming from the banquet hall, and my stomach grumbles in anticipation. I've already made certain there will be plenty of chocolate cake for every single guest and hopefully, leftovers as well.

I thought I'd be nervous, but all I am is excited. Standing in the front of the throne room is my father, in a place of honor. Beside him is Nathan's family, their grins so exuberant that they seem almost to glow. It's the sun in their skins, I think to myself.

There is a camera at the back of the hall, live-streaming the coronation throughout the Winter courts. Nathan ordered special TVs to spread throughout the kingdom so we could share our special day with everyone.

Because of thoughtful gestures like this, I know he will be an amazing consort for our people.

The opening ceremony passes by in a blur as we stand next to each other on the dais, facing the gathered crowd.

Soon, it is my turn to speak. I step forward, gazing into the eyes of the people gathered before me. They are silent as my voice echoes through the throne room.

“Thank you, honored guests of the Northern and Southern Courts, for gracing us with your presence today. I stand before you, a humble Fae, here to claim my place as your Queen. I don't claim this position lightly, but do so with the desire to see the Winter Court become everything I know it can be.”

Closing my eyes briefly, I inhale deeply. Now the anxiety is hitting.

"Will you, as representatives of the Winter Court, accept me as your Queen and my husband as my consort?"

Silence.

My heart is pounding, and Nathan tugs on the bond between us, his fingers running down mine as we wait.

A moment passes.

Then two.

Then the crowd speaks as one, "We will."

Snowflakes begin swirling from the ceiling as dozens of tiny owls and ospreys made of snow fly through the room. They all land on us, their wings beating the air momentarily before they explode, showering us in snowflakes. They melt instantly, disappearing into our skin.

Tingles spread through my entire body, and when I look at Nathan, I know he feels the same. His eyes fill with absolute wonder as he grabs my hand and pulls me in for a kiss, his tongue sweeping my mouth as we stand before our subjects. Behind us, cheers erupt through the room.

My father steps forward, a look of intense pride on his face.

"Please welcome, for the first time, the Winter Court Queen Elva and her consort, Prince Nathaniel."

Riotous cheers and applause fill the air as we step off the dais, hand in hand. Nathan leans into me and brushes his lips against my ear.

"I would do it all again for you," he whispers. "I love you, my Queen."

I turn to him, my eyes swimming with joyous tears. "I love you too. You make me whole."

We grin at each other and walk forward into the future. It feels so right. I don't know if Fortuna wove this path for us, but I'll light a candle for her the next time I visit her temple. I'll do anything to keep Nathan at my side.

EPILOGUE

One Year Later

"N*athan, if you don't get out here, I will steal your baby!"* Cherie calls through the door. I groan and roll over, untangling myself from my wife. Elva is wearing a silky blue nightgown, and her eyes are closed tight with sleep.

From beyond the door, I hear Cherie croon. "*You are the most perfect little princess in the world, right? Aren't you? You'll make your auntie prove all those human tales* true." She draws out the last word, and I roll my eyes.

Cherie and Mattias have spent most of their marriage in and out of FaeTility clinics (Trademark for exploitation assholes.) I keep telling her to relax and that a child will come in its own time, but Cherie is a force that could never be tamed. In the end, I conceded to mind my own business. It is their choice, after all.

I just want to make sure that she is happy and healthy.

A knock sounds at the door, followed by more gibberish from Cherie. I growl, beyond annoyed at my sister.

"Is something wrong with Taneisha?" Elva awakes with a

start, transitioning from blissful sleep to being fully lucid in less than a minute. I draw her into my bare chest, gently kissing the top of her head.

"Nothing is wrong. I am here, my queen." I hold her tight until her breathing calms, and she eases back into her restful slumber.

I can't help but kiss her as I slide out of bed and pad into the hallway in my shorts. I don't pull on a robe because… I like to feel the fresh air on my skin. What can I say?

My mother's house in the Summer Court is large, old-fashioned, and comfortable. The artwork is so bright it threatens to blind me as I exit my room, squint, and look around for Cherie and my daughter.

A high-pitched squeal sounds downstairs, and I grin. As quietly as possible, I walk down the stairs and into the family room, where Cherie and Taneisha are playing on the couch.

"You know, sis, Elva hasn't slept this well since that little princess in front of you was born. I hope you know I appreciate it." I lean against the wall and cross my arms as I speak.

Cherie looks up at me and pretends to wretch. "*Gods, Nathan*, can you put some clothes on? You are going to damage this girl psychologically."

I laugh and join them on the floor. Mine and Elva's daughter, Taneisha, is trying and failing to grasp some wooden cubes that are too big for her hands. Cherie and I take turns placing the heaving block into her palm. When she holds it for over a few seconds, I'm filled with such a fierce sense of pride that I can barely contain it.

Parenting tiny Fae is wild. Their progress is so clear and so inspiring. I would gladly burn cities or sacrifice myself to keep my daughter safe.

I'd only ever known a love like that once before: for her mother.

"Sup, Nate?" Mattias saunters into the family room, dressed in attire similar to mine. He's relaxed a lot in his time with my sister. I would never tell him, but I like him. He's the opposite of boring.

I nudge Cherie with my elbow.

"What?" She says aggressively.

"You didn't say anything to him about his outfit?"

Mattias looks visibly confused, and Cherie giggles—which causes Taneisha to giggle alongside her. "Why would I say anything to my husband? He's so *sexy*."

"Who's... sexy?" Elva comes in and plops down behind my back. She is still in her thin nightgown. Winter Fae have odd definitions of modesty compared to Summer Fae.

"Apparently, I am," Mattias says. Elva looks him up and down and laughs.

"I guess beauty is in the eye of the beholder," Elva says with a small smile.

His cheeks turn red, and everyone else erupts in laughter. I wrap my hands around my stomach and groan. My sides might split from mirth. "Shut—up—" I manage to get out. "I don't want to wake up Lucinda."

This time, Elva is the one that speaks. She rubs her forehead and chuckles to herself. "We were up pretty late last night. I don't think she'll live for a few more hours."

I roll my eyes, "Could you please stop drinking Faerie Mead with my mom?"

"Actually, Elva, *could you keep* drinking Faerie Mead with my mom?" Cherie mimics me, and I push her over. "Hey—ow. Calm down, you grumpy king. We both know it makes her chill."

"Yup," Mattias contributed.

When our laughter died down again, I met eyes with Elva and saw the odd flicker of sadness under her happiness.

I put my palm on her knee. "Are you ready to go?"

"Clearly not, Nathan." The Queen of the Winter Court smirks. "You are not either. Let's hurry, I want to get there before anyone else."

"Are you heading to the hot springs?" Mattias asks. I nod.

"We'll watch Neisha!" Cherie offers, and Elva smiles as she thanks her.

The gleam in my wife's eye makes my stomach twist with excitement. Before I know it, I am bounding up the stairs and pulling on a pair of swimming shorts.

Once we are safely in the car with one of Elva's guards, we set out to our favorite spot. After we were married, Cherie told Elva exactly how to get to this place so we could have some privacy during our first visit with my mom, Lucinda.

The Summer Court is in full bloom, and I would be lying if I said I didn't enjoy the warmth that was just so... available. Living in the Winter Court is beautiful, but the endless days of ice were brutal on my skin after a few months.

When we neared the natural preserve, a Summer Fae in a black suit greeted our driver. After a few moments, they ushered us into the most exclusive area in the whole park.

I always make sure to pay for that kind of luxury, even though Elva claims she couldn't care less.

Once we finish unloading the car, we head over to the lush, natural oasis. The springs are draped in thick, leafy green vines and delicate white flowers. Small hummingbirds flutter in and out of the cave-like enclosure. Inviting steam rises from the water.

No sooner than the guard closed the protective, invisible gate than Elva slipped out of her clothes. I glance nervously to the outside, knowing full well that the gate prevents everyone from looking in.

Elva's hips sway as she walks, and I admire her. Her body had changed with both the pregnancy and the birth. A new story is written across the perfect lines of her skin.

She smiles at me and eases into the water. The sight of her enjoying herself makes me burn with delight.

I follow close behind and sit on the stone next to her. We lay there for a while until the space between us becomes unbearable. We enjoy our slow, lazy kisses before our movements become more intimate.

When we finish, chests heaving and hair tousled, she rests her head on my chest.

"I'd never imagined how beautiful marriage could be before I met you, Nathan."

Her words made me smile. "You know how many years I wasted going on the same dates with different people over and over again until I wanted to pull my hair out."

"Oh? You don't think what we have is repetitious?" She quirks an eyebrow.

"Absolutely not, my love. Staying with you is teaching me about real life. We've been together long enough to have seen the ugly parts. Sometimes I'm annoying, sometimes you're cruel," Elva swats me playfully, but I continue, "I won't lie—it's unpleasant sometimes. But it is never boring. You already know all of my old material. With a long relationship like this, things die and then are rekindled, and that shared process of rebirth deepens the love. It's hard work, but it's worth it. What we have is far warmer and more fulfilling than anything I've experienced before."

Elva stares at me with wide eyes. It's a long moment before she whispers, "Keep speaking like that, and you may find yourself trapped between my thighs once more."

The way she says it catches me off guard, and we laugh. But then, the sadness returns for a moment.

"What is it, my love?"

Elva lets out a breath, preparing herself. "I haven't heard from Helena yet."

I nod slowly. She mentions this often. "Are you ready to try to visit Aqualis? I don't think they've removed the price on my head."

She shakes her head. "I have reason to believe she isn't there—she hasn't been there for a long time."

I blink. "Where is she then?"

"I don't know, but I want to find her." Elva hesitates and avoids my gaze. "I've been meaning to ask you about that actually. I don't know how to say this..."

A few moments pass. "Say it, my love," I coax her.

"I think I need to go searching for her. But, Taneisha..." she trails off again, and I nod.

"Elva, you know you can hire someone else to look. It's not just Taneisha, it's your entire court. We both have responsibilities."

She nods thoughtfully. "What if I had a lead, but that lead would expire soon? I would only be gone for a week, tops."

"Well then, I'm coming with you."

She flicks her gaze over to me. "And what of our daughter?"

"Her very capable aunt and uncle would be dying to spend the week with her. We will send guards, too. She would be fine, Elva." I brushed back some hair from her eyes. "Sweetheart, you give your whole soul to that little princess. One week will not make you less of a mother. But you are kidding yourself if you'll be going without me."

She bites her lip, and I go a little bit insane. "Do you mean that?"

I kiss her once again. "Of course. When do we leave?"

THANK YOU FOR READING!

Want to know what happened to Elva's best friend, Helena? Check out A Court of Seas and Storms! Releasing October 18th, 2023.

If you enjoyed the story, please leave us a review!

Also by Elayna and Daniela

We also write our own series! Check them out below:

The Binding Chronicles

Elayna R. Gallea—Upper YA/NA High Fantasy Romance

The Blood Tournaments

Daniela A. Mera—Young Adult Dystopian Fantasy Romance

The Ithenmyr Chronicles

Elayna R. Gallea—Upper YA/NA High Fantasy Romance

Entangled with the Enduar

Daniela A. Mera—New Adult Fantasy Romance

The Divinity Chronicles

Daniela A. Mera—Upper YA/NA High-Fantasy Romance

The Sequencing Chronicles

Elayna R. Gallea—Young Adult Dystopian Fantasy Romance

Acknowledgments

We want to thank the readers that made this book a reality. To our ARC and Beta Readers, know that your comments and encouragement really propelled us onto finishing and publishing our novel.

To our writing group partner, author Sydney Hunt. She is our cheerleader and close friend. We also want to thank R.L. Davennor, Nisha J. Tuli, and Cassie Alexander for bouncing ideas off of.

We are so grateful for the talented and hilarious Stacey McEwan (@stacebookspace), who gave us the original idea for the book.

Of course, we would be no where without the support, inspiration, and love from our incredible families. They were very cool with our joint-custody book baby.

Thank you to Elayna's family: Aaron, Britanny, and Jack.

Thank you to Daniela's Family: Josué, Jacqulyn, Grant, Érica, and Victoria.

About the Author

Daniela A. Mera is a word-smith living between Nevada, USA and Hidalgo, Mexico, living out her own fantastical dreams one day at a time. Sign up for her newsletter to get updates and free novellas or extra book chapters!

For print version, visit:

www.danielaamera.com

facebook.com/AuthorDaniela.A.Mera
instagram.com/authordaniela.a.mera
amazon.com/~/e/B09JDDZQX7
goodreads.com/authordanieaamera

ABOUT THE AUTHOR

Elayna R. Gallea lives in beautiful New Brunswick, Canada with her husband and two children. They live in the land of snow and forests, near the lovely Saint John River. When Elayna isn't reading or writing, she can be found teaching French online to her amazing students. Tap the image or click here to see more of her work!

www.ingramcontent.com/pod-product-compliance
Lightning Source LLC
Chambersburg PA
CBHW020340310726
48979CB00015B/2449/J

* 9 7 8 1 9 6 0 3 4 3 1 2 3 *